Honest
Secrets

Muna Shehadi's lifelong love of reading inspired her to become a writer. She got her start in romance but is excited to be making her debut now in women's fiction.

Muna grew up in Princeton, New Jersey, lives in Wisconsin, and has a much-loved summer place on the beautiful coast of Maine, all of which she couldn't resist featuring in her Fortune's Daughters trilogy.

For more information, visit her website: **munashehadi.com**

In the Fortune's Daughters trilogy:

Private Lies
Hidden Truths
Honest Secrets

Praise for Muna Shehadi:

'A wonderful read with evocative descriptions and enough family secrets to create a gripping journey of discovery'
Woman

Honest Secrets

Muna Shehadi

REVIEW

First published in 2021
by HEADLINE REVIEW
An imprint of HEADLINE PUBLISHING GROUP

1

Cataloguing in Publication Data is available from the British Library

ISBN 978 1 4722 5875 5

Typeset in Sabon by Avon DataSet Ltd, Arden Court, Alcester, Warwickshire

Printed and bound in Great Britain by Clays Ltd, Elcograf S.p.A.

Headline's policy is to use papers that are natural, renewable and
recyclable products and made from wood grown in well-managed
forests and other controlled sources. The logging and manufacturing
processes are expected to conform to the environmental regulations
of the country of origin.

HEADLINE PUBLISHING GROUP
An Hachette UK Company
Carmelite House
50 Victoria Embankment
London EC4Y 0DZ

www.headline.co.uk
www.hachette.co.uk

To Isabel, for being herself.

I'd like to acknowledge my fabulous editor Kate Byrne at Headline Publishing, who guided me through the *Fortune's Daughters* trilogy with unfailing skill and support. Diana Roberts and Stanley Pendleton deserve warm hugs for their hospitality and fascinating discussion of a boatbuilder's life. I'm also grateful to Laura Erickson-Schroth for her excellent book *Trans Bodies Trans Selves*, which aided me in my research; and I salute the world's transgender community for its bravery and determination to be recognized. Many thanks to Laura Iding for passing along just the right anecdote at just the right time. And a million more thanks to my husband, Mark Stodder, for reading every word of all three books, laughing and crying in all the right places, and generally being the best.

Honest Secrets

Chapter 1

July 28, 1993 (Wednesday)

So many busy times. Three girls and a full, fabulous career. I get run ragged and don't have time to write this diary. But it's so important to capture my amazing life.

We are just back from another trip to our beautiful house on the Maine coast. The girls love it so much. It's a joy to set them loose on the rocky shores, and to explore in the woods. So different from the beaches in LA, where I have to watch them like hawks. Men ogle Olivia, developing a woman's figure already at age twelve, and it's all I can do to keep Rosalind from killing herself by swimming out too far. At least Eve is content to sit by me and build sandcastles.

At our place in Stirling, there are no male predators to get in the way of Olivia's joy, and no other teenagers for whom she feels obligated to ditch her sisters in order to look cool. The water is too cold for Rosalind to drown herself in, and Eve is happy building little houses out of rocks, twigs, leaves and moss.

Daniel and I relax. When we bought the place, we promised each other not to bring work up here, even if it means that some years we can only stay a week. This year the weather, tides and our energy levels all came together and we managed to have a clambake. I thought I'd die of happiness being around my wonderful family. My beautiful girls and my handsome husband look even more beautiful and handsome in the light of a Maine sunset.

I was almost sorry when we had to come back to chaotic in-the-spotlight reality. Except for how much I love that too.
La Prima Donna,
Jillian Croft

Olivia Croft faced the TV camera, features arranged in her best happy-hostess expression, eyes slightly wide and alert, mouth ready to smile. Inside she was slowly and systematically falling apart. When they came back from commercial, she'd be making her very last appearance on the show she'd created from scratch, pitched to the studio and starred in for the past five years on LA's channel 53. *Crofty Cooks* had been her focus, the crew her family. Her wide array of guests, chosen from among ordinary citizen-cooks of Los Angeles, had enriched her experience of her home city. Most importantly, hosting the show had scratched Olivia's performing itch, as the years spun along and stardom didn't happen. *Crofty Cooks* had kept her in the public eye and away from her nagging feelings of not living up to her potential, not fulfilling her dream or her mother's expectations for her career. When that mother had been one of the world's biggest movie stars, being one of its smallest hurt.

For this last episode, Olivia had chosen all things kids. Tips on how to sneak vegetables and wholegrains into treats, commentary from pediatricians on sugar consumption and its health consequences, plus segments taped earlier in the week featuring some of LA's kid-friendly, healthy-food restaurants. Live on today's set: six kids, ages four to eight, helping to make the recipes, reacting to the treats, providing hilarious opinions on which foods they thought were healthy.

What are good greens to eat? *Mint ice cream! Green M&Ms! Pistachio pudding!*

'Ten seconds, Olivia.' John, her stage manager, on whom she had a crush because it was impossible not to, flashed both hands.

'Thank you.'

A little girl – Amber, her name tag said – bolted from the table in Olivia's TV kitchen, where she and her guest-starring friends were sharing a 'decently nutritious' cake Olivia had baked earlier, made with wholegrain flours, pureed prunes for additional fiber and sweetness, and cocoa powder. Olivia snatched her up and held her, tickling her tummy to make her giggle.

'Five seconds.'

Olivia waved Amber's frantic mother back. Then, impulsively, she bent forward – couldn't help herself – and inhaled the sweet little-girl smell she craved. Maybe without the show she would be more relaxed, and she and Derek would finally conceive. About the only silver lining she could find. At thirty-nine, she was terrified her window of fertility was closing. Another window closing.

When God closes a show, he opens another audition. One of her mother's many invented sayings. Please let her be right.

'Three, two . . .' John's fingers continued the countdown toward what Olivia liked to think of as 'blastoff'.

'Hi, everyone, welcome back to *Crofty Cooks*. This adorable little girl I have in my arms right now is Amber.' Olivia turned to the child. 'I have had the best time today. How about you, did you learn anything important?'

Amber nodded, a blob of blue low-sugar frosting smeared on her cheek. 'Cake is good.'

'Well done.' Olivia's heart was positively melting. No, pining. The little body felt so natural and right in her arms.

She'd planned to do another couple of weeks of shows centered on the problems and joys of feeding children, but . . .

She turned back to address the camera, bolstering her wobbly smile. 'Today's kids are the world's tomorrow. We need to give them the best possible start. The fewer sweet foods they eat, the less they'll crave sugar. For all you lucky moms-to-be, yes, that includes what you eat when you're pregnant.

'So give your babies a big hug today.' Olivia squeezed Amber, relieved when the little girl didn't shriek for Mommy. 'Promise yourselves that you'll feed them well. And if you're like me, struggling to have children, or childless for other reasons, then make sure you're spoiling other people's kids with love and fun activities, rather than with sugar.

'Thank you so much for joining me today.' She covered a crack in her voice with a quick throat-clearing. 'I love you all. Eat well! Amber, wave bye-bye with me?'

She and Amber waved goodbye, then, as the credits rolled over the still-live shot, Olivia put Amber down, took her tiny soft hand and led her back to the table full of cake-smeared kids, taking time to crouch down and say a word or two to each one.

John announced that they'd gone to commercial.

It was done.

Olivia forced her stiff lips into a smile. Parents stepped on to the set and collected their little ones, competing conversationally with audition schedules, dance lesson achievements, and diet plans. Amber's mother, a sweet-looking blonde who stood out for her reticence among the stage-mother crowd, sidled cautiously toward Olivia with her daughter on her hip, as if she worried that getting too close to even such a minor celebrity could hurt. Olivia smiled warmly, much preferring this shy approach to that of fans who seemed to think they owned her – touching her, telling her dull stories about their families, insisting on multiple selfies. The proliferation of cameras was a pox on Olivia's privacy, though it wasn't bad for her ego.

'Hi there . . .' She peered at the woman's name tag. 'Jeanine.'

'I wanted to tell you how much I love your show.'

'Thank you.' Olivia had wrestled with whether to let the audience know that today's episode was her last, but had decided against leaving viewers with the image of her bawling her eyes out. Letting fans like Jeanine down was devastating, but the suits in charge had spoken. Her best hope was to exit with dignity intact. 'Thank you so much.'

'My neighbor was on with you once. You remade her grandmother's turkey tetrazzini recipe. She still uses your version.'

Olivia beamed, as if making a turkey-tetrazzini difference in the world had been her life's goal. Olivia Croft was an actress, not a cook. 'That is so good to know.'

'I also wanted to tell you . . .' Jeanine shifted Amber to her other hip. 'I met your mother once.'

'Really?' Olivia's smile grew more natural as warmth spread through her, along with the inevitable sadness.

'I was ten. I wanted so much to be an actress. I saw her on the street. She was so beautiful, even off screen.'

'Yes.' Olivia nodded proudly. Mom had turned heads everywhere she went. Walking down the street with her, Olivia had felt like a queen.

'Seeing her was so unexpected, and I was so excited, I tripped at her feet. Literally. I was mortified.' Jeanine laughed, rolling her pretty blue eyes, cheeks pinking. 'But she was so gracious. She not only helped me up, she stayed there talking to me, asking questions about what I was interested in, encouraging me to work hard, to keep going.'

'That was Mom.' *Never surrender* was Jillian Croft's mantra, thumped out on Olivia's eardrums over and over until Mom was sure her eldest daughter had internalized the concept.

Jeanine shook her head in awe. 'Jillian Croft, the biggest star in the world, and she acted as if she really cared who I was.'

'She did care.' Olivia reached to straighten the lace collar of Amber's pink dress. 'She was an incredibly genuine person, and she loved kids.'

'She was a huge role model for me.' Jeanine pressed her lips to Amber's forehead in an unconscious mom-kiss that made Olivia sigh with envy. 'Acting never worked out for me, but . . . anyway, I wanted to tell you.'

'I'm so glad you did, Jeanine.'

'And thank you for having Amber on your show! Can you say thank you, Amber?'

Amber shook her head, no. Jeanine looked horrified.

'Amber has had a busy day.' Olivia laid a hand on the child's impossibly soft arm. 'You did really well on the show, sweetheart. But you probably want to get out of here now, right? Go home and play? Maybe take a nap?'

Amber nodded enthusiastically. 'Play.'

'All right, thanks for helping me. Bye-bye.' Olivia waved until they were out of the room, the last guests to leave. As her adrenaline receded, tension and fatigue surged in to take their rightful place alongside her grief. Thank God her sisters had flown in to be with her, Rosalind from New York, Eve from Boston. Derek was out on location in Montana somewhere. If Olivia had to go back to an empty house right now, she'd drink a fifth of Scotch and barf all afternoon. Instead, while she was busy on the set, Eve and Rosalind had gone shopping for a picnic lunch that the three of them would be taking to Zuma Beach.

She said fond and devastating farewells to the crew, making sure she spoke to everyone by name, mentioning in particular the fine job they'd done to make her life easier. Mom had taught her that too. *Never forget what people do for you, no matter how small.*

Finally she walked over to where her sisters were waiting, anticipating the relief of being around people she could flake out on if she needed to.

'You were fabulous.' Rosalind, her free-spirit brunette middle sister, wrapped her arms around her, baby of the family Eve waiting to take her place.

Rozzy looked surprisingly normal today in a pair of knee-length pink shorts with a plain yellow top. Usually she pushed the boundary of fashion so far that it nearly snapped. Eve, on the other hand, generally dressed as if she hoped she would disappear – muted colors and classic styles. Today she was chic-blond visible in navy-flowered capris and a simple white tee. Both of her sisters' lives had changed substantially for the better over the past year. Olivia's had changed, too, substantially for the crappier.

'Thank you. Thank you both for coming.' She returned her sisters' hugs fiercely, fighting the emotion in her throat. 'Now let's get the hell out of here.'

She started toward the exit, Eve and Rosalind hurrying after her.

'Are you okay?' Eve asked.

'Not thinking about that now.' Keeping tears back by the sheer force of hating them, she stalked through LA's typically perfect June weather toward the tiny lot where she'd parked for the past five years. 'Let's go party in Malibu.'

'Oh, fun.' Rosalind sighed with pleasure. 'It's been years since I heard anyone say that.'

Olivia dug her phone out of her purse to see if there were any words of support or comfort from Derek. 'Probably because it's been years since you've been back here.'

'Gee, now *there's* a possibility.' Rosalind sounded more amused than annoyed. It was hard to get a rise out of her. Eve, however . . . like taking candy from a baby.

Nothing from Derek. He couldn't have forgotten about today. On the other hand, he *was* a man.

One email from Susan, the studio receptionist. Olivia halted about two feet from her car, a bright red Audi RS7, which she adored for its luxury and speed. In LA, your choice of vehicle was as important as your house – because you spent about the same amount of time in each.

'What is it?' Rosalind asked.

'This is weird.' Olivia held up her phone. 'I got an email from the studio receptionist. Guess who just called looking for me?'

'Steven Spielberg?'

'Martin Scorsese?'

'Ha . . . ha.' She gave her sisters her famous stink eye. 'Weirder than that. Derek's ex-wife, Jade.'

'Are you in touch with her?' Rosalind unlocked the car, then passed the key to Olivia.

Olivia passed it back. 'You drive. I'm changing in the car. And no, of course not. They've been divorced for like twelve years. We've been married eight. I never even met the woman.'

'Oh no. Not me. I hate driving in LA.' Rosalind pushed the key toward Eve.

'Forget it.' Eve held up her hands, refusing to take it. 'That is strange about Derek's ex. You don't think *he's* in touch with her, do you?'

'Not that I know of. But it was a decently amicable divorce, so I wouldn't care if he were. Who knows?' Olivia climbed into the back seat, where she'd stashed her beach clothes before coming to the studio that morning. 'C'mon, guys, let's go. *Eve*, you drive.'

Eve slouched into the driver's seat, grumbling.

'Rosalind, how can you hate driving in LA?' Olivia kicked off her Walter Steiger pumps. 'You live in New York!'

'I don't *drive* in New York.' Rosalind got into the passenger seat. 'I'm not insane.'

'Debatable.'

'Ha ha.' She pulled out her phone. 'Let me figure out the fastest route.'

'There's GPS in the car, use that.'

'Nah, I'm used to this.' Rosalind tapped at the screen and studied it. 'Faster to go the inland route, but only by fifteen minutes. Let's take the coast. It's awful traffic through the city, but not bad after that.'

Olivia unbuckled the wide leather belt she'd used to accessorize her Caroline Herrera sheath dress. Of the three girls, she was the only one who had learned anything about fashion, in spite of their mother's best efforts at teaching all three of them. *Clothes can make the best of a bad situation.* 'Where did you go to get lunch?'

'Bristol Farms in West Hollywood.' Eve checked the traffic, then hit the accelerator. The V8 engine shot the car forward, making her shout with nervous laughter. 'Your car is on steroids!'

'We bought grilled artichokes, tabouli, cheeses, a baguette, grapes, choco—' Rosalind squealed. 'Watch out!'

'I *am* watching out. *He* wasn't.'

'We grew *up* here. You got your *licenses* here.' Olivia wriggled out of the dress. 'What happened to your LA driver balls?'

'Fell off when I moved,' Eve said. 'Boston's nuts, but I don't take my car in to the city.'

'We last drove here over ten years ago. Traffic is much worse now.' Rosalind plugged her phone cord into the car's USB port. The electronic voice came on and gave directions. 'Eve and I couldn't believe how bad it's gotten.'

Olivia nodded, pulling on her bright pink bikini bottom. 'It is definitely worse. I'm seriously thinking about buying another house to escape to. Either northern California or Maine. We were dumbasses to sell Mom and Dad's place in Stirling.'

'Maybe . . .' Ever-diplomatic Rosalind. 'Kind of a lot of memories there.'

'You guys want to go in on it with me?' Olivia unhooked her bra and replaced it with the bikini top.

'I'd love to have a place there,' Eve said. 'It's an easy drive from Swampscott.'

'Depending on where you buy,' Rosalind said. 'I assume you mean on the coast. Maybe near Dad and Lauren.'

'Of *course* the coast. You think up near Grandma Betty in moose world?' Olivia finished dressing, covering her bathing suit with a lacy white tunic, while Eve tackled the fun of trying to get somewhere in Los Angeles along with too many of its four million people.

'Any more auditions in the works, Olivia?'

'One.' She tried to sound like that didn't devastate her. 'For a film about aliens. A high point in a low career. If that doesn't pan out . . . I don't know. I worry that stress is interfering with our baby-making.'

'Taking a break might be smart.' Eve sped through a yellow light. 'I can see that being the problem.'

Rosalind turned with a wide grin. 'I can't wait to be this poor kid's crazy auntie.'

'You might pop one out before I do.' Olivia buckled her seat belt and settled back against the headrest. A break might sound good, but the role of a lifetime could pop up while she was snoozing. As Mom would say, *You can't lead the pack of wolves if you're a kitty-cat.* 'Has Bryn proposed yet?'

'Nah.' Rosalind waved away the suggestion. 'Even if we do get married any time soon, I want to wait to have a kid.'

'Don't wait too long is all I'm saying.' Olivia sighed, watching buildings and storefronts go by, then let her eyes close, suddenly exhausted. Her sister had met Bryn, a sculptor and all-around fabulous guy, the previous fall, when she'd bravely traveled to New Jersey in search of her birth mother. 'You never know how long it will take.'

'True . . .'

She was dimly aware of her sisters continuing to chat, then the car stopped and Eve turned off the engine.

Olivia forced her eyes open to discover they were in the parking lot at Zuma Beach. 'Whoa. How long was I out, an hour?'

'Just about.' Rosalind pushed open her door, letting in a glorious sea breeze. 'Woo-hoo! I *love* this beach. It is *so* great to be back.'

'It really is.' Eve got out of the car. Olivia scrambled to join them. Zuma was one of her favorites too, nearly three miles of beach, seldom crowded, with gentle surf excellent for swimming.

They unloaded the picnic, blanket and towels from the trunk and found their perfect spot on the wide expanse of sand, gulls soaring overhead, a warm breeze blowing in from the tumbling ocean.

'Swim or eat first?'

'Eat!' Rosalind put a hand to her stomach. 'I'm starving.'

'Sounds good to me.' Eve laid out the blanket and started unpacking. 'Olivia, you sit there and be pampered.'

'That is one of the few things in life I am truly expert at.' She stretched out on a towel and spritzed her hair and skin with Clarins sunscreen. 'How's the architecting coming, Eve?'

'Slow, but not bad.' Eve opened a container of drool-worthy grilled artichoke hearts, a vegetable straight out of paradise as far as Olivia was concerned. 'I got another Washington Island job yesterday.'

'No kidding!' Rosalind was slathering on the Coppertone. 'That is awesome.'

'You might as well move to Wisconsin,' Olivia said. 'I'm sure Clayton would love it.'

Eve shrugged, pointedly ignoring the bait. Olivia was dying to know if Sex Had Happened with the man Eve had met on the island early last spring.

Of course, it would be extremely rude to ask. 'So have you and Clayton gotten over yourselves and had a good boinking yet?'

'Olivia!' Rosalind clapped her hand over her mouth to hide her grin.

Eve's stink eye was nearly as good as Olivia's.

Olivia cracked up. 'Just impatient for you to be happy.'

'You'll be the first I don't tell. Anyway, it's a good job. An interior renovation design. I'll probably take it. As for moving there, no. Wisconsin's a nice state, and Lake Michigan is pretty cool, but . . .'

'It's just a lake.' Olivia gestured at the surf, greedily inhaling the moist air. 'I've lived here all my life and I am still amazed that I have access to beaches like this whenever I want. I was born for oceans. Mom loved them, too. More than Dad, I think.'

Her sisters exchanged glances. Olivia refused to let that stop her. Since last summer, when the three of them had discovered that their mother had been unable to have children, Eve and Rosalind had become awkward talking about Mom. As if she wasn't really their mother anymore.

As far as Olivia was concerned, Jillian Croft was Mom, end of story. If she'd resorted to being . . . creative about how she'd produced kids that everyone, including her kids, thought were hers, more power to her.

Of course it wasn't that simple. Hiring women for your husband to impregnate while you wore pregnancy costumes was pretty messed up. But thinking about ethical complications made Olivia tired, especially when they involved a woman she'd both idolized and adored. So . . . load it on a rocket and shoot it up to Planet Denial. She hadn't even told Derek.

'The beach was the only place in California Mom would *always* go incognito, remember? She didn't want anyone interrupting her sun and surf time.' Olivia thrust her fingers into the sand and brought up a warm handful. 'She'd bring me to Zuma to dig when I was little. I was determined to reach China, and so disappointed that I never had enough time to get all the way.'

'That is adorable.' Eve handed over a slice of baguette smeared with something pure white that tasted goaty and fabulous. 'I don't really remember Mom on a beach.'

'You were so young when she died.' Olivia chewed, familiar sadness muting some of her cheese pleasure. Eve had been eleven when their mother accidentally overdosed on her medication just before midnight on New Year's Eve 2001. Rosalind had been sixteen, Olivia twenty. Olivia had known Mom for longer than either of her sisters, and had been closest to her, most notably in their shared love of and ambition for acting.

'Where's Derek this time?' Rosalind helped herself to another artichoke and more cheese. It drove Olivia crazy how much Rosalind's sturdy ex-gymnast's body could absorb without getting any sturdier. Eve was worse, always underweight, though she'd lost the scary-thin figure she'd had before she ditched her icky boyfriend and found Clayton. At least these days, with the stress of Olivia's mysterious infertility and her show being cancelled, Olivia was where she liked to be on the scale, and could eat cheese with only minor guilt.

Okay, major guilt, but she could double her workout later. In a city of sticks masquerading as women, she didn't need her weight to be the reason she wasn't being cast.

'He's in Montana. He had to find a ranch for a movie about special-needs kids learning to ride. The director had all these ideas about exactly how big the ranch had to be, what color, what "vibe", what this, what that, how many trees, how many trails, how many horses. Drove Derek crazy. But he found it.' Olivia was proud of her husband. He loved his job as a location scout, and she loved that he was gone a lot. Their marriage worked much better when she was missing him, then really glad to see him back. Repeat as needed.

'I'm dying to know what his ex wanted.'

Olivia pulled out her phone. 'I can't remember if she left a num— Wait. Another email from Susan.'

'Don't you have a flunky to read your emails for you?' Rosalind asked too sweetly.

'Gone.' Olivia spoke briskly, so she wouldn't seem as upset as she was. Her assistant Donna had taken another job, and Olivia had had to face the fact that with the show closing, there was no point hiring another. 'Oh my God, Jade called *again*, and is asking me to call back. She said it's important.'

'Whoa.' Eve stared over a forkful of tabouli. 'That's strange. Is Derek okay?'

'Of course he is.' Olivia's heart started pounding. 'Why would anyone contact *her* if he wasn't?'

'Well, call her back,' Rosalind said impatiently. 'I'm dying to know what she wants.'

Olivia felt uneasy. She wasn't sure why, but she really didn't want to know what her husband's ex thought was so important. 'Right now?'

'Why not?'

She couldn't think of a reason, so she squinted down at the message, annoyed that she was finding small print harder to read these days. 'Okay, I'll call her.'

Jade answered on the first ring. 'Olivia.'

'Hi, Jade, what's up?' Olivia wasn't going to waste time with small talk. Derek and Jade had been college sweethearts, married and divorced within a year, no kids, no hard feelings.

'I saw *Crofty Cooks* today.'

'Oh.' Olivia rolled her eyes at her sisters, then moved closer and held the phone out so they could hear Jade telling her how great the episode was, or that she had an old family recipe she wanted featured and fixed on the show-that-no-longer-was. 'That's nice.'

'The part about the infertility. You and Derek. I can't . . . I'm sorry, I'm so upset.'

Olivia frowned. *She* was upset? 'Okay.'

Rosalind got on to her knees and waddled closer to hear better.

'You've been trying?' Jade asked.

'Yes.' *Obviously.*

'I can't believe this.'

Olivia and her sisters exchanged glances. 'Jade, what are you talking about?'

'Derek never wanted kids.'

Olivia spluttered. 'Well, *obviously* that changed. Why are you calling me?'

'I'm sorry. I'm sorry, I'm doing this so badly.'

Olivia mimed throwing the phone into the sand, expecting Rosalind and Eve to snicker. They didn't. 'Doing *what* badly?'

'During our marriage, Derek didn't want kids. So he . . . he had a vasectomy.'

Eve and Rosalind gasped and reared away as if they didn't want to hear another word. Olivia stayed frozen with the phone to her ear, trying to wrap her brain around what Jade had just said.

'That is ridiculous.' Her voice came out too high and not nearly rude enough.

'I'm so sorry, Olivia. I couldn't believe it when you said you were having trouble. It made no sense. And then . . . I mean, I know Derek is capable of . . .' Jade made a sound of exasperation. 'I'd better leave it there. You must know him by now. Better than I do.'

Rosalind and Eve were looking at Olivia with identical expressions of somber acceptance. They actually believed what they were hearing.

This was crazy.

'He must have had it reversed. After you divorced.' Though the success of that operation wasn't guaranteed. And why wouldn't he have mentioned it? 'He *had* to have had it reversed.'

'Maybe. But he was so definite about not ever wanting kids. I'm sorry, I just wanted to make sure you knew. He can be . . . Well, he wants what he wants when he wants it. You must know that by now.'

Fear turned on its heel and became anger. 'You know what? I don't want to discuss my husband with you anymore.'

'No. No. Of course. I'm sorry. I just wanted you to know.'

'Yeah, thanks.' Olivia ended the call and let out a vicious laugh. 'Well, *that* was a waste of time.'

'Olivia . . .' Rosalind was looking at her with sympathy that was like a red flag to a bull.

'My husband did *not* have a vasectomy.' Olivia's goat cheese did cartwheels in her stomach. 'There is no way he'd put me through all these years of absolute hell on *purpose*. No way.'

'The doctor said there was nothing wrong with you . . .'

'*Or* him.'

Eve's face was ashen with worry. 'Did the doctor tell you that? Or did Derek?'

Olivia stared defiantly, hating her for her logic. Derek had told her.

'Maybe that's why the doctor refused to try artificial insemination. And why Derek wouldn't agree to do *in vitro*.' Rosalind looked as ill as Olivia felt. 'Maybe they both knew it was a waste of time.'

'Our doctor is a saint. He would *definitely* tell me if Derek was the problem.'

'Privacy rights.' Eve said the words like a death sentence. 'It's not legal for a doctor to disclose health information without the patient's permission.'

'What I want to know is why the bleep *Derek* didn't tell you.' Rosalind had her hands on her hips, avenging angel in pink and yellow. 'If it's true, and he's put you through this on purpose, I will—'

'I'll help you,' Eve said.

'No. No. He would *not* do this to me. If he had a vasectomy, then he had it reversed. I'll call him right now and ask. End of story.' Olivia picked up the phone, trying to decide how to phrase the question, then realized there was no way to phrase it. 'What am I doing? I can't ask him. I will insult him beyond belief by acknowledging I could ever believe such a thing. Which I don't.'

Rosalind and Eve looked unconvinced.

'Plus, if you ask him, he'll just deny it.' Rosalind collapsed back to sitting. 'He must know you have no proof. He can paint his ex as vindictive, his word against hers, blah blah blah. You won't know if he's telling the truth or not.'

'But I *do* know. I do. I know.' Olivia knew she sounded *this* close to breaking down. 'There is some completely normal and logical and good explanation for all this.'

Eve bit her lip, looking so beautiful it was actually unfair. 'I think you just heard that explanation. From Jade.'

Olivia got to her feet, shaky and sick, furious that her miserable day, which this lovely family picnic had been about to turn around, was now even more miserable. 'Why should I trust *her* over my own husband? How do I know she's not just vindictive and messing with me?'

'Twelve years after an amicable divorce?' Rosalind said. 'Why would she suddenly turn vindictive?'

Olivia could not stand the fact that her sisters were both being so calm and rational about something this crazy. They should all be wailing and running frantic circles in the sand. She might start doing so at any moment.

'If I can't ask Derek what's going on, how am I supposed to prove that this is all some weird ploy by Jade to mess with my head?'

They had nothing.

'See?' She threw her hands up in exasperation. 'It's impossible.'

They sat in dismal silence, the exhilarated shouts of kids charging and retreating from the waves providing a surreal soundtrack to their thoughts.

'Wait!' Rosalind held up her hand, eyes lit. 'There *is* a way. I just figured it out.'

Chapter 2

What an epiphany I had today. My psychologist friend Josie was talking to me about a mental illness I had never heard of. Narcissistic personality disorder.

This is my mother.

On the one hand, great, monumental relief. My horrible childhood in that house and my horrible relationship with her was not my fault. I'm going to write that again: Not My Fault. *Running away from home at seventeen was not an act of cruelty to her; it was an act of self-preservation.*

This knowledge is freedom. Such freedom! In all my therapy sessions, I have talked about me me me *as much as they wanted, but when they asked questions about my parents, I'd mumble about how they were strict. I didn't want to say more. I couldn't bear to tell even my therapist about my deformity, which was always in the back of my mind when talking about my mother, the great and terrible Betty Moore. She didn't think I should know what was wrong with me. She didn't even want the doctor telling me. She must have thought my physical disorder would reflect badly on her. Her her* her.

That's the freeing part of this new understanding of my mother. On the other hand, there is no cure for narcissistic

19

personality disorder, which means that what I have wanted my whole life – to make Mom see, to explain, to get her to understand me and love me – is impossible.

How do you let go of a lifelong fantasy? I guess you shove it away and you grieve. The irony is that the public sees me as the embodiment of all of their fantasies come true. This is the role I play for them. They can't begin to comprehend my daily hell.

Olivia bent down and opened the oven, lifted a corner of the foil covering her largest sheet pan and poked the pork ribs.

Perfect. Tender, but still with some chew.

She pulled the pan out and laid it on her five-burner professional-grade Wolf stovetop, which she loved with a somewhat unnatural passion. All the ribs needed now was a final heating on the grill and another basting with her special barbecue sauce concoction, a hybrid of all her favorites. Fresh chilis for fruity heat, molasses for depth, vinegar for an acid kick, and ketchup because, well *obviously*. This type of sauce required it.

Cooling on the kitchen table: cornbread. Organic Pastures butter to slather over it sat softening on the counter.

Still simmering on the stove: collard greens, flavored with a Berkshire heritage ham hock.

For dessert, resting under Olivia's favorite etched-crystal cake dome: a triple-layer coconut cake.

Derek's favorite meal, the kind he grew up eating in Biloxi; the type of food Olivia only made in her house on special occasions because of the appalling number of calories in each and every dish. All those dishes in one meal spelled fat, and therefore general unemployability, if not a heart attack.

She doubted she'd eat much.

Outside on the custom-designed patio, the teak table was

already set. Their wedding china with the cobalt-blue and gold rim sat on blue fabric place mats, flanked by Mom's silver, which neither Rosalind nor Eve had wanted, and which Olivia had, desperately. Accenting each place, a monogrammed pink linen napkin whose color echoed the orchid centerpiece and pink tapers in crystal candlesticks. Ready for Derek's favorite IPA from San Diego's Stone Brewing Company, Waterford pint glasses.

Everything was ready. Derek was due home from the airport any minute.

Olivia wanted to puke.

Two weeks earlier, when Rosalind had suggested this diabolical plan on Zuma Beach, Olivia had rejected it out of hand. She was not going to play games with her husband. If they had issues, she'd confront them head-on. Faced with her righteous anger, Rosalind and Eve had gradually and reluctantly backed down.

But. The seed they'd planted took root and grew, day after day.

If Derek had done this monstrous thing to her, this unbelievably cruel and vicious thing . . .

Olivia closed her eyes, gripping handfuls of her dress's red rayon skirt. She hadn't told her sisters of her change of heart, hadn't told anyone; could barely believe even now that she had taken it this far. Please, please let her end this evening reassured and deeply ashamed that she'd ever suspected Derek of anything but normal male selfishness.

Their marriage hadn't been perfect, but Olivia had promised to stick by him, and she very much wanted to honor that promise. Unless he'd put her through the most miserable, anxiety-producing years of her life on purpose.

She shook her head, refusing to believe, because it simply

could not be possible; in which case, this meal would become a real homecoming celebration instead of a trick.

Please, God . . .

Her phone chimed. Another text from Derek.

Be there in five. Shit. After Montana, LA is like being crowded into an elevator with unshowered marathoners who have fleas.

Olivia smiled. Yes, the poor man suffered from the male defect gene, like all of them, but he could be funny and charming, and her heart still fluttered when he walked into the house after a trip, the way it had the day he'd walked into the bar at Vincenti Ristorante in Brentwood, where she'd been on a hot date with a glass of Nebbiolo. Not just fluttered: sang. Derek had asked her to marry him that very first night and every night after for the next three weeks, until she'd given in and accepted him on the condition that they have a long engagement.

Eight years later, after their fabulous pull-out-the-stops wedding in Hawaii, it all came down to tonight. Their marriage. Her trust. Everything.

Her smile faded as she texted back. *We can always move to Montana.*

Rather bathe with scorpions

All right then. You're stuck with traffic. See you in five.

Five minutes.

She used the first-floor bathroom to make sure her makeup was perfect, and that her hair fell just so around her face and shoulders. It would be hard to look glowing when she was so scared, but Olivia was an actress. She'd make this work. Mom would have been able to. Mom would have been able to look carefree juggling live grenades if that was what was required of her.

If you can't stand the heat, fake it.

The garage door rumbled open.

She took another moment to try and settle her skittering nerves, then walked toward the back of the house with her best casual stride. By the time she stepped out on to the patio, Olivia had a wide smile in place, heart pounding so fast she felt woozy.

In the driveway, Derek had already opened the trunk of the Porsche Boxster she'd bought him for their fifth anniversary and pulled out his suitcase. Her handsome husband. Tall and dark, thick hair pulled back in a neat ponytail, he wore a black silk blazer over black jeans and black boots.

Totally hot.

He closed the trunk, hoisted his case and took two steps up the path before he saw her.

'Hey.' He dropped the case, broke into a grin, then a jog, then a full-tilt run that made Olivia recoil, squealing, even though she knew he'd stop in time, lift her off her feet and kiss her until her lipstick was all over both of them, leaving her breathless and laughing.

How was she supposed to believe this man had betrayed her?

'Hello, wife.' He still had his arms around her, forehead pressed to hers.

'Hello, husband.' She managed to get the words out, horrified that she could have suspected him of such base behavior. Derek loved her. He *adored* her. She should be feeling like the luckiest woman in the world. She couldn't wait to put her doubts to rest, to tell her suspicious, judgmental sisters how wrong they were.

'You are the sexiest woman in the state of California.' His hands skimmed down her back to rest on her ass, and he pulled her close to feel his erection.

Olivia's giddiness vanished into thoughts of what she'd want to do to that bulge if she found out he'd been knowingly shooting blanks into her month after month, year after year.

'Dinner's ready.'

'Dinner can wait.' He yanked up the hem of her dress.

'Not this one.' She pulled back. Absolutely no sex until she had her answer.

'There isn't a dinner out there that can compare to the hot dish *you* are.'

'Ribs, cornbread, collards, coconut cake. Sex later.' She lifted her eyebrows as if waiting for his decision, when in fact the power here was all hers.

'Aw, hell.' He glanced at the table, did a double-take. 'Wow. What's the occasion?'

'You're home. And I have something fabulous to tell you.'

'Hmm, let me guess.' He snapped his fingers. 'You bought me a yacht so we can watch Wednesday's fireworks from the bay?'

'Uh . . . good idea, but no. Come in. Have a beer, something to eat. We'll talk later.' She turned toward the kitchen, somehow managing to sound as bouncy and excited as she should be. Jillian Croft's daughter, after all. 'You hungry?'

'Starving. Crap food on the plane. I barely ate. Oh my God, it smells good in here.' He grabbed her from behind and pulled her back against him. 'It's good to be home.'

Olivia turned for a kiss, laid a hand against his stubbled cheek. 'It's good to have you here. For a while, right? Beer?'

'That'd be great.' He let her go and followed her into the kitchen. 'Yeah, next up I'm finding interiors for a short film set during the Dust Bowl. Right here at home.'

'Nice.' She poured him a beer, fixed herself another Scotch on the rocks. Macallan twenty-one-year-old fine oak. Because it was that kind of an evening. She'd already downed a quick belt before he'd showed up. Dutch courage, Mom called it, though where the Dutch got that reputation for bravery, Olivia had no idea.

'Man, look at that cake.' Derek swaggered over to the dome and touched its polished crystal surface wistfully. 'You are a professional, babe. This is totally amazing.'

'Gifted amateur.' Olivia sipped her Scotch, smooth and deeply comforting. 'Just welcoming you home.'

'Thanks.' He took a long drink of beer, Adam's apple rising and falling around the Philip Sidney quote he had tattooed around his neck: *Either I will find a way, or I will make one.*

'Ready to eat?' She took the foil off the ribs. 'While these are grilling, we can start with your mom's pickled shrimp.'

'Oh my God.' He picked up the tray, took one step, then turned back, looking worried. 'All my favorites . . . You're sure it's not bad news and you're cushioning the blow?'

'Nope.' She smiled lovingly, hoping she wasn't overdoing it. 'The opposite.'

Derek's high cheekbones relaxed. 'Cool. I'll get the grill going.'

'Thanks.' The second his back was turned, Olivia drained her Scotch and poured herself another. She took the vinegar-and-lemon-spiced shrimp and onion mixture from the refrigerator and carried it to the table, grabbing the Macallan bottle to bring with her at the last second. While Derek put the ribs on to heat and char, she served appetizer portions on to lettuce-lined plates.

'So, babe . . .' Derek sat, picked up his fork and speared a shrimp. 'What's this you have to tell me?'

'Well.' Olivia sank into her chair and sipped Scotch to ease her dry throat. 'First, I got a call last week from Cherie.'

This part of the evening's tale was true. The call from her agent had come at the perfect time.

'Really?' He chewed, then closed his eyes. 'Aw, man, these are good. What'd she want? Did you get a part?'

'*LA Morning* is doing a segment on infertility. Someone on their team must have heard me mention our troubles on *Crofty Cooks*. They want me to appear.'

'Yeah?' He forked up two more shrimp. Was his face carefully blank or was he actually not reacting because there wasn't much to react to? 'Well, okay. I guess. Honestly, I'm not crazy about us having our personal life out there like this. I mean, this stuff is between us, you know?'

'Yes. But.' Olivia put her elbows on the table, watching him eat, too nervous to join him. 'A lot of women struggle to conceive. The more it's talked about, the better. People should know it's not just happening to them. The more public the issue, the more pressure for research to help people like us.'

Derek nodded, chewing while he speared three more shrimp, stab, stab, stab. He ate fast when he was uncomfortable. Not conclusive, but bothersome. 'I'd rather you didn't, babe, but it's your career, your move. You know I'd never stand in your way.'

'Yes. I do know that.' Acid escaped into her words. She drank some water, thinking longingly of her Scotch.

'Well, that's good news. I mean, I guess.' He looked a little confused. She didn't blame him. Time to stop stalling. She had to get this over with so they could relax and enjoy the meal she'd prepared.

'There's just one problem.'

'Yeah?' Derek looked up from his plate, dark eyes curious, maybe wary. 'What's that?'

She made sure her smile sparkled. 'I'm not sure I'd be such a good guest.'

'Why's that?'

'Well . . .' More sparkle. This was it. In the next several seconds she could torpedo her marriage and her life.

Was this really what she wanted to do?

She stared at her husband staring back at her. His jowls were softening, just a bit. His hairline was receding, just a bit.

What if she wasn't destined to grow old with this man after all?

'Because . . .' She forced her features into warmth while her insides turned to ice. 'I'm pregnant.'

Derek didn't move. He didn't blink. He stared blankly as if he'd just had an aneurysm that had taken out his brain. Then he swallowed so hard she could hear it across the table.

She couldn't hang him yet. Not yet. He might be stunned by delight. That could happen. Right?

'Isn't it a miracle?' She pushed back her chair, put her hands protectively on her flat belly. 'Right here. Our child. The one we—'

His chair scraped back. He jumped to his feet. 'You're fucking kidding me.'

Olivia couldn't move. She sat, hands protecting her empty uterus, trying to take it all in, trying to think logically enough to take the sensible next step. *Was* there one, besides running him over with his Porsche?

Her fondest hope had been that he would take her into his arms and swear to be the best father the world had ever seen, so Olivia could call her sisters for an extremely satisfying neener-neener, proud that she'd stood by her man, delighted that his ex was a lying whore.

Her second fondest hope had been that he'd admit to the surgery, but, *Oh darling, what a miracle! The reversal of my vasectomy was worth every penny! I did it for you. I did it for us. I did it for this moment!*

You're fucking kidding me did not make her fondest-hopes list. Not even in last place.

Yet on some deeply depressing level, Olivia must have

expected this. Had she truly believed in Derek's innocence, she would never have pretended to be pregnant. At least one person in this marriage wasn't capable of cruelty.

She forced her lips to move. 'Of course I'm not kidding. Why would I joke about something like this? It's what we've wanted for so long.'

Derek turned away, hands on his hips. When he whirled back, his face was murderous. 'How . . . ?'

'Derek!' She stared up at him in blank amazement, an acting tour de force. She wanted to drop to the ground on all fours and scream, *How could you do this to me?* at the top of her lungs. Instead, she brought off a perfect, convincingly uncertain laugh. She was channeling Jillian Croft tonight. She could feel her mother's on-screen confidence and integrity in every cell of her body. 'What do you mean, how? Insert male penis into female vagina, agitate until orgasm, right? Isn't this what we've been doing every month?'

'You bitch.'

Olivia's jaw dropped, her eyes widened into shock, act two of this nightmare farce, which was playing out exactly as her sisters had envisioned it. Only ridiculous, naïve, head-in-the-clouds Olivia had believed her husband wouldn't turn out to be a poop-eating dirtbag. '*Excuse* me?'

'Who is it?'

She stared at him as if trying to understand, which wasn't hard, because she *was* trying to understand. How could she have been married to someone for this long and have no idea who he was or what he was capable of doing to someone he had sworn to love, support and protect?

'Who is who?'

'The guy you're cheating with.'

Olivia picked up the Macallan, poured herself a good shot,

then lifted it and tossed it back. She slammed the glass on the table and stood. 'What kind of logic is that, Derek? How does "Darling, I'm pregnant" lead to "You must be cheating"? What could possibly make you think I've—'

'It's not mine. And you shouldn't be drinking. You'll make it retarded.'

'Oh, *that's* adorable! Spoken like any woman's dream guy.' She gave him her mother's haughtiest look of scorn. 'I'll drink however much I want. And since I haven't had sex with anyone else since I met you – and unless I impregnated myself, which, given that I'm not a sea horse, is unlikely – *you* are the father.'

'I'm not the father.' His eyes were blazing with rage. 'Who is he?'

Olivia backed around her chair and held on to it. She needed something else between them besides the table for support. She was shaking with fury, more anger than she'd felt toward any human being since she'd picked up the phone as a teenager and heard her father talking lovingly to a woman who wasn't her mother. Even more angry than when Dad introduced Lauren to his daughters with some bullshit story of having met her a year after Mom died, and Olivia recognized the same voice from that phone call. She had forgiven her father, might conceivably someday forgive Lauren, too.

But she would never, *ever* forgive Derek.

'There is no father.' She heard herself laughing in a way she was pretty sure she'd never laughed before, which was not at all pretty. 'There is no baby, Derek.'

'What the—'

'Do you want to know why there is no baby?'

Shock registered on his face. Soon, when he figured out she'd tricked him into admitting he was the World's Biggest Dickhead, he'd be furious again. For now, she had the advantage.

29

'There is no baby because for the past *four years* of infertile misery, of doctors' appointments and specialist consultations and tears and hopes and constant, *constant*, unrelenting failure, you neglected to tell me that you *could not have a child*.' Her voice broke. Goddammit. She had to stay strong. She had to hang on to her outrage. If she cried, it was over. He'd comfort her. He'd sweet-talk her. He'd try to convince her of his reasons and how it was for the best.

She *hated* him. As she'd hated very few people on this earth and hoped she'd never hate again. Lovely hate. Beautiful hate. Strength-giving, delightful hate.

'I'm wondering why you thought that little detail was not important in our struggle to conceive.'

'Who told you I couldn't have a child?' He swept his chair to the side. It leaned sickeningly, then toppled slowly, as if it had been shot. 'That's bullshit. Where is this coming from?'

'The dictionary.' She smiled, as if she were enjoying herself. 'V is for vasectomy.'

'I did *not* have a vasectomy.' He could even say it looking straight at her.

How many other lies had he told her over the years?

She didn't want to know.

'Oh, I believe you.' She raised her eyebrows, trying to look earnest, praying he couldn't see her shaking, and that she would get through this without crumpling into grief. Or barfing, unless it was all over his black silk, which *she'd* paid for. 'Or I will believe you, when you tell me why you just reacted as if the child had to be someone else's.'

Even Mr Lying Bullshit couldn't think fast enough to refute that one.

'Because, Derek?'

He tried. His eyes darted back and forth, trying to find a loophole. Trying to gain back the upper hand.

Olivia lunged for her glass and the bottle of Scotch. She and Macallan were going to have a long, intimate night together. Alone. 'I'd like you to pack up your stuff and be out of his house in an hour. Since I paid for pretty much everything you own, you can do it that quickly, I think.'

'Babe—'

'My lawyer will be in touch about our divorce.' The D word shocked her, hurt her, even though she'd planned to say it. There was no other way. Not after this.

'Divorce? What the fuck?' Awww, she'd stunned him. Flattened him! What was so bad about what he'd done that she'd give up on their True Love just like that? Women were so touchy about stuff! Those hormones, Jeez, what guys hadda put up with. 'You're throwing away ten years of marriage—'

'Eight, Derek.'

'Whatever-the-fuck, Olivia. Eight years of marriage over *this*?'

She nodded. The more angry he got, the easier it was for her to stay calm. The more she was able to stay calm, the better her defenses. 'Yupper-dupper-doodle.'

'Come on. *Come on*.' He was thrashing now in the net of his own making. If only she could enjoy it without this dreadful, howling pain. 'You can't be serious. We have so much going for us!'

Olivia laughed bitterly. Funny Derek! Hilarious Derek! He did not see this as a big problem in their relationship! 'You *lied to me*. You stood silent *for years* while I suffered. You knew how to fix it, but you didn't.'

He had the nerve to put on his aw-shucks face. 'Babe, I—'

'*Worse*.' She interrupted with no compunction. This was

31

her show. 'I wanted to have kids soon after we married, back when I was in my early thirties, and you kept putting me off. We had plenty of time for that, you said. I'm almost forty now, Derek. And the chances are pretty good that I won't find someone else to impregnate me before it's too late. You stole from me the thing I wanted more than anything in my life.'

'Give me a fucking break. Your life? Your life has been *easy*. You grew up in a house with more money than—'

'Oh, here we go. The boo-hoo poor Southern boy routine! You were so hungry you slept on spikes and ate your best friends, waaaaaah!' She stared as viciously as she knew how. 'Then you married me, and guess what? *Your* life became easy, too!'

'That's not what—'

'Except now, Derek, because of the brilliance of my father, who apparently saw you for the shit you are and insisted I get you to sign a prenup, now you are going to have to go back to the indignity of being *middle class*.' She hissed the last words as if they were a death sentence, then looked pointedly at her watch. 'And by the way, you now have only fifty minutes to get out of my house.'

'Okay. Okay. I'll play your little power game.' He righted the toppled chair, then pointed at her. 'But I know you. A couple days, you'll be begging me to come back. You're so fucking high-maintenance, you can't last a *week* without someone telling you how beautiful you are and how talented and how incredibly *special*.'

His twisted face made him uglier than she could have imagined him being. It made her wonder what she'd ever seen in him, even knowing that after he'd left, all the memories would come roaring back and make this terrible grieving worse.

While Derek banged into the house, then bumped and

swore and thumped around in their bedroom, Olivia stayed in suspended animation, holding her glass of melting ice like it was a magic crystal ball that would turn the clock back to a new world in which none of this had happened.

God, how she wished none of this had happened.

Finally he came back downstairs, lugging one of the ridiculously expensive suitcases she'd bought him last Christmas, when his brown eyes had lit up at the sight of the Louis Vuitton brown checkerboard. She'd bought it for him because she loved making him happy, because money was something she took for granted, even knowing that only a handful of people in the world were able to do that.

Would he miss her money as much as he missed her? Or more?

He'd miss the sex. So would she.

He stood for a moment on the patio, at the edge of the path to the garage, watching her, probably trying to figure out if she were cracking already. 'Babe—'

'You'll hear from my lawyer.'

His face shut down. 'I'll hear from *you*. You know my number.'

'I'll pass it along to him.'

He stalked furiously out to the garage and flung the Vuitton into the back seat of the Porsche, then backed down the driveway and squealed up the street.

Child. He was a child. Apparently she'd had one all along.

The growl of the motor receded. Olivia turned away, toward their house. Her house.

So.

Her husband was gone.

Moving like a zombie, she cleared the patio table, took the charred ribs off the grill and tossed them, along with the rest of the shrimp, the collards and the cornbread. She couldn't see herself ever wanting to eat any of those dishes again.

Work done, she stood uncertainly in her clean state-of-the-art kitchen, hating the silence. She headed again for the Scotch, in spite of her wise inner voice telling her alcohol was the worst next step.

She poured anyway. Generously.

Now what? How did you fill the hours left open and blank after your life had fallen apart? Television?

She giggled and swallowed more Macallan. Damn good Scotch.

Unfortunately, Derek knew her better than anyone. Olivia didn't do grief well. Nearly twenty years earlier, summoned from a party in the wee hours of New Year's Day, her father's voice on the phone, high and strange. 'Olivia, come to the hospital. Your mother had an accident.'

The drive from Redondo Beach to Cedars-Sinai had been the longest of her life. In the ER, her father, ashen and shaky, suddenly older, 'You need to be brave.'

Olivia had made such a scene, her father had begged the ER docs to sedate her.

Brave? She wasn't brave.

Another sip, kicking off her Balenciaga pumps.

Well. Couldn't stand here all night.

She turned and came face to face with the coconut cake, still in its glass dome on a corner of the counter, frosted virginal white, decorated with more of the orchids adorning the table. Waiting like a bride for her groom on their wedding night.

Olivia staggered back, hit the wall and slid down into a helpless, Scotch-pickled mess.

Derek.

Chapter 3

Another movie! Another star turn! The parts haven't quite dried up yet, even though I'm well into my forties. It's criminal what happens to women's careers. Get rid of them when the wrinkles start, never mind that older women are, as I am now, at the height of their power and craft. I will nail this role to the wall.

I'll be playing a woman living in the California desert in the 1870s who loses her husband to a bad guy he trusted. The bad man rapes her. She has a child, a son she rears to kill his father. I'll have to play her young and then older. I'm so excited! I want to do all of my own stunts, even on the horses. I've been doing lots of research. I want to rent a cabin somewhere out in the desert, preferably near Lone Pine, since that's where the movie will be filmed, and immerse myself in that world. Just see how it feels, like becoming Laura Ingalls Wilder. I sure loved those books when I was little. Back then, I read everything I could get my hands on, which wasn't much. First time I walked into the New York Public Library, I was sure I'd died and gone to heaven. I must have wandered for an hour with my mouth hanging open. Gawking country girl that I was!

The bad news is I'll have to go off my meds for the filming.

I can't be on them and act. Just when things were feeling really good.

 Bipolarly yours,
 Jillian

Olivia pulled open the door to the audition waiting room, bracing herself for all the other tall, long-haired, nearly-forty attractive women who'd already be there, making her feel like another stalk of corn in Kansas.

At least she was used to it.

'Hi.' She beamed around the room, expecting and getting two responses: none, or you-talkin'-to-me? She kept her gosh-I-love-being-here smile in place while signing in with the receptionist, then chose a seat between two other corn stalks, hoping she didn't look as if she'd been curled up fetal bawling her eyes out for the past week.

Good times, good times. She hadn't cried this much since her mother died. Deep, ugly grief pulling out tears that went on and on until she was sure her body couldn't produce more. After brief interludes of exhausted peace, her throat would cramp, her chest heave, and off she'd go again.

Like having an endless emotional stomach flu.

Feet flat on the floor, she put in her earbuds and started a track of soothing ocean sounds to center her and discourage conversation. To better imagine herself in a beautiful beachy place, she closed her eyes, reciting the lines her agent had sent, even though she already knew them perfectly. The wait for her turn could be anywhere from a few minutes to many, many minutes, depending on who had or hadn't shown up.

Honestly, she'd gone back and forth over whether to take this audition at all. In the end, she'd done what her mother had ingrained into her since she was old enough to show promise on stage: *Every failure means you're one step closer to success*. This was a small studio, only one B-list star, but it was work, and she needed something to do besides dehydrating herself.

When she was very little, she'd wanted to be a chef. She'd spent hours in the huge kitchen of their Beverly Hills house with Emma, the lovely and very patient cook Mom had hired. Emma had taught her basic techniques and how to develop recipes from ingredients on hand. Olivia had been obsessed, until Mom had seen her on stage for the first time in a school play, and swooped in to inject her with the acting bug.

Olivia still hadn't recovered. For most of her life, she'd been sure that stardom awaited her. Why wouldn't she be? Mom had been coaching her, teaching her, preparing her for what she spoke of as 'the inevitable' since Olivia could remember. *Choose the parts* you *want, Olivia. Don't just run around auditioning for everything as if you're desperate. If you work hard and pay attention, they'll come to* you.

Olivia had taken the advice to heart. Not only did it come straight from the top, but what kind of parent would lie to a child about something that important? Deep down, she had expected to ascend the heights even more easily than her mother, because Olivia wasn't battling mental illness or addiction. There would be no whispers behind her back, no confessional talk-show appearances during which she had to apologize for her behavior, thank her loved ones and fans for supporting her, acknowledge the doctors and staff who'd helped her see the light, and tout her beautiful new life of sobriety. Then go back to using and have to do it all over again.

Olivia would get it absolutely right from the beginning.

Directly out of a theater major at UCLA, where Dad taught, brimming with confidence, she'd refused to work as an extra. Had turned down bit parts. Turned down student film projects.

Turned down commercials. Finally her agent – her first one – told Olivia that she wasn't interested in working with someone who wasn't interested in working, and dumped her.

Agent's fault! Clearly an amateur! Olivia's mother knew best. All Olivia needed to do was work hard and never, ever give up.

However. Owing to what was undoubtedly a giant mistake, the movie world didn't seem to understand that she was destined for greatness. Gradually, painfully, over the years, she'd let go of her prima-donna certainty that she would win the world over, and became willing to start at the bottom.

Except by now, the bottom didn't want much of her either.

Without her cooking show, without her husband, without the beautiful babies she could have been nurturing for the past five years, she needed to make this career work. At thirty-nine, with a theater degree, years of courses, workshops and community theater, bit parts in bad movies and even smaller parts in large ones, she was trained for nothing else. Wanted nothing else. Except children.

Never surrender.

The audition room door opened, making every perfectly coiffed head in the room turn, every perfectly made-up face brighten into an expectant smile.

An exhausted-looking woman with bad hair peered at her clipboard. 'Lacey Desiree?'

Olivia barely held back a snort. *Lacey Desiree?* Why pick a porn-star name for legitimate acting?

Lacey glanced her way. Olivia gave a big smile and held up crossed fingers. *Hope you suck!*

'Thanks!' Lacey swept past and into the room, flipping badly highlighted hair behind her shoulders, bracelets jingling. Bad idea. The noise could get on to the tape and annoy everyone. Why take a chance like that?

Olivia settled back into her ocean sounds, reclosing her eyes, going over the lines again: *We shouldn't be doing this. Not with the aliens so close. They'll be able to smell our bodies.*

Christ. Did these scriptwriters read what they'd written? Out loud? Didn't they ever think, 'Gee, that sounds sort of stupid, and clichéd and utterly unrealistic; maybe I should try again until I hit on something a character would *actually say*?

Apparently not in this film.

Deep breath in. Deep breath out. Thoughts wandering. Derek threatening.

Go away.

The worst part of the week hadn't been the rage over his betrayal, though that had been super fun, a particularly slicing pain. The worst had been the parade of good memories. Why couldn't Olivia focus on the fact that Derek was underhanded and self-serving and routinely made less than a quarter of the effort needed to keep their marriage fresh, and that he made a weird smacking sound when he ate?

No, she remembered the fun times, the loving times, the feel of his warm naked body curled around hers in the bed they'd shared for the better part of a decade. Their travels, to Greece, to Tuscany, to Ireland, to Spain, to Paris several times. The parties they gave, the friends they made together, the mornings alone making love, reading, laughing at the silliness in their heads, at the silliness around them. Olivia and Derek against the whole wide world, safely bonded together until death.

He adored her. All her faults, all her neuroses, all her narcissism and childish impulsiveness. He loved her anyway.

Who else ever would?

The grief started again. Her eyes shot open, staring. She set her jaw.

Absolutely. Not. Now.

The door opened. Lacey Desiree sailed through, color high in her hollow cheeks, eyes shining.

She thought she'd aced the audition. But something as crazy as the shape of your nose could be the thing that disqualified you.

Olivia had been taught not to take rejection personally, which had nothing to do with the fact that she always did. *Use that anger, Olivia, use it to be even better next time. There will always be a next time . . . unless you stop trying.*

She was really good. She was still trying. She had to focus on that.

The door opened again.

'Olivia Croft.'

A murmur in the room from those who might not have recognized her, but who knew her mother's name, which Olivia had taken in preference to the Braddock surname she was born with. So far, she hadn't been able to figure out if it helped or hindered.

'Coming. Thank you.' She yanked out her earbuds and shoved them into her pocket, keeping friendly eye contact with the bad-haired exhaustion waiting to usher her into the doubtless stuffy room. Different stuffy rooms, different exhausted employees, different roles, same range of nerves and hopes.

'Stand there.' The woman pointed to a navy X of tape on the floor.

Olivia obediently stood there. From the three cranky bored people sitting on chairs wearing this-will-suck expressions, she picked one she hoped was the casting director – sitting straightest, nicest T-shirt, coolest hair – and aimed at him her biggest smile. 'Hello. Thank you for having me. I'm Olivia Croft.'

'Yeah. Olivia, uh . . .' The guy looked down at his desk, shuffled through papers, picked up a stapled sheaf and held it out to her. 'We're having you read for Melanie today.'

'Sure.' Panic sprouted. She took the pages from him, radiating calm. *Who the fuck was Melanie? Why didn't they tell Olivia's agent about the change? How could she do her best reading unprepared?*

'In this scene, Melanie is trying to convince her daughter Martha not to go after the alien.'

'Can you tell me something about her?'

He looked exasperated. 'She's Martha's mother. She wants to prevent Martha from going after the alien.'

'Ah.' Olivia nodded pleasantly and looked down at the script's first line, which she should have seen coming . . .

Martha! Don't go after the alien!

Just kill her now.

She read as best she could, putting everything into saving her beloved Martha from certain death, deep-down furious that she was having to come at this cold, when she'd already worked so hard on worrying whether aliens could smell her body.

'Thank you.' The maybe-director interrupted her last line. 'Can you scream for us, please?'

'Scream.' She felt her smile freeze and pushed it back into warmth. 'Like happy scream, scared scream, angry scream, erotic scr—'

'Just scream, please, Ms Croft.'

His condescending tone pissed her off, pushed her too far toward the edge. Admittedly, over the past few years, Olivia's edge had gotten several feet closer. 'Okay, then.'

She bunched her lips, closed her eyes and curled her fingers into fists, picturing Derek the last time she saw him, on his way out of their home and her life, sneering with hateful confidence that within days Olivia would be begging him to come back.

Then she screamed.

Quite impressive, if she did say so herself. Also very loud. And long, very long. As long as her strong diaphragm could make it. By the time she straightened up from where she'd finished – doubled over nearly to the floor – her face had turned hot and her ears were ringing.

Four startled pairs of eyes stared back at her.

'Jesus.' The cameraman's hands were over his ears.

No one looked bored or exhausted anymore.

You're welcome.

'Uh.' The casting director shifted in his chair. 'Thanks. That'll be all today.'

'Thank *you*.' Olivia strode out of the room, through the silent cornfield, all of whose stalks were staring with an unforgettable combination of awe and horror, and out into the beautiful southern California sunshine, feeling almost human for the first time all week. Maybe she ought to sign up for scream therapy. Good stuff. Right now, she didn't even care if she got the part or not.

In fact, she felt strong enough to do what had to be done: call family and let them know what had happened. She'd tell her sisters about successfully springing Rosalind's trap. But she'd have to tell her father the whole story, from the beginning.

Blech.

This past week of grieving alone was uncharacteristic, to say the least. Olivia did not do alone well. Anytime she felt something strongly, she needed to tell someone: her parents and sisters when she was little, her best friends in her teenage and college years, then boyfriends and her husband later.

Derek had obviously disqualified himself as her confessor. Her friends from Life Before Derek had been absorbed over the years into motherhood, leaving Olivia on the outside. She and Derek had socialized as a couple with other couples, which made those friends poor candidates for crying to on her own. Her sisters and father would be lovely and sympathetic, but since none of them had ever really liked her husband, they'd all be thinking the same thing: that Olivia was better off without him.

Therefore, Olivia had cried alone, not ready to hear those words. She hadn't been feeling better without him. She'd been feeling like a garlic clove smashed flat with a cleaver.

Back in her car, she headed to Santa Monica Pier, where she parked and jogged out on to the warm sand. Mid morning, not overly crowded. A few surfers, moms with their kids, teenagers, probably tourists as well. She peeled off her alien-bait blue cotton sweater, kicked off her matching blue loungers, and plunked herself down without a towel. Who cared about getting dirty? Then she jabbed at her phone to call Dad. He'd be angry she hadn't called sooner, but that was his problem.

The second his deep voice answered the phone, her strength, her anger, her resolve disappeared and she reverted to her smashed-garlic persona.

'Daddy . . .' A childish wail that embarrassed her.

'Olivia.' She could imagine him perfectly, bushy gray brows lifting in alarm then dropping into concern. 'What is it? What's happened?'

'Derek and I are getting a divorce.' The horrible word made it too real. Divorce! She was going to be one of *those* people, whose marriages had failed, who'd bailed on matrimony after promising before God that they wouldn't.

'He left you?'

'I kicked him out.

Her father chuckled. 'Attagirl.'

Hadn't she predicted this? Her sisters would react the same way, though at least they'd know better than to do it out loud.

'Dad, this is my *marriage* we're talking about. The man I

loved – still love.' Though not as much. Love couldn't survive such a betrayal intact.

'You're too good for him, Olivia. I've always known that. I'm sorry for your pain, but I'm glad you figured it out before you got too old to find someone else.'

Too old? Dad had remarried at sixty-four! Her father was many things, and sexist was one of them, though he wasn't the worst of his generation.

'The reason we couldn't have a baby was because Derek was sterilized. Before we met.'

'You kicked him out for *that*?'

Olivia sat ramrod straight on the beach. Dad wasn't himself. Maybe after his stroke last summer he didn't really understand. This wasn't the father she knew, the one she'd run to when Mom was in a dark place, the one who always took time to give her a consoling hug, who spoiled his adored little princess rotten. 'How could you say that?'

'It happens, Olivia. Some guys don't produce enough of what it takes. That's not his fault, and it's certainly not a reason to divorce him. I'm surprised at you.'

Aha! She got it now. 'No, no. Not sterile, steril-*ized*. He had a vasectomy during his first marriage, and didn't think to mention it.'

Silence stretched on the other end. Olivia waited, praying he didn't make light of her misery again.

'That . . . *bastard*. He put you through . . . all that? For that . . . long?'

'Yes.' She bit her lip, worried by the odd pauses between his words, but relieved that he was on her side after all. She needed him. 'I couldn't kick him out fast enough.'

'Princess . . . you . . .' He made a terrifying gasping sound that had Olivia on her feet in under a second.

'Dad? Daddy? What's happening? What's wrong?'

Lauren's alarmed voice sounded in the background, then closer, her words unintelligible until they suddenly sounded clear in Olivia's ear. 'I'll call you back.'

The line went dead.

Dammit. *Dammit.*

Olivia whirled around, whirled back, hand to her temple. What had she done? He had recovered so well over the past year; she'd thought he was strong enough. What if he was having a serious medical crisis? What if she had killed him?

She sank back on to the sand, dazed and terrified. What now? She wouldn't be able to get across the country fast enough to help him, though she'd go in a heartbeat if she thought he needed her.

Lauren would call. She had to. She'd better.

God, the waiting . . .

She desperately wanted Derek. If the little dickhead hadn't insisted she couldn't last more than a week without him, she might have given in, though it galled her to admit it. He'd done her a twisted favor by taunting her. Pride kept her from caving now.

Why hadn't Lauren called yet to tell her everything was okay? Olivia wanted relief, the release of this horrible tension and guilt. Why hadn't she just called her sisters and left Dad out of it? Her neediness had put her beloved father at risk.

Her phone rang. Lauren. Olivia couldn't answer it fast enough. 'What happened?'

'He's fine, Olivia. He had some heart arrhythmia. We're getting it checked out, but he's fine, breathing normally now, with a steady heartbeat.'

'Thank God. Oh thank you, God.' She collapsed on to her knees. 'I was terrified. I thought . . .'

'He shared with me what you told him.' Lauren cleared her throat. 'I'm so sorry. That must be terribly—'

'I'm fine. Thank you. Or I will be. Just getting through it.' Olivia did not want sympathy from this bland-but-devious person who had wormed her way into Dad's heart and bank account. 'Should I come see Dad?'

'Your father is fine. There was no emergency. But if you need a place to get away, my brother Stuart lives in Belfast. He has a big place with a guest house. I can check if it's occupied. You'd be close to us there. Just under an hour.'

Olivia rolled her eyes. Oh yeah, she'd love to hang out with Lauren's relatives. 'You sure Dad doesn't need me?'

'Seeing you will only work him up again.'

Olivia narrowed her eyes. 'I thought you said he was fine.'

'He is, but you upset him and that's not a good idea,' Lauren said mildly. 'He needs quiet while they figure out if he should have a pacemaker.'

Olivia pressed her lips together. Pacemaker? That sounded serious. 'Can I speak to him?'

'No. Give him time.'

'I want to know he's okay.'

'I just *told* you he was.'

Exasperating control freak. Olivia would never understand how her father had turned from someone like Jillian Croft to someone like Lauren. It was like giving up caviar for head cheese. 'I want to hear his voice.'

Lauren sighed. 'All right. I'm giving him my phone. Please watch what you say.'

As if she wouldn't.

'Olivia.' His cracking voice made him sound about two hundred.

'Hi, Daddy.' Hers made her sound about twelve.

'You tell that cocksucker husband of yours that if I were younger, I'd beat him to a bloody pulp.'

'No, don't worry. It's fine. I'm fine, really.' Tears started in Olivia's eyes and wouldn't obey her order to retreat. Had she ever lied to him that baldly? 'Well rid of him, as you said.'

'You'll find someone better. You're young and beautiful.'

'I know I will. This is for the best.' She swiped at her tears, annoyed when more spilled out to take their place. It took all her training to keep her voice level and steady, breath supporting her diaphragm. 'It's a beautiful day. I'm standing right next to Santa Monica Pier. Remember when you took me fishing here?'

'Sure.' He sighed. 'Sure . . .'

'You take care of yourself, okay, Dad?'

'Olivia.' Lauren's voice again. 'He needs to rest.'

'Yes. I know he—' She forced herself to dip into her reserve tank of manners and civility. 'Thank you for letting me speak to him.'

'I understand. And I'm sorry about Derek. Your father is right. He wasn't good enough for you.'

And you're not good enough for my dad.

'Thanks.' Olivia kept her voice brisk and ended the call. She wiped away the tears, took a moment to center herself and make sure she was breathing deeply and cleanly. She'd call her sisters. Get this news out and over with.

When did she get to have fun emotions again?

She dialed Rosalind first. Rosalind would respond exactly the way Olivia needed her to. Rosalind was a brick. Even when she'd been dyeing her hair rainbow colors and flitting all over the planet, she'd been solid where it counted. Eve, though . . . Eve was quiet and slightly mysterious. Quiet and slightly mysterious invariably made Olivia feel she was being judged.

'Hey, Olivia! I was just thinking about you. Worrying, actually. How is life post-show?'

'Peachy. I just barfed all over an audition.' She was immensely grateful to her sister for not immediately asking about Derek's sperm.

'Aw, crap, I'm sorry. Did you really do badly or did it just feel that way?'

'I have no idea. I don't even really care anymore, you know. It's just so old. And I have so much else happening right now.'

'Bad? What is it?' That was Rosalind. Immediately ready to offer support.

Olivia's insides warmed. 'You and Eve were right about what Jade said.'

She told her sister the lurid details, knowing Rosalind would be going through the pain with her every step of the way.

'Oh, Olivia. I'm so sorry. I still cannot believe he lied like that for so many years, when having a baby was so important to you. I swear, I don't know what is wrong with people. Why can't everyone be normal?'

Olivia snorted. 'What, like us?'

'You know what I mean. Honest and fair and . . . I don't know, *decent*! I watched that documentary of Fred Rogers the other night, have you seen it? I'm telling you, I cried my eyes out, wanting everyone to care that much and be that kind.' She sighed. 'So what now? What are you going to— Hey, why don't you move out east for a while, closer to Eve and me? Just till this all settles. I know you still want to try for a movie career. But maybe you need a break.'

'Maybe.' The day was so sunny and hopeful, it seemed absurd to be in such darkness and despair. 'I don't know. I have no idea.'

'Have you told Dad?'

'Just now.' She couldn't bring herself to confess that she'd nearly killed him.

'What did he say?'

'He was pissed. Lauren said I should go hang out with her brother in Maine. Like *that* would fix anything.' She didn't even know why she was mentioning it. 'Isn't he a drunk?'

'No, no, that's the other one, Ben.'

'How do you know so much?'

'I don't know. She told me along the way.'

'Hmph.' On Olivia's list, asking Lauren about herself was below extracting grossness that wouldn't go down the InSinkErator.

'You've been saying how much you miss Maine. Staying with Stuart might be the perfect chance for a break.'

'I can't think of anything more depressing. Leave my house and yoga instructor and manicurist and masseur and stylist?' She waited for Rosalind to laugh. When she didn't, Olivia decided not to be insulted. 'And how do you know her brother's name?'

'He and his wife Georgia were at Dad and Lauren's wedding, don't you remember? Tall, silent guy, cute Southern redhead.'

Olivia had no recollection at all. 'Blocked it.'

'Yeah, that was a tough day for you. For all of us. You know, Bryn and I don't have anything important going on right now. I could come out to see you.'

'No, you were just out here. I'll be fine. Really.' She loved that it was so easy to keep reassuring people of something she barely believed herself. What was ahead for her foreseeable future but boredom, loneliness and grief?

'I'm worried about you.'

'I'm tough. Like Mom. What doesn't kill me makes me—' Her choice of words appalled her. Mom's troubles *had* killed her.

'Makes you wish you hadn't said that?' Rosalind chuckled

drily. 'You could come visit me in New York, then. I've got plenty of room. There's a lot more going on around here than at Stuart's.'

Her sweet concern had started wearing down Olivia's defenses; another tearfest was threatening, one she refused to burden her sister with. Olivia was *just fine*, after all. 'If things get too bad, I might take you up on that. Thanks for listening to me whine.'

'Oh, no. Whining is "boo-hoo, bad hair day". This is not whining. This is serious and life-changing.'

That about summed it up. 'I should go, Rozzy.'

'I'll call soon, okay? And if you need me, please pick up the phone. I'm a plane ride away.'

'Thanks.' Olivia had to clench her teeth against the tears. Rosalind was the best. She deserved every ounce of happiness she'd found with her birth family and Bryn. 'Love you.'

'Love you too. Hey, do you want me to call Eve for you? I know how awful it is to have to spread this kind of joy around.'

'No, no, I'll call her, thanks. Probably later today.' Olivia said goodbye, allowed this latest batch of tears thirty seconds, then dried her eyes and tipped her head back to feel the sun on her swollen, splotchy face. Not for too long – she didn't have on sunscreen – but enough to enjoy the warmth and light.

Too short a time later, she forced herself to retreat toward shade, feeling calmer, saner and hungry for the first time in days. Weeks. Since Jade's call during the picnic on Zuma Beach.

But she wasn't hungry for just any food. She was hungry for an In-N-Out burger with fries, animal style – onions, cheese and Thousand Island dressing ladled over.

Bring it on.

Carrying her blue shoes, she strode back to her car, putting them on before following GPS instructions to the nearest

In-N-Out, on West Washington Boulevard. By the time she parked and got in line, she was practically salivating.

Her phone rang. Cherie, her agent.

Olivia gasped. Did this mean a callback? Had they so admired her scream? Adrenaline kicked into high gear. Was it part of Murphy's Law that success found you only when you were on the verge of hitting bottom? Maybe she had been so ripped open by grief, she'd given the audition of her life.

'Did I get a callback?'

'What? No. Oh, no, sorry, Livvy. I've heard nothing.'

No. Olivia was bloody sick of that word. And of being called Livvy, even though she'd corrected Cherie about a hundred times. But she wasn't in a position to sneer at anyone.

The line moved forward. She stared up at the menu board she still knew by heart. Maybe she'd get a Double-Double burger. Definitely fries. Definitely animal style.

'How was your Fourth celebration last week?'

Miserable. 'Super fun. Yours?'

'Super fun! You're ready for Wednesday, riiiiight? *LA Morning*?'

Oh crap. She'd be on TV in less than two days. This food would make her blow up like a balloon. She'd still be fat on Wednesday. And probably have sprouted a zit. 'Of course.'

'They want you in a dress. Not fancy. Professional, but still feminine. Okaaaay?'

The guy ahead of Olivia stepped up to place his order as employees scurried behind the counter to keep up with the demand.

'Yeah, sure.' A dress? Not a suit with a nice big jacket to hide her post-indulgence bloat?

'They want you there at seven. Be early, okaaaay?'

Olivia wanted to scream, *Of course I'll be early. I've been doing this forever.* But Cherie was probably her last-chance agent. She had fired or pissed off all the others.

'Okay, sure, thanks for the reminder.'

The guy in front of her moved aside. Olivia stood where she was, staring at the woman smiling expectantly behind the counter.

Olivia was five-ten with an hourglass figure – her normal weight should be between a hundred thirty-five pounds and one sixty-five. Normally she weighed one twenty-seven, probably less now due to the stress. But a casting director had once called her pudgy. The camera added ten pounds.

She couldn't eat this. Nor could she cry between now and Wednesday, or her eyes would puff. What the *hell* was she doing?

'Get me out of it, Cherie. I can't go through with this.'

'*What?*' Cherie nearly screeched the word. 'You have got to be kidding me, Olivia. Tell me you are kidding me.'

Olivia wanted to throw a double-double tantrum of grief. Animal style.

You'll be great someday, Olivia, truly great, maybe even greater than I am. If it doesn't hurt along the way, you're doing it wrong.

She sighed. 'Of course I'm kidding you. I'll be at the studio on Wednesday. Early. In a dress.' Pretending to be infertile. Pretending that her husband wasn't the biggest nightmare that had ever been pulled from a uterus.

She closed her eyes, light-headed with hunger and fatigue.

'Ma'am?' The woman behind the counter wasn't even pretending to be patient. '*Ma'am?* Can I take your order?'

Olivia opened her eyes and gazed up at the menu board, stomach growling.

Never surrender.

She turned and left the restaurant.

Chapter 4

October 15, 1993 (Friday)

Disaster. They want me to do a nude scene in Solitary Vengeance, *even though it's known throughout the industry that I don't do nude scenes. They don't understand why. They think I'm a prude. A prude! I hung a topless portrait of me in our house. But even if the only people who see me full-frontal are the cameraman and the director, that's two too many. They'd see I don't look normal. They'd see there's something wrong. They might tell someone. They might tell everyone.*

I can't risk that. I need to pull every string possible to get around this while maintaining my reputation for absolute devotion to the integrity of my art and of the script. If people found out the sickening truth of my body, it would blow my career and life apart.

If all else fails, I will happily throw the biggest prima-donna tantrum of my career. I've come all this way without anyone finding out, and have three beautiful daughters everyone thinks are mine.

I am not risking any of that. The shame would kill me.
Determinedly yours,
Jillian

*

Olivia stood in *LA Morning*'s pleasant green room, trying to look placid, along with the two other nervous people in the room. One, a middle-aged man in a badly fitting suit, stared straight ahead, fingers drumming his thigh. The other, a young woman in jeans, heels and a yellow blouse with a plaid collar, slouched in her chair, face glued to her phone.

A jug of water sat in one corner, along with fixings for tea and coffee. Potted plants decorated another, and entertainment-industry magazines were strewn over end tables between cushioned chairs that Olivia avoided for fear of getting wrinkles on her dress. She'd worn jeans over here and changed in the bathroom, putting on her heels first so she wouldn't have to bend over with the dress on.

Another lesson in total glamour from the totally glamorous Jillian Croft.

Last night, Olivia had slept badly and been too upset and anxious to eat breakfast. Over the past two days, she'd put a tremendous amount of time and energy into not crying, which meant she also wouldn't allow herself to relax. Sleeping pills and Scotch at night. No massages. No therapy. No meditation or yoga. Nothing that might allow her brain time to think about the disaster that was her life. She'd taken extra exercise classes, gone shopping and shopping and shopping, and had lunch with a friend she hadn't seen in years, who managed to talk about something other than her above-average-in-all-things children for several minutes in a row.

In one very welcome development, having kicked the reason she couldn't have children out of her life, Olivia had felt less bitterness and envy hearing about Catha's kids. After all, there was no reason Olivia couldn't still have children of her own, though at her age she didn't have a lot of years to mess with.

In spite of the Derek apocalypse, she knew she wanted to

marry again, to get it right, as her parents had. She was meant to be someone's wife. As much as she'd adored Bill Chandler, the distinguished divorcé she'd been dating before Derek, she'd broken up with him when it became clear his promises of marriage were nothing more than lies he wanted to be true.

Olivia paced the length of the room, picked up a *Forbes* magazine and put it down, ignoring the admiring gaze of the middle-aged man sharing this limbo. On her return pace, she stopped by the mirror to check herself once again. Stress and lost sleep had made her cheekbones a bit too sharp, the shadows under her eyes resistant to all but the heaviest application of makeup.

The good news was that all her not-crying had paid off. Her eyes were clear and non-puffy. When she'd stepped on the scale that morning, she'd seen with a surge of both shock and fierce satisfaction that her weight had dropped to one twenty-three, making her outfit – not quite the conservative look the studio had asked for – fit like a dream.

If she did say so herself, she looked incredibly hot. The figure-skimming dress showcased her breasts like the elegant pair they were, and its emerald color complemented the unusual light brown of her eyes and her hair's auburn shade – the same her mother used.

Regardless of the deep-down shame she'd felt at being unable to conceive, Olivia was intent on broadcasting the message that infertility did not make a woman any less of a woman. Mom had been living proof of that.

A scruffy guy with intentional bedhead, ragged jeans and a baggy black shirt came into the room holding a clipboard. Olivia beamed at him, trying to hide her panic. What was he, twelve? Thirteen? Probably twenty-five. They looked younger and younger every year.

'Jacob Thalston? We're ready for you.'

'Yes. Yes. That's me. Thank you.' The middle-aged man adjusted his tie, rose slowly and walked reluctantly to the door – a soul to be damned.

Olivia wilted into relief, wishing she hadn't been a good soldier and come in so early. She'd much rather be anxious at home than in this supposed-to-be-cozy room where she had to pretend calm.

God, she was nervous. Not for the cameras – being in front of the camera was her job, her passion, her life – but over having to lie about something so personal as her body, which was pretty hard to divorce from whatever else defined her. She couldn't imagine how her mother had been able to pull off living a lie, not just once, but over and over again, wearing the prosthetic pregnancy tummies three times, being interviewed, gawked at, written about, smiling her brilliant magnetic smile, seemingly unperturbed by her deception.

If her mother could pour it on for the right reasons, then Olivia could as well.

She shook out her arms, rotated her head one direction then the other, making exaggerated chewing motions to keep her jaw loose, all while breathing deep into her abdomen, trying to find some way to restore equilibrium, not caring if she looked like a dork.

Unfortunately, the usual techniques weren't working. She still felt edgy, not centered in herself. Her stomach growled so loudly the young woman looked up from her phone.

Delightful.

'Sorry.'

'No, no problem. I'm starving too.' She stretched and stood, her shirt clinging to reveal a small baby bump. 'Is there a restroom, do you know? My bladder is the size of a lima bean.'

Olivia pointed to the exit door, green with envy in the green room. A baby! The woman must be there to give the segment its happy ending. 'Out there, turn right.'

'Thanks.'

The second she was alone, Olivia pounced on her phone to dial Eve. Her youngest sister had recently admitted that she'd spent years battling anxiety and panic attacks over the fact that an utter scumbag producer friend of Mom's, Silas Angel – least appropriate last name ever – had molested her when she was a girl. If anyone could give Olivia on-the-spot advice on coping with these ridiculous jitters, Eve could.

'Hey, Olivia, I'm streaming *LA Morning* at my computer, waiting for you to come on. There's some shrink talking now. What's up?'

Olivia hesitated, trying to choose her words. This was not a situation she relished. She was always the competent in-charge older sister, leading the way for the younger two, especially after Mom had died.

Get over yourself, Olivia.

'I'm on next. Just . . . feeling anxious.'

'I'm not surprised.' Eve sounded totally surprised. 'This isn't your show.'

'It's not that. It's that I'm going on as a spokesperson for infertility when I'm no longer infertile. Or probably not. It feels like a lie.'

'Oh. I see. But you and Derek *were* infertile together. So you're not really lying.'

'I know. But I'm . . .' She drew in a breath. 'I'm still having a tough time.'

Eve made a sympathetic sound. 'Logic has nothing to do with anxiety, or we'd all be able to talk ourselves out of it.'

'I was wondering if you had any advice. Some technique that worked for you.'

A short silence that Olivia wasn't sure how to interpret. 'Sure. Of course. You already know about relaxing and breathing and posture, right?'

'Yes, yes, I'm doing all that.' She didn't mean to sound irritable, but having to ask Eve for help made her cranky. 'Standard actor training.'

'Then try this. My therapist calls it self-soothing. You take stock of your anxiety and act as if you were a friend of yours suffering the same way for the same reasons. Tell yourself what you'd tell that person. It sounds weird and feels stupid, but it really works.'

'You mean like "Gee, Olivia, it's fine that you're going out there to lie to half the country"?'

'Exactly like that. And it *is* okay. When they asked you to be on the show, you believed you had a problem – you just didn't know it was Derek. Remind yourself of that. Tell yourself you have a lot to offer women just by having survived all those years of disappointment. Whatever you would say to help another Olivia.'

'I'll try. I guess.' She rolled her head side to side, trying to lengthen tight neck muscles. 'Thanks, Eve. I appreciate the help.'

'You're welcome.' The same tone of voice Eve had used earlier, slightly surprised. Or amused. Or both. 'I think this is the first time you've ever come to me for advice.'

'Oh. Well.' Olivia had no idea what to make of that.

'I love it, actually.' Eve's voice softened into affection. 'It means a lot.'

It did? Why? Was Olivia such an awful older sister? She and Eve did seem to push each other's buttons, but she wouldn't have thought asking for psychological help would be any kind of breakthrough. 'Well, good. I'll try it.'

'Good luck. Call again if you need to. Marx and I are driving over to Washington Island in a few days. They've broken ground for Aunt Shelley's cottage.'

'Hey, that's exciting. Your first design in the flesh, so to speak.' This past spring, Eve, along with her dog Marx, had been sent by Lauren the Manipulator up to Washington Island, Wisconsin, purportedly to work for a childhood friend of hers who – gee – turned out to be Eve's biological aunt. Lauren apparently didn't think Eve should have a choice as to whether she wanted to find her birth family or not. If Lauren had tried something like that with Olivia, Olivia would have decked her. 'How is Shelley?'

'She seems fine. It will be great to see her. I'll be spending a couple of weeks up there, working with the new client.'

'And seeing Clayton?'

'Clayton will be busy in Chicago,' Eve said primly.

'Oh.' Olivia rolled her eyes. 'I assumed—'

'But he'll visit as often as he can.' She chuckled wickedly.

'Yee-haw.' Olivia grinned triumphantly, first genuine smile of the day. 'Get together for some hot action, for God's sake, will you? This whole "friends first" thing is ridiculous.'

'I promise you'll be the last to know.'

Olivia managed a laugh, thanked her sister again and ended the call. She'd try the self-soothing, see how it worked. Turning from her corner-facing exile, she resumed her deep breathing, weight centered on both feet, posture straight.

Olivia, my lovely, I understand why you are shaking like a pathetic amateur, but I promise you are doing the right thing for the right reasons. Your mom would be incredibly proud of you.

Repeated, added to, the technique worked pretty well. Her shoulders lowered even farther, her adrenaline backed off some.

Not bad.

Scruffy Guy opened the door again, ushering through the good doctor, now walking with the confident stride of someone who'd made it out of hell without so much as singeing an eyebrow.

Scruffy glanced at his clipboard. 'Olivia Croft? We're ready for you.'

'Great.' She smiled to show how thrilled she was, wishing she could feel likewise. 'I'm ready for you, too.'

He held open the door, then led her into the cavernous room, one half of which housed the familiar *LA Morning* set, with Bob Allen and Barb Vardham in comfy teal chairs, a low table with glasses of water in front of them, a fake view of LA behind. Overhead the ceiling bristled with variously angled lighting fixtures. Just like the *Crofty Cooks* studio, only twice the size and probably fifty times the budget. Unlike *Crofty Cooks*, there was a small studio audience there to watch the fun.

'When we go to commercial, you'll get called. Feeling okay?'

'Of course.' She grinned at Scruffy, determined to seem in control no matter what, silently thanking her sister for the boost to her calm. 'It's all very familiar.'

'And we are in commercial.' The stage manager beckoned in Olivia's direction without giving her a glance. 'Next guest up, please.'

Olivia walked proudly on to the set, where Bob and Barb waited with carefully expectant, done-this-too-many-times expressions.

'Hi there. I'm Olivia Croft. Nice to meet you both.'

'Hi, Olivia. Thanks for joining us today.' Barb, who looked enough like a Barbie doll to make her name ludicrous, held out a stiff hand for a plastic shake.

'Good to meet you, Olivia.' Bob was stout 'n' hearty, with

expertly coiffed dark hair and gray so perfectly placed at his temples, Olivia suspected it had been painted on. 'I was a big fan of your mother's.'

'You, me and the rest of the world.' She took her seat on the guest chair, adjusted her skirt, tilted her together-always knees to the left and swung her hair back over her shoulders. Familiar pre-show gestures that felt strange in this unfamiliar setting.

'And we're back in three . . . two . . .' Mr Stage Manager counted down the rest of the way silently, then pointed: *Go.*

Barb brightened into joy. 'And we are back, with a very special lady. Olivia Croft, Jillian Croft's oldest daughter. You know her locally as the wonderful hostess of *Crofty Cooks*. Welcome, Olivia.'

'Thank you for having me.' Olivia smiled at Barb, then at the camera, supposedly in her element but clenching her hands in her lap, still disoriented and with the barest beginnings of panic.

She refused to bomb this interview. Not an option. If for no other reason, in case Derek was watching.

'We're talking today about a difficult topic, one that is often hard for people to discuss. In-fer-ti-li-ty.' Bob half sang the syllables and swiveled to face Olivia, showing appropriate concern. 'Tell us, Olivia, how long have you and your husband struggled to conceive, and is that battle ongoing?'

Ongoing? She'd better dodge that one. 'My husband and I had . . . have been trying to conceive for the past five-plus years. We've been to every expert, had all the tests and found nothing abnormal. It just didn't happen. *Isn't* happening.'

Christ. Her panic intensified, which pissed her off. *Come on, Olivia.* At least get the damn tenses straight. This was not like her. She was a pro.

Never let them see you ugly.

'Wow, you know that must be almost harder than if they found something, am I right?'

'Yes, you are, Barb, absolutely. Because there is *no reason* we can't conceive.' She had to grit her teeth on that one. Sweat pricked her scalp and under her arms. 'Infertility is never easy, but if there's something specific wrong, you can fix the problem or get to a place emotionally where you can accept the problem as unfixable. We didn't have that. Don't have that . . . didn't.'

Make up your mind.

'Your mother had trouble conceiving, is that right?'

Olivia whipped her head over toward Bob, immediately in guard-dog protective mode. 'Why do you say that?'

He looked mildly taken aback. 'We found an article from *People* magazine announcing your birth. In it your mother stated that it took her and Daniel Braddock seven years to conceive you.'

Thank God. 'Right. Yes. Sorry, I forgot about that.'

'Any connection there, do you think?' Bob asked.

'To my mother? No. No.' Olivia cleared her throat, mind racing. 'No. My mother just, uh, she was able to fix . . . the problem.'

Crap. *Crap.* She was never at a loss for words in front of a camera. Never. Mom had drilled and drilled her in every possible interview situation until Olivia could respond coherently no matter what came at her. Mom would be mortified to see her best pupil screwing up like this.

'Obviously Jillian Croft fixed the problem or you wouldn't be sitting here.' Bob gave a hearty TV-host chuckle, which Barb matched with perfect timing. The audience obediently joined in. Because yeah, that was so funny.

'Now, Olivia.' He sobered instantly. 'Before you came on,

we were hearing from Dr Thalston that couples experiencing fertility problems go through a range of emotions, and that this . . . difficulty, if you will, represents a loss of control over their lives that can have profound psychological consequences.'

'That's right, Bob.' Barb shook her head mournfully. 'He described a cycle of disbelief, anger, sadness, guilt, blame, anxiety and depression. Can you corroborate any of that from your experience with your husband, Olivia?'

Could she? Was it safe to? How did she want to play this? She couldn't decide.

Shit. She had to say *something*.

'Oh. Yes. Those . . . all those things. Those emotions. We felt them all.' She was sweating freely, teeth clenched harder, stomach roiling, smile staling.

Fuckarini. She was bombing. Olivia Croft, who chatted like a magpie on camera, who loved the attention, loved the chance to shine, to be witty, beautiful and all-around fabulous, was sitting here impotently, brain fuzzing with confusion and shame.

And then anger, delicious, strong, life-giving anger came into the mix, acting like a cerebral defogger. 'It was one of the hardest things we ever faced as a couple.'

'How long have you and Derek been married?'

'For*ever*.' She made it sound like the nightmare it had turned into.

Genuine laughter from the studio audience. Bob and Barb joined in uneasily. Apparently they hadn't anticipated interviewing a bitter bitch.

Get used to it.

'Seriously, how long?' Bob asked.

'We've been married eight years. This changed our relationship. No question.'

No question whatsoever, and she hoped the bastard was watching and sweating in his overpriced shoes.

'Would you say that fighting this battle together has brought you and your husband closer?' Barb leaned forward, anticipating the happy-ending answer that Olivia should right now be composing in her head, to give all the people watching what they wanted to hear.

Would she say this had brought her and her husband closer?

Olivia's mind slowed to a crawl. She stared at Barb's overly white smile and became so full of rage at the prick who'd put her in this position that she didn't give a shit what happened, either to her, to the *LA Morning* show, or to anyone else. 'No.'

Barb's eyes widened.

'I'm sorry to hear that.' Bob looked about as sorry as any host would who was about to get juicy controversial gossip on his show.

'I imagine this would be rough on any couple.' Barb did her best to look sympathetic, but the gleam in her eyes was unmistakable.

'In fact.' Olivia was starting to enjoy herself, but not in a fun way; in the way you enjoyed smashing plates or slashing the tires of an enemy. 'We are getting a divorce.'

Bob faked a gasp. 'Oh no. I guess that can happen, though, huh? The strain of not knowing what was wrong, why you weren't able to conceive? It must have been rough.'

Olivia let out a laugh that sounded like a Pomeranian being strangled. 'It *was* rough. But you know what was really rough, Bob? You know what was – and is – really, *really* rough?'

Bob clearly did not know. And just as clearly couldn't wait to find out.

'We're getting a divorce *because* I found out why we couldn't conceive.' She imagined Derek wetting his $600 jeans as he realized what she was about to do, what she'd had no intention of doing until she got on this program and faced her first on-stage meltdown in front of the living-dead nightmare that was BobandBarb.

Olivia . . . Her wise inner voice told her to take the mature route, not to drag herself down to Derek's level.

'So you *did* find out what was wrong?' Barb leaned closer, smelling a ratings bumper. 'If you don't mind me asking, what was the problem?'

Olivia told her wise inner voice to shove its head up its own ass. Revenge would be so sweet she could almost taste it.

'My husband Derek had a vasectomy.' Her voice broke. 'Years ago. Before we were married.'

Low murmurs from the audience.

Exhaustion and fear got the better of her. Tears gathered and fell – involuntary, but God, what great theater. She put her hands to her cheeks, a victim overcome, and delivered her next line in a quavering whisper. 'He never told me.'

Chapter 5

January 18, 1994 (Tuesday)

Daddy had to have emergency heart surgery. I had to leave the set and fly up to Bangor immediately, then drive like crazy to the hospital in Greenville (in the snow!), but of course immediately wasn't soon enough for Mom. Christina was already there, what took me so long? Christina lives in Maine! Of course she was there sooner! I didn't bother pointing that out. What's the use?

Daddy looked so strange lying in the hospital bed. I was trying to think if I've ever seen Arnold Moore anything but upright and strong. They say the surgery was a success, but that he'll have to be careful from now on. It's hard to imagine him being careful. He's worked his whole life with his hands and body.

Mom was horrible to me. She will never forgive me for leaving home without telling her, no matter how many times I say that until I had my own children, I had no idea what I'd done, that I was only thinking of me, and that I regret it with all my heart.

Not entirely true, of course. If I had told her my plans, she would have locked me up somewhere. I had to remind myself over and over that nothing I do or say will make a difference.

It's just so hard, when seeing other people's points of view comes so naturally to me, to realize that she really and truly can't see anyone's but her own. It's easier just to think of her as a bitch, but that's unfair because she is simply saying what is true to her.

The house looks terrible. Where did all the money go that I sent her? All the beautiful appliances and furniture I thought she'd like? It's nowhere. She must hate me so much.

Sadly,
Jillian

The shitstorm began slowly. First, the eager reactions from Barb and Bob on set as they pretended shock and sympathy, practically chortling with joy. How did Olivia react to finding out Derek was sterile? How could he do such a thing? What would she do now? Had this ever happened before to a couple? They wanted to hear from their viewers.

Olivia had no idea how she'd answered, what else she'd said. She'd been too wired, too full of danger adrenaline. Along with a twinge of guilt at having stooped so low, there'd been fierce joy that she'd gotten the sweetest possible revenge on Derek for the soul-crushing lie he'd inflicted on her and their marriage, knowingly destroying her most cherished hope, apparently with no guilt or remorse.

The hint that something larger was brewing started with the call from Cherie shortly after Olivia arrived back at her too-big, too-empty house in Brentwood. Drained and numb after the traffic-slowed ride home, she changed into sweats and tried to think of something to do rather than face the lonely blank that was the rest of her life. Her certainty that she'd struck a blow for justice had dwindled into doubts and worries about the fallout, about how much damage she might have inflicted on any hope of a quick, relatively painless divorce. With luck, no one had seen the damn show, or would care about her problems if they had.

'Livvy, you hit gold todaaay.'

She was standing in front of the refrigerator, head telling her body to eat, body refusing like a truculent toddler. 'I'm not sure that's what I'd call it.'

'Bob and Barb are thrilled. Their phones and website lit up like *crazy* after you were on. They said they'd never seen anything like it. You're the tragic heroine of the moment.'

Olivia gave a bizarre half-laugh. 'You're kidding me.'

Her phone beeped with another call. Eve.

'I'm not kidding, honey. This puts you in the national eye. I can see half the producers in town fighting for this story. It could be gold for us.'

'Wow.' She laughed again, slightly hysterical. She'd wanted to be famous, not infamous. Cate Blanchett, not Lorena Bobbitt.

'Oh my God, *TMZ* is calling. I gotta go. I'll call you baaack.'

Olivia put down her phone. Closed the refrigerator. Tabloids. That was bad. But okay, okay. Damage control still possible. She'd refuse to be interviewed. Spilling Derek's secret might be excusable once – temper, raw emotions – but giving interviews . . . gross. She couldn't do that. Even to him.

Olivia's phone rang again. Rosalind. 'Hi, sweetie.'

'Olivia! God, was that something! I was cheering like mad. You go, sister. He deserved every second of that honesty!'

Olivia laughed, that same choking Pomeranian sound. 'I sorta lost it up there.'

'You were *great*. Completely real. It looked like you were fumbling at first to protect him, and then broke down and had to admit the truth. I loved it.'

Hope rose. If everyone saw it that way . . . 'Thanks.'

'Do you know if Derek was watching?'

Olivia cringed. 'I'm sure I'll find out.'

'Ugh, yeah. Hope that's not too ugly.'

'Oh, it will be.' She opened the refrigerator again, her sister's cheerful support fooling her stomach into thinking it could manage some food. Yoghurt, anyway. She pulled out a carton of raspberry and reached into a nearby cupboard for granola.

'If you need Eve or me to show up and pummel him, you just let us know. What a poo-ball. He deserved everything you gave him. I'm so proud of you.'

Olivia smiled, spooned the yoghurt into a bowl and over it sprinkled a generous handful of granola. 'Thanks, Rozzy.'

She carried the yoghurt into the living room, ignoring Cherie's callback, wondering when this horrible combination of hating her husband and missing him would let her alone. She'd split him in half, missing the Derek she'd created in her mind, hating what had turned out to be the real one.

Except it wasn't even that simple.

Sitting on the sofa, she looked around her as she ate. She'd have to redecorate, refurnish the house, get rid of everything she and Derek bought together. It would be easier to push back the pain if she wasn't constantly reminded of him here, seeing all the objects with stories attached, thinking of the times they'd made love on the sofa where she sat, or hung out cuddled together in the easy chair, Olivia perched on his lap, the two of them sharing wine. The painting they'd both fallen in love with in a tiny gallery in Milan. The rug they'd bought from the merchant in Casablanca.

How much more of the planet would she have to redecorate? They'd traveled all over as their careers permitted, eaten and drunk the finest wherever they went. Skied, sailed, swum, climbed, hiked and made love all over the world.

The bastard.

At the height of her yoghurt-and-misery, Eve called again.

'Have you been googling yourself lately?'

Olivia snorted, unwilling to admit how often she did just that. But not lately. 'I have better things to do. Why?'

'You're going viral.'

Olivia put down her bowl. 'You're kidding.'

'Online news stations have picked up the story. It's spreading like mad.' Eve sounded anxious. 'People are . . . reacting.'

'Reacting?'

'Most people are totally outraged on your behalf.'

'They should be.' Olivia sat straighter on the couch. 'What are the rest doing?'

'They're not real happy.'

'Well, whatever. It's none of their business.'

'You go on TV and say something like that, it's sort of too late for privacy.'

Olivia slumped back against the cushions. She preferred Rosalind's reaction. 'Okay. How bad is it?'

'Bad. I think you might need to apologize or something.'

'*Apologize!*' She stood up so abruptly she banged her knee on the table leg and bent down to rub it fiercely, Mom's solution for any kind of injury. 'I have to apologize for my life having been ruined by my husband?'

'Olivia, it's really bad.' Eve sounded terrified. 'People are threatening you.'

Olivia sat back down, feeling suddenly woozy. Anonymous bashing – the basest level of humanity, and the most cowardly. 'Threatening *me*?'

'Yeah. I would . . . I don't know. Maybe go spend the night with a friend?'

'Are you *kidding* me?'

70

'No, Olivia. It's scary.'

'I'm going to look. I'll call you back.' She put her phone in her pocket and raced upstairs for her laptop to see how bad it was.

Bad.

Yes, some people loved Olivia and hated Derek. But some people also hated her. They wanted her to hang herself. Shoot herself. Or *they* wanted to hang her or shoot her. Or hang her first and shoot her during.

For the next couple of hours, she stayed where she was, riveted by the horror and the sheer speed of information, true and not. Yes, she'd seen it before, but like most human drama, such a different animal when it was happening to her.

Derek had been tweeting, denying everything, calling Olivia a liar, a bitter, unbalanced woman out for revenge after he'd asked her for a divorce.

Jade chimed in, identifying herself as Derek's ex-wife, defending Olivia, insisting the vasectomy story was true.

Derek called Jade a liar too, another bitter woman.

He seemed to marry a lot of those.

Angry men rose in throngs to defend poor Derek from vindictive bitches. Some wanted to kill Olivia and Jade. Others wanted to rape, then strangle them. Gang-bangings, good old-fashioned bludgeonings, lynch mobs, public torture and beheadings.

So many intriguing methods!

Such fabulous imaginations!

Others chimed in. It was Derek who deserved those tortures, not Olivia, not Jade. Babies were offered up to Olivia for adoption. Various techniques for castrations were suggested for Derek.

A nurse who used to work at the Beverly Hills clinic where

Derek and Olivia had been receiving fertility treatment joined the fun. She'd known about Derek all along, and thought him the most disgusting human being she'd ever encountered. How dreadful it had been, with privacy laws tying her hands, to watch Olivia suffer for so long! She wanted to kill Derek with her bare hands. God would certainly send him to hell.

More opinions. More clips. Amused local anchors mentioning the story just before going to commercial, the ha-ha portion of the broadcast.

Olivia's misery was the country's ha-ha portion.

On and on she read, until she was so freaked out she had to stop, slamming down the lid of her laptop, breath coming irregularly.

This was a disaster.

This was terrifying.

God, she wished Mom was around. Mom would know exactly how to handle this. Mom knew how to handle everything.

When her phone rang, she jumped, then peered anxiously at the display, chiding herself for being paranoid. She guarded her cell information rabidly. Only family and close friends knew the number.

It was family.

Shit.

She straightened her spine. 'Derek.'

'What the fuck is your problem?'

'I'm fine, thanks. How are you?' She rose from the chair and started pacing their – *her* – bedroom.

'I'm totally fucked and it's your fault.'

'*You* are totally fucked? Do I have any children? Do I?' Her voice had risen to a panicked shriek. *Don't make it worse.* She forced her range down an octave. 'Look. You did a horrible thing to me. I lost my temper and did a horrible thing to you.

This isn't how either of us should have behaved. But we can call it even now. We don't have to keep—'

'Even? You call this *even*? I just came out of the bank and some woman *spit* on me.'

Olivia's skin prickled, ashamed at her immediate thoughts: he'd gone to the bank? Should she shut down their accounts?

Dear God, had it really come to this between them? 'Women are not going to love you for what you did.'

'Women aren't supposed to *know* what I did.'

Her temper rose again. 'What kind of defense is that for lying to me for so many years? Boo-hoo, I got caught?'

'Shut up, just fucking shut up for once in your pampered silver-spoon life.'

Olivia gasped. Never, ever, in all their married years, no matter how angry he'd gotten, had Derek ever spoken to her like that. She backed up until she reached the room's corner, the wall solid and cool at her back. '*What* did you just say to me?'

'All you care about, all you've *ever* cared about, is yourself. It's been sickening having to cater to that for all these years.'

Bang.

After what he'd done to her, deliberately withholding the child she wanted so badly, Olivia would have thought it impossible that Derek could hurt her any more. She wanted to crumple to the floor. Instead she grabbed on to the only strength she could access – her anger.

'Who were *you* looking out for when you hid the fact that you're sterile? Me?'

'I couldn't tell you.'

'Why?'

'You would have left me.' His voice was barely recognizable as that of the man who could whisper such tender words, a shaky, ugly growl that chilled her. 'You wouldn't have stayed with me if you knew.'

'That wasn't your decision to make.'

'It was my only choice.'

Olivia put her hand to her forehead, squeezing her eyes shut, trying to calm herself enough to concentrate. 'So then . . . you were afraid of losing me?'

She didn't have to wait for his sickening laughter to know that she was being a stupid romantic fool.

Derek had never wanted kids. Derek had never wanted *her*, not really. Their marriage, which she'd entered into with all her heart, was all about the life she could give him, and probably always had been. The doting and adoration? An act, so that she would keep him around. So she would pay for every toy the poor boy from Mississippi had ever wanted.

She wanted to get down on her hands and knees and hit her head against the wall until her brains liquefied in her skull and she could stop thinking and stop feeling.

It was all she could do to loosen her throat enough to make sound. 'You stayed for the money. My money. That's what this marriage was about.'

He took in a long breath, and if she'd thought she was a stupid romantic fool before, she was triply so now, because she actually hoped – *actually hoped* – that he would tell her not to be an idiot. He'd been angry. Of course he loved her.

'You need to apologize. Publicly. Broadcast an apology and say you were angry and you made everything up, that you were wrong. You need to do that, Olivia.' There was no mistaking his threat. '*Right. Now.*'

Or else . . . ?

'Right now, Olivia. It's the fucking least you can do.'

She slid down the wall, thinking of the good times, the happy times. The even better times. And the infuriating times, the miserable loneliness she'd felt being his wife, trying to fill that emptiness with a child. How stupid she'd been. How deeply in denial.

'No, Derek. The *least* I can do is *this*.' She jabbed at the phone to end the call and tossed it face down next to her on the hardwood.

Half an hour later, she was still sitting in the corner of the room, Derek's threats and those of the Internet ragers growing and swirling in her brain until she was paralyzed by fear.

Her father had taken her to LA Opera back when she was in high school, to see *Otello*, Verdi's opera based on the Shakespeare work. Olivia had loved it up until the third act, in which Desdemona prepares for bed, then is wakened by her husband, who sings how he's there to kill her, and that she should prepare for her death. Olivia had buried her head in her father's shoulder, unable to watch, as she'd been unable to watch that scene in any other version of the story since. No matter how many other violent or otherwise horrifying twisted movies she'd seen, nothing had chilled or haunted her quite as thoroughly as this man calmly and deliberately going about strangling the woman he loved.

Her phone rang again. She jerked in fear, bumping her head against the wall, letting out an undefined syllable of surprise.

What if it was Derek again? What if he was outside?

She turned the phone over as if there was a scorpion hiding underneath.

Lauren.

For the first time ever, Olivia answered her stepmother's call with some eagerness. 'Hi, Lauren.'

'There's a redeye to Bangor leaving from LAX tonight. I bought you a ticket. My brother is expecting you. Go now.

Before reporters show up at your house, if they're not there already. Before any crazy person gets hold of your address. If you go now, you can just make it. Please, Olivia.'

A thousand protests formed in her mind, then a thousand more, but the only reaction she could muster was to scramble to her feet, already thinking of what she could pack, and two words she'd never said to Lauren with anything approaching this depth of sincerity.

'Thank you.'

Chapter 6

May 19, 1994 (Thursday)

My work in Solitary Vengeance *is the best I've ever done, even better than in* Dangerous Fall. *I'm so so so excited! After this I know there will be more offers. I can't wait to get at them! Forget a slow slide into obscurity; I have proved that I can last, and that I can only get better.*

As soon as the movie wraps, Daniel and I are planning to take our first trip without the girls, a second honeymoon in Greece. I have scripts to read and he'll have papers to edit, but if you're doing your job on a balcony overlooking the Mediterranean, how much can it feel like work?

If I have my way, this trip should keep whoever Daniel is fucking out of his bed for the rest of his life. I plan to be absolutely fantastic in every possible way.

Fantastically yours,
Jillian

Olivia pulled up to Stuart and Georgia Patterson's house, where she'd be serving her sentence until the world calmed the hell down and let her back home. Packing and leaving so abruptly last night had been hellish. Arriving here in the beloved vacation state of her childhood had been a relief. Like crawling part way back to that childhood, when she'd been free of responsibility, happy in the bosom of her family, and half the world didn't want to kill her.

The Pattersons' large white Victorian sat regally on a gentle hill at the end of a long sweep of driveway branching off Route 1. In spite of Olivia's tense exhaustion and pounding headache from self-medicating with Delta's adorable bottles of Woodford Reserve bourbon on the overnight flight from LA, when she got out of the white VW Jetta she'd rented at the airport, she still took the time to close her eyes and fill her lungs repeatedly with Maine's remarkably clear coastal air, tinged with scents of fir, salt and sea. An intoxicating smell that her Pacific, for all its wild tumbling glory, lacked.

Another breath, then her nostalgic respite was cut short by the opening of Stuart Patterson's front door, revealing a middle-aged redhead with blue eyes and freckles, wearing overalls camouflaging whatever figure she had and a sunny big-toothed smile.

'Welcome, Olivia. Welcome.' The woman Olivia assumed was her step-aunt, Georgia, bounded down the steps, arms outstretched.

Apparently Georgia wanted to hug her.

Olivia managed a smile and leaned down, nearly knocked off-balance in her high-heeled boots by Georgia's enthusiastic squeeze. She had a lot of strength for such a tiny woman. The top of her head barely made it to Olivia's collarbone.

'I'm so glad you came to see us.' Georgia drew back, holding on to Olivia's arms, searching her face. 'You poor thing, what you've been through.'

'Thanks. It's very nice of you to put up with me.'

'No, no, it's nothing.' Traces of a Southern accent made Georgia's voice lilting and musical. 'Come in, come in. Let me help you with your bag.'

'Bags.' Olivia found the appropriate button on her key set, and the trunk obediently rose to reveal her bright red suitcases.

'Three!' Georgia laughed. 'Honey, around here you need underwear, two pairs of shorts and seven shirts, laundry once a week.'

'I left in a hurry. I had no idea what I was doing. I brought everything.'

'You're fine, you're fine. We've got lots of room. This house is too big for the two of us. It'll be so good to have another person around.' She hoisted the larger two suitcases as if they weighed nothing. 'Stuart's parents gave us this house. Between you, me and a gatepost, I'd rather have something smaller, but sometimes you don't get to choose. Prices are much higher in Belfast now than when my in-laws bought, so this house is pure gold. Come this way.'

That much chatter in another context or from another person might have set Olivia's teeth on edge, but coming from this bubbly, exuberant woman with the singsong speech and warm eyes, the torrent of words was an unexpected comfort. For one thing, it meant Olivia's fried brain wouldn't have to come up with much to say. And it was a relief to find out that Georgia was on her side in the horrific debacle sweeping the nation. Or if she wasn't, she was too polite to say otherwise.

'Let me take the suitcases, Georgia. They're crazy heavy.'

'They certainly are.' She started toward the house with quick, sure steps. 'Am I carrying your husband's body?'

'Tempting, but no.'

'Probably wise. The smell could get real unpleasant.' At the top step, she pulled open the screen and pushed through the front door with her hip. 'Did you have lunch?'

Olivia followed her into the pale-yellow foyer. 'Crab roll at McLaughlin Seafood in Bangor.'

'I love that place.' Georgia jerked her head toward a wooden staircase. 'I'll take you up to your room. You can rest as long as you like. Those overnight flights are the pits.'

'Thank you so much for letting me hide here.'

'Heavens, it's the least we could do.' She started climbing. 'Honestly, I trust my husband a hundred percent, but you hear something like what happened to you, and it chills you inside and out. You start thinking, "She probably trusted *her* husband too." So where does that leave you?'

'Not-trusting.' Olivia loved the house on sight, the glimpses of invitingly furnished high-ceilinged rooms around and beyond the staircase, whose creaky steps had been worn nearly to bare wood in the middle. A comfortable place, the perfect feel if you had to interrupt your life to seek refuge.

'Not trusting is no way to have a marriage.'

'Agreed.' Olivia followed her hostess into a large room with a four-poster bed, rocker and desk, and a lovely view of the bay and the Belfast harbor opposite. 'That's why I'm going to stop being married.'

'Don't blame you one bit.' Georgia hoisted the largest suitcase on to a luggage stand. 'So here you are. Normally we'd have you stay in the guest house, but Duncan's with us, and we sure can't kick him out.'

'Duncan.' Olivia mentally searched for information about Lauren's family and came up empty on that name.

'Duncan and our son Nate grew up together, like brothers. Duncan even lived with us his senior year of high school after his family moved to Florida. He's like a second son to Stuart and me. His son Jake is probably our only shot at a grandchild, since Nate is too busy with his restaurant in Portland – his own place. It's what he's always wanted, but I swear that boy has no time for anything else.'

'Ah.' Olivia only half followed the torrent of information, since the sight of the lilac-decorated quilt on the bed was so inviting.

'You have your own private bathroom just there. I left your towels hanging on the rack behind the door. Let's see, what else.' Georgia stopped to think. 'Well, Jake hangs out here while his dad works at the boatyard. That's my husband's business. Jake's napping right now, but he'll be up soon. Duncan and his wife have been separated for a while. They're going through a divorce.'

'Oh, I'm sorry.' The standard response, though now that Olivia was about to do the same, she recognized that there were cases calling more for congratulations than sorrow. She wasn't yet feeling congratulatory about her own situation, but at least now she could imagine that happening someday.

'Yes, it's a shame.' Georgia's lips pressed together. She put her hands on her hips, surveying the suitcases, but Olivia got the impression she wasn't only thinking about luggage. 'I should find you another rack for your suitcases.'

'No, no, please don't bother.' Olivia stifled a yawn, guiltily wanting this lovely, welcoming woman to shut up and leave her alone.

'If you're sure. The dresser here's empty.' Georgia opened the top drawer, then the next, as if to prove she was telling the truth. 'Closet's got plenty of room, too. Unload into there, then we can put your suitcases in the attic if it'll save you some space.'

'Thank you so much.'

'Okay, I think that's everything.' Georgia opened her arms for another squeeze-out-Olivia's-breath hug. 'Rest well. Come on down and find me when you're settled. We'll have a get-to-know-one-another chat.'

'Yes. Thanks. Sure.' Olivia was down to monosyllables. But at last Georgia was on her way out, carefully closing the door behind her, leaving behind blessed silence.

So.

Olivia looked around the room, decorated for someone more frilly and country-casual than she was. Home sweet home for who knew how long. A week? Two? She couldn't have landed in a place much more different from LA, but at least she had a strong emotional and family connection to this state, both from summers northeast of here in Stirling, and from trips to see Grandma Betty, her mom's mother, way north inland, in the relative isolation of Jackman. Olivia probably felt more at home here than anywhere that wasn't California.

Half an hour later, after unpacking her massive overload of supplies, toiletries and clothes into the dresser and closet, and shoving her suitcases out of sight, she fell on to the bed. It was fabulously comfortable, outfitted with thick down pillows, as far as Olivia was concerned the only pillow worth considering.

Rolling over, she stared up at the high white ceiling, following a crack on its meandering journey, wispy here and there with strands of gray cobweb that hung down like Spanish moss.

What would she do here?

She could visit her father and Lauren at the old folks' home, about an hour away in Blue Hill. She'd brought her laptop. She'd brought books. She'd brought a blank notebook in which to scribble any ideas for a new show, or a book, or . . . whatever next step she might take.

What next step *would* she take?

Mom had prepared her for everything, except what to do if that 'everything' didn't work out. How many other kids were out there who'd so far been unable to fill their monstrously talented parents' shoes? Did they feel the same way she did?

Could she start a support group? Failed Creative Kids of Uber-Parent Successes. Acronym: F*CKUPS.

Olivia allowed herself a smirk. Enough negativity. She was alive, she was healthy, she had a loving family, and she wasn't yet at the point of giving up on her career.

There. Better?

Nah. That shit never worked.

She'd try Eve's self-soothing technique. *Olivia, you have been through hell, granted, some of it of your own making. This is not the time for major life decisions. Just relax out here in your favorite state and something will come through.*

When God closes a show, he opens an audition.

Better?

Yes. Nice, actually.

Examining the ceiling became dull. Her eyes closed.

A kid's shouts and pounding footsteps jolted Olivia awake. Apparently both she and Jake were up from their naps.

She washed her face in the old-fashioned deep-bowled bathroom sink and reapplied her makeup, glad she'd brought her lighted mirror. A quick brush through her hair, then she was as ready for an evening with strangers as she ever would be. Georgia had been nothing but warm, but Olivia was anxious about how Stuart would feel. Who knew what Lauren had told him about her rarely pleasant eldest stepchild? Olivia's stay would be so much easier if he hadn't already been turned against her.

Two steps from the door, her phone rang. She peered at the display and groaned, considered not answering, but . . . Lauren probably wanted to know she'd arrived safely. Olivia had called her father from her layover in Philadelphia and had been relieved to hear him sounding stronger. She should have texted them when she arrived.

'Hi, Lauren. I'm here at the house.'

'Just making sure. Your father is resting. He appreciated your call this morning.'

Olivia curled her lip. She hated when Lauren took over her relationship with Dad. 'Yes, he told me.'

'When are you coming to Blue Hill? Daniel is anxious to see you. He worries.'

'I don't know. In a couple of days? I need to recover a little first. I'll let you know.' She should thank Lauren again for providing this place, but the words stuck in her throat.

'All right. Take care, Olivia. Get some rest. I'm . . . sorry about what happened on the show.'

She stiffened. 'How much does Dad know?'

'All of it. He says he's proud of you for hitting back.' Her tone and careful enunciation made it clear she didn't agree with her husband. But since she had not the smallest spark of spirit inside her, she'd never say so, just sit there judging Olivia in pink pudgy silence.

'All right. I'd better go help Georgia with dinner.'

'She's a good cook. You'll have a nice meal. And if you need anything, Olivia, you can—'

'I'll call Dad tomorrow, thanks.' She tossed her phone over to land on the bed, and let out a long, loud growl of frustration.

A squeal of fright sounded outside her door, followed by a light thud.

Jake apparently had an enquiring mind and good ears.

She opened up to find a small boy, probably three or four years old, flat on his butt as if he'd fallen on to it, staring up at her open-mouthed.

'Hello. I'm Olivia. Did I scare you?'

'I thought you were a bear.'

'Hmm.' He was incredibly cute. Brown eyes and a curling

mouth. Olivia's bad mood lifted. She squatted down. 'Take a close look. Do you still think so?'

He shook his head, strands of brown hair flying straight out.

'I didn't know you were out here or I wouldn't have made such an angry noise.'

'Okay.' He stared at his sneaker. 'Why were you angry?'

Because my stepmother is a passive-aggressive nightmare. 'Sometimes when I'm tired, I get mad over little stuff that doesn't really matter. Don't you?'

'Ye-e-e-s.' He tilted his head back and made a goofy face that brought on Olivia's first real smile of the day.

'Were you out here trying to check me out? Like a spy? See if you could find any secret information?'

His eyes lit up. 'Yeah! Super-spy man!'

'Cool. I bet I can guess your name.' She closed her eyes and pressed fingers to her temples. 'I'm thinking . . . Jake.'

His eyes popped, then narrowed. 'Gorgy told you.'

'Maybe . . .' She pointed to the middle of her chest. 'Can you guess *my* name?'

'I *know* your name. You just *told* me.'

'C'mon, guess.'

He giggled, dropping his head to one side. 'Olivia!'

'Nope. It's Olivia. Guess again.'

'I *said* that!' He let out a cascade of laughter. 'Olivia!'

'Nope. It's Olivia. Guess again.'

He nearly fell over. 'It's Oliv— It's Frank!'

'Bingo. Good for you.' The kid was sharp. She was in love with him already. 'So you hang out here with Georgia while your dad's at work?'

'Yeah.' He folded his skinny arms across his chest, no longer laughing. 'My mommy and daddy don't live together anymore.'

'I'm sorry to hear that, Jake.' She touched his arm. 'But

sometimes it's the right thing to do, to keep your mom and dad from being really sad. I'm getting a divorce too.'

'Did you have a man caught inside you?'

Olivia felt her eyes go wide. 'Uh . . .'

'My mommy had a man caught inside her. It made Daddy sad and sometimes angry.'

Olivia struggled not to react. Unless this child had walked in on Mom and her lover, which was unlikely unless they were criminally careless or stupid, there was absolutely no reason he should know that his mother had cheated, let alone in such detail. Someone had been careless around him at a time when his welfare should have been top priority.

Thank God her split involved just her and Derek. Their crappy decisions and bad behavior would hurt only themselves and each other.

'Divorce is hard. But your mom and dad will always love you the same amount.'

'Yeah.' His head bobbed. He scratched a mosquito bite on his leg. 'They tell me that all the time.'

Well, that was good at least. Olivia got to her feet. 'I think I'm supposed to help Georgia make dinner. Can you show me to the kitchen?'

'Yup.' He scrambled to his feet. 'It's downstairs.'

The kitchen was beautiful, spacious and modernized, while still maintaining some Victorian character, which kept it from feeling out of place in the house: white cabinets with brass and wrought-iron handles, and a painted tin-tile ceiling with a delicate iron chandelier centered over a round table and matching carved wooden chairs. Stunning taste.

'Gorgy, Livia is here. I heard her growling.'

'Is that right?' Georgia grabbed a towel and turned from the sink with a wide smile. 'Hi, Olivia. All settled in?'

'Yes. Thanks, it's perfect. So is your kitchen.' Olivia gestured around her. 'I could live down here.'

'Sometimes I feel like I do.' Georgia pulled open the door of the immense stainless-steel refrigerator. 'Would you like a beer or a glass of wine? The boys should be home soon.'

'They're not boys, Gorgy.'

'No, I guess not. I'm going to have wine. Olivia, what would you like?'

'Glass of wine works for me, thank you.' Olivia was admittedly a bit of a wine snob, inspired by her father. Daniel Braddock took the subject very seriously. French if possible, Italian and Spanish second; do not even talk to him about those upstart winemakers in his adopted state. But at the moment, she would drink cooking wine if it would help her through this evening.

Georgia handed her a glass of white. 'I have a fabulous wine guy over in Rockport, about half an hour south of here. He's taken my education in hand. This is a Muscadet from France's Loire valley. Hope you like it. I think it's perfect for these long summer days.'

Olivia took a sip and smiled, delighted to have landed in a house that took good wine advice. 'Very nice. Fruity but dry.'

'Ha!' Georgia clapped her hands. 'That's exactly what he said. Me, I think it tastes good. What do I know? I grew up in a Baptist family. We drank milk or water.'

'I drink milk or water, too,' Jake said. 'Am I Baptist?'

'No. Count yourself lucky.'

'Okay.' He pointed to himself. 'One. Lucky. Can I have juice?'

Georgia gave a throaty laugh that showed naturally white teeth. 'Well done, Jake. And yes, you can.'

'Where did you grow up, Georgia?' Olivia tasted the wine

again, glad she'd have such delicious help relaxing. 'I assume the South.'

'You assume correctly.' Georgia glanced back from the refrigerator, smile crinkling her blue eyes. 'Take a guess which state.'

'Not Georgia.'

'That's the one.' She shook her head, dimples denting her cheeks, and poured a plastic tumbler a quarter full of cranberry juice. 'My younger brothers and sisters were all named after Georgia counties. Macon, Clarke, Gwinnett, Liberty and Floyd. My parents are crazy.'

'Can I have wine too?'

'Not till you're older, punkin.' She diluted the juice with water and handed it to Jake, along with a plastic bowl containing a few peanuts still in the shell. 'This okay for now? Your daddy'll be along soon.'

'Yah.' He sat on the floor and absorbed himself in the process of cracking and splitting nuts.

Georgia gestured to Olivia's glass. 'More wine?'

She was startled to realize she'd nearly emptied it. 'Yes, please. Long day.'

'After what you've been through, you are welcome to as much as you need.' She topped up the glass generously. 'Oh, here they are.'

'Daddy!' Jake jumped up and tore out of the kitchen.

'He is *so* cute.' Olivia started toward the abandoned peanut bowl.

'No, no, don't you dare. You're the guest here.' Georgia lunged and got there first. 'He is cute. He's taking the divorce pretty well, too, though it's not easy for any of them. As you know.'

'I do.'

'Hey there, Stu.' Georgia's face lit up at the sight of her husband. 'Look who arrived safely. Your niece and I have been getting acquainted.'

Olivia could see how she might have overlooked Georgia in the crush of people at Dad and Lauren's wedding, but she should have remembered Stuart. He was a barrel-chested man, six-four or five, easy, bringing into the room a smell of outdoors, chemicals and man. His neck was probably the size of one of Olivia's thighs. Thinning salt-and-pepper hair fled from a wide forehead over eyes startlingly like Lauren's, but darker blue. On his upper lip was a mustache that traveled around his mouth to cover his chin. Handsome guy. Impressive presence.

He turned from kissing his wife.

'Olivia.' He extended an enormous hand, not smiling, but she couldn't tell if he was hostile or just reserved. 'Good to see you again. Lauren's kept me up to date on you and your sisters over the years.'

'Nice to see you, too.' Olivia's worries that Lauren had poisoned her chances with Stuart were not relieved by the flat way he spoke to her. 'Thanks for taking me in. Life in LA was a little nuts.'

'I'm sure,' Georgia said sympathetically. 'People are idiots.'

'Some more than others.'

Olivia opened her mouth to agree politely when she caught the reproving glance Georgia sent her husband. Was he referring to *her*?

Fabulous. She'd taken refuge from wolves in a grizzly's den.

Head high, she gave him a blinding smile. 'Isn't that the truth? You never know where they'll turn up.'

Georgia gave what sounded suspiciously like a snort. Stuart had the decency to drop his gaze, though color crawled up his face, exactly as it did on his sister's when she was angry, uncomfortable, or embarrassed. Toss-up as to which he was feeling.

'I'll go clean up for dinner.'

As soon as he was out of sight, Georgia rolled her eyes. 'Do *not* let that big ol' lunkhead bother you. I love the man to death, but he *is* a man, and therefore he has no idea what he's talking about. I'll set him straight later, don't you worry. He won't make a mistake like that again.'

'He didn't bother me.' Olivia was lying. Having to hole up here among Lauren's family was humiliating enough. Doing so in even a half-hostile environment would be intolerable. She'd rather put on a wig and plastic nose-glasses and check into a motel.

Jake's chattering grew louder, then he appeared in the kitchen, pulling after him a stunner of a guy, younger than Olivia – she'd guess mid thirties. Dark hair. Brown eyes. The fit look of a guy who worked with his hands and body for a living. Sexy stubble and an incredibly sensual mouth.

Some woman had cheated on *that*?

'This is my daddy.'

'Olivia Croft, meet Duncan Reed.'

'Hi.' He gave a curt nod, hands stuffed in his jeans pockets, sending out an even chillier vibe than Stuart.

'Hi, Duncan.' She offered her hand, daring him to ignore it. 'I hear you're an honorary son of the family.'

'I guess.' He dragged out a hand and shook hers reluctantly, without making eye contact.

Obvious why his wife had cheated on him: he was a rude pig. A gorgeous rude pig. 'Good to meet you. Your son and I had a nice talk earlier, didn't we, Jake?'

'I heard Olivia growling, Daddy. Like a bear.' Jake crouched down, face in a snarl, claws extended. 'Raaaaaahr!'

'Just like that.' She beamed at Duncan, hoping he'd see how friendly she was and lighten up a little. 'He's a smart kid. You must be proud of him.'

'Yeah, thanks.' Daddy took a step back, unsettled rather than charmed. 'Ready to go, Jake?'

'Can't you stay to dinner?' Georgia asked. 'Lemon chicken and rice, nothing exciting. Olivia, I figured your first night you'd rather have something simpler.'

'Yes, you—'

'Thanks, but we're heading home.'

'Aww!' Jake scowled at his father. 'What are *we* having?'

'Burgers.'

'Not *again*.' His adorable face screwed up in disgust. 'That's all we *ever* have since Mom left.'

'Yeah? I seem to remember a pretty great batch of spaghetti last night.'

'I made plenty.' Georgia smiled fondly at Duncan. 'We'd love to have you.'

'Please can we stay? Please?'

'Not tonight.' Duncan scooped up his son. 'Say bye to Georgia. And no whining.'

Jake bit off what was probably going to be an expert whine and hung his head, poking at a button on his dad's shirt. 'Bye, Gorgy.'

Olivia opened her mouth to say goodbye too, then changed her mind. She'd had just about enough rejection, and there was bound to be more from Stuart during dinner.

'See ya tomorrow, Jake. Bye, Duncan.' When the front door closed behind father and son, Georgia sighed. 'I was hoping they'd stay. I worry about that man.'

'He's taking the divorce hard? Not that I've ever heard of it being easy.'

'That's true. And yes, he is taking it hard.' Georgia bent and took a beautifully browned platter of chicken pieces out of the oven. 'I wouldn't say he and Sam were the ideal match, but they seemed right for each other. She just . . . Well, what can you do? I shouldn't be gossiping.'

Yes, you absolutely should be. Olivia spread her hands. 'How can I help?'

'Everything's ready. I'll bring in the chicken, you can grab the wine. Stuart'll be down soon.'

'Okay.' Olivia gulped the rest of her glass and filled it back to its previous level before following Georgia into the high-ceilinged dining room, whose three windows framed gorgeous views of the house's sloping yard and a charming gazebo Olivia hadn't noticed from her window.

The massive oak table had been set for five. Georgia put the chicken on a hotplate and swept away the two extra place settings, leaving three at the end with the best views.

'Have a seat.' She pointed to one of the upholstered antique chairs and took the one opposite. The head of the table was apparently reserved for the house's lord and master.

Olivia sat, praying her charm would work better on the lord and master than it had on Duncan, or she'd be finding a lot of excuses to miss dinner.

'Duncan go home?' Stuart came into the dining room and took his seat without looking at Olivia, his graying hair neatly combed back, sweatshirt and boots exchanged for a blue polo shirt and clean jeans.

'He said he couldn't stay.'

'Right.' He reached for the serving tongs and hovered them over the meat. 'Dark or white, Olivia?'

'Dark, please. Not much. I'm more tired than hungry.' And anxious and freaked out, and really wanting to drink a lot more than she should in front of these people.

Stuart chose a thigh and used a spoon to pour a buttery-looking sauce over it, then served her a small amount of rice from another pot and steamed carrots flecked with what smelled like coriander. 'Thank you, Stuart. Georgia, this looks so good.'

'It's simple. I'm a simple cook. Not like you.'

'No, no.' Olivia waved her compliment away. 'Exactly like me. My show was all about simplicity. Simplicity and good health, for cooks of all levels.'

'Oh, but you're *trained*. I just grew up watching Mama in the kitchen.'

'Not trained. I grew up watching in the kitchen, same as you, then practiced. But I'm really an actress, not a chef.' She took a bite of chicken, delighted to find it exactly as delicious as she'd planned to say it was. 'This is so good. It's hard to get the lemon flavor to really pop.'

'Well, thank you very much.' Georgia looked pleased.

Stuart kept his eyes on his plate, eating steadily.

Winning him over would take work. 'How did you two meet?'

'On an airplane.' Georgia beamed at her husband, who forked rice into his mouth and loaded up again, still chewing. 'We sat next to each other on a flight to Atlanta. I was going home after visiting an uncle; Stuart was taking a look at a boat on Sea Island. I knew the second I laid eyes on him that he was the one for me.'

Olivia emptied half her glass to fight the stab of pain. She'd also known the instant she laid eyes on Derek. Why did love at first sight seem to work out for everyone but her? 'How about you, Stuart? Did you know right away?'

Stuart shrugged. 'She was cute.'

'Hey!'

He sent his wife a grin. 'You were.'

Georgia rolled her eyes. 'To answer your question, Olivia, yes, he knew. We didn't stop talking the entire flight, or pretty much any of the weeks after it, until he came down to Georgia, met my parents and proposed.'

'What did they think?' Olivia drank more wine, then reminded herself that food was more important. It just didn't feel that way.

Georgia looked over at her husband with shining eyes. 'They thought we were pretty crazy.'

'We were.'

'Oh, you.' She pushed at his massive forearm. 'We've done just fine. Though I'll tell you, Olivia, over my first winter here, I nearly lost it. I think I threatened to move back home about every other week.'

'Every week.' Stuart helped himself to more water.

'So we made a deal.' Georgia passed Olivia a basket of rolls that looked home-made and smelled fabulous. 'I'd stay if I could spend at least part of each winter somewhere warmer. When we were younger and Nate was in grade school, we could only leave during his vacations, and we could only afford to stay with my family down south. Those were the lean years, huh, sweetie?'

His answer was a nod.

'Now we go wherever we want, January through March, and I'm happy as a steamer clam. It's beautiful here in the summer, I love it. But I do not want to test my sanity that way again.'

'You should retire to southern California.'

Stuart looked disgusted. 'Too many people.'

'That's true, but—'

'Too many *weird* people.'

Olivia emptied her glass to keep from telling him her latest definition of 'weird'.

Georgia offered her husband the rolls. 'What would you like to do while you're here, Olivia? I'm happy to show you around the area.'

'You don't have to entertain me. I'm very independent. And . . .' she looked pointedly at Stuart, surprised to find him with his face out of his food, actually looking back at her, 'I'm guessing you haven't spent much time hoping I'd move in with you without knowing when I'll leave. I promise I'll stay out of your way.'

Stuart put down his fork and folded his hands, elbows on the table. 'You're family and you're in trouble. It's right that you stay here.'

'Okay.' She gestured at him with her glass. 'But you're telling me Lauren didn't have to twist your arm?'

'Of course not,' Georgia said.

Stuart's right eyebrow twitched. 'Some.'

Olivia smiled drily. At least he'd allowed himself to be honest. 'Well, I'm grateful. And I'll be gone as soon as this all blows over. Sooner if you want me to be.'

'No, don't be silly.' Georgia waved away her offer. 'It'll be a treat for me to have someone to talk to who's over four.'

'I'm over four,' Stuart said.

'Sometimes I'm not so sure.' She grinned at her husband. 'But you're gone all day, and I get to feeling lonely sometimes.'

'You never told me that.'

'You never asked.'

He grunted, and helped himself to another roll.

Olivia poured herself more wine. She'd had enough that she'd stopped caring what they thought. She'd buy them more the next day. A case. Maybe two, and stash one in her room.

Go on a bender that would last the term of her exile.

Stuart stared pointedly at the more-empty-than-not bottle as Olivia put it back down on the table. 'If you're thirsty, we have plenty of water.'

Olivia froze. *Fuckarini*. Did he really just say that to her?

'We also have plenty of wine, Stuart.' Georgia's gentle reprimand carried remarkable weight.

'I do not tolerate drunks in this house.'

'That's not a problem.' Olivia lifted her glass, face hot with anger. 'Because I haven't even *begun* to get drunk.'

Stuart put his utensils down again. 'In my house—'

'Stuart, Olivia is a grown woman who has just been through hell. If she needs to blow off steam, then I think what you mean to say is that she's welcome to, because our house is a safe and loving place to do it.'

His eyebrows went up coldly. 'Is that what I mean to say?'

'Yes, Stuart.' Georgia folded her arms. 'It is.'

'You know what?' Olivia got to her feet. 'I think I'm going to take my obnoxious presence upstairs and put it to bed. Thank you very much for the delicious dinner, Georgia. Stuart, you and I will figure this out. I'll see you both in the morning.'

She took two steps toward the door, then changed her mind, marched back to the table, grabbed her glass *and* the bottle, and headed upstairs to her room.

Chapter 7

June 29, 1994 (Wednesday)

Daniel and I had such a fabulous and relaxing vacation. I think I gained about ten pounds in two weeks. But being there, without pressures, with only each other – it was like old times. It was perfect. There is no way he can want anyone but me now. I feel safe for the first time in so long.

Coming home, I have never been so glad to see anyone as my girls. It hurt to be away from them, though we called often. They are each a piece of my heart. They deserve a better mother, but no one could love them as much as I do. Even if they didn't come out of my body, they are my children. *They belong to me. I will never, ever allow them to belong to any other woman.*

Happily,
Jillian

Olivia couldn't sleep. The bed was comfortable, the ocean scents blowing through the open window heavenly, the sound of waves hypnotic, her sleeping pill useless. She was claustrophobic, rigid with tension, mind refusing to quiet. She hadn't worked out in three days, hadn't meditated or been able to follow any of the usual comforting routines that wore out her body and quieted her brain. Eve's technique was effective, but wore down under the onslaught of worry, and Olivia ran out of patience.

All the shit she was able to keep at bay in active daylight had been sitting patiently, waiting for the cover of sedentary darkness to spring out, grab hold and start tearing at her mind.

Grief over her marriage, terror that she'd be alone for the rest of her life. Never be a success, never have children, never be able to trust any man again. A three-ring circus of pain, self-pity and regret.

Olivia threw off the covers and sat up abruptly, still a little drunk. She couldn't lie here anymore or she'd lose it completely. She had to get outside. The air, the ocean, the good smells and embracing innocence of the natural world might help calm her. Anything was better than the misery treadmill she'd been running on here.

She dressed quickly, then picked up her phone to use as a flashlight, treading as softly as possible in the hallway and down the creaky stairs, though even if she woke Georgia or Stuart she doubted either would come after her. Georgia would figure she was hungry. Stuart would assume she was after more alcohol.

Ooh. One more glass, sipped slowly by the water . . .

But this wasn't her house, and it wasn't her wine.

Outside in the cool, sweet air, the idea grew in appeal. Maybe there was a package store open late. A search of the Internet turned up a twenty-four-hour Mobil station four minutes away that had beer, wine and an agency liquor store.

Hallelujah.

At her car, she stopped, gripping the door handle. Had she really sunk this low? Sneaking out to buy booze at midnight in a strange town? Needing to get drunk in order to deal with her emotions? Needing to exhaust herself in order to sleep?

Yup. She had.

Ten minutes later, she returned clutching the mortifying brown paper bag containing a fifth of Jack Daniel's. Tiptoeing around the back of the house, she walked down the path bisecting the wide grassy yard, past a small shed she hadn't noticed before, and the cute-as-a-button gazebo. By the shore, near an enormous cedar, she found steps down to a wooden platform. Here the water wasn't bounded by the immense craggy ledges and boulders of the Candlewood Point property in Stirling, but by potato- to melon-sized stones, among which were a few ledges large enough to sit on and dangle her legs. The moon had set, the tide looked to be about halfway in – or out; she hadn't been here long enough to acclimate to its rhythms.

Settled in a decently comfortable position, she unscrewed the top of her Jack and took a burning, flavorful mouthful, felt the sweet warmth flow into her chest. Mmm. So lovely, she took another sip.

The cool air was soft, the smells and ocean noises familiar and comforting. Olivia leaned back on her elbows. Stars crowded the moonless sky, infinitely more than were visible in Los Angeles, reminding her of the nights her family had lain outside on the wonderful big ledges on their property, listening to the swish and gurgle of the waves, watching for falling stars, Mom and Dad in one spot, Olivia, Eve and Rosalind closer to the water, giggling with excited anticipation. The meteors tore across the sky, sometimes in thrillingly large streaks of white, sometimes small enough that only one or two of them caught the display. Bursts of loud *oohs* and urgent pointing at what was already gone. *Did you see that one?* Then waiting and waiting for the next, and the next . . .

Olivia tipped the bottle up to her mouth again. The glug of whiskey tumbling through the bottle's narrow neck brought back more memories. That same sound on those same star-gazing nights.

Mom, drinking whiskey. Sharing sips with Dad, the two wrapped in each other's arms, the girls huddled together for warmth, under a blanket it if was really cold. Sometimes Dad would have to help Mom back up to the house, his arm under her elbow, coaching her over rocks and around roots on the path. So strong. So gentle. So in love.

Olivia's mouth opened in a sudden and involuntary howl of grief, whiskey trickling down her chin, on to her shirt.

She lurched forward, hanging her head down, letting the rest of the mouthful splash on to the shore. Another spasm of terrible grief, another moan turned staccato by racking sobs she couldn't control.

How had she come to this?

Olivia was the golden girl, the daughter most likely to ascend to the heights, money protecting her from want, her confidence and ambition enough to pave the rest of the way. After a brief goth period, Eve had returned to herself, low-key to the point of wanting to remain invisible. Rosalind scattered herself widely enough to stay on the fringes of whatever she wanted to try. Olivia was the one to dive straight in, immerse herself in the very core of what the life she wanted had to offer.

Now Rosalind and Eve were blissfully paired, futures bright, with solid and satisfying achievements behind them and ahead. They'd have families. Adorable babies who'd complete their lives.

Another howl, interrupted by something landing very close to her, bouncing, tumbling, stopping abruptly, caught at the intersection of the rock she sat on and the one next to her, making her squeak with fear.

Then silence.

What the—

She turned on her flashlight. The searching beam found the missile almost immediately: a square box of Kleenex.

Olivia twisted around, left then right, peering up at the shore. Georgia? More likely Stuart. Georgia would come all the way down and offer the tissues in person.

But the Pattersons' bedroom was on the other side of the house, a long way up the hill. She remembered how dramatically sound traveled in Stirling, but still, she couldn't imagine they'd been able to hear her.

'Would you mind keeping it down?'

Olivia let out another startled squeak and scrambled unsteadily to her feet, squinting at the figure at the top of the bank. Duncan? How had he heard her? Where was his house? How loud had she been?

And really? That was his reaction to a woman in terrible distress? *Would you mind keeping it down?* She put her hands on her hips. 'Thanks for the tissues. And for your sweet concern.'

'You scared the shit out of my kid.'

Her indignation melted. Aw, crap. Growling behind a door, now howling in the night. Olivia owed Jake a month of coos and cookies. 'I'm sorry. I couldn't help it.'

'Everyone can help it. Just close your mouth.'

Even through her sudden blaze of temper, Olivia's jaw dropped in to a decidedly not closed mouth. She was unable to believe this guy could be such a prick. 'Are you even *human*?'

'Last I checked.'

'Check again. And next time stop to think about *why* someone might be sobbing her eyes out in the middle of the night and show a little compassion.'

'I know why. You brought the whole thing on yourself. I don't feel sorry for you.'

She shouldn't be dumbfounded. She'd read the online rants, seen the threats. It was just so different meeting one of the Great Unfeeling Assholes in person, someone so immune to a fellow human in terrible pain. 'People like you make the world such a kind and loving place.'

'What did you expect would happen, airing your dirty laundry on TV? That everyone would feel sorry for the poor little rich girl who didn't get what she wanted?'

The world turned red. 'Are you *kidding* me? Did you really just say that?'

'Private matters should be kept exactly that.'

She was consumed by the need to hurt him back, land a blow that would disable his awful, judgmental power. 'Why am I not at *all* surprised that your wife cheated on you?'

Suck on that, baby.

'Cheated on me? Who told you that?'

'Your son.'

'What did he say exactly?'

'Who *cares* what he said *exactly*. I would have cheated on you too, right in front of you.'

His hands went to his hips. 'I want to know what he said.'

She struggled with her rage and lost. 'Fuck you.'

'*I want to know what my son said to you.*' He started down the steps.

Olivia stepped back, nearly overbalancing, then folded her arms and glared up at him, afraid now but determined not to show it. She'd been stupid, as usual. He was stronger. She was alone and knew nothing about him or what he was capable of. 'He said . . . that she had a man caught inside her.'

Duncan stopped with his hand on the railing. A sound reached her. It took a while for her to realize that he was laughing. 'That's brilliant.'

What the— She couldn't believe he found it funny. His poor wife. Olivia wanted to find her and conspire to bump Duncan off. 'Oh, hilarious. I'm sure Jake enjoyed it too. Did you take video so he could watch?'

'Stop.' She could sense his rage from the way his body stiffened. 'Now.'

'How did you get any kind of custody?'

'I said stop. That is none of your damn business.'

'Oh, I see.' She was on a roll now. 'But my problems are yours?'

'You told your problems *to the entire world.*'

Olivia wasn't sure she'd ever been this furious. She wanted to run up the stairs and sink something long and sharp into his gut. This was why it was a really bad idea for people with tempers to have guns. She would have cheerfully unloaded a couple of chambers into him, just to get the sneer off his face. As long as she could undo it immediately.

'Listen, you son of a bitch.' She was heading for the stairs. What she would do when she got up them, she had no idea, but her legs were moving of their own accord. She stumbled in the dark; the bottle slipped from her hand and smashed on the rocks a second before she followed suit.

Goddammit.

She struggled to her feet, aware of Duncan pounding down the stairs.

'Leave me alone.'

'Christ, you're drunk. Stand up.'

'I *am* standing up.' She was screaming. 'Get *away* from me.'

'You're bleeding.'

'I'm not *bleeding*.' She started crying. 'Get *away* from me. I fucking *hate* you.'

'Duncan. Sam.' Stuart's voice boomed down from the yard. 'What the hell are you doing out here? We have a guest upstairs.'

'Your guest is right here.'

'Olivia?' He sounded stunned. 'I thought you were inside.'

'She's hurt.' Duncan's voice was contemptuous. 'Won't let me touch her.'

'Why are you fighting with her?'

'He's an asshole,' Olivia called out.

'You need someone to look at that cut.'

'I'm not bleed—'

'There.' Duncan pointed.

Olivia looked down to see her forearm covered with blood. She started crying again. 'I want to go home.'

'Stuart? What's happening?' Georgia sounded frantic. 'Olivia's not in her room.'

'We have a little situation here.'

Georgia's gasp was loud enough to make it down the stairs, followed by her light steps. 'Good Lord in heaven, child, you are a mess in blood. Hold your arm up.'

'She was drinking.'

'Well, of *course* she was. I would be too.' Her arm came around Olivia. 'Don't you be judging what people do in grief, Duncan. Not everyone can stuff it away like you can. What Olivia's doing here is a lot healthier than the way you handle it.'

Olivia waited for Duncan's sneering comeback. He stepped back, hands on his hips, but said nothing. Apparently he respected Georgia, at least.

'I don't know what went on here, but I would bet my backside that you owe Olivia an apology. I expect it from you first thing tomorrow morning, hat in hand. Now get back to your boy. Shame on you, leaving him like that.'

'She woke him with her yowling. He was scared.'

'So you left him *alone*?'

'I didn't think—'

'Obviously.'

Georgia's tone left Duncan with his first uncertainty since his righteous-man-rage appearance. Olivia felt like cheering. 'He had his comfort bear and his music. He knew where I was, and that I—'

'Go back. Now. I'll see you in the morning, young man. Hat in hand.'

Duncan turned and climbed the steps two at a time, then strode back along the path toward the woods Olivia had thought marked the boundary of the Pattersons' property. His cabin must be back through there. She made a mental note never, ever to go near it.

'Let's take a look at that cut.' Georgia held Olivia's forearm up to the beam of Stuart's flashlight. 'See if you need a stitch or two.'

'No, no, I don't.' Now that her antagonist was gone, the battle over, Olivia started shaking, teeth chattering. 'I'm so sorry I woke—'

'It's long but not deep. Might be some glass still in there. Come up to the house and I'll take care of it.'

'I'm so sorry. I'm so—'

'Shh, you're fine. Just fine. We'll get you cleaned up and back in bed. Everything will look better tomorrow, I promise. You've had a terrible shock, and everything happened so fast, you haven't had time to process any of it. Come on now. Stuart, help her.'

Stuart clumped down the steps and took Olivia's uninjured arm. She didn't bother protesting. Her feet weren't behaving properly and, given Stuart's size, if she stumbled or fell, he could grab her with his thumb and forefinger before she hit the ground.

'Th-thank you.' Her stupid jaw wouldn't let her talk. 'I don't know h-how that all h-happened. I got so angry. He g-got so angry.'

'Shh, you're fine, you're fine.' Georgia stroked her back as they walked. 'Don't waste your energy talking, and *don't* blame yourself. You're in a bad place right now, and so is Duncan. So we're going to forget all about it.'

'Why are you so nice to me? I don't deserve it.'

'Because she's a saint.' Stuart's words left no question that if his wife wasn't there, Olivia would be bleeding out on the rocks.

'You bite your tongue. I am no such thing. Here, careful of the grass, it might be slippery.'

'I woke you.'

'No, no, we weren't asleep,' Georgia assured her.

'Yes, we were.'

'*Stuart! Not* helping.'

'I'm sorry.' Olivia's voice came out a pathetic whisper. She was never, ever getting that drunk again. Swear to God.

Georgia must have put her to bed somehow, because the next morning Olivia woke up in it, her arm clean and bandaged, with a vague memory of being forced to drink about two quarts of water before she was allowed to pass out between the sheets.

Sunlight was streaming in under the shades. Given that her bedroom faced southwest, that meant the day was well under way. Olivia squinted painfully at the old clock radio next to her bed. Nearly noon.

Groan.

She got out of bed, nausea churning her stomach, the well-deserved headache pounding at her temples, and grabbed a clean batch of clothes, recoiling at anything she might have been wearing the previous night.

In the quaint bathroom, complete with a claw tub that must be original to the house, she popped aspirin, drank more water, and took a quick shower under the strong spray, rebandaging the cut on her arm, which stung but was healing nicely.

Somewhat revived, she came downstairs, hoping like mad that Stuart was gone, and that Duncan had either decided not to apologize, forgotten to apologize, or had given up when he found out she was still in bed.

'Morning.' Georgia jumped up from the chair in the kitchen where she'd been reading a novel with an embossed rose on the cover. 'Did you sleep okay? How do you feel? How's that wound?'

'A mere scratch. And I feel better than I deserve.'

'No, no, you beat yourself up plenty last night. I texted Duncan; he'll be up from the yard shortly to apologize, and then we're starting over, all of us.' She moved to the stove and filled a kettle. 'Coffee?'

'Yes, please.'

'What sounds good for breakfast? I have a blueberry coffee cake, made with Maine berries – not fresh; those aren't in till August, but frozen from last year. If you'd rather have toast and honey, that's available too. Mama always made that for us when our tummies weren't at their best.'

'That's fine. But let me make it. I don't want you to—'

'No, no, this first morning you're our guest. After that I'll let you fend for yourself, all right?'

'Yes, thank you.' She loved Georgia. If she and Stuart ever divorced, Olivia was proposing.

The hot toast had just landed on her plate when the front door opened, and Duncan appeared in the kitchen.

Without thinking, Olivia put her napkin on the table and stood.

He walked toward her, stopped a couple of feet away and put his hands on his hips. She was so flustered, she couldn't do more than glance up, but it was enough to notice yet again that he was an absurdly beautiful man, watching her from wary brown eyes, just darker than hers. 'Morning.'

Olivia forced herself to lift her chin, wanting to give him the sneering stare he deserved, but out of respect for Georgia, she'd make it easier on him. 'Good morning.'

'I . . . wasn't in a good place last night. I apologize for insulting you. I'd had a hell of a day and was angry. It was not right to take it out on you.'

'Thank you.' She glanced down at the table, mortified to feel a blush coming on. 'I wasn't at my best either. I'm sorry for the things I said. I shouldn't have taken my crap day out on you either.'

He took a step forward and held out his hand. 'Okay.'

'Okay.' She shook, forcing herself to do the mature thing and meet his eyes, only to get zapped with unwelcome attraction. Could chemistry like that only go one way? She hoped so. The last thing she needed was to have to fend off another jerk.

'Aww!' Georgia stood with her hands clasped. 'That was adorable. Like exchanging vows!'

Olivia and Duncan turned to glare at her in shared horror.

Georgia gave a shout of laughter. 'I'm just messing with you. Y'all are hilarious. Thank you, Duncan, you did good. Thank you, Olivia, for being so gracious.'

Olivia smiled, glad she'd chosen the high road, wondering how many sticky situations in this house had been smoothed over or avoided by Georgia's kindness and force of will. Olivia could learn a lot. 'No problem.'

Duncan nodded, shot Olivia an unreadable glance and left the room.

Relieved that was over, Olivia sat back down to her breakfast, hoping Duncan wasn't going to be hanging around the house often, though she wouldn't mind the view. Maybe if he never opened his mouth again . . .

'Where's Jake this morning?' She bit into the toast and nearly swooned. 'Mmm. Did you make this bread?'

'I sure did. It's my grammy's recipe. Jake's at his friend Betsy's house for a play date. He'll be back soon for lunch.'

Olivia finished eating and drank some orange juice followed by a cup of Georgia's excellent coffee. It was stronger than she generally liked, but that morning she needed the extra boost.

'What's your plan today?' Georgia was preparing lunch for Jake. 'Recovery and settling in?'

'Pretty much. If there's anything I can help you with, please let me know. I don't want to feel useless, or like a burden.' Olivia held up her hand to stop Georgia's protest. 'I mean it. I can help with cooking, I can do housework. I can help watch Jake.'

At the last one, Georgia's eyes brightened. 'Really? You'd want to do that?'

Olivia nearly laughed. 'Are you kidding? I would *love* to.'

'Well.' Georgia headed for Olivia's empty plate. 'Quite honestly, I could use a break. I love him, but I did my time raising Nate, and there are days I want to sit and do whatever it is without being interrupted.'

Olivia's spirits rose higher than they'd been in days. Something she could do! To kill time, to feel useful, and to begin to pay back her wonderful hostess some of what she owed her. She stacked up her dirty dishes before Georgia could reach them and went to put them into the dishwasher. There were limits to how much she could stand being waited on. 'I'd really love to help.'

'Done – oh, shoot.' Georgia's expression had fallen. 'I'd need to ask his mama and daddy first.'

'Ah.' Olivia poured herself another inch of coffee from the pot. 'Well, *that* should go well. I made a magnificent first impression on Duncan.'

'Hmm . . .' Georgia bunched up her mouth, scrutinizing Olivia as if she could will a solution out of her. 'Tell you what. You do a trial run here next week for a couple of days, under my supervision; see how you manage, and how Jake takes to you. If I vouch for you, we'll have a better shot at getting Mom and Dad to say yes.'

'That would be wonderful.' Olivia was so excited she had to keep from dancing around the kitchen and risk looking as if she had no grip on reality. Again.

'And . . .' Georgia fixed her with a look, 'it wouldn't hurt if you were nicer to Duncan.'

'I will be.' Olivia put a hand over her heart. 'Sweet as sugar.'

'Settle in today and over the weekend. Take a walk, explore Belfast. It's such a cute town. You can start on Monday. Jake's here each weekday but alternates nights and weekends between his mom and dad every week. This is Mom's week, except for last night when she had an appointment and couldn't get a sitter.'

'It sounds perfect.' Olivia was positively gooey with gratitude. 'Thank you so much, Georgia.'

'You're the one doing me the favor.'

'Not true. I owe you. For taking me in. For . . . last night.' She grimaced, still mortified by her behavior.

Georgia laid a warm hand on her shoulder. 'To tell the truth, I wasn't sure what to expect when you showed up. But the minute I saw your face, I knew you were a good person in a bad spot, and that we'd get along just fine. So much pain in you, but also courage and plenty of kindness.'

'Yeah, courageously drunk and kindly screaming.'

Georgia's blue eyes crinkled under her fading red curls. 'Maybe go easier on the booze?'

'I'm way ahead of you.' Olivia rubbed her temple. 'I'm keeping to my limit from now on, I promise.'

'All right then, young lady.' Georgia nodded firmly. 'We have ourselves a deal.'

Chapter 8

March 28, 1995 (Tuesday)

I didn't get the Oscar. Dianne Wiest got it for Bullets over Broadway. *She is an amazing actress, but I really wanted this one. I wanted that validation. I wanted the goddam statue. Who knows if another script that good will come my way again. When they announced her name, I was so disappointed I nearly cried. Then my sweet little Eve, not even five yet, but with such a big brain in her head, saw what was happening and said, 'Camera, Mom.' She notices everything. I was able to smile in time and look gracious and happy for Dianne, even while wanting to scream and rip the statue out of her hands. Dianne works hard, is a very classy lady, and did a superb job on her movie.*

So did I on mine, goddammit. So did I on mine!

I'm going downstairs to have a drink. Just one.

J

'I need more rocks!'

Olivia grinned at Jake's imperious tone and set off to find another batch. Jake was building a 'swimming pool' to capture the tide when it came back in. Olivia was gathering the bigger rocks and Jake was instructing her where to put them. She had warned him the water would still be able to escape between the piled-up stones, but he clearly thought her grasp of physics lacking and went about carefully plugging any cracks he saw with smaller pebbles, adamant that his luxury pool was only a high tide away from being ready to float in.

Olivia had spent a pleasant, relaxing few days without a single mental breakdown. She'd almost forgotten what it felt like not to be on the verge of throwing herself off a precipice. Most of the cloudy, damp weekend she'd spent resting and reading, but she'd gotten in a few good mood-lifting runs, and had explored the town – in sunglasses and a low hat, though no one had done more than glance her way.

Belfast was charming, its main street – appropriately called Main Street – lined with stately red-brick buildings from long-ago centuries, and its neighborhoods full of equally wonderful old houses. As far as Olivia was concerned, architecturally speaking, New England beat LA's pants off. Even commercial buildings here were elegant works of art.

The town had an uneven history in economic terms, but was clearly thriving now. Gigantic yachts were parked by the wharf at the bottom of Main Street's steep hill, ready to follow the channel out to Belfast Bay and beyond. Flowing into that bay under a high, narrow bridge was – wait for it – the Passagassawakeag River. Generation after generation of elementary and middle-school kids must have had a blast giggling over that one.

This afternoon, having watched Olivia and Jake play for the last couple of days and approved heartily, Georgia had grabbed an hour to have a quick coffee with a friend, utterly thrilled that she'd be able to sit and enjoy their conversation without having to worry about an antsy four-year-old wanting her to be done *now*.

Olivia and Jake were becoming fast friends, mostly because Olivia obeyed all his commands – what wasn't to like? She and Stuart seemed to have reached a place of mutual strained civility. Olivia had stopped baiting him, and he'd started ignoring her as much as possible, which suited her fine. Duncan, she hadn't seen, which suited her even finer.

'There.' Jake placed one last pebble. 'I want to fill it now.'

'Uh . . .' Olivia glanced at the rock-strewn trip to the water, rapidly becoming longer as the tide went out. She wasn't really excited about hauling buckets of water over unstable footing to pour into a pool that would empty immediately. 'Why don't you wait for—'

'And I need my bathing suit.'

That she could do. When the pool thing didn't work out, she could distract him by letting him splash around at the edge of the harbor's ocean/river mix. 'Where is it?'

Jake pointed toward the trees where Duncan had emerged last Thursday night wanting to strangle her. 'In Dad's new house.'

'I don't think we should go in there.'

'Why?'

'I don't . . . have a key.'

'It's not locked.'

'Okay. Uh . . .'

'Is there a problem?'

His question made her laugh. 'Is that what your mom or dad says when someone's confused?'

He nodded enthusiastically, his smile a perfect Cupid's bow, then took her hand and tugged. 'Come on. I hafta get my suit.'

How could she say no to this adorable child? 'All right. Let's go quickly, though.'

'Okay!'

They climbed the stairs to the bank and followed the well-groomed path, leaving bright sunshine to trudge through the woods to a small clearing where a simple white barnlike structure stood – what Olivia would guess was a renovated boathouse.

'In here.' Jake opened the screen door and turned the knob.

Olivia froze. 'Is your dad at work?'

'Yah.'

'You're sure the door's not locked?'

He threw her a look as if she was speaking Swedish. 'My dad and me need to get in.'

She was about to point out that keys were a really good way not to get everything you owned stolen, but thank God remembered how often she'd frightened poor Jake already, and how much kids liked to repeat things they'd learned to their parents, who wouldn't appreciate her terrifying him over burglars. 'Of course. Great. Let's go.'

She followed his eager footsteps inside.

Definitely a boathouse. One large room, a kitchen area to the left, wood stove and living room beyond it to the right. Toward the back, an attic-type stepladder led to a loft area. Jake was already climbing. 'Dad and my bedroom is up here. We have a skylight. We can see stars at night.'

'That's awesome.' She stood near the kitchen, arms folded over her chest, feeling like an intruder, terrified Duncan would unexpectedly show up and, unaware that Georgia had okayed Olivia's babysitting trial, accuse her of kidnapping, or breaking-and-entering, or whatever else his disdain cooked up. She'd have to be pleasant to him if she wanted him to trust her with his son. Though Sam, Jake's mother, would be coming to pick him up later that evening. Olivia might have better luck securing her permission first.

Looking around while noises of Jake's search floated down from the second floor, she noted that the kitchen and the rest of the downstairs were spare, with minimal decoration: only necessary items apart from the raft of toys scattered near the fireplace, hardly a sign that someone had moved in for more than a night or two. It smelled really good, though, like woodsmoke and aftershave. Probably like Duncan.

She tightened her arms around herself, still spooked. 'You ready, Jake?'

'Yup.' His little body appeared at the top of the steps. She moved instinctively closer, but he climbed down without hitch or hesitation, wearing a bright blue bathing suit with fish and navy turtles navigating around his butt. 'I have to get my bucket.'

Adorable. She wanted to reach out and gather him in a fierce hug, inhale in his neck, kiss his soft cheeks, and . . . freak him out again! Maybe after they'd been buddies for a while she could indulge. For now, no more mistakes.

'Let's go!' He charged out of the house with his little blue bucket, and Olivia followed, closing the front door behind her carefully, heart not slowing until they were safely back through the woods and had climbed down to his swimming pool. She made the perilous journey over slippery rocks down to the water and back, and dumped the tiny amount of water into his pool. 'Oh no!' Jake was crestfallen. 'It didn't stay! I need to get more little rocks.'

Olivia helped him gather a few, then announced that she was taking a break and sat on the wooden platform at the bottom of the steps, watching him work, waving away mosquitoes investigating her exposed skin.

'Jake?' A deep female voice from up above them, its owner not yet visible.

'Mom!' Jake's little face jerked around in delight. '*Mom*, I'm down here. Come see my pool!'

'Coming.'

Olivia stood abruptly, trying not to look guilty. Mom was early. Mom wasn't supposed to arrive for another hour or so, when Georgia would be back and could introduce them. Now Olivia would have to explain why Jake was hanging out with a stranger.

Sam came into view. Olivia's pleasant expression turned to shock. Unless there was another person right behind him, Jake's mother was a man. An extremely handsome man, younger than Olivia, effeminate, with big brown eyes, fantastic lashes, and a funky haircut, long on top and close to his head around his ears. He was clean-shaven, with a triple-pierced ear and a tattoo of symbols on his forearm that she was too far away to be able to decipher. On his slender body he wore tight jeans and a royal blue T-shirt with gold lettering: *Belfast Lions.*

Olivia forced a welcoming expression back on to her face, thoughts crowding, chief among them: *Holy shit, Duncan's gay?*

'Hi, Jake, sweetie.' Sam looked at Olivia, and for a second his expression turned fearful before he started down the stairs. 'I'm Sam. You must be Olivia.'

'Hi, Sam. Jake and I have been playing today. Georgia went to . . . She said I could—'

Wait, how did he know her name?

'I made a swimming pool, Mom. Come see. Come see!'

'Coming in a minute.' Sam stopped next to Olivia. 'I texted Georgia to let her know I was coming to pick Jake up early. She told me you were here and that you were fabulous with him. It's nice to meet you.'

'Thanks.' Olivia couldn't take her eyes off this beautiful

man. Not only because he was stunning, and not only because she was battling unwelcome dismay at the idea that Duncan was gay, but because there was something compelling and . . . different about him.

'Look at your pool, Jakey! Wow, did you do this all by yourself?'

'Livia helped.'

'You both did a great job. Thanks.' Sam grinned up at Olivia, and the answer was right there, camouflaged in all but his smile.

Jake's mom was transgender. Born a woman, changed into a man.

My mommy had a man caught inside her.

No wonder Duncan had been mystified when Olivia mentioned his wife's cheating. No wonder he'd wanted to know Jake's exact wording.

Sam did have a man caught inside him, the man he'd become, or was still becoming. His voice was low enough to pass, and his biceps were fairly well defined, peeking out below his sleeves, but his facial hair, visible as stubble, was like that of a fifteen year old, patchy and fine. Olivia wasn't going to stare at his chest, but her impression was that his breasts had either been flattened or surgically altered.

'I'm sorry to hear about your . . . mess, Olivia.'

'Thank you.' She forced herself to stop staring and act like a polite human, thinking that Sam's own mess, though private, had probably been harder to acknowledge and get through than hers. 'It was messy.'

'You're as beautiful as I expected. Like your mother.'

'Thanks.' Olivia waited for the pain of being reminded that she and her mother were not biologically related, but she was so rattled it didn't come. She had encountered transgender women in California – one was a huge fan of *Crofty Cooks* –

but not many transgender men. Or maybe she just hadn't recognized them. Either way, she should be coping better with meeting this one.

'*Mom!*' Jake's impatience had reached shouting point.

'Coming.'

To Olivia's relief, Sam walked over to examine his son's pool.

She sat down on the platform again, trying to regain her composure, which lately had been taking too many unauthorized leaves.

Sam bent over the swimming pool, the rounded curves of his ass clearly feminine.

Olivia's thoughts jumped straight to the place she'd spent the better part of the last year avoiding.

Mom.

Jillian Croft had been a kind of hybrid herself, born with undescended testicles she was told were pre-cancerous tumors that had to be surgically removed. No uterus. No ovaries, though her breasts developed normally, as did her features and shape. She certainly appeared to identify as a heterosexual woman. But she wasn't wholly female.

What had this transition been like for Sam? What were the thoughts and feelings in his brain that had so absolutely refused to accept his physical form? How much similar gender confusion had Jillian hidden away?

Sam was a whole woman, fully equipped to have a child but with a brain so strongly male he was willing to take the hormones necessary to erase everything feminine about his appearance. Inside that body had lived – maybe still lived – all the female organs denied to Jillian Croft. Like so many things in the world, it wasn't fair.

Sam laughed with Jake, then patted him lovingly on the back and made his way back to where Olivia was sitting. He smelled of aftershave. Very masculine. For all Olivia's determinedly liberal views on sexuality and gender, she found something about him very disconcerting.

'I hear you'd like to help watch Jake.'

'Yes.' Olivia managed to hide shakiness behind her on-camera smile. 'Only if you and Duncan are okay with it. Georgia could use a break. I'm around for a while and need something constructive to do. Jake is adorable.'

'He is.' Sam sat with his legs spread, arms resting on his thighs, hands clasped between his knees. 'Every parent thinks his kid is something special. I'm no different.'

'I guess by now you've read on the Internet how much I love and want kids.'

'Yeah, wow, that's been something.' He leaned down to pick a stalk off a spiky plant growing from a rock, and bit off the end. 'If I can be blunt . . .'

'Please be blunt.'

'My only worry is that you might not be at your most . . . patient right now.'

Who had told him? Georgia? Duncan?

'No. But being around kids is a totally different dynamic. Jake centers me. His joy and his immersion in each moment are really good lessons.' She laughed self-consciously. 'I'm probably sounding totally Californian right now.'

'No, I get it. He does the same for me.' Sam tossed the stalk away, rubbed his hands together. 'I asked him how he liked playing with you and he said, "She's good," which is high praise. I'll need to talk to Duncan, though.'

'Of course.' Olivia should say something about what had happened between them last week. 'I wanted to—'

'Mom? Can we come back tomorrow after the tide's been here?'

'Mom's taking tomorrow off. We're going fishing with Uncle Thomas, remember?'

Jake grew still, brown eyes – so much like his father's – round and troubled. Olivia sensed a big storm brewing inside the little body. 'But I need to see if the water stayed in my pool.'

'How about we come by real close in the boat on our way out and you look through the binoculars?' Sam mimed the gesture through fingers bent into circles. 'That okay?'

'Yeah!' His face cleared and he went back to playing.

'Five more minutes, okay, Jake?'

'Awww!'

'Five,' Sam said firmly.

'Oh-kaaaay.' He was clearly disgusted.

Happily, their exchange had given Olivia time to work out what she wanted to say. 'Your ex and I had a little . . . disagreement.'

'Georgia told me. Sounded like neither of you was at your best.'

'You could say that. I didn't get the feeling Duncan was thrilled to meet me, and it went downhill from there. Not that I was blameless. At all.'

'People are often like that, judging not from the facts but from emotions. I'll let you in on his secret – Duncan's got a chip on his shoulder about rich, beautiful women.' Sam seemed amused by this. 'His high-school girlfriend lived on Islesboro, big island south of here. Her family was rich like you wouldn't believe. Duncan was crazy about her. He used to steal boats to get over there when the ferry wasn't running. Her family hated him as a match for her, and didn't try to hide it. Clara dumped him when she went to Vassar. Duncan always felt the family pressured her into it.'

'That's a long time to hold a grudge.'

121

'He's proud.' Sam turned and examined Olivia. 'She looked sort of like you, too. Tall and voluptuous, though she was darker. The only woman who ever broke his heart.'

'You didn't?'

Sam's eyebrow quirked, his eyes dancing. 'I'm a man.'

'Right.' Olivia laughed louder than necessary, because he was a very attractive man, and was making her a little fizzy smiling at her this close, which was incredibly unsettling. She got to her feet. 'Thanks for telling me. It helps to know that story.'

'Sure.' Sam got up too. Easier when they were on their feet, since he only came up to her forehead. 'He's proud but not unreasonable. Give him time. Okay, Jake. Time to go.'

'Awwww!'

'Getty balls and choggy cake tonight.'

Jake gasped in delight, body freezing rigid, mouth open, eyes lit. 'Getty balls and choggy cake!'

'His baby words,' Sam said. 'Spaghetti and meatballs and chocolate cake, which is actually brownies, but that's what he always called them.'

'Sweet.' Incredibly sweet. Olivia shut down cravings for her own mispronouncing little one. It would do her no good to cry over getty balls. She'd have her own kid someday, or she wouldn't. 'What do you do, Sam?'

'During the year I'm a high-school science teacher here in Belfast. In the summer I find whatever I can to earn a little extra money. Right now I'm helping out in a hotel office in town.' He turned to his son. 'Jake. *Now!*'

'I'm *coming*!' They watched his little body negotiate the walls of his pool, then scamper toward them. He walked on the uneven, sometimes wobbly surfaces as if he were on asphalt. Olivia had experienced the same thing in Stirling, her brain subconsciously gauging rocks ahead for flat surfaces, always scanning for the next safe footfall.

'I'll talk to Duncan, tell him I saw you with Jake and how good you are with— *Oof.*' Sam bent nearly double as Jake leapt on to the platform and barreled into his legs. 'Careful, Jake. He'll be fine with it, I'm sure.'

Olivia pictured that conversation and wasn't so sure.

Hi, Duncan, I was thinking of letting Olivia—

No.

'Actually.' Olivia rubbed in a smear of sunscreen she'd missed on Jake's back. 'If it's okay, I think I should talk to him. I don't want you asking while his entire experience of me has been a drunk, furious mess.'

'Not a bad idea.' Sam's eyes softened into that feminine smile. 'Though I bet you make a gorgeous drunk, furious mess.'

The eye contact was charged and unbearable. So was Olivia's frisson of pleasure at the compliment. She was dead straight, though, and Sam wasn't *really* a man, at least not . . .

Wait. But if he was in love with Duncan when he was a woman, then he'd be gay now, right?

Or . . .

Olivia had no idea how it worked. But she was kind of freaked out that Sam was getting to her like this.

'Thank you.' She stuck out her hand, formally, forcefully. 'It was nice to meet you, Sam.'

'Same here.' He gave a firm shake. 'Jake, can you turn around and thank Olivia for helping you with your pool?'

'Thank you for helping me with my pool.' The little boy's earnest, sweet face nearly undid her again.

'You're welcome. Maybe we'll get to play together again soon.'

He ducked his head into a nod that ended with him staring at his water shoes, swinging his arms back and forth.

'Let's go, buddy. You coming up to the house, Olivia?'

She chickened out, not wanting to walk next to Sam after her bizarre reaction. 'I think I'll stay down here a while. It's so peaceful.'

'Sure.' One last sweet smile, and the male mother and his son climbed the stairs.

Olivia sat watching the water, enjoying the sunshine, inhaling the sweet, calming sea breeze, until she heard Sam's car drive away. Then she went up to the house, relieved that Georgia wasn't back yet. She got a glass of water in the kitchen and took it upstairs to her room, where she flung herself on to the bed to check on the Internet whether she was still adored and loathed as much as before, or whether the storm had abated.

Her stomach sank, along with her mood. Debates were still raging. Derek's rights had been violated by Olivia's on-camera airing of his private medical information. Olivia's rights had been violated by a husband secretly denying her the child she craved. People called for her stoning. People demanded his waterboarding.

Let. It. *Die.*

At least here, lying on the lilac quilt on the four-poster bed with gulls cackling outside and salt water stretching across the peaceful green view, Olivia felt like she was in the eye of this hurricane, instead of being blown and pelted from all sides.

Determined not to check again for several more days, she listened to her voicemails, one from Rosalind and one from her agent. Rosalind was concerned about her. Cherie was gleeful, announcing that every talk show in the country was lining up begging to have Olivia on as a guest. 'The world wants you, baaaabe. This is your moment. Call me, call me, caaaall me.'

Olivia closed her eyes. After the mistake of revisiting her shitstorm, just the idea made her tired. She should call her agent back. She should make a plan for what to do when she returned to LA. She should make a plan to visit her father and Lauren. She should make a plan to visit her grandmother, only an hour and a half away.

Instead, she dialed her sister.

'Olivia, sweetie, how are you doing? I can't believe how nuts people are. It's disgusting. Are you holding up okay? I hope you're staying away from the worst of it. You need to recharge.'

Emotion rose at the warm sympathy in Rosalind's voice. 'I'm doing all right.'

'Would it help if I came to visit?'

The idea of a familiar and beloved person around was so tempting. Olivia had opened her mouth to say *yes, please*, when maturity kicked in. This was her mess. She couldn't ask Rosalind to be part of it.

'No, no. You stay put. I'll be fine. I'm better already. Seriously. I just have to get through the rest.'

'Oh, but—'

'Actually, tell me something.' Olivia raised herself up on to her elbows. 'Have you ever met a transgender person?'

'Not knowingly. I mean, I've seen them around, who hasn't?'

'I met one today. A transgender man.'

'Uhhh . . . which one is that again? A man turned into a woman? Or—'

'No, the other way. This guy was . . . It was freaky. I was attracted to him.'

'Uhhh . . . that sounds really complicated, Olivia. Are you sure you're in the right place to—'

'No, no, no, not attracted sexually, just a weird reaction. I'm too straight for that.' She grinned wickedly. 'Except if I got drunk enough.'

Rosalind snorted. 'Yeah, do me a favor, if you go at it with this guy, do *not* tell me about it. I'm still traumatized from finding out about Mom not having a vagina.'

Olivia shot to sitting. 'Huh? I thought . . .' She was immediately mortified. No female reproductive organs; what did she think that included?

'Not enough of one anyway. They had to stretch her.'

'Oh God.' Olivia let herself fall back on the bed. 'Poor Mom!'

'She did it for Dad.'

'I don't want to hear any more.' She rolled to her side, resting her head on her hand. 'Actually, I do want to hear more. I think I'm getting closer to being ready. Do you think Mom considered herself a real woman? Does a transgender woman consider herself a real woman?'

'What is a real woman? People are people. Once you start with definitions, you're already defeated. It's too complicated.'

'Okay. But . . . what do you think about how it all works? Genders, I mean.' She was not sounding coherent, nor intelligent, unsure what she was really asking.

'I think there's a continuum. Female brain with all appropriate body parts at one end. Male equivalent on the other end. Perfect hybrid in the middle. All kinds in between.'

Olivia rolled off the bed, went to the window and looked out at the water and the evergreen-covered hills beyond.

'When I thought I couldn't conceive, I felt like I wasn't quite a whole woman either.'

'Excuse me, but phtttttttttttttttttttpt.'

She laughed. 'I mean, I was still a woman, obviously, but I *felt* as if I was more inward on the continuum. Not at the total-woman end.'

'That must have been hard. But it makes no sense. We're not defined by our ability to have children.'

'Yes, you're right. You're right.' She turned from the window, leaned against the wall, frustrated at not being able to articulate what she was getting at.

'What do you think of Lauren's brother?'

'Stuart? He hates me.'

'Oh, come on.'

'He does. Lauren probably warned him what a bitch I am. His wife Georgia is a doll, though. Oh, and Stuart has a totally hot guy who works with him. He also hates me.'

'For what?'

She told her sister the bare details of the fight with Duncan and the forced apology, making it more amusing than it had been, and leaving out the bleeding.

'Oh, nice work.' Rosalind was laughing. 'You have such a talent for self-destructing.'

Olivia was taken aback. Self-destructing? Since when was any of this *her* fault? Getting drunk was absolutely her responsibility, yes. And outing her husband on TV. And losing her temper . . .

Oh.

'I'd love to see you try being nicer to yourself, Olivia.'

'How about I hop into a bubble bath. That nice enough?'

'It's a start. Have you seen Dad yet?'

'No, I've sort of been avoiding the trip.' Guilt showed in her tone. 'I'll go soon, though.'

'I could come with you.'

'You could.' She turned back to the view, feeling claustrophobic without its space and distance. 'We could go see Grandma Betty too.'

'Ew, why?'

Olivia grinned. Chatting with her sister was like therapy. Much better than getting drunk. 'I love Grandma Betty, she's a hoot.'

'You go, then. Eve went up there. She's still traumatized.' Rosalind made a shuddery sound of horror. 'You want to be cured of your love for her? Read Mom's first diary, the one I got. You'll also learn a lot about Mom's condition and her feelings about it. I'll send it to you if you want. When I made the copy for Eve, I made one for you, too.'

'Even knowing I didn't want any part of it?'

'I hoped you'd change your mind someday. I think you'd find it really interesting.'

'I'm not . . . Not yet.' Olivia pushed back her hair and found her hand trembling. Time for a change of subject. 'How's Bryn?'

'Perfect.'

'Of course.' Olivia grinned, even as she battled a predictable pinch of envy. 'Thanks for calling to check on me, sister dear. Tell Bryn I said hello. Send him my love. And save plenty for yourself.'

'I will. Love you too. Take care, Olivia. I'll call again soon.'

Olivia stood for a long time clutching the phone. She already regretted asking her sister for information about Mom. Childish, yes, but she wanted to keep Jillian Croft in her memory exactly as she already existed there: luminous, graceful, beautiful, and so talented she made everything she did look easy, whether it was a viciously difficult role in a film or hosting a hundred people at their Beverly Hills house and making every guest feel special.

She wanted to keep intact memories of the two of them on the rare occasions they went shopping together, just mother and daughter, leaving Eve and Rosalind behind. Olivia had reveled in the way sales clerks rushed over, anxious to please. *Is this your daughter? She looks just like her mother.* The way other customers reacted, either studiously pretending not to notice who'd just walked in, or gawking, some hesitantly asking for autographs, others acting as if Mom knew and loved them exactly as they thought they knew and loved her.

Olivia wanted to keep thinking back to the good times, the makeup lessons Eve and Rosalind had rolled their eyes at or avoided, and the dated advice: *Always emphasize your bosom, it's your best accessory. Wear a bra to bed so your boobs never sag. Make sure you do exercises to keep them uplifted.*

She and Mom had been a team, bonded by their mutual love of all things staged and all things girlie. So yes, she might learn a lot from reading Jillian's diaries.

But she couldn't think of a single reason to want to replace her treasured version of Mom with anything less perfect.

Chapter 9

February 9, 1997 (Sunday)

I'm sitting in bed, watching my sleepyheads all around me. Rosalind is snoring, just getting over a cold. With their eyes closed, they look so much like the babies they used to be. I was remembering the silly songs Daniel and I made up for the three of them. 'Livia the Faboo Baby', 'Everything's Coming Up Rosalind' and 'Amazing Eve Grace'. How we laughed.

I've been back from rehab for three days now. I feel better and stronger than I have in a long while. This time I know I can make sobriety stick. For my girls' and my husband's sake if not for mine. I owe them that. If I have to repeat those words to myself a million times a day, I will.

To celebrate being back, I told the girls we'd have a movie night here in my room, since Daniel is in New York speaking at a conference. I would have liked to go with him, partly because I love that city so much – everything good started for me there. And partly to make sure he sleeps alone. Something or someone is on his mind. Again? Still? I don't know. I'm hoping that me being sober will keep him home.

The girls and I watched Bringing Up Baby. *I popped some popcorn and let them have ice cream and we all watched and giggled and snuggled together until they fell asleep. I hope these nights are what they remember of me. Not the rest. I feel so much shame that so much of the bad karma in their lives comes from me. I would much rather be the source of their joy.*

    Jillian

Downstairs, Georgia was at the kitchen counter cutting up kale, wearing a faded red apron that said, *Kiss the Cook*. She looked over with a smile when Olivia walked in. 'Hi there. Were you napping? Looking after Jake pulls all the energy out of you, doesn't it? I feel fresh as a daisy thanks to you. Usually by this hour I want to put my feet up and go into a coma.'

'I did doze for a while. I was also talking to my sister.' Olivia helped herself to a glass of water. 'Anything I can do for dinner?'

'Sure, if you want to wash and dry lettuce for a salad.' Georgia pointed to a couple of heads, bibb and romaine, lying next to the sink, along with a salad spinner. 'I pulled a lasagna out of the freezer for dinner. Seemed easiest since I was away this afternoon.'

'I love lasagna.' Olivia finished her water and put the glass in the dishwasher. 'You were only gone an hour or so.'

'Well, it felt like forever. Such a luxury to be able to finish sentences, thank you.' Georgia bent over her work. 'So . . . I guess you met Sam.'

'Yes.' Olivia picked up the bibb lettuce and pulled off several leaves, then tore them into bite-sized pieces and dropped them into the spinner. 'That was a surprise.'

'I meant to be here when y'all met, so I could have talked to you first. I should've said something sooner; it just never seemed the right time to discuss her.' Georgia made a sound of exasperation. 'I know, I'm supposed to say "him", but I just can't do it yet. I've known Sam her whole life, since she was a baby girl, then a little girl, then a teenage girl, then a young woman, then Duncan's wife and Jake's mother. Now I'm supposed to switch?'

Olivia started on the romaine, not sure how to respond. It wasn't her place as a guest to deliver lectures on tolerance and acceptance. 'It must be difficult.'

'I'm sure I'll come around eventually, but this part is so hard. It's barely been six months since she left Duncan. I don't know when she started taking the hormones. She was so beautiful, too. And now . . . My God, it doesn't seem natural.' She lifted the cutting board and used her knife to swipe the chopped kale into a waiting saucepan. 'Maybe it's because I didn't grow up with this whole transgender thing, but it makes no sense to me. How can you be born female, marry, have a baby, and then suddenly think you're a man?'

Olivia added romaine to the spinner while working out a careful response. Given that Georgia generally seemed like a gentle, understanding person, Olivia would assume this rant was more about getting complicated feelings out than true condemnation. She would bet Stuart wasn't the most willing conversation partner on the subject. Either that, or he ranted all the time and Georgia never got the chance. 'I don't claim to know much about it. But I'm pretty sure it's not sudden. More like finally getting up the nerve to admit the truth.'

Georgia put her knife down and braced her arms against the counter as if she were trying to push it through the wall. 'I know you're right. I do. It's just that sometimes it's hard to be supportive and act like this is all wonderful and freeing for her, when I have so much worry about Duncan, and even more about Jake.'

'Jake seems okay. He seems great, actually.' Olivia wasn't sure whether to simply listen, offer comfort, or try to educate, not that she was remotely an expert. The last person who came to her with a big problem was her college best friend Angela, whose husband had cheated on her for the second time. That had been easy: *He's an asshole, leave him.* 'Jake is young enough to take this in his stride. It would have been harder on him if Sam had waited till he was older.'

'But when he starts school in the fall . . . Lord, the questions he'll be asked. "Why is your mom your dad?" I worry he'll be bullied.' She sounded close to tears. 'I don't get why Sam had to do this. She was always a tomboy, ever since she was old enough to run after her four brothers. No sisters. Her mother is very feminine, but she's a lawyer, not around much. Maybe the combination . . .'

Olivia cautioned herself to speak carefully, thinking of her own mother, also very feminine. 'I'm pretty sure it goes a lot deeper than that. Genetically, I mean.'

'Yes, of course it does. Don't listen to me, I just get so upset.'

Olivia ran water into the bowl to rinse the lettuce. 'It must be upsetting for everyone. But—'

'Poor Duncan is a mess having to watch his pretty wife grow a beard. Can you imagine? This is a small town, too. People talk.'

'They do.' Olivia was getting tired of walking a neutral tightrope. 'Seems like Sam is handling it pretty well.'

'Of course Sam is. She's getting what she wants.'

That was it. Olivia turned and made eye contact, though she made sure her voice stayed even and her face kind. 'He's revealing who he believes he is. Who he most likely really is.'

Georgia sighed heavily. She turned to her spice cabinet and started poking at the jars. 'That's what everybody says. I love Sam to death, I really do, but for her boy's sake, for her marriage's sake . . . well, I just wish it was all different.'

'I would bet Sam does too.' Olivia lifted the lettuce-filled basket out of the water and let it drain while she searched for her next words. 'Was Sam happy before he started transitioning? In the marriage? In himself?'

'Well, no. There were troubles.'

'They would have gotten worse.' Olivia fitted the lid on the spinner. 'That's much harder on a kid than a happy parent.'

'True.' Georgia sounded doubtful.

'What does Stuart think?'

'He thinks it's all New Age bullshit. But that's how he was raised. He and Duncan don't talk about it.' The front door opened. 'Oh gosh, here he is now, and me running my mouth off and not concentrating on dinner.'

Stuart's heavy tread sounded in the hallway. Olivia spun the lettuce vigorously. Stuart being home meant Duncan was home. Duncan being home meant that at some point soon, she would need to talk to him about letting her watch Jake. Talking to Duncan was only barely below thumbscrews on her list of preferred tortures.

'Hey, honey.' Georgia's voice was all Southern sunshine. 'How was your day?'

'Fine.' Stuart nodded curtly toward Olivia.

It was on the tip of her tongue to say, *Mine was fine too, and yours?* Instead she tipped the collected water out of the spinner and spun again until her arm ached and the lettuce was probably a bruised, mushy mess.

'Dinner will be ready in about an hour. I'm late getting started. Olivia watched Jake while I went to get coffee with Maxine.'

Stuart's bushy eyebrows rose. '*She* watched Jake?'

'She did, yes.' Olivia sent him a charming smile. 'First I pulled out all his fingernails and then I set him on fire.'

'Olivia!' Georgia let out a startled giggle. 'Stuart, do not listen to her. She was perfect with him. Sam met her, and she approved, too.'

'We built a swimming pool down on the beach. Jake was very proud of it.' Olivia brought the basket of ultra-dried lettuce over to Georgia. 'I'd like to make it a regular thing. It will help your wife and give me something fun and useful to do here.'

'Sam's fine with it?' Stuart opened the refrigerator and pulled out a Budweiser. 'What about Duncan? He fine with it too? After your behavior the other night?'

Grrrrrrr.

'You know what? I was planning to talk to Duncan later, but suddenly I feel like going right now.' Olivia stalked out of the kitchen. 'I'll be back for dinner, Georgia.'

'No need to hurry. It'll keep.' As Olivia reached the front door, Georgia's voice changed. 'Stuart, I could cheerfully strangle you. What the hell were you—'

Olivia closed the door on the rest of the scolding, resisting the urge to slam it. If that man was sent by God to test her patience, he was doing a bang-up job. She should probably go ahead and reserve her spot in hell right now. Before the excuse of going to see Duncan had popped into her head, she'd been about to tell the bull moose where to put his antlers. *And* his bull.

Unfortunately, now that she was out of the house and there didn't seem to be any thumbscrews around, she really did have to attempt to make nice with Dickhead Duncan. Worth doing, though, since she not only wanted to watch Jake, but she wouldn't mind being able to bump into Duncan on the property or at dinner without her stomach trying to digest itself.

She picked a strong stride, head high, arms swinging, down the slope toward the shore, then on to the path through the woods, where her hell-bent march startled a red squirrel into stuttering fury. At the boathouse, she knocked without hesitation and put her hands on her hips. Then put them down. Too confrontational. She should channel Lauren during this visit, be utterly bland and invariably pleasant.

After all this, the jerk better be home.

The door opened halfway. The jerk was home, and he took her breath away. No, not really; she could still breathe, but her heart did launch into an energetic tap number. He must have showered after work, and his face was shiny clean, hair damp. She'd bet he smelled deliciously of aftershave and/or soap. He wore tight jeans and a loose T-shirt, and absolutely did not deserve to be that hot, or to have such an effect on her.

If he was surprised, disappointed, annoyed to see her or all three, he didn't show it. 'What's up?'

'I'd like to talk. Powwow. Forge a truce. A neighborly day in this beautywood, and so on.'

Duncan hesitated, while Olivia kept her face as sincere and neutral as possible, since along with hoping he'd let her in, she was also wondering what he looked like naked.

'Okay.' He moved back from the door, which she'd guess was as close to an invitation as she'd get. *Come into my parlor, said the spider to the fly.*

She stepped into the familiar surroundings, thought about mentioning she'd been there before with Jake, and decided against it. 'Nice place.'

'Old boathouse.'

'That's what I'd guessed.'

'I was about to have a beer. Want one?'

'Sure. Thanks.' So far, so good. While Duncan went over to the half-size refrigerator, Olivia looked around again, because watching him was too unsettling. The toys scattered by the fireplace during her last visit had been gathered and deposited somewhere else; otherwise, the spartan interior was still spartan. 'You must miss Jake when he's with your . . . ex.'

'Yup.' He popped the top off a bottle. 'Need a glass?'

'Yes, please.' She took both from him. 'What's this?'

'A beer and a glass.'

Olivia gave him a look. Okay, it was a dumb question. But if he'd have the decency to stop being so attractive, this would be a lot easier. She was determined to act professionally and impersonally during this visit, agree to disagree if that was the best they could do, and leave with a firm handshake and good feelings.

'Belfast Bay Brewing Company, Stone Crab IPA.' Olivia finished reading the label and took a nervous gulp, then another. 'Nice. Not too hoppy.'

Duncan gestured her to the red futon sofa in the living area and sat on a chair to one side, leaning forward, elbows resting on his thighs, reminding Olivia of Sam's posture earlier that day on the shore. A man pose.

She took her time arranging herself and had another big swallow of beer for relaxation purposes, wishing he'd put music on. The dead quiet made every word seem to count more.

'Since we both know I wouldn't show up like this for a purely social visit, I'll get to the point.' Deep breath. 'I'd like to give Georgia a break and watch Jake now and then while I'm here. Georgia is okay with it. Sam seems fine too. Obviously I need—'

'You met Sam?'

She put aside annoyance at the interruption. 'Yes. When he came to pick Jake up today.'

They stared at each other, a strange game of chicken. Who'd acknowledge the obvious first?

A gull burst into raucous laughter not too far away. Something ran over the roof.

Olivia decided it had to be her, or she might grow old and die here. 'This must be a difficult time for all of you.'

'That's exactly why I don't want what I've seen of you anywhere near my son.'

And they were off! A fabulous start to the match.

Olivia let out an unfortunate nervous chuckle. How the hell would Lauren respond to that? Or her sweet diplomat sister Rosalind? 'What you've seen of me won't be anywhere near your son. That's why I'm here, to show you who *would* be around him. Georgia has seen that person with him. Sam has seen that person with him. I love kids and I am totally aware of what's off limits around them.'

She lifted her drink to hide her smirk of satisfaction. Beautifully put if she did say so herself. Furthermore, she was telling the truth.

Duncan stood and turned to face the boathouse's sliding doors, open now to the early evening. 'What am I supposed to say?'

Oh for crying out loud. 'How about what you're thinking?'

'You don't want to know that.'

Okay then. Olivia kept her expression sweet, though sour was starting to tempt her. 'You might be surprised.'

'You want me to change my opinion of you in one conversation to get what you want.' He turned back to her. 'I would guess you pretty much always get what you want.'

Olivia counted to ten.

Ten wasn't enough. What an asshole. 'You know what would help? If you stopped talking to me like a misogynist with a chip on his shoulder the size of Islesboro.'

His eyes narrowed. 'Islesboro.'

'Sam told me about Clara and your issue with rich girls.'

Duncan's jaw set. 'That is *not* in play here.'

'Really?' She made him hold her gaze. 'Really really *really*? You are deep-down sure that you have no prejudices against me based on my looks, income level or upbringing? The fact that I am not only from California but from LA and deep into celebrity culture makes no difference? This is all a legitimate reaction to my behavior on one extremely difficult night? Behavior which I have already owned and apologized for?'

He drained his beer. 'I need another one. You?'

'Yes, I do.' She downed the rest of her first with shaky hands. God, he pissed her off. And she wanted to sleep with him. The same toxic combination she'd soon be in the process of divorcing.

Duncan closed the refrigerator, padded back over the plank flooring in his still-bare feet, and handed her number two. Then back to his side of the ring.

And there they sat. And there they drank more beer.

'Okay.' Duncan rubbed at his temple. 'You're probably right.'

Olivia smiled politely, instead of taking the victory lap that tempted her. 'I get it, I really do. When I met you, I assumed you were a blue-collar laborer with no education and terrible taste in everything.'

His eyes flashed until he saw she was kidding. 'Okay. Point taken.'

'Then we understand each other.' She toasted him with her glass. 'Progress Made Tonight in Talks Between Warring Factions.'

He *almost* smiled.

'Why don't you tell me your story?' There wasn't a man alive who didn't love talking about himself. 'I know you grew up here. Georgia told me your parents moved to Florida your senior year of high school and you moved in with her and Stuart. What else? How did you get into boatbuilding?'

He considered his beer, and for a horrible second Olivia thought he was going to blow her off and they'd be back to square one.

'I went to The Landing School, here in Maine. One of the few accredited boatbuilding schools in the world.' Pride crept into his voice. 'I got my associates degree there, then my BS at Southern New Hampshire University. In technical management. Then I captained for a while, first for a guy in Florida, then a guy in St Thomas.'

Olivia thumped a hand to her chest. 'Captained meaning you drove someone else's yacht all over the place?'

'Sailed.'

'Sailed, sorry, but my God.' She was starry-eyed at the very thought. 'That has to be a dream job. Yachts? St Thomas? What made you give that up?'

He shrugged. 'I got tired of it and missed home, so I came back and started working for Stuart.'

'You don't miss sailing?'

'I have a boat.' The pride again. 'But I also have a hometown.'

Olivia nodded, touched by that, thinking of how on their first meeting Derek had jumped all over himself to tell her as much as possible about his life, most of which turned out to be exaggerated or made up to impress her. She was pretty sure everything Duncan had just told her was swear-on-the-Bible accurate. A good feeling. 'After you came home, you married Sam, and the rest I know?'

'Pretty much.' He glanced at her unwillingly. 'What about you?'

She nearly laughed at his discomfort. He probably expected a twelve-chapter novella on All Things Olivia. 'For me it was acting, acting, acting. I graduated from UCLA with a degree in theater, raring to go, sure that LA would drop at my feet. It didn't. Success, failure, success, failure, cooking show, more failure, marital explosion. Now I'm here.'

His look of surprise made her want to be smug again. 'Sounds like you haven't always gotten what you want.'

'Who does?'

He scratched at his ear. 'People who don't want anything?'

Olivia cracked up. He was funny. Humble. Hot. By the time she left Maine, she might almost like him. 'Very profound. Very Zen.'

'Yeah, you Californians don't have all that stuff sewn up.' He almost smiled again, clearly less worried that she might attack him, which made being alone with him in this little cabin a lot more intimate. Which made her want to attack him.

'When did you meet Sam?'

'We grew up together. She's the kid sister of one of my buddies.' He scowled down at the floor. 'And to answer your next question, no, I didn't see the man thing coming until she told me.'

'That was not my next question, because it's none of my business. But I'm sorry. Really. It's not quite the same, but I didn't see Derek's vasectomy coming either.'

He pressed his lips together, then relaxed abruptly. 'That must have sucked.'

Empathy! She was on a roll. And feeling nicely loosened up by the fact that he was easier around her, and that she was more than halfway through her second beer. 'It did suck. Enough for me to go ballistic. As you saw.'

'On camera.'

'I was not planning to do that. It happened.' She tapped her head. 'Temper. Always had one. Also bad impulse control.'

'And you want me to say it's okay that you watch Jake?'

Crap. Olivia had laid her own snare that time. 'I'm never like

141

that around kids. It's like how you approach fine crystal; you know you have to be careful. Completely different from the way you pick up a plastic cup.'

'Fair enough.'

He was starting to impress her. He seemed able to admit to his mistakes and his flaws. More than that, around him, Olivia had found it easier to admit to hers. She was trying to think of a single confrontation with Derek during which either of them had done anything but clamp down on his or her position as hard as possible. It had been about winning, not discussing. So twisted.

'If finding out about Derek's vasectomy was hard, I'd think finding out your wife was a man would be fairly apocalyptic.'

His face shut down. 'Yes.'

'Still is?'

'Some days better than others.'

Olivia tried to imagine how she'd feel if Derek admitted to being female.

Nope. Couldn't do it.

'I didn't realize he was transgender until he smiled.' She replayed their encounter in her mind: the smile, the big, beautiful eyes in the mostly masculine body. The way he'd made her feel. 'It was strange, talking to him, standing that close to him, smelling his aftershave and trying to understand. I mean . . .'

Olivia stopped herself in time. What had she just said about impulse control? Direct, fully open line from brain to mouth.

'You mean what?'

'He was . . . I mean, he's very . . . attractive.'

Duncan's eyebrows went up. 'Tell me you didn't make a pass at her.'

'*No*, God, no, nothing like that.' She could feel herself blushing. Why had she started this? 'It was just . . . confusing.

Disconcerting. Like what the hell is going on and who am I?'

'How do you think *I* feel?' The words exploded out. 'I'm still attracted to her, and she's a *man* now. What does that make me?'

'Someone going through something really complicated.'

He rubbed his hand through his drying hair, making it stick up adorably in all directions, and they sat in silence, not quite as awkward as before. Olivia helped herself through it by indulging in sexual fantasies involving her and Duncan and the chair he was sitting on. In short, she wanted to rip her clothes off and ride him like a cowgirl. Unfortunately, that would be yet another in a long series of Worst Ideas Olivia Ever Had. She was here to gain his trust. Now was not the time.

Though . . . later on might be.

As if he'd heard her thoughts, Duncan looked up from his beer and met her eyes. The chemistry between them roared to life so violently that this time she really couldn't breathe. The sexual fantasy she'd been enjoying for the purposes of idle amusement started to turn into the promise of serious business.

She waited for her wise inner voice to scream at her, to tell her absolutely not in a million years of Sundays. This time, Olivia promised herself, she would listen.

The voice was silent.

Three beats. She'd wait three beats for him to look away. If he looked away, she'd keep the conversation going. If not . . .

One. Two. Three.

He didn't look away.

She put down her nearly empty glass and took a deep breath. 'Do you have condoms in this house?'

Duncan looked startled, as she'd expected him to, but not repulsed. 'Uhh . . .'

'Because I need one.' She pulled off her shirt and tossed it on to the couch. 'My life has fallen apart. My husband turned out to be a gold-digging user. My career flushed itself. And today I was hot for a transgender man.'

He didn't move, watched her with slightly narrowed eyes, but his body was rigid, the atmosphere still electric.

Maybe this was one of her *best* ideas.

'And I would think . . .' she unhooked her bra, let it fall next to her shirt, 'that since your life has fallen apart too, and that you get hot for the same man, you might also need a little . . . affirmation.'

She stood up and kicked off her flats, unbuttoned her jeans. Duncan hadn't moved. Nor had he taken his eyes off her.

'No strings. Quick. One and done.' She stepped out of her jeans. One leg. The other. Tossed them aside. 'Neither of us needs to make our lives any more complicated, but we do need this. Afterward, we go back to talking and acting as if nothing happened. Those are the rules.'

He swallowed audibly.

'So.' Her panties joined the pile. She stood facing him, hands on her hips. 'Are you in?'

Duncan's eyes wandered up and down her body. He took a leisurely swig of his beer and pointed toward a corner of the cabin. 'Medicine cabinet. In that corner. First shelf.'

'Excellent.' She smiled coolly, heart beating like a jackhammer. 'Be right back.'

The condoms were where he'd said. Olivia extracted one, along with several tissues from a box on the counter, then walked back, holding up her booty triumphantly.

Duncan had taken off his shirt and was in the act of pulling down his jeans and underwear. His chest was broad and well developed from a lifetime of physical work, thighs muscled and thick. His erection pointed straight at her.

The man was a work of art.

'Sit.' She pushed at his chest until he was back in the chair, put the pile of tissues on the floor next to them, then handed him the condom and straddled the lower part of his thighs, waiting as he put it on. 'Ready?'

He rested his hands on either side of her hips, small smile curving his lips. 'You're crazy.'

'We both are, which is why this is such a good idea. One of the best I've had all month.'

'From what I've gathered, that's not saying much, but okay.' He put his hands to her waist and pulled her toward him like she weighed twenty pounds. 'And to answer your question, yes, I am ready.'

She grabbed his shoulders and climbed on, grateful for her strong thighs. The earth didn't move, but there was excitement and intense pleasure, and the moment of attraction to Sam was swallowed up in the certainty of Duncan's utter maleness, and of Olivia's utter femininity.

The whole thing took about ten really, really wonderful minutes.

Olivia stayed collapsed against him for as long as she dared, savoring the masculine arms around her, the press of her breasts against a warm, hard chest, the joy of feeling skin on skin once again.

A swell of emotion was all the warning she needed. She was *not* going to ruin her best seduction ever by bursting into tears.

Instead, she allowed herself to press her cheek against the warm column of his neck, then reached for the tissues and stood carefully, handing him half.

'Well.' She blew out a breath, forcing herself not to tremble. 'That's better.'

'I would agree.' He offered a half-smile, disposed of the

condom and cleaned himself up. Olivia walked back to her scattered clothes and dressed quickly, while he did the same.

'So.' She sat back on his couch and picked up her beer with an unsteady hand. 'What were we talking about?'

His eyebrow quirked. 'Are you really that unaffected?'

'No.' She took a swig of beer she didn't want. 'I'm trying not to cry.'

He rubbed his jaw. 'First time with someone since your separation?'

'Given that my separation was three weeks ago, yeah, I should hope so.'

'First for me too, since Sam left.' His voice grew husky. 'Unexpected. But necessary.'

'I really did only come here to ask if I could watch your son.'

Duncan grinned. 'Strangely, I believe you.'

Truce established. Maybe even some trust. 'I'm glad to hear that.'

'Now.' He came over and sat on the futon, half facing her with his arm draped over its back, close enough that she wanted to lean into his fingers. 'Tell me again why you want to watch Jake.'

This time he was really asking, so she took time to form her answer. 'When I'm with him, the crap goes away. He has no expectations of who I am. Even more to the point, he doesn't care who I am. Also, I want to help Georgia for her extraordinary generosity to me. And I want some time during this weird exile during which I'm not continually stepping in my own shit.'

He gave a couple of slow nods. 'Okay.'

Hope rose. 'Okay?'

'Isn't that what I said?'

She was able to smile then, not her camera-ready smile, but

a natural grin of happiness. 'It is what you said. Thank you, Duncan.'

'You're welcome.' He gazed at her until the sight of him and her feelings became unbearably wonderful. 'You are a piece of work, Olivia.'

'I certainly am.' She stood, reluctantly, wanting to hear him say her name again. 'I should get back up for dinner. But I'm glad I came.'

He snorted. 'Me too.'

She laughed, which felt really good. It had been a long time since she could do so from pure enjoyment. Even if this high was temporary, she'd done the right thing.

For once.

'Thanks for hearing me out, for letting me watch Jake, and, uh, everything else. This was a really nice way to start a truce.' She reached the door and turned back. 'Have a good evening.'

Duncan nodded. 'You too. Anytime.'

Her heart gave a leap. Anytime?

He went back into the house and she walked up the hill, peaceful and glowing. The sun was on its way down, shadows long, colors deepened, rosy hues reflecting off tree trunks and branches. So beautiful. So restful being here, far away from hectic crowds and their constant jarring noise and demands.

In the years after Mom died, Olivia hadn't wanted to return to this glorious coast, afraid of memories from the place Jillian Croft was happiest. Later in life, after Dad and Lauren moved here from California, she had not only been avoiding the two of them, but with her life established in LA, Stirling seemed too isolated, too cut off from everything that was happening across the globe. Inconsequential. Unreal. A movie set of a place.

It had taken everything she loved most in LA betraying or denying her to make Olivia realize her mistake. She felt closer to her mother in Mom's native state. This part of the world now spoke in a way that seemed honest and important in comparison to the ant farm she'd lived in for so many years.

Or maybe she was romanticizing the place from a really great mood because she'd just gotten laid.

Regardless, she was in love with the Maine coast again. She would enjoy the evening ahead, chat with Georgia and let Stuart's grumpiness roll right off her. She might even sleep well.

As she reached the Pattersons' front door, her phone rang.

She pulled it out, hoping for Eve or Rosalind. She'd like to be able to speak to them in this better frame of mind, reassure them with more certainty that she was going to be okay, because tonight she'd gotten a real taste of how that could someday be true.

Her adrenaline burst into action. Hope, fear and guilt rushed in to spoil her blissful mood. The call wasn't from either of her sisters.

It was from Derek.

Chapter 10

August 4, 1998 (Tuesday)

My sister is diabetic. Mom knew, but of course she didn't tell me because it had nothing to do with her. I flew up to see Christina immediately when she told me. I knew she was diabetic during her pregnancy, which can indicate a risk of developing the disease later, especially if you don't take care of your health. Christina has gained a lot of weight. I don't think she's been following the diet properly either. I worry she is depressed and doesn't care enough.

I wonder sometimes if having her give up her child was the wrong thing to do. I saw how she looked at baby Olivia that first time we went back to visit. It broke my heart – and chilled it. I never left them alone after that. People in terrible grief can do desperate, uncharacteristic things. After that trip, she showed frighteningly little interest in her niece, as if by ignoring her she could pretend she didn't exist. I offered to hire her a life coach, but she looked at me as if I were an alien. I don't think she leaves the house often enough. I don't think she dates. I know for sure she sees too much of Mom. That man who got her pregnant and left did serious damage to her – as if Mom didn't do enough to both of us.

If Christina still had her daughter with her, would things be different? I'm still not sure I made the right choice regarding Olivia. But Christina didn't want to keep her baby. I can't be blamed for that, though Mom would find some way, I'm sure.

I need my sister to stay healthy. She has always been a true friend to me, and those are in such short supply. I am never sure if people actually care about me, *rather than what I might be able to do for them.*

Jillian

Olivia stared at the phone so long she had to jump to answer it before Derek went to voicemail. Why was he calling? To apologize? To admit he had loved her after all? To reconcile? Her ridiculous heart leapt at the thought, and she had to tell it to get real. Had she learned nothing? She was reacting from exhaustion, wanting to regard the past few weeks as a particularly bad patch amid years of a decent if not spectacular marriage. High points and lows like everyone else's, but both of them committed and both of them faithful.

Oops! Until just now!

She allowed herself a grin and a small thrill. She *had* learned something. If reconciliation was what Derek had in mind, she looked forward to telling him to screw himself.

'Hi, Derek.' She managed exactly the surprised and breezy tone she was hoping for. If all it took to qualify for a movie role was the ability to sound the opposite of how she was feeling, Olivia should be a star by now.

'Hey there, baby.'

Olivia gritted her teeth at the familiar greeting in his deep, slightly raspy voice as if nothing had happened, as if he was once again calling from location to catch up, see how she was doing, report on his day. Given how much he traveled, weeks of their relationship happened during phone calls that started just like this one.

She pushed through the front door and strode past the dining room, where Georgia and Stuart were eating lasagna, pointing to her phone and mouthing, 'Sorry.'

Georgia waved her on her way with a smile and a thumbs-up. Stuart didn't turn around.

'What's going on?' Olivia started climbing the stairs.

'Oh, nothing. I just wanted to call and see how you were doing.' He sounded his everyday self, sincere, casual, intimate.

'I'm fine, actually. Better every day.' *In fact, Derek, I just got laid.* Tempting, but Olivia couldn't bring herself to stoop that low. What if he'd been banging other women since the day he left? She'd be back where she'd started emotionally, just as she'd managed to begin her climb out of the pit. 'How are *you* doing?'

'Still picking up the pieces.'

'Yeah.' She found the exchange bizarre, like leaders of warring nations doing an affectionate check-up on each other's mental health.

'I just had an interesting talk with a woman who called me. She knew your mother. Or knew of her.'

'Okay.' Olivia went into her room and shut the door, annoyed that he seemed to think they could chat together as if nothing had happened. 'That narrows it down not at all.'

'True.' His laughter turned nervous, no longer casual, no longer sincere. Olivia paused by the bed, staring out at what was going to be a spectacular sunset, weighing the wisdom of telling Derek to fish or cut bait. 'She had some information I think you'd be interested in.'

'Okay . . .'

'About your mother.'

Olivia made an exasperated noise. Bloody showbiz people. Always the drama. 'Will you get to the point, Derek?'

'I'm looking at a piece of paper that proves Jillian Croft was a man-woman hybrid. That she had balls at one time, and that none of you are her real kids in spite of all the lies she and your dad told the press and the world.'

Olivia took in air, then sat on the bed so hard she bounced.

This could not be happening. He was talking about the document she and her sisters had found last summer, the 1969 diagnosis of eighteen-year-old Sylvia Moore with complete androgen insensitivity.

'How did you get that? Where did you find it?'

Derek's triumphant chuckle exposed Olivia's terrible mistake. The little prick had been bluffing. There was no way he could have that paper. The only copy was safely with Rosalind in New York. The original had been destroyed decades ago by the doctor's staff.

She wanted to scream. Instead of playing it cool, denying the whole thing, calling him a trash-raking moron pathetically searching for revenge, she had calmly handed him all her remaining power on a silver platter.

'What do you want?'

'Aw, Olivia. Come on. This isn't . . . I'm not trying to blackmail you.'

'Really? That's so sweet.' She wanted to hire an assassin. How could she have been married to this guy for so long and have no idea what he was capable of? The idea that she'd been bracing herself to disappoint his hopes of a reconciliation made her sick. 'You just decided to let me know because you knew it would make me feel so good?'

'Look, babe.' He had the gall to sound impatient with her. 'I'm in desperate shape right now. I need to . . . I need to assure my future, is all.'

'Oh, I see.' She was choking on the words. 'But this isn't blackmail at all.'

'No.' He sounded boy-scout earnest. 'No, I just—'

'Jesus, Derek. Grow a pair and admit it.'

'I'm not . . .' He stopped for a breath and came back calmer. 'I'm not threatening you or anything.'

'Oh, thank you! Thank you so terribly much. You decided to let me know you had this paper, which I don't think you do, and you happen to mention that you need to assure your future, but you're not threatening me or blackmailing me. Super!'

He sighed, as if this criminal stuff was taking a lot out of him. Poor baby! 'I just need a place to live. You own the house.'

The little shit. 'Nice, Derek. Very nice. All those years together and this is what it comes to?'

'What did our marriage mean to you when you told the world I couldn't have children?'

Olivia's mouth opened, then closed. She could say nothing, she could say everything, she could say, 'You did it first, so you deserved it, you poopy. Neener-neener.'

No point.

She'd been playing with fire when she got back at him so publicly. She'd had no idea how hot he could burn, but this was her consequence: total incineration.

What had Rosalind said about Olivia's talent for self-destructing?

She flashed back longingly to her relatively carefree walk from Duncan's boathouse in the peace of a sunlit evening. She thought about LA, about the career-that-still-wasn't, about the long years she'd spent in pain and frustration. And she made an instinctive, impulsive and bizarrely freeing decision. She was never going back there. Not to live. That life was over. The movie business was newly thriving in other places, like Atlanta, or Vancouver. Or she could try to forge a theater career in New York, or Chicago. No more banging her head against the same brick wall. She was done.

'Take the house. You can't have a thing that's in it, but you can have the house. Sell it, buy a condo, and you're set for life, longer if you buy somewhere cheaper than LA.'

'Sure, sure. Yeah, okay. That's good, that's good.' He sounded truly bizarre now. Was he guilty? On something? Who cared?

'But I want a signed paper saying that's it, Derek, you're done, and you won't ever use that information against me again.'

'Yeah, sure. Sure, I can do that.'

Her stomach roiled. He wouldn't. He would never give up that much power. Olivia had been a naïve idiot to ask. 'Okay, then. We're finished.'

'Yeah, yeah. Thanks, Olivia. I really appreciate this.'

Aw, gee, Derek, you're welcome. Pleasure doing blackmail with you.

'I gotta go.' She ended the call, getting an adolescent thrill from being the first to hang up, which lasted all of a nanosecond.

This might be only the beginning. There was nothing stopping Derek from using the information about Mom's condition any time he wanted to. Need a vacation? Pick up the phone and get one. A yacht with crew? Sure! Olivia was good for it.

It was possible he wouldn't, possible that he'd sell the house in LA and live contentedly forever after on the millions it would bring. But knowing about Mom's condition gave him the last word, the power to keep Olivia as his cash cow until death did them part. He didn't even have to put up with her moods and tempers and self-centered demands anymore. He had it made!

Olivia would be tied to the little bastard forever. He knew exactly how she felt about Jillian Croft's legacy, and how hard she'd fight to protect it. He had her right where he wanted her.

She let loose a string of curses that would have impressed a rapper.

Where had he gotten the information? Who else knew? Mom would never have told a soul, neither would Dad. Grandma Betty was still in total denial and Christina had died a decade ago.

Who had slipped up, and to whom? Neither Rosalind nor Eve, she was sure. Rosalind's boyfriend Bryn would never betray her. Neither would Rosalind's birth mother, Leila, or her half-sister, Caitlin. Did Eve's almost-boyfriend Clayton and his daughter, Abigail, know? Eve's aunt, Shelley Phillips? Eve certainly trusted all of them, and she was a hard sell on trust.

Lauren? Even as Olivia's outrage started building, she knew it wasn't Lauren. Dad's personal puppy denied him nothing, and whatever Olivia thought about how their romantic relationship had started, there was no question that Lauren adored Daniel Braddock. She'd never risk exposing him to that level of stress and misery. Especially over this past year, when his health had been so shaky.

So who? Even if one of the people in Jillian's inner circle had inadvertently been overheard, what were the odds that would happen around someone sleazy enough to want to give – or sell – the information to a shithead like Derek?

Olivia should call her sisters, see if together they could figure out what scum had found out Mom's secret. Maybe they could discredit him or her in advance, stop this nightmare from happening. Derek could say Olivia had acknowledged such a document existed, but he couldn't prove it.

155

Too risky. Maybe he did have his hands on it, or could get his hands on it. They had to protect Mom from exactly the kind of speculation and gossip she'd gone to such extreme lengths to prevent. Her remarkable legacy, tarnished by her addictions and recovery efforts and her untimely death, would be further damaged by outrage, ridicule, satire, who knew what else. More gossip, more malice, more reporters in the family's faces demanding details of her condition, of the cover-up, of the three sisters' births. They'd come after Leila, too, and Shelley, neither of whom had signed on for this.

Olivia had to call her sisters.

Her bile rose. How could she? Her relationship to Eve and Rosalind had been steadily improving over the past year. Now this. They'd be furious with her, both of them, and she deserved it. If she'd kept her mouth shut on camera, none of this would have happened. She could have quietly divorced her snake of a husband and ridden off of Sunset Boulevard into a new life. How many more people did she have to make hate her this month?

Olivia would find some way to handle this alone. Maybe Derek would be satisfied if she agreed to publicly retract her statement about his infertility and admit she'd made it all up out of spite. But what if that still wasn't enough? There might be no end to this. Monthly payments, weekly payments – he knew the size of her fortune. He knew the size of her sisters' fortunes too, since Mom's estate had come to the three of them equally. What was to stop him plundering all of it?

Olivia fell back on to the welcoming mattress. Her life had become a TV melodrama. Up next: the scene in which she had to descend the stairs and eat lasagna with people she'd known for a ludicrously short time, pretending her life hadn't just taken yet another full rotation down the crapper.

God, she needed a drink. The beers she'd had with Duncan – had that even been this century? – were long gone. She couldn't overdo the booze around the Pattersons again. If only she hadn't broken the bottle of Jack on the rocks. She could have a few sips to smooth out this horrible pain and tension. Just a few. Maybe quite a few.

She groaned. No, no, not remotely healthy and even less smart. She couldn't start relying on alcohol for coping. In that regard, Mom had been a role model of a different kind. Instead, Olivia would do what she did best: pay a visit to her favorite place, the beautiful Planet Denial.

None of this had happened. Derek hadn't called. Last week, Olivia had decided straight from her beautiful, generous heart to gift him the house. She didn't need to tell her sisters, because Derek was satisfied and would never need to resort to blackmail again.

She sat up, keeping her spine straight, closed her eyes and took deep breaths, letting the tension flow out of her body with each exhale, continuing to push away negative thoughts like so many crumbs flicked off her lap.

In. Out. In. Out.

Olivia was strong. Olivia was resourceful. Olivia was well educated. Olivia had a loving family and plenty of money. Olivia would do fine. Especially if there was red wine served with the lasagna.

In. Out. In. Out.

Her lips curved into a smile. Speaking of in-out, what was Duncan doing right now? Had he put their encounter out of his mind? They'd been blisteringly hot together, passion brought on by their mutual anger, misery and deprivation. Even more erotic than the make-up sex she and Derek had about every other week after another marital blowout.

Olivia opened her eyes with a smile. She was ready for dinner.

'Hey there.' Georgia looked up from her salad with concern. 'Everything okay?'

'Peachy.' Olivia smiled warmly at her hostess, then lustfully at the bottle of Chianti on the table. 'Sorry I'm so late.'

'No, no, it's fine. The lasagna's keeping hot in the oven.' Georgia started pushing back her chair. 'I'll just run—'

'Georgia—'

'You sit. I'll get it.' Olivia headed for the kitchen before Stuart could finish telling his wife not to wait on her. She was holding tight to her inner peace, and was not in the mood for any more male buttheads to shatter it.

She brought the lasagna back into the dining room, and served herself in the silence.

'Well.' Georgia pushed the salad bowl closer to Olivia's plate. 'I hope you like sausage.'

'Love it.' She didn't, and tonight it smelled like indigestion waiting to happen. However, she was not going to give Stew-y here any more ammunition to use against her, so she would not pick out the pieces, even if she was up all night.

'Wine?' Georgia picked up the bottle. Stuart made a sharp movement.

Oh for God's sake.

'Yes.' Olivia bestowed a chilly gaze on Mr Butthead. 'I'd love some.'

'How was your talk with Duncan?' Georgia finished pouring and set the bottle down within easy reach.

Olivia hid a smirk. 'He thinks it would be fine for me to help watch Jake.'

Georgia clapped her hands together. 'Oh, isn't that great. All that free time ahead! I've been wanting to get back into knitting. Do you knit, Olivia?'

'Nope.' She finished chewing a mouthful and swallowed. The lasagna was delicious, moist and cheesy, studded with decently small bits of sausage, spinach and mushrooms. 'Not a knitter.'

'I learned when I was a kid, from my grammy. We'd sit in the living room – she called it the parlor – and her hands would be flying, making such beautiful lacy patterns. At first I spent the whole time dropping stitches and asking her to fix them for me. But I finally did get the hang of it.'

Olivia downed a good gulp of wine, anxious for its soothing effects. 'What about you, Stuart? What were you into?'

Georgia laughed. 'Stuart has always been about boats. Duncan too, from the moment he met his first one.'

'Is that right?' Olivia kept her gaze on the Mute Butthead. 'Tell me about that.'

He shrugged. 'I like boats. Grew up liking boats, learned to build them, and that's what I do.'

'I'd love a tour of the boatyard sometime.'

Stuart gave a brief nod and got up from the table with his empty plate.

Olivia lowered her glass. Okay. That was just shitty. 'Hey, Stuart?'

He paused on his way out of the room.

'Do I need to apologize for being me? Because the problem is, I don't know how to be anything else.'

He looked blank. 'Sorry?'

'Sweetie, I don't think we understand what you're saying.'

Olivia sighed. How could they not understand? Explaining would be excruciating. 'I was trying to have a conversation with you.'

Stuart screwed up his big weathered face. 'What are you talking about?'

Georgia burst into laughter. 'Oh, I see. He's like that with everyone, Olivia. Don't you pay him any attention.'

Olivia's outrage wavered. 'Oh.'

To her surprise, Stuart's face split into a grin. 'Thought you were special, huh?'

She snorted, letting him see her amusement. 'I am *supremely* special.'

'I'll get Duncan to give you a tour sometime.' He left the room with his plate.

Georgia rolled her eyes. 'Such a chatterbox I married. Give him time. He doesn't warm up to people quickly. And you blew in here on such a storm. He's intimidated.'

'*Intimidated?*' Olivia didn't buy it for a second. 'Well, I'd try to be sweeter, except for the fact that I'm not sweet. He'd do better with either of my sisters.'

'Tell me about them.' Georgia poured herself another inch of wine.

Olivia caught herself drinking too quickly and picked up her water instead.

Blech. So *watery*.

'Rosalind is an artist and free spirit. She lives in New York, but met the love of her life last summer, a sculptor, so she spends a lot of time with him in New Jersey. In Princeton.'

'Oh.' Georgia was obviously disappointed. 'I was hoping she was single. My Nate is also a free spirit. He's a chef down in Portland, I think I told you. Works all hours. He needs a good woman to distract him from the kitchen.'

'That's a hard life.'

'Among many hard lives. What about your other sister?'

'Eve is the quiet one. She and I tend to butt heads.' Olivia jabbed a thumb toward her chest. 'I'm the bossy older sister.'

Georgia made a face. 'I had one of those.'

'We're awful. I know.' She chased lasagna down with another sip of colorless, flavorless liquid. A last sunbeam cut into the dining room and made the ruby depths of Georgia's wine glow.

See? Even God wanted her to drink.

'Where does Eve live? What does she do?'

'Boston. She's an architect.'

Georgia perked up. 'That's not far from Portland.'

'Yeah, but she met a guy last spring . . .'

Georgia threw up her hands. 'That's it. I'll never have grandbabies.'

'Nate is your only son?'

'Yes.' Her face clouded. 'We tried for more, but it wasn't God's plan for us.'

'It wasn't Derek's plan for me either.'

'Oh, mercy.' Georgia cringed. 'I shouldn't have—'

'No, no.' Olivia helped herself to salad. 'It was my clumsy way of saying I feel your pain. Not being able to have kids . . . it's not the worst thing in the world, but there are a lot of times when it feels like it.'

'Sure are.' Georgia rotated her glass, causing the wine to swirl, making Olivia's mouth go Pavlovian. 'I hate to ask this, I know you get asked all the time, but . . . what was your mother like at home? As a woman and as a mama? I admired her so much.'

Olivia nodded. She had this answer down pat, because yes, she did get asked all the time. 'She was a remarkable woman, very strong, devoted to her art. She knew what she wanted and never let anything stop her, but she was so elegant, and so charming, and so beautiful that her strength never felt abrasive or forceful. My dad used to say she could charm the spots off a leopard.'

Georgia's face shone, a look Olivia was used to. People

always wanted their idealized views of a celebrity validated. 'And as a mother?'

'She had battles. I'm sure you know about those. But she always had time for us. She and I were like . . .' She held up two fingers tightly together. 'Same tastes, same passions.'

'What were those?'

'Acting, of course. Movies. Theater. Everything was about stage and screen for me. Acting lessons, voice lessons, dance lessons, all preparing me for the big career I haven't had yet. We both loved to shop, stereotypical I know, but it was so fun.' The ache grew in her chest, reliable as Old Faithful. 'Most of the time a personal shopper would bring things to the house and we'd pick, but sometimes when Mom was in the mood, we'd go to stores. You should have seen the clerks running. Mom owned the place. Then we'd go home and giggle about how she'd slayed everyone with her diva routine. She'd stand just so. She'd speak just so. She'd come out of the dressing room in outfits that suited her and pose, pretending she was hoping for approval, and everyone would swoon over her. It was so fun to play starlets together.'

'Did your sisters enjoy it too?'

'Nope.' Olivia laughed, drank more fucking water, then gave up and picked up her Chianti. 'Neither of them. I got the diva genes.'

A jolt hit the pit of her stomach. She'd gotten none of her mother's genes. That particular part of Planet Denial was getting harder to inhabit. It didn't help that Mom had pointed out their resemblance constantly to anyone who would listen, doing it so naturally that Olivia wondered whether by that time Jillian was even aware that she was lying, or if she'd disappeared into the fantasy role of birth mother so completely that it had become her truth.

With another shock, Olivia realized that she might be able to find the answer to that question in the diary Rosalind had been sent anonymously from an address in Saratoga Springs, New York, a copy of which was all set to be mailed when Olivia wanted it. Or Mom's second diary, the one equally mysteriously sent to Eve on Washington Island, also ready for when Olivia chose to read it.

Maybe she'd be ready soon. The rest of her world had crumbled; why not make it worse?

She drained the rest of her wine, reached for the bottle . . . then offered it to Georgia and finished her water.

Chapter 11

December 27, 1998 (Sunday)

I'm drinking too much. I'm taking too many Valium. I can't control my temper. I'm horrible to Daniel and then more horrible. I need to figure out a way to stop this overindulgence. I think from now on I will stop after three drinks, and try to wean myself down from the pills. If I can keep it under control, I will be fine, and not have to go to rehab again. I can't go a third time. Once or twice the public can forgive and forget. More than that and you're just a loser drunk.

Olivia woke early to the sound of much-too-near crows having an animated conversation. *Croak, croak, caw, caw.* Was it fair that one of the most common birds on the planet had one of the loudest, ugliest songs?

She would have designed things differently.

A bleary squint at the clock radio by her bedside showed 6.45. Her window showed bright light sneaking around the shade's uneven edges. The past two days, since her night with Duncan, had been cloudy, warm and humid. A pretty day would be a nice change.

Olivia hauled herself out of bed, shuffled to the window and raised the shade. Sunlight poured over the opposite shore, turning the sea blue and the pines a gold-tinged green. Leaning close to the half-open window, she inhaled the light, clear air coming in through the screen. If there had been a storm the night before, she hadn't heard it, but the humidity had definitely broken, leaving the kind of fresh-washed start-over day that made it impossible to be grumpy. Even when your ex was blackmailing you.

She yawned and went to pick up her phone to check her text messages.

From Washington Island, Eve had sent a picture of Marx at the edge of a giant foundation hole that would someday be her Aunt Shelley's cottage, and reported that it was miserably hot in the Midwest.

Olivia's agent wanted to know whether Olivia had changed her mind about being on *Good Morning America*. Cherie couldn't keep them hanging on foreverrrrr. And what about the magazine interviews? And why hadn't Olivia called her baaaaack?

Because Olivia was not interested in any more publicity. She had learned her lesson the not very easy way, at the cost of her marriage, house and plans for the rest of her life.

Her next-door neighbor in LA very kindly wrote to tell her that her house had been egged.

Oh please. A week and a half later, people were still in an uproar? Someone else needed to screw up and get Olivia off the radar. Though she thought it would be fine if the eggs kept coming after Derek moved back home.

She told Eve to pet Marx for her, told her agent she was not interested, thanked her neighbor, then went on to check the current state of the media frenzy. Nothing new, though the #metoo movement had taken over and the whole mess had moved from being a championing and/or condemnation of her and Derek in particular to a condemnation of women by men and men by women.

The Internet had taken the good old-fashioned practice of shouting in the privacy of your own living room at all the idiots on TV, radio or newspaper, and sent that rage soaring out to land in everybody else's living room. At least Olivia was gradually becoming less of a target, though she still felt like the legendary Mrs O'Leary's cow, who'd started the Great Chicago Fire of 1871 by kicking over a lamp.

With luck, Olivia could emerge from her exile sometime soon, though so far she'd been oddly unmotivated to make the necessary plans for the next phase of her life. Probably because she had no idea what that would be.

She showered and dressed quickly – not bothering with makeup or hairstyling – in black cotton shorts from one of her favorite LA boutiques, added a white scoop-neck top with ruffled cap sleeves that just covered the tops of her shoulders, and slipped into her favorite pair of Teva sandals, sturdy, waterproof, safe for rock-clambering, and best of all, not ugly.

After a quick trip to the bathroom and a tooth-brushing session, she visited the kitchen, where she grabbed one of the banana and walnut muffins Georgia had baked the night before and an apple. Coffee would have to wait until she came back. She felt restless, edgy; she needed to sit by the water and breathe Maine air to clear out the online ugliness lingering in her brain.

Down on the shore – she'd considered the gazebo, then changed her mind when the mosquitoes seemed bearable – she sat on the little wooden platform at the bottom of the stairs where she'd chatted with Sam. There must have been a storm, or rough water at some point, because all Jake's hard work on his pool had been tumbled flat. He'd be so disappointed.

She ate her muffin and apple, enjoying the lowered humidity and cooler temperature, watching the breeze ruffle the tide, and boats big and small making their way in and out of the harbor. Breakfasting like this reminded her of Stirling, where the family had eaten many meals by the water. She and Derek had taken plenty of picnics down to the Pacific beaches in LA, but had to share that shore with wall-to-wall houses, shops and throngs of people. In Stirling, with acres of unpopulated forest around and no other houses in sight, the great outdoors had felt as if it existed only for the Braddocks.

Olivia's last trip to Candlewood Point, the previous summer, had been dominated by the immense task she and her sisters had inherited after Dad's stroke, of clearing out the family house for sale. Difficult, often painful work, filled with memories and discoveries; some wonderful, like the clipping from *People* announcing Olivia's birth, others not so wonderful, like Mom's diagnosis.

She lowered the half-eaten apple, suddenly and violently homesick for the family property. Dad had wanted to sell even before he got sick; he and Lauren were tired of the responsibilities of home ownership and had planned to invest in a cottage at the Pine Ridge retirement community where they now lived. His stroke had meant an immediate move, and the girls had been so upset and overwhelmed by his crisis that getting rid of the house felt more like a relief than a loss.

So short-sighted.

A beautiful wooden sailboat appeared on its way out of the harbor at the same time an idea struck her. She pulled her phone out of her back pocket and opened Google Maps, typed furiously and grinned at the result. It would take less than two hours to drive from here to their old house. Why not? It wasn't as if she had anything else to do. Jake wasn't around on Saturdays, and

Stuart and Georgia would probably welcome a day of Olivia-free relaxation. Stuart certainly would.

If the family who'd bought their property wasn't around, Olivia could roam the shore whose rocks she knew like they were rooms in her own home. If the family was there, maybe one of its members would let her at least look around. If not, enough summer people owned houses on Candlewood that she'd be able to find some uninhabited place to hang out. She could buy a picnic, a lobster roll somewhere, maybe at one of the places she and her family used to visit. Jordan's or Ruth and Wimpy's outside Ellsworth, or Tracy's in Sullivan. She'd be able to surround herself with wonderful memories, dating back to some of her very earliest.

Energized, she jumped up and threw the rest of her apple into the ocean for the fish. Fish probably didn't eat apples, but that was what Mom had always said when she threw in the last crust of her sandwich or the pit from a plum. *To feed the fish!* Then she'd laugh and clasp her shapely calf, bright scarf tied around her big straw hat, toes painted the same ruby red as her fingernails. Posing perfectly without giving it a thought. Jillian Croft wore her movie-star glamour like a favorite shirt, comfortable and effortless, to throw on as soon as she awoke.

Being back in Stirling, on Candlewood Point, would almost be like visiting her.

'You're up early.'

Olivia started at the sound of Duncan's voice, then turned nonchalantly, nerves buzzing, mortified that she hadn't bothered with hair or makeup. *Never let them see you ugly.* 'So are you.'

'I have things to do.'

'Me too.' She stood tall, heart thumping, noting his lazy swagger and the way his jeans hugged his thighs. She hadn't set eyes on him since they'd been together, and she hoped he wasn't planning to come closer and get an eyeful of her blotchy skin, skimpy lashes and the bags under her eyes.

Luckily, he stopped at the top of the stairway. From that vantage point, Olivia probably looked only mildly horrifying. 'Whatcha doing down there?'

She made a sweeping gesture toward the ocean. 'Watching. Breathing. Existing. Trying not to think too much.'

'Good things for a Saturday morning.' He leaned against the handrail, relaxed, casual, but she could see the energy coiled inside him. Tightness around the jaw. Shadows under his eyes. He could undoubtedly see the same in her. Even when she did have makeup on.

Messes, both of them.

A sudden breeze blew hair across her face and she pushed it back, wishing he'd go away. She hated how vulnerable and unprepared she felt for this encounter, and not just because of how she looked.

'How did you sleep?' Lame, but someone had to say something.

'Not great. I had . . . dreams.'

'Nice dreams?'

Instead of answering, his eyes held hers, lips slightly curved, and Olivia knew exactly what kind of dreams he was talking about.

Adrenaline fizzed through her system. She wanted to invite him down to the platform and give the passing boaters something *really* fun to watch.

With a different man at a different time, she might just do that. But she'd made a deal with Duncan. No strings. One and done. Those had been her rules, and she needed to play by them, certainly to save her sanity and probably his as well. Given their current mental states, infatuation could grow and turn too quickly into unhealthy dependency.

Duncan broke their gaze, looking out toward the sea. 'What are you up to today?'

'Driving to Stirling. Know where that is?'

'Sure I do.' He pointed back over his head. 'Way up, past Milbridge.'

'Our family used to own a house on Candlewood Point. I always felt happy and peaceful there.' She shrugged. 'Maybe the magic still works. How about you?'

'I have work to do around the house. I was on my way up to see if I could borrow some tools from Stuart. Mine are in storage.'

'He and Georgia aren't up yet.'

Duncan grinned down at her. 'Yeah, I don't really ask anymore. You coming up now? I'll walk back with you.'

Olivia froze, then told herself sternly to grow up and climbed the stairs, reluctantly preparing to show Duncan what no man except Derek had ever seen: Olivia, nearing forty, without makeup.

Chin up, she stood calmly in front of him, in spite of the fact that he was fulfilling her worst fear by staring at her with those killer brown eyes as if he'd never seen her before.

Olivia jammed her hands on her hips. 'Didja lose something in my face?'

'*You* did.' He moved his hand near her cheek, an intimate stroke even without touching her, one that left her skin tingling. 'All that crap you wear.'

'Crap?' She pretended outrage. 'Do you know how much that "crap" costs?'

'Way too much if you look better without it.'

Ridiculously pleased at the compliment, she pushed past him

up the grassy slope toward the house. Crap indeed. He could look at her ass instead. No makeup there either.

'You going to be around for dinner tomorrow night?' he asked.

'Yes, I think so. Why?'

'Stuart and Georgia invited me.'

'Oh.' She turned to him in the shade of the gazebo. He'd already seen her face; she wanted to see his while he answered her question. 'Do you want me there or not?'

He shrugged, expression giving nothing away. 'All the same to me.'

'Okay.' She couldn't tell if he were being honest or polite, and was uncharacteristically shy about asking. 'I'll probably play it by ear.'

'Sure.' If he was disappointed, he didn't show it, which annoyed her because she'd childishly wanted him to be.

She turned and kept walking. She needed to keep her crush under control. Chemistry like theirs was dangerous. In Olivia's perfect world she'd make sure that shaky-limbed, fizzy rush only happened around a person's true soulmate.

While she was at it, she'd make crows sing like thrushes.

'This is my stop.' Duncan paused at the path to the shed. 'Have a good trip. Maybe I'll see you tomorrow night.'

'Thanks.' She gave him a casual wave, a cool smile, and let herself back into the house, thinking wistfully about all the wild sex they could be having.

If she continued to behave this maturely, her life was going to bore her to death.

Upstairs, there were still no signs of Stuart or Georgia. Olivia put on her makeup, avoided the hair issue by pulling it into a ponytail, and grabbed a pair of jeans and a light jacket in case Candlewood Point was cooler or too full of mosquitoes. She had bug spray but could always stop in Ellsworth for one of those electrified rackets that zapped the itchy nuisances to hell where they belonged.

Car keys, purse, phone, note for the Pattersons informing them of her plan . . . and she was ready to get the hell outta Dodge.

The trip was smooth, both familiar and not. Familiar because it was Maine, unfamiliar because the family usually flew to Bangor and rented a car, so the route between Belfast and Ellsworth was new. From there, however, pretty much every twist and turn had some memory attached. She avoided the Google-recommended inland shortcut on Route 182 and stuck to Route 1, which was how her father had always driven, he and Mom in front, girls buckled in the back.

The atmosphere was always happy, convivial. Since she wasn't working, Mom would be taking the meds that leveled her moods. All of them would be in a state of excited anticipation, pointing out familiar sights along the route, each of which brought them closer to the place they adored. Ray Murphy, the Chainsaw Artist, with nightly live shows, almost next door to Ruth and Wimpy's restaurant with the giant lobster out front. The singing bridge into Sullivan, now silent, but which before its refurbishment had a surface that produced three distinct tones under a car's spinning tires. The whole family would sing along with the changes in pitch.

The closer Olivia got, the more excited she became, as if she were still a girl or teenager in the back seat, on the first drive up that year. This trip felt exactly as she'd hoped, like a voyage back into better times, into the bosom of her family, bringing her mother vividly back to life.

In Milbridge, she stopped at Chipman's Wharf for a container of fresh crabmeat, and at the local Shop 'n Save she bought rolls, the smallest jar of mayonnaise she could find, and a few other items for a picnic lunch. Then she continued on toward and past the tiny town of Stirling until she came to the turnoff down Candlewood Point.

As soon as she made that turn, she could hardly sit still, singing loudly along with a Norah Jones CD, windows rolled down to let in the sweet air. The car sped with her eagerness, now on the narrow bridge over mudflats where the ocean would swell in for its twice-daily trip to peak tide. Now through blueberry barrens, ripening berries on their way to maturity, then into the thick woods that blanketed the rest of Candlewood, reducing the ocean view to now-and-then glimpses through the trees.

The pavement ended, a much-anticipated milestone, and her Jetta bumped over gravel and sand. Driveways appeared and receded, mostly summer places. One sharp curve, then the next, which revealed the wide pebbled beach providing the first clear view of the bay. Olivia slowed to a stop as Dad always had, to drink in the sight, proof that the family was mere minutes from its destination. After the beach, there was only the final climb through the sun-dappled woods to their part of this heaven.

Olivia had been astonished that her erudite father, having grown up and lived in the culture-clogged megatropolises of New York and Los Angeles, had chosen this isolated, relatively primitive place to retire. And yet . . . maybe he had been trying, as Olivia was today, to recapture the times when his movie-star wife and family had been happiest. Before Mom's toughest years began. Before he turned to the unremarkable Lauren for whatever it was he needed from her. Olivia would like to think that was the case.

Over the final few yards, Olivia's mood changed, her bouncy

excitement becoming a deep, quiet pleasure. She parked at the top of the driveway and sat for several minutes, remembering how much her mother had loved this first approach every summer, how giddy she'd get during the trip, starting from the plane's initial descent into Bangor. *Trees! Look at all the trees!*

When they arrived at the house, she'd jump from the car almost before it had stopped rolling and take huge, greedy breaths. She'd bend and stare at her daughters through the window, eyes bright with happiness, cheeks flushed, already impatient that her family wasn't moving fast enough. *Smell that air. Just smell that air. Oh my God, it's fabulous. My lungs are lighter, I swear they are.* Then she'd throw her arms wide, laugh her beautiful, musical laugh and call out as if there was someone there to welcome them: *We're here! We're back!*

While their father dutifully began to unload the car, Mom would rush with the girls down to greet the water – a quick hello and more exclamations over the view – before she ushered them back to help Dad carry in suitcases and supplies, turn taps to bring down water from the well, light pilots on the stove and water heater. Mom would hurry upstairs for the box of favorite items she deemed too precious to leave over the winter: her copper pot, special hand-painted vases, the tide clock that she'd wind every day to keep track of the motion of the sea, what remained of Dad's grandparents' china, an iron chandelier that held eight candles to light the dining room, and the long-handled snuffer the girls fought over when it was time to extinguish those flames.

Olivia had inherited some of Mom's treasures. The copper pot sat on her kitchen counter in LA, filled with ripening fruit. One of the vases held flowers in her living room. The crazy soup tureen from the Braddock china set was in one of her cupboards somewhere. Where had the rest of it gone? She'd missed so much by not being able to help clear out the house last summer. Her work had been all-consuming. Preparing and performing in a weekly live show was a lot more than just the hour in front of the cameras. She'd also been trying to get pregnant.

Given how *that* had turned out, her time would have been much better spent making sure pieces of her and her sisters' precious and irreplaceable past were appropriately saved and divided.

She pushed open the car door and emerged into the sunlight, stretching and inhaling with as much pleasure, if not as much noise, as Mom used to. Such great smells, better and richer here even than Belfast. Christmas-tree firs, damp earth and decomposing leaves, moss and ferns, sea salt and the rich, slightly fishy tang of low tide.

Best smell on the planet.

Fingers crossed, she tiptoed cautiously down the long driveway lined with low blackberry plants, berries still red and sour. No car. A good sign. Whoever had bought the place wasn't here, at least not now. August was a more likely choice for summer people, when the chances of one of Maine's famous fogs had lessened, the blueberries were ripe, and fall was gathering to pounce at the end of the month.

Another few steps. There was the boulder near the house where she and her sisters had played Queen of the Hill until Eve fell off and sprained her wrist. Any second Olivia would be able to see the screened-in back porch where the family had eaten so many meals, breeze blowing across their spectacular bay view, bringing its sea scents to mingle with the aromas of their dinner. Soon after, the mottled grey of the house's shingled exterior would come into view, with its heavy dark-green shutters. If those had been opened, the owners would be coming back, possibly any minute. If closed, Olivia was fine spending the day here.

Mouth stretched in an expectant grin, she hurried forward. And stopped in horror.

The new owners had torn off the beautiful shingles and installed cheap beige aluminum siding, replaced the heavy green shutters with shiny black ones that didn't look like wood. The original single-pane wavy glass windows had been ripped out in favor of modern energy-efficient models. The weathered cedar deck was now a gray composite eyesore. The porch's wonderful open-to-the-world screens had been smothered by metal and glass windows and doors that could be purchased in any home improvement store.

Olivia's heart broke. *Oh Mom.*

After her death, when Dad had retired here, some changes had happened. Lauren had replaced threadbare rugs worn by years of happy feet, faded curtains, uncomfortable antique furniture and long-outdated if wonderfully romantic kitchen equipment. In doing so, she'd turned the inside from a charming, quirky delight into suburban normalcy, which Olivia still hadn't forgiven her for, even understanding that what worked in a summer house wasn't desirable all year around.

But this. This was rape, pillage and looting all in one. The elegant if slightly worn charm of the place had been ruined.

Olivia turned her back on the atrocity and was met with another rude shock. A large number of the majestic firs and cedars in front of the house had been felled to provide clearer sightlines to the water. Mom had been adamant that the massive network of roots was needed to prevent erosion. To paraphrase: if anyone needed to see the ocean, he or she was welcome to drag his or her lazy ass down to the shore and take a goddam look.

Olivia made herself move toward the water on the familiar narrow path, bumpy with rocks and roots, snaking through blueberry bushes, Queen Anne's lace and goldenrod. At the bunchberry-strewn shore, she stopped, surveying the rocks that sloped toward the sea, now about ten yards out, making its gradual way back twelve vertical feet to high tide.

At least the shore was the same. They couldn't ruin that. There was the sandy strip where the Braddocks had held their clambakes. There was the ledge where they ate meals when the weather cooperated. There was Olivia's favorite tide pool, a magical world of barnacles, snails and brine shrimp propelling themselves through forests of maroon and green seaweed. Further out, the same uninhabited islands, thickly furnished with pine and birch. The same pea-sized houses on the far-off shore, easy to ignore.

Olivia clambered over the rocks she knew so well, searched the tide pools, waded ankle-deep in the freezing water to hunt for starfish and mussels. Then she sat, mutely watching the movement of the glittering buoy-strewn expanse, tide pulling one way, river currents another, gulls and cormorants doing their gull and cormorant thing, lobster fishermen working their traps.

At one, she ate her lunch. At two, she started a walk around the property and along the edge of Candlewood Point. By four, she could no longer pretend that being there was enjoyable. She was lonely and tired, of nostalgia and of grief, of nothing staying the same, of searching for something without knowing what it was and always coming up empty.

Sick and desolate, she returned to her car. Her hand was on the key when Eve called. Olivia considered not answering, unwilling to spread her lack of joy around, but curiosity got the better of her. Her sister and Clayton *had* to be a couple by now.

She sat straight, supporting her voice properly so it wouldn't sag into misery. 'How are you doing, Evie? Is it great being back in Wisconsin?'

'It's pretty great. Hot, but supposed to cool off soon. The island is really nice in the summer. Much more going on than in April.' Her sister's normally even tone had taken on a distinctly chipper bounce. That could only mean one thing.

'I take it Clayton was pretty glad to see you?'

'Seems like.'

In spite of her mood, Olivia found herself grinning. 'Fan-freaking-tastic! What happened?! Tell me everything!'

'Where are you? The reception is crappy.'

'Candlewood Point. At the house.'

Eve gasped. 'You're kidding. Are the owners there? How does it look?'

'They're not here.' She wouldn't tell Eve about the devastating changes. Chances were none of the Braddock sisters would come here again. Olivia would allow the place to remain whole in Eve and Rosalind's memories. 'I had lunch on our picnic rock.'

'Awww!' All the nostalgia Olivia was no longer feeling showed up in her sister's wail. 'I miss it.'

'Tell me about Clayton. You're together now, I assume? Finally?'

'Finally?! We were both just out of crappy relationships when we met. It was smart to be cautious.'

'No, no, no, it's *never* smart to be cautious. Look how super well that has worked for me!' She waited for Eve to stop laughing, wishing she found it as funny. Maybe she would someday. 'Tell me how it happened.'

'He invited me over for dinner, and—'

'You wore your good underwear.'

'I did.' Eve giggled. She giggled! Her happiness was doing a lot for Olivia's mood. 'Clayton made an amazing meal. He's such a good cook. Roasted duck that he put into this incredible warm salad, oh my God.'

'You're making me hungry.'

'With lots of delicious wine, lifted from his father's cellar.'

'You're making me thirsty.'

'And then, we were still talking, I don't remember what about. He is so easy to talk to, and I was all blah blah blah, and then he shot up like he'd forgotten something on the stove, which is what I thought had happened. But then he headed right for me, pulled me up and kissed me like he was going to *die* if he had to wait another second.'

Olivia hooted. Her sister was clearly out of her mind with joy. Eve had actually just shared! With details! 'Did you ever get to dessert?'

Eve giggled again. 'Much later.'

'Oh sweetie, I am *so* happy for you.' She was. And also envious. Not of the sex; sex was easy to get. All a woman had to do was find the nearest guy and say yes. But of that other thing, the knowledge that you were starting something with a really good person that might just last forever.

Her sister chatted on about her aunt Shelley and the Eve-designed cottage-to-be, her new client and how she had to feed words into his mouth in order to get any to come back out.

At some point she must have remembered that while her life was coming up sunshine and roses, Olivia's was coming up poison ivy and dog poop.

'Ack, listen to me, I need to shut up. How are *you*, Olivia?'

'No, no, I love hearing you so happy. I'm doing fine,' she lied beautifully through her teeth. 'Lauren's brother and his wife are knocking themselves out for me, and their house is beautiful. Belfast is adorable.'

'Did you get the diaries yet?'

Olivia went on alert. 'Mom's diaries?'

'Yes, Rosalind and I sent them to you.'

'You sent them?' She sounded panicked. 'I told Rosalind I wasn't ready.'

'Oh. Well, she told *me* that you were.'

'Oh, for—' Olivia stared out the window at the beautiful fern-strewn woods that were no longer part of her. 'Rosalind seriously overstepped.'

'Hey.' Eve spoke gently. 'You don't have to read them until you're ready.'

'It's just the principle of the thing.' She was close to tears after a bunch of days without any, and it pissed her off. 'What part of "I'm not ready" was hard for her to understand?'

'She loves you, Olivia. And respects you. I do too. But we both think it's really important that you understand Mom better. More than that, though, I think . . .'

Olivia waited, understanding that it was still hard for Eve to articulate thoughts centered around their mother. She'd twisted her molestation by one of Mom's producer friends into fierce bitterness against Jillian Croft that had only recently abated, partly, to her enormous credit, through weekly therapy sessions, and partly, Olivia thought, by opening up to let the clearly remarkable Clayton in. Eve had been a new person since they met.

'Rosalind and I feel as if the three of us should be going through this together. Right now, you're the one on the outside. We don't want you disconnected from us any— We don't want that.'

Any . . . more? It was true. Olivia had always been on the outside, more so since last summer, when she'd issued a moratorium on the subject of Mom's infertility. 'I'll try.'

'You have *plenty* to cope with right now. More than plenty. More than anyone should. Take your time. But when you are ready, do read them. I wish I had a *lot* sooner.'

'Yeah, okay.' By now, Olivia just wanted off the phone. 'Kiss that man for me. I can't wait to meet him.'

'That will happen! In the meantime, if being at Stuart's gets awful for any reason, Washington Island is a good place to be anonymous, and I'm sure you'd be welcome at either Clayton's or Shelley's.'

'Thanks.' *Wisconsin?* Cheese and cows and sausages? No, thanks. If Olivia had to be in exile, she'd do it here in the state she loved.

She said goodbye to her sister and started the car. Back to Belfast. Back to dinner with Georgia and Stuart and Duncan.

What had she expected to find here? That Candlewood Point was truly magic? That her mother's ghost would be waiting to comfort her and make all her troubles go away? This was just a place with trees, like many others in Maine, with typically beautiful views and rocks and sea life, with a house made of concrete and wood and brick – and now aluminum siding – like many, many others. None of her memories were here. Olivia had brought those with her.

She drove away, from the property, from Candlewood, from Stirling, without looking back. Whatever she'd been searching for, Olivia was beginning to realize she'd have a much better chance of finding it if she kept herself facing forward.

Chapter 12

March 23, 1999 (Tuesday)

I can't stop at three. I should care, but I don't, which makes me feel horrible, because of course I do care, just not when there's a drink in front of me. Then nothing matters but getting it down as fast as possible. Of all the conditions I have, this is the worst. I don't know how to beat this one. I can take pills for bipolar, I could stretch my younger body to make a vagina, I could fake getting pregnant – but this one is winning. I will probably die young and be remembered tragically, like Marilyn Monroe.

I don't want to die. I want to live and see my girls grow up. My beautiful soulmate Olivia will be an actress like me, a fine one I'll be so proud of. She told me she wanted to be a chef. A chef! I told her women can't be chefs, that that world is too sexist. Why start off your life fighting a losing battle? I told her she was born to be on screen, like her mother. She is so beautiful, the camera will adore her. Eve will be an architect and build fine things around the world that will last forever. Rosalind . . . she could go in any of a thousand directions. And does, regularly. My sweet, cheerful, bouncy girl. I want to see their daughters grow up, too, even if it means I have to become a grandmother someday, which is too horrifying to contemplate.

Daniel is for sure having another affair. I am probably

driving him to it. I love him and I hate him and I don't blame him and I do. If I didn't have my girls, I would not have anything to live for.

Olivia walked up to the Pattersons' front door, holding the bag of groceries she'd bought on the way home from Stirling to contribute to the household.

She knocked, then waited impatiently. There had been tourist traffic on the way back, so the drive had been slow, and getting to the bathroom was her current goal in life.

No answer.

She rang the doorbell, humming a frantic little tune, straining for the sound of footsteps.

Nothing.

What if Stuart and Georgia had gone out? Neither of them had given her a key. If she stood here much longer, she'd pee herself.

This time she knocked *and* rang the doorbell, still humming, as if that would help her bladder hang on. Dum-dee-dum-dum.

No answer.

In desperation, she turned the knob, which gave easily. For heaven's sake. Georgia and Stuart didn't lock their front door? At least Duncan's boathouse was deep in the woods. These people were nuts. Olivia couldn't imagine feeling that safe. Even if she lived in a convent, she'd worry about that one psycho gardener who might be secretly armed.

She pushed into the house, feeling a little like an intruder. In the yellow foyer, someone had dragged a chair out from the kitchen; on its cushioned seat sat two FedEx packages and a note from Georgia. *These came for you this afternoon. Stuart and I are having a dinner and movie night. Help yourself to whatever you'd like. There's leftover lasagna . . .*

The note went on, Georgia describing practically the entire contents of her refrigerator and cabinets, and all the different ways and in what combinations Olivia might or might not be in the mood to eat them.

What a good person she was. Stuart was lucky. So was Olivia.

She put the note and groceries down in the kitchen and ran for the first-floor bathroom. Good thing Eve had warned her the diaries were on their way, so she hadn't torn the envelopes open expecting something she might actually want.

Two minutes later, she was back in the foyer, hands on her hips, scowling at the packages. She shouldn't be annoyed with her sisters, but she was. No one was forcing her to read her mom's diaries, but this felt like it. After today's trip to Stirling hadn't provided the comfort she'd hoped for, Olivia didn't really want to delve into any more complicated emotions.

To put it mildly.

Back in the kitchen, she unpacked her goodies. Two bottles of a nice Central Coast Chardonnay and two bottles of Pinot Noir from the same area; a bag of fancy mixed nuts flavored with cayenne and thyme; chicken, rosemary, leeks, bacon and another less expensive white wine for the stewpot. Olivia would make one of her favorite braises and serve it with sautéed snow peas and chive biscuits. A nice dinner, and the least she could do to begin to repay the Pattersons for their kindness.

She could even offer to cook it the next night, giving Georgia a lazy Sunday. With Jake not around, Olivia needed things to do, and nothing centered her and took her out of herself more than cooking. Except maybe sex.

Speaking of which, Duncan had said he'd be at tomorrow's dinner. She'd love him to—

Olivia rolled her eyes. Oh, great idea! Try to impress the man with her kitchen skills! Maybe she could volunteer to clean his house, too, or do his laundry. She was skidding on her ass down too many slippery slopes as it was. She needed to cut that kind of thinking right out.

After she'd put away the groceries, she poured herself a glass of the Pinot and took that and a bowl of the nuts out to the glassed-in back den overlooking the lawn and the gazebo, both extra pretty in the early-evening light.

She sat in a rocking chair facing the window and had a sip of wine. Ate a nut – a cashew.

Nice. Relaxing.

Another sip of wine. Another nut. This time an almond.

Her thoughts drifted. What did the diaries contain? What had her mother written in private, straight from her brain and heart on to the page, with no acting, no posing?

Olivia shook herself. She'd been over this. She didn't want to read them. *Think about something else.*

She got up and went to one of the red-curtained windows. The bay was lovely, dark blue against the green of the shore. She was so glad the weather had held today.

Back to her seat. A sip of wine. A pecan.

Maybe tomorrow would be as pretty. She hoped the heat on Washington Island broke soon too, for Eve's sake.

Dammit. While the diaries had been safely in other states, Olivia hadn't given them a thought. Now that they sat a few yards away, they were beckoning, piquing her curiosity and testing her resolve.

She looked around for a magazine to read. Or she had books upstairs. Or she could listen to music on her phone.

She sighed and put down her glass. Or she could read her mother's diary.

Back in the foyer, she picked up the top package, from Rosalind. If Olivia remembered correctly, this diary covered Mom's early years, from high school through her marriage to Dad.

She opened the flap and peeked cautiously inside, as if Rosalind might have mistakenly included a tarantula.

A book, identical to the copy Rosalind had given Eve last May for her birthday, bound in blue leather with a simple title embossed in gold: *Sylvia*. Inside, typed versions of the original pages. Her mother had never touched this.

Olivia brought the diary over to her wine to introduce them. Since they were going to be spending quality time together, they might as well be friends.

So. She opened the book, trying to decide if she were brave or stupid, and ending up settling on both. The first entry, she skimmed, afraid of reading carefully.

Today I got the absolute best *news in the world and the absolute* worst. *The best was that I got the part of Sarah Brown in the spring musical,* Guys and Dolls! *The lead role and I'm only a* sophomore!

I would have been so happy today, like up-in-the-clouds happy all day long, but then the worst thing also happened . . . Nan got her period. She was the only one *left in our* whole *grade, besides me.*

I'm crying writing this . . . I hope I read this someday and laugh at how worried I was, when I was young and silly enough to think there was something wrong with me.

I think there's something wrong with me.

Olivia's hand trembled reaching for her wine. She downed the rest of the glass, poured herself another and read the entry again, more slowly this time, registering her mother's joy and her fear.

This was going to be a rough ride. She should put the book down, cork the wine and get something to eat.

Since all those were very wise ideas, Olivia ignored them and kept reading, turning pages raptly in spite of the pain. The more she read, the more she missed her mother, and the more she ached for all Jillian Croft had been through – how she'd hated her body, how she didn't understand why she'd been born different from the girls around her, how she'd been victimized by an uncaring and neglectful mother. Neither Grandma Betty nor the family's doctor had shared Mom's diagnosis with her, nor had either made any move to comfort or counsel her, even when Mom had surgery to remove the undescended testicles she thought were cancer.

Olivia almost gave up then. At the very least, her enthusiasm for visiting Grandma Betty hit an all-time low. What kept her reading, what drew her in most forcefully, was her mother's unshakeable confidence in her talent. Her understanding of and dedication to her craft was remarkable for someone her age, someone with no access to lessons or coaching. Her risk-everything plan to run away from home and aim for the top school in the biggest city had worked.

How many people had taken similar risks? How many of them actually became stars or even made a decent living? Jillian had beaten incredible odds.

Olivia was proud, and doubly ashamed that she hadn't been able to follow in those great and awe-inspiring foot-steps. This was a true actress, a genius of her art. Olivia, mean-while . . .

Well, she'd tried really, really hard.

She caught herself and rephrased. *Was trying* really, really hard. These weeks of hiding represented a brief timeout. A recharge.

It took a sip of wine to soothe her burst of annoyance, then she put down her glass and read on. And on. She read about her mother's first encounter with Daniel Braddock, how he saw something special in her, offered to coach her. How they fell in love, how he proposed. How the first time they tried to make love . . . disaster.

Then Mom's heartbreaking final entry after the diagnosis:

I'm not normal. I do not have a hymen. I do not have a vagina. I do not have ovaries, never had ovaries. I had testicles removed. I'm a hybrid man-woman, with the reproductive capability of neither, a freak of nature in a pretty package. I will never have my own children to love and nurture and teach about the joys of being human, to be every bit the mother mine wasn't.

The only way that I can become a real woman is to play one in the movies.

Olivia couldn't close the book. She couldn't leave her chair. She couldn't even see for the tears.

Why had Rosalind sent this to her? How was being devastated by the truth of her mother's childhood going to help Olivia in any way, or bring her closer to her sisters?

What was the *point*?

She grabbed her glass and the bottle and went back into the kitchen, poured herself another glass, then stopped, put the bottle on the counter and leaned both hands on its edge, head bowed.

Rosalind did not mean to hurt her. Rosalind wouldn't hurt anyone. Neither would Eve.

Careful not to spill any, Olivia poured her full glass back into the bottle and recorked it. She ate lasagna straight from the refrigerator, washed down with sparkling water, which at least had more flavor than plain.

Better. Somewhat. She was still restless, still emotionally churned up.

What was there to do in this town on a Saturday night? Dancing? Live jazz? Roller-skating? Greased codfish relay?

She grinned, clearing her plate to the sink. There was a codfish relay every summer in Milbridge, the town in which she'd bought her crabmeat and groceries that morning. Contestants in hip boots and yellow slickers relay-raced carrying, you guessed it, a greased cod, which they'd pass to fellow team members, along with the outfit, amid a whole lot of cheers, jeers and hilarity. Mom had loved the event, making sure the family went every year they managed to be in Stirling at the end of July. She'd wear dark glasses, old jeans and a sweatshirt, hair tucked under a Red Sox baseball cap in an attempt to blend into the casual crowd.

A sudden soft knock at the door made Olivia jump, a tap-tap-tap like a secret communication. Whoever it was could go away. Georgia and Stuart weren't home.

She put her plate and silver into the dishwasher.

The knock came again. Tap-tap-tap. What was that about? Why didn't the caller just push the bell?

Creepy.

Olivia put away the lasagna and was wiping down the counters when the front door opened.

She gasped and jumped back so she wouldn't be visible from the foyer, looking desperately around for a knife. Or a place to hide. Or both.

Fuckarini.

189

This was why people needed to lock their doors! What was wrong with them? And why hadn't she locked it?

Steps sounded. Someone had come in. On the counter opposite her – Georgia's knife block.

Three . . . two . . . one . . . Olivia lunged, pulled a chef's knife from the top of the block and held it out in front of her. She'd taken martial arts. Once. A long time ago. She might remember some of it. Maybe.

'Olivia?'

Her breath blew out in an enormous sputtering gust. 'Jesus, Duncan.'

He appeared in the doorway, wearing jeans and a close-fitting white T-shirt that did nothing to slow her heart. 'What's with the knife?'

'You nearly got it between your ribs.'

'Yeah?' He bunched his mouth, obviously trying not to smile as he gave her a slow once-over. He had that look in his eyes, the predatory one he'd had earlier that day. The one that gave her the shaky-fizzies. Something else was different about him, too, but she couldn't place it. 'What'd I do this time?'

'Scared me to death.' She was still breathing hard, but now the fear mingled with attraction to become ridiculously exciting.

Duncan needed to get ugly. Fast.

'I knocked.'

Olivia shook her head disdainfully. 'You Belfast people have no idea what the real world is like.'

'Fine with me.'

She put the knife away and poured more wine. 'Now look what you did. I'd stopped at two.'

'Why?'

She glared over at him, but it was hard to stay irritated when he was standing there looking so hot and so adorably amused at her expense. 'This means you're going to have to drink too.'

'Suits me.' He held up a six-pack he'd brought with him. 'I knew Stuart and Georgia were going out tonight. I thought you might be . . . lonely.'

Oh. My. God.

Olivia turned back to face him. 'Are you talking about what I think you're talking about?'

He popped the top of a beer with a flourish and gave her a lazy grin that answered her question.

'What about our rules? One and done?'

He shrugged. 'Is that really what you want?'

What *did* she really want? How was she supposed to know in this state? She really wanted Duncan, that was a given. She really wanted him to make the world go away again. To be able to pretend they were normal people having a normal time together doing what normal men and women did – except she was no longer sure what made a man or woman normal.

'It's dangerous, Duncan.'

'Why?'

'Because, I don't know, we might . . . get used to it.'

He took a step toward her, expression making it clear how stupid he thought that comment was. He seemed cockier. Less closed down. 'And that would be bad because . . . ?'

'Because we might . . .' Dammit, she'd had this worked out earlier today. Something about dependency. 'Because we'd get to like it too much.'

He laughed that time, and she had no excuse not to join in, because she sounded patently ridiculous. 'You worried you'll fall in love with me, Olivia?'

She made a sound of derision. 'About as big a chance as you falling in love with me.'

191

'So?' Another few steps and he'd be close enough to touch. She really wanted to.

Instead, she took a careful sip of wine, trying to cut through her id-driven impulsiveness to find out what her inner voice had to say.

Her inner voice appeared to be as horny as she was.

Olivia held her breath, then let it out on a long sigh. Okay. Worst case, she'd fall for him a little, and get hurt. In the meantime . . . well, *look at him*.

'Hmm.' She put on her full smoldering-sexuality act. 'As a matter of fact, I am a little lonely.'

'Yeah?' He stepped closer.

'Uh-huh.' She took out her elastic and shook her hair loose as sensually as possible. 'Got anything particular in mind?'

Duncan snorted and looked around. 'Wait, are we in one of your mom's movies?'

'Ha!' She liked that he'd called out her bullshit without cruelty. 'Have you *seen* any of my mom's movies?'

'A few. She was *something*.'

Olivia tipped her head, frowning at him. 'Can I ask without fishing, ask seriously . . . Do I remind you of her?'

'Hmm.' He examined her through narrowed eyes. 'Almost.'

'Almost?'

'You have her look, though not her features; her sensuality, her strong presence. But not . . .' Duncan furrowed his brow, circling a hand to coax out the right word. 'Not her intensity.'

'Yeah.' Olivia turned away and put down her glass. 'I couldn't get that part right.'

'I hurt your feelings.'

'I asked you. I'm not blaming you for answering.' She heard the thunk of his beer hitting the counter.

192

'You are . . .' He turned her to face him, standing about six inches away. 'Extremely sexy.'

Olivia melted, because even though he must have felt he had to say that, he'd made an effort to sound convincing. 'I was thinking the same thing.'

'Really.'

'Oh yes.' She moved until her mouth was barely an inch from his, feeling his breath on her lips. 'I am *extremely*—'

She ruined the joke by cracking herself up, including an extremely unsexy snort, which made her laugh harder. Duncan stepped back, shook his head at her, then lunged forward, grabbed her around the waist and lifted her. She squealed, a blatantly fake protest she belied by wrapping her legs around his waist and her arms around his neck to make carrying her easier. Not that he seemed to need help.

God, this was fabulous.

'Would you like to be made love to in a bed?' His eyes glittered with fun. 'Or screwed on the counter?'

Olivia blinked demurely, shivery with excitement. 'Yes, please.'

He laughed and carried her over to a lowered section of the counter near the opposite wall, where Georgia had set up a chair and laptop in front of a row of cookbooks. He set her on her feet. 'Last one naked loses.'

'What if Stuart and Georgia come home?' Olivia jerked down her shorts and panties.

'Nope.' He pulled off his T-shirt, let it fall to the floor, attacked his button fly. 'They texted me to see if I wanted to come with them. Seven-thirty show, run time one hundred and thirty-two minutes.'

Olivia burst into giggles, nearly getting tangled trying to take off her top and bra at the same time. 'You checked?'

'I was sitting alone in the boathouse, my buddies all coupled up tonight.' His jeans flew across the kitchen. 'I figured you'd be alone too, your own friends thousands of miles away, and it seemed really stupid to waste a beautiful night not with you.'

She'd never heard him talk this much or this openly. Either he'd already had a six-pack or she'd passed some kind of test. 'I might have to start thinking of you as a romantic, Duncan.'

'You might be right.' His warm, slightly devilish smile made her chest fluttery.

'I win.' Naked, Olivia turned abruptly to spread her shirt over the counter and scrambled on to it, arms reaching, wanting him to push away all her disappointment and confusion and self-doubt.

They went at it savagely, as they had previously, bodies finding the best angles and rhythms for each other's pleasure, Duncan waiting for Olivia's climax like a true gentleman. A true gentleman boinking a woman he barely knew on someone else's kitchen counter.

They came down together, panting, laughing a little self-consciously.

'Mmm.' Olivia took hold of the back of Duncan's neck and brought their foreheads together for a brief connection. 'Thank you. That was fantastically therapeutic.'

'For me too.' He brushed hair back from her forehead, a tender gesture that made her chest flutter again. Then he grabbed up a bunch of tissues from the box Georgia had on her kitchen desk so they could clean up.

And there went the flutters.

Duncan took Olivia's Kleenexes from her and tossed them into the trash, then came back, confidently and gloriously naked, hands on his hips, with the reluctant look of someone about to ask a favor or confess to a crime.

194

'I don't know about you, but . . .' he cleared his throat, 'I, uh, would kill to be able to hang out in bed with someone instead of alone all the damn time.'

Olivia drew in a surprised breath. 'Wow.'

He glanced at the stove clock. 'We have about two hours before the movie's over. Does that appeal to you?'

'God, yes.' She let out a stupid half-laugh, thinking of how many times during the past weeks she'd woken up craving Derek's body against hers. Even knowing that if Derek's body *had* been against hers on any of those nights, she would have screamed bloody murder. Duncan's body, though . . . 'Like you wouldn't believe.'

'How's your bed upstairs? Or would you feel more comfortable at the boathouse?'

She frowned, then shrugged. 'Doesn't matter. As long as we're safely separated when Stuart and Georgia come back.'

He held out his hand to help her off the counter. 'If we go upstairs, we don't have to get dressed.'

'Sold.'

They took the party up to her room, putting their drinks on the nightstand then diving under the covers, Duncan on his back, pulling Olivia close, their legs tangling, two near-strangers giving each other happiness at a time when life's supply had run short.

'Oh man, you feel good.' He pressed his chin to her temple. 'The crazy things you miss when you're single.'

'No kidding.' She forced herself to be conscious of everywhere their bodies intersected, the maleness of his skin against hers, the blissful feel of being warmly held between cool sheets. 'I want to know what changed your mind about me.'

'Who said I changed my mind about you?'

'For one thing . . .' She gestured to the lack of space between their bodies. 'And you're really talking to me tonight. It's better than fighting.'

'I don't know, that was pretty fun.' He put a hand under his head, stared up at the ceiling. 'To answer your question, Georgia gave me a talking-to. That started it. You not being a jerk when I apologized, and Sam saying you were really good with Jake – those helped. But it was at the boathouse, when you took off your clothes, that I finally saw the goodness in you.'

Olivia pretended to try to push him away. 'You disgust me.'

'Men are the way they are. Nothing we can do.'

'Damn shame, too.' She ran her hand over the hard planes of his chest, thinking through what he'd said. Thinking of the male–female difference. Of her mother. Of Sam. 'Will Sam become that way? I mean more aggressively sexual?'

He groaned. 'Do we have to talk about this?'

'Yes. Because I want to know.' She propped her head up on her hand, brain filling with more questions. 'Do the hormones change the way—'

'Why don't you ask her?'

'Him.'

'Whatever.'

'Because I don't know him well enough.'

'You don't know *me* well enough.'

'All right, all right.' She sat up and reached across him for his beer and her wine. 'Here. Drink.'

He pulled himself up, arranging pillows behind them so they could both lean back comfortably.

Olivia took a sip of wine, then put the glass down next to her. The taste had become harsh, acidic, and no longer appealed. 'How long have you known about Sam wanting to change?'

'Why do you want to know all this?'

'I have good reasons. Important reasons.' She met his gaze squarely. 'Personal ones.'

His eyes widened. 'Don't tell me *you're* thinking of transitioning.'

'Me? *Me?* You think I'm—' She pinched him when he chuckled. 'Someone close to me was . . . Well, it's complicated.'

'Your husband?'

'God, no. He's way too much of a jerk to have any female in him.'

'*Hey.*'

'Score one.' She drew her finger down an imaginary chalkboard.

'About Sam.' Duncan grimaced and rubbed his forehead as if the subject gave him a headache.

'I won't ask a million questions. Just the basics. If you really don't want to talk about it, that's fine. But it would . . . I think it would help me process some of what's been going on.'

'Basics. All right.' He drank from his beer, put the bottle back and folded his arms across his fabulous chest. 'Sam was always a tomboy. She grew up here with four older brothers and a strong dad. I'm close to one of her brothers, Caleb.'

'Georgia told me that much.'

'I'm just getting started, you mind?'

She batted her lashes. 'Pray do continue.'

'Sam got picked on a lot by her brothers and at school for not being feminine enough, whatever that means. I defended her a couple of times.' He scratched his head, let his arm drop as if the motion had exhausted him. 'I guess she had a crush on me, but I didn't pay much attention. As she got older, when I was in high school, we became friends. She hung out sometimes with Caleb and me. Then—'

'She got boobs and you fell in love with her.'

He glared at her. 'Give me *some* credit.'

'Okay, okay, sorry. What did happen?'

'She got boobs and I fell in love with her.'

Olivia burst out laughing, glad she'd put her glass down or wine would be spreading all over Georgia's spotless white sheets. 'Let me guess. Because you're a guy, and guys are just like that.'

'Yeah, well.' He gave her the grin that flipped her stomach. 'Nature makes us this way for a reason. Survival of the species and all that.'

'So you married her . . .'

'I did. I loved her, we were friends, it seemed like a good match. And actually, it was good.' He spoke matter-of-factly, not as if she'd been the great love of his life. 'We had a lot of fun together.'

Olivia kept her smile on, irritated by an unwelcome twinge of jealousy. For heaven's sake, the guy was allowed to have loved his own wife. She and Derek had had plenty of good times, too.

'We agreed to wait a couple of years before kids, to make sure we were solid. Then . . .' He sighed, mussing up his hair, which made him look rumpled and absolutely edible. 'Sam kept putting it off. She – she *was* a she then, as far as I was concerned, so don't correct me.'

'I'm just lying here.' Lying there feeling her interest in the conversation shifting, from wanting information for her own purposes, to wanting Duncan to have the chance to tell this story. She sensed he didn't get the chance often. Or maybe ever.

'Sam started making excuses. She wasn't sure she could be a good mother, she wanted to pursue a PhD, et cetera. I tried being patient, but it was hard and confusing, since the excuses didn't seem real, and we had always been completely honest with each other.'

'Or so you thought.'

'Exactly. She went into therapy to figure it all out. I found out later that she freaked badly when she realized what her truth was, and instead of owning it, exploring it, she pushed it away. After that appointment, she came back absolutely gung-ho about having a baby. I was thrilled. She got pregnant quickly, and just as quickly freaked out again. She hated her bigger breasts, the big belly. I'd heard that women can find the changes hard, but this seemed . . .' He blew out a breath. 'I mean, she *hated* it, she thought the whole process was foreign and disgusting. After Jake came, it was the same with nursing. It made her miserable. I finally told her to stop. We limped through a couple more years together, really bad years. She became more and more depressed. Cutting herself. Talking about suicide.'

'God, Duncan.'

'It was bad.' His body tensed next to her. 'I was angry. I'm embarrassed to admit the ugly things I said to her – to *him*, at that point. I still get frustrated. I still think bad thoughts and get hard-headed about him changing. But I think . . . that's pride talking. Even when we were doing okay, I could imagine something better. Deep down I knew things weren't right, but I didn't want to admit it.'

'You're human.' She stroked his arm, feeling him relax some, touched that he needed this from her, glad she could give the gift of hearing him.

'Bottom line . . . he's happier now.' Duncan quirked an eyebrow. 'You might say he's a completely different person.'

'Ha ha.' Olivia pressed her lips to his shoulder. 'I'm sorry you had to go through that.'

'We got Jake. I can't be too sorry.'

'No. He's very special.' They got Jake. Olivia waited for Old

Reliable envy to hijack her good feelings, and was pleased when it didn't. 'Thank you for telling me all that.'

'You're welcome.' He reached for his beer, took a long drink and finished with a satisfied *ahhh*. 'I didn't want to talk about it. But everything seemed to pour out.'

'It can only help.'

'Georgia's always at me for keeping stuff in.' He touched her cheek, eyes warm and vulnerable, a far cry from the cold pair Olivia had met that first day in the Pattersons' kitchen. 'I seem to feel safe with you.'

The depth of Olivia's reaction to his gaze and his words nearly panicked her. He'd given her a gift, too, of his trust. She was not worthy of anything so precious. It was too much.

This was the reason she'd wanted to say no downstairs. She'd been wrong thinking it was about the sex. Sex was not the danger here.

'I'm glad.' She kept her voice light, reached for his bottle and took it gently away. 'It's time.'

'For what?'

'You gave me a choice downstairs. Screwing, or making love. The screwing, we already did.' She moved over him, kissed his forehead, his proud cheekbones, and finally allowed herself a brief taste of his mouth. 'Let's make this last until the movie's over.'

Chapter 13

June 12, 1999 (Saturday)

I think someone is stealing from me. I can't find some of my jewelry. Someone is watching me, too, I can feel it, I just can't tell where they are, or how they're doing it. Is it someone with a telescope trained on my house? Is it a ghost? God? Aliens? I'm afraid I'm going crazy. I'm terrified all the time.

I know Daniel is cheating. I know it. I sniff at him to see if I can smell her. I tear his room apart and put it back together. I find nothing. He is too good at hiding. He tells me where he's going, face so smooth and without a trace of guilt. How did he get to be that good an actor?

I made such a mistake tonight. I couldn't bear the loneliness and the silence and the feeling of those eyes on me and the fear of losing Daniel. I called all my friends. Josie wasn't home, neither were Alice or Isabel. Not home.

I called Mom. Why why why? Why won't I learn? I was just going to chatter, but I broke down and it all came out, about Daniel, about how I want to kill him or myself, that it can't go on like this. She told me to stop my crying and look the other way. He was doing what men do. When I told her I couldn't, she said, 'You always expect everyone to love you all the time. Not everyone will.' I said, 'Yes, Mom, you taught me that very well.' Just before she hung up on me, she said she'd never met anyone so cruel.

She'll probably never talk to me again. If only I could stop wanting to talk to her.

At least I got in one really, really good zinger. Let her remember me that way if that's what she wants. The bitch.

Olivia turned her face to one side, making sure she got an even dose of the sun's rays. Not for tanning – she would never subject her skin to that damage – but the warm weight was blissful on her liberally sunscreened skin.

Today had been a pretty good day. Last night she and Duncan had made the most of the hour they had left with a slow, sensual exploration of each other's bodies, followed by a blissful time curled around each other under the sheets.

Best part? They'd said a fond goodnight and separated with no drama, nothing but the quiet certainty that this was there if either of them needed it. Olivia couldn't believe how lucky she was to have found the perfect hook-up. The generous part of her hoped Derek had done the same. Maybe if he was happier, he would leave her alone and help make their divorce an easy one. If any divorce could be easy.

That morning, she'd slept late, then taken a leisurely five-mile run along the coast. Afterward, in the Pattersons' basement, she'd worked on upper-body strength with a dusty weight set Georgia told her Nate had bought in high school to bulk up for a girl he wanted to impress. Following all that exercise, she'd made herself a protein-rich lunch to help maintain muscle mass so she could rock her bikini into the next decade.

There was still time before she needed to start cooking dinner, a privilege she'd won only after a polite battle with Georgia, who seemed to think Olivia needed a longer rest before she tackled anything as taxing as cutting up chicken. It being another gorgeous day, Olivia had decided to spend at least part of that time immobile and utterly self-indulgent after her hard physical work of the morning. So she'd come down to the shore with Georgia's latest issue of *Cook's Illustrated*, chosen a likely rock for her towel, and had been reading and lazing, feeling happier and more content than she had in what seemed like forever.

Content was good. Content suited her fine. She should be worrying about having to call her lawyer. About whether Derek would try to blackmail her again. About whether to tell her sisters that somehow word had leaked out about Mom's condition. About what to do with the rest of her life if she really never went back to LA.

But right now, she wanted to float like a beautiful iridescent bubble way above her troubles. All too soon she knew she'd bump into one of them and pop again into a sloppy mess.

She dozed briefly, half aware of the surrounding noises of boats, gulls, flapping cormorants – all good sea sounds – then woke and stretched her stiffening body luxuriously. No matter how much she exercised, it always felt like an uphill battle against her body's insistent attempts to become fat and flabby. In her ideal universe, once everyone achieved a desired level of fitness, they'd be able to stay there for the rest of their lives.

While she'd lazed, the sun had climbed higher and so had the temperature. She sat up to catch a breeze, then stared warily at the clear, languid water inviting her to jump right in. Not fooled. 'Swimming' this far north consisted of trying to get up the nerve to submerge, then staggering out as quickly as possible, shivering and gasping. At least that was how she and her sisters used to swim off Candlewood Point. Do-not-even-try in June. I-dare-you in July. Painful-but-possible in August.

The water might be warmer in this protected harbor than it had been on Candlewood, but it would still be damn cold.

She stepped off her sunning rock and waded in up to her ankles, her Tevas protecting her feet from barnacles and sharp edges.

Yep. Damn cold. She took one cautious step farther, feeling for stable footing on the rocky bottom, then a few more, up to her knees, where her resolve wavered. In this chill you had to dive right in and suffer the consequences. No thinking it over.

Mom used to stand at the water's edge, fill her lungs with air and let it out in a bellow as she ran into the sea up to her thighs, then fell forward to go under. A few strokes, her pale arms flailing and splashing, then she'd emerge, shrieking and laughing, hugging herself as she ran toward her towel, sometimes held for her by Dad, who claimed his anatomy wasn't suited to frostbite.

Spurred on by the memory – if Mom could do it, she could – Olivia bent down to submerge her forearms.

Brrrrr.

Soon. She'd dive in soon.

One . . . two . . . three . . .

No, not yet.

One . . . two . . .

Maybe if she waded out a little farther.

One clumsy step on to a wiggling rock made the decision for her. *Whoosh*, the shock of the icy water drew the air out of her lungs in a surprised yell. She managed to keep her head out, avoiding makeup run, then, giggling madly, struggled to get her footing back, floundering nearly under twice in her attempt to exit the icy hell.

She made it, climbed back on to her rock and took off her

water sandals. This was the good part, the part that made the torture worthwhile, when your body warmed up again in the sun, skin tingling and alive. 'Like you're glowing,' Mom had said.

'Like you're dying,' Dad had responded. 'None of you would have been born if I indulged in such idiocy.'

Olivia's smile drooped. She'd managed to push away the diary's contents in the afterglow of her evening with Duncan. She didn't want to think about how Dad had actually conceived her and her sisters. Rosalind had found her birth mother. Eve had discovered that hers had died. Olivia still wanted the physically impossible: to be the miracle baby who'd sprung fully formed out of Jillian Croft's head, like Athena from Zeus's.

She should really call Dad this afternoon. She'd been so full of her own troubles and of adjusting to being here, she'd neglected him. Maybe she could—

'Tell me you didn't go into that water on purpose.'

Her worries fled in a rush of adrenaline. Duncan was coming down the stairs. 'Of course I did. It was fabulous.'

'Crazy summer people.'

'You don't swim?'

'In Florida. In Virginia. In St Thomas. Not here.'

'How come?' She smiled a welcome, moved over on her ledge and patted the space next to her.

'I have a brain.' Duncan sat, but on the rock's far edge. The magnetic energy and confidence of the previous night were no longer in evidence. He looked solemn and tired. 'Been busy today?'

'Worked out, lazed.' She wanted to stroke his back to make him feel better. 'I'm cooking tonight, though.'

'You any good in a kitchen?'

'Uh . . .' Olivia gave him a look. 'I had a cooking show?'

'Isn't everything in LA fake?' He glanced mischievously at her breasts.

Olivia chucked a sandal at him, missing deliberately. 'Those are real.'

'I know that.' His smile faded quickly. 'I wanted to talk to you about tonight.'

'Okay . . .' She found herself tensing.

'I don't want Georgia and Stuart to know about what we're doing.'

Oh for heaven's sake. Were they in high school?

'You want to hide our *engagement*?' She clutched at her chest. 'I'm *crushed*.'

He ignored her theatrics. 'It's just that they're pretty traditional.'

'I get it, Duncan.' Olivia wanted to pummel him, tickle him or pinch him, whatever would bring back the man he was last night. 'I can keep my hands off you for an hour or two.'

'Right.' He stood.

'*That's* why you came down here? To tell me to stay away from you?'

'Always the romantic.' He walked back over to the stairs and gave her a brief wave. 'See you tonight.'

'Right.' She was annoyed, but not enough to keep from staring at his very fine ass moving up the steps.

At the top, he turned. 'Actually . . . I warned you for a different reason.'

'What's that?' This better be good.

He mumbled something she didn't catch.

'Huh?'

He sighed. 'I *said*, "Because I'm not sure *I* can keep my hands off *you*."'

He was out of sight before Olivia could get her brain rebooted to respond.

My goodness. Not much on conversation today, but the man could certainly communicate.

After he left, however, Olivia's rock felt less like a refuge and more like the island of Naxos, with her as the abandoned Ariadne. Resigned and cranky, she gave up reading and lounging, gathered up the sandal she'd chucked at him, and stalked up to the house, aware that she should not be letting Duncan's mood influence her own.

Back inside, she took a quick and soothing shower to wash away the salt, lotion and crabbiness, and came downstairs clutching her phone and a portable Bluetooth speaker, eager to start prep work. She hadn't cooked in way too long. Being alone in a kitchen with her thoughts and some really good music had always been her happiest place. Unlike acting, this was something she was free to do virtually whenever she wanted, and in whatever style she preferred. When she wasn't working on a film or commercial project as well as *Crofty Cooks*, she and Derek ate like royalty every night, to the point where he sometimes begged for meatloaf and mashed potatoes.

The second she stepped over the kitchen threshold, Georgia appeared from the den.

'Need help?'

'What were you doing back there?' Olivia strode across to the counter, set up her speaker and plugged in her phone. 'Don't tell me you were relaxing.'

'Guilty.'

'Get back to it.' She selected St Vincent and David Byrne's joint album, *Love This Giant*, and went over to the refrigerator to get out the chicken, leeks and bacon. 'You're taking the night off.'

'Are you sure?' Georgia looked doubtful.

'Absolutely. This is where I live. Staying out of a kitchen too long makes me twitchy.' She brought the chicken over to the sink. 'You're doing me a favor.'

'I *was* considering taking my book out to the gazebo.'

'Go. I'm pig-in-shit happy. Seriously.' Olivia removed the bird from its confining plastic, then became aware that Georgia hadn't yet left. She looked over questioningly.

'One more thing.' Georgia took two steps into the room. 'I have a surprise for tonight. But I'm thinking I ought to clear it with you first.'

Olivia tested the edge of one of Georgia's knives and nodded approvingly. Dull knives were like slicing with rocks. 'If it's a male stripper, I'm all for it.'

Georgia giggled madly, face flushing. 'Mercy, it is *not* a stripper. I rented a movie to watch after supper.'

'Sounds fun. What movie?'

'*Friendship Never Dies.*'

Olivia let out a startled laugh. She'd done some of her best acting in that movie. 'Really? You'd want to watch that?'

'Of course we would. But you've probably seen it a thousand times.'

'Actually.' Olivia patted the chicken dry with paper towels. 'I've never seen it.'

'*What?*' Georgia thumped both hands to her chest. 'You're kidding.'

'I never watch my movies.' Olivia began cutting up the chicken, wondering what Duncan would think of her performance, then telling herself to stop with the Duncan-everything. 'Mom never watched hers either.'

'Well, bless your hearts. I never imagined. I'd probably never *stop* watching myself. Why don't you?'

Olivia paused her butchery. 'Because if I never see it, then my performance stays perfect in my mind.'

'That can't be why your mom never watched. Her performances *were* perfect.'

'They wouldn't have been to her.' Olivia began separating the poor chicken's legs into drumsticks and thighs. 'But I don't mind if we watch tonight. Thanks for thinking of it.'

'You are welcome.' Georgia took one step back. 'So . . . you're sure I can't help?'

'Go.' Olivia pointed the way with her knife. 'Relax.'

Georgia's dimpled smile bloomed. 'Thank you, Olivia. I don't know when I've had a Sunday afternoon to myself.'

Olivia snorted in disgust. 'Get Stuart to take you out sometimes.'

'He likes Sunday dinner at home.' Georgia folded her arms, looking exasperated. 'It's what his blessed mother did.'

Olivia growled. 'Tell him you're not his blessed mother.'

'You know what?' Georgia fluffed up her curls with attitude. 'Maybe I will. Funny how you do things without thinking until someone holds a mirror up to you. Thanks, Olivia.'

'Enjoy your book.' She finished cutting the chicken, wondering why men who'd grown up in the last half of the twentieth century still acted as if it were 1940. Was it simply that their hormones made them less nurturing, more liable to think of themselves before others? Men-will-be-men, as Duncan had implied last night?

Obviously Olivia was generalizing wildly, but if that was the case, did those hormones play into why Jillian Croft, despite the fact that she inhabited the ultimate female presence, had no use for a woman's traditional role around the house? The girls were brought up as much by their father as their mother and had seen both parents manage equally high-powered careers.

Probably a far-fetched theory, but as more studies of gender proceeded, Olivia would be curious to see how much of male/female behavior was guided by the relative proportions of chemicals in each person. What kind of woman would Mom have been without her condition? How much of her in-your-face femaleness was inherently part of her – her clothes, her flirtatious behavior around men, the topless portrait that hung in their Beverly Hills mansion – and how much an overcorrection to what she perceived as her deformity? *Not a real woman*, she labeled herself in the diaries, and yet to many people, Olivia included, she was the epitome of womanhood.

As soon as dinner was under control, Olivia would call her father. Maybe she could get him to talk about Mom.

She hurried to brown the chicken pieces in a Dutch oven, following their turn in the pot with bacon until crisp, and leeks until soft. Prep done, she layered everything in the pot along with garlic and rosemary, poured over the less expensive bottle of Chardonnay she'd bought the previous day, and put the Dutch oven on the stove to simmer.

The smells were already fabulous. Olivia had gotten this recipe from their household cook, Emma, who had copied it down from an episode of Julia Child's *The French Chef*. Any time Olivia wasn't tagging along after Mom, she was sitting in the kitchen watching Emma perform her magic, or experimenting clumsily herself. If not that, she was watching the Food Network, or devouring cookbooks as if they were novels – until the day her mother caught her reading an issue of *Gourmet* she'd bought at the drugstore, and firmly substituted Uta Hagen's *Respect for Acting*.

Point made. If Olivia wanted to get ahead, she could not spend time on frivolities.

While the chicken simmered, she switched St Vincent for

Jenny Lewis, then turned her attention to dessert, slicing peaches into a bowl and mixing them with sugar, ground ginger and a touch of cinnamon. Next, she put together an oatmeal-walnut streusel, flavored with chopped walnuts, crystallized ginger and a pinch more cinnamon, her movements rapid and precise, enjoying the control and her skill at juggling several dishes at once, honed over many years of practice.

While the peach crisp baked, she started on the chive biscuits, also Julia's recipe, cutting butter into the dry ingredients using Georgia's food processor. Purists strongly insisted there was no substitute for using two knives or a pastry blender, but Olivia equally strongly insisted that a normal person had no patience for that level of fussiness. She'd put her pie crusts and biscuits up against anyone else's.

Biscuits in the oven, Olivia silenced Jenny Lewis and at last called her poor father. She'd been a terrible daughter. She should have called days ago, and should already have planned a visit.

'Olivia!' She loved the way he roared her name, a weaker lion than he used to be, but still communicating his joy at hearing her voice. 'We're having a grand time monitoring your kerfuffle. The world has gone insane.'

'I'm trying not to notice.'

'How are you liking Stuart's place? Nice solid guy. His wife Georgia is lovely too. A real peach.' He laughed at his joke, which was good, because as much as it was wonderful hearing him laughing again, Olivia wasn't inspired to join in.

'I'm very comfortable here.' She rushed to change the subject before he insisted on finding out her opinion of Stuart. 'I was thinking about you earlier, when I went in for a swim.'

He made a choking sound. 'You're crazy. Just like your mother.'

'I've been thinking about her too.' Olivia began pacing the

kitchen, then turned abruptly at the sight of the desk where she and Duncan had spent quality time the previous evening. She couldn't think about that with her father on the phone. 'Do you miss her?'

'Of course I do.' His voice grew more gentle. 'But she's been gone a long time.'

Olivia frowned. So? Jillian was still incredibly vivid in her brain, and she'd known her mother half as long as Dad.

'I miss her too. Especially up here.' Olivia leaned against the counter. She had to be careful not to upset her father again. But the diaries had raised so many questions. 'Dad . . .'

'Yes, chipmunk?' His alternative nickname, because her hair was red and she talked too much.

'Were you happy with Mom?'

His hesitation made her blood run as cold as the sea she'd been splashing in. 'Your mother was a complicated woman, Olivia. There were hard times for all of us. Me, you and your sisters. Happy wasn't always the right word. But I loved her.'

Olivia turned around to lean on her elbows. That wasn't the expected answer, and it certainly wasn't the desired one.

'You're happier with *Lauren*?'

'Yes, I am.' His sharp tone was in reaction to her incredulous one.

'But Mom was—'

'When are you coming to visit, princess? You're practically next door. People here won't care who you are. Half of them are too old to notice.'

'I'll come soon, Daddy. But I was thinking—'

'How soon?'

She wanted to shriek at his unsubtle method for keeping her from asking about Mom. 'Tomorrow? I have stuff to do in the morning, but—'

'What time should we expect you?'

Olivia made a childish face. *We?* 'How about I take you out to lunch, Dad? Just you and me?'

More hesitation, which already felt like rejection. 'That would hurt Lauren's feelings.'

Tell it to someone who cared. 'I never get to talk to you without her around.'

'She's my wife, Olivia.' He didn't raise his voice. He didn't have to. The same way he never had to specify a punishment to his daughters; he'd just say, 'Or else . . .' and they'd obey.

'I'll see you a little after noon.' She ended the call, furious that she'd let him shut her out, and that she'd put herself out there for rejection and gotten it. *Bang, bang, I shot you down.*

Her mother had worshiped Dad, adored him. If Lauren hadn't come nosing around, if Dad had been able to give Mom his full support, she might have stuck at sobriety. She might have been persuaded to take her meds full-time, especially after the work dried up. With the girls out of the house and off to college, Mom and Dad might have rekindled their romance, traveling the globe, living *la dolce vita.*

Olivia restarted Jenny Lewis. Ifs and mights over things that happened decades ago. Useless to think about.

She took the snow peas out of the refrigerator, and the biscuits out of the oven when they were lightly browned. Shortly before six, Georgia came back in, claiming she could smell heaven coming from the kitchen, and insisted she do something to help. Olivia let her cut up vegetables for the salad while she made a mustard vinaigrette. Apparently it was not possible for Georgia to be completely supplanted in her own kitchen, which Olivia found completely understandable.

At six, Duncan arrived wearing new jeans and a blue-and-white-striped linen shirt. His eyes flicked over Olivia disinterestedly, while he made a polite comment about dinner smelling good. Olivia made sure she responded the same way, tempted to sneak in a knowing leer but honoring his request that she be careful.

Stuart clomped into the room, yanked the refrigerator open and handed Duncan a beer with a warm – for him – greeting. The two men stood in the corner talking business until Olivia couldn't stand it anymore and pushed flatware into Stuart's hands and napkins into Duncan's.

'Table needs setting. You know where the plates are.'

Georgia looked up from her cutting board with wide eyes that softened into amusement. 'Well.'

Stuart scowled at his wife as if Olivia's sin was her fault, but allowed Duncan to push him into the dining room.

'Thank you,' Georgia said. 'I should have trained him better. But he was raised by a mother who did everything for him, so it was a constant struggle to get him to pitch in. Most of the time it's easier to do it myself.'

'I understand.' She didn't. But Georgia and Stuart's marriage wasn't hers. Thank God.

When the men had finished, Stuart mixing up spoons and knives, Olivia brought the food in and asked them to sit, which they did promptly, on the same side of the table. She served the chicken and biscuits before taking her seat, beaming in response to the compliments.

If she was talking about the food, dinner was a success. The chicken was tender and flavorful, the biscuits crisp on the outside, buttery and soft within. Duncan and Stuart had seconds; Stuart had thirds. The peach crisp was spicy, warm and comforting, not too sweet, served with generous scoops of vanilla ice cream.

If she was talking about the conversation, not so great.

Predictably, Stuart was no help. Duncan tried, but was clearly uneasy, rarely meeting Olivia's eyes, even when she was pelting him and Stuart with questions about boatbuilding and repair and remodeling. Finally she gave up and chatted with Georgia about recipes and favorite meals.

Thankfully, the second Stuart's second helping of peach crisp disappeared, Georgia clapped her hands. 'We have a special treat tonight for after-dinner entertainment.'

'What's that?' Stuart was clearly suspicious.

'I found one of Olivia's movies.' Georgia smiled proudly. 'We can watch her be a star.'

Duncan and Stuart's heads turned toward Olivia like tennis spectators following the ball. Olivia kept her exterior calm, while nervous excitement had its way with her insides.

'She must have seen it enough times already.'

Olivia rolled her eyes. One of these days she was going to dump a tray of ice cubes down Stuart's pants. 'Actually, Stuart, I've never seen any of my movies.'

'Never?' Duncan looked surprised.

'You must have.' Stuart looked skeptical.

'Why? Why must I have?' Olivia was quite sure *she* looked pissed.

'Stuart, if she says she hasn't, she hasn't.' Georgia patted Olivia's arm.

'How many movies have you done?' Duncan asked.

'Six.' She brought up her fingers to count on. 'Lines in four and roles in two. In this one I'm the heroine's best friend, who dies. I was good at dying.'

'Like your mother.' Georgia smiled until she tuned into the shocked silence round the table and gasped. 'Oh, my dear girl. I meant in the movies.'

Olivia started breathing again. 'Of course you did.'

'Her best was when she passed away in *Dangerous Fall*. Lord have mercy.' Georgia patted her chest. 'I cried my eyes out for weeks every time I even thought of it. *Don't stop bailin'* . . .'

'. . . *'til your boat's plenty dry*.' Olivia finished the line with her and they both laughed.

Duncan raised his eyebrows. 'What does that mean?'

'Never give up,' Olivia told him. 'Mom's character said it to the paralyzed man learning to walk again, and he says it back to her when she's diagnosed with cancer.'

'Sounds like tons o' fun,' Stuart said acidly.

'It's a tragedy!' Georgia retorted. 'Much more civilized than all those movies you like, where they blow up everything they don't shoot.'

'Did she ever give up?' Duncan asked.

'In the movie she dies of cancer.' Olivia allowed herself a smile at him. 'In real life she certainly never gave up.'

'Don't get me wrong,' Stuart said. 'I did admire your mom. She was beautiful.'

Beautiful. Men like Stuart would never understand. Olivia smiled pointedly. '*And* incredibly talented.'

'Speaking of which, let's go see our resident movie star.' Georgia pushed back her chair. 'I'll get the food put away, but we'll do the dishes later. I can't wait.'

'No, no, we can all help.' That time Olivia didn't stare pointedly at Stuart, but she wanted to.

To her surprise, he did help, wrapping and storing leftovers while the rest of them cleared up the meal and the kitchen.

'Thanks for helping, Stuey.' Georgia put a hand to his cheek and gazed at him lovingly. 'You're a sweetheart.'

'Yeah, I'm not so bad.' His turn to look pointedly at Olivia, who gave him a conciliatory half-smile, still withholding final judgment.

'Let's go watch.' Georgia led the way out of the kitchen. 'I'm so excited.'

In the living room, Olivia summoned the power not to sit next to Duncan on the poufy leather sofa. For one thing, she hated poufy leather sofas. For another, being in the dark next to him would get her all worked up and she might start pawing at him. So she perched sedately on one of the upholstered chairs clear on the other side of the room.

As Georgia pushed the endless number of buttons on the endless number of remotes to get the movie queued up, Olivia fidgeted, feeling like a prisoner about to hear her verdict. She was proud of what she'd done in this film, but it was fairly excruciating having to watch it in front of people she cared about impressing.

Friendship Never Dies was a tearjerker about a woman named Alantha, played by Missy Taylor, an actress whose career had gone about as far as Olivia's. Her character had to come to grips with demons after she rescued her best friend Jane from drowning only to watch her die in an accident she herself had inadvertently caused. Sappy plot, but it made for great emotions, and a fabulous scene in which Olivia as Jane got to grant whispered forgiveness to her friend while trapped in the passenger seat of a convincingly mangled car, covered in fake blood.

Olivia leaned forward as the movie started. It was not only her best work, but also a film with decent production values. She wouldn't have to be embarrassed by any of it.

The opening credits rolled over twangy guitar music, and disappeared. Alantha and Jane appeared in the shot. Everyone clapped and hooted. Olivia grinned, buzzy with adrenaline.

Alantha started talking while Olivia-as-Jane listened earnestly. They were on their way to go swimming at LA's Redondo

Beach. When the young women casually dropped their towels to reveal skimpy bikinis, a wolf whistle rang out in the room.

'Duncan!' Georgia turned to frown at him. 'Be respectful.'

He mumbled an insincere apology.

Olivia was dying to send him a wink, but her first line was coming up, one she'd never forget: *Wow, look at that rip tide.* She'd worked hard to say the words with just the right combination of fear and anticipation, having conjured a backstory for her character that included thrill-seeking since an early age, and a couple of near-death experiences.

Here it came . . .

'Wow, look at that rip tide.'

Olivia went rigid at the same time the others in the room cheered. Flat, amateur delivery with about as much emotion as a robot. A wooden arm flung toward the ocean, her mouth open in a comical O of astonishment.

It got worse.

Maybe not worse, but it didn't get better. Olivia sat in bewildered silence, watching as the stupid plot unfolded. Every scene in which she appeared, Georgia would comment. *There you are, Olivia. Oh, this is so exciting.* Duncan and Stuart stayed silent.

Not soon enough, about a third into the movie, Jane had her big death scene, the one Olivia was so proud of, the one she insisted her agent use as an audition piece.

Only slightly less awful.

Her on-screen eyes closed. Her body went limp.

Georgia burst into applause. 'Fabulous! Wonderful. I'm so proud of you.'

Olivia was not proud of her. She was mortified. Because having finally watched what was supposedly the best thing she'd ever done, she'd learned something horrifying.

The reason she never got big roles wasn't because of prejudice against her famous mother or father, or her height or figure or features, or bad timing or bad luck.

After all the study, all her commitment to the craft, all her mother's faith in her and the encouragement of everyone around her, she was simply unable to act, moving and speaking like a middle-schooler in the play from hell.

No wonder when she'd declared a theater major, her father had urged her to choose something else, anything else. At the time he'd said he was trying to protect her from the ravages of a life in film.

Maybe he was trying to protect her from the failure he saw coming two decades ago.

She'd inherited none of her mother's talent. None!

The movie spun on, Olivia sitting stunned by the thought, appalled at the degree to which she'd been fooling herself for the past year. Athena out of Zeus's head?

Be serious.

It was time to accept a truth that hurt far worse than her lack of talent, one her younger sisters had already embraced but which Olivia, even after reading Mom's diary, had pushed away, never truly internalized.

There was nothing to inherit from her mother. Biologically speaking, she and Jillian Croft, the woman she'd spent her whole life vainly trying to become, had absolutely nothing in common.

Chapter 14

October 27, 1999 (Wednesday)

I've had such a shock. I still can't breathe. I was going through an old box – I've taken to hiding my best jewelry now, in case someone breaks in – and found a medical book on complete androgen insensitivity that Daniel must have bought me way back when we were so young and so miserable over my diagnosis and so starved for any kind of information. He meant to be kind, but I couldn't look at it, I couldn't bear it, so I put it away. I don't know if he read it. If he did, then either he didn't notice, or he's the cruelest son of a bitch in the world.

In it is a naked picture of a terrified teenage girl, black bar over her eyes to disguise her identity. But I know what I look like. I remember when they took this picture. I remember how frightened I was, how cold the room was, how desperately I wanted my clothes back on. How brusque and unfriendly the people were. They didn't explain why they were taking the picture. They didn't explain anything.

This is why they took it, without my permission or understanding. My body is a symbol of deformity for the medical world to gawk at.

I need a drink. I need five.

*

After *Friendship Never Dies* crawled to an excruciating finish, its audience sitting in a stupor of polite boredom, everyone jumped up as if released from a torture device, Olivia fastest of all. The movie clocked in at barely an hour and a half, but every minute added another layer of misery to her misery.

Why had she kept expecting to be a star in the face of so much evidence that she never would be one? Why had no one told her it was hopeless? Why had her agent kept her on all these years? If that was her best role and it was that bad, how did she keep getting auditions? Just because of her parents?

Somehow she made it through the rest of the evening, refusing coffee, accepting compliments from Georgia and one carefully worded comment from Stuart about how he'd never seen someone familiar in a movie before and how it shattered the illusion of reality. Duncan called it a 'great experience', but sent her a few cautious looks in the kitchen, as if he expected she might grab up a knife and sink it into her chest.

The idea had occurred to her.

For all her public proclamations of being a failure, under-neath, she'd enjoyed them, deep-down convinced that someday, *someday*, this dream of hers would come true. Maybe not as an ingénue anymore, maybe not until she had white hair and took the world by storm in some artsy-fartsy Sundance festival favorite. She might have to wait a long time, but success would come. Success was her destiny. All the discouraging, exasperating, infuriating bumps along the way could never quite extinguish that glowing certainty.

Never surrender.

As soon as she could politely get away, Olivia went up to her room and closed the door. Tonight the lovely room felt too warm, confining. She was miserably homesick for a space that belonged only to her.

She paced, desk to closet, feeling on the brink of collapse but not quite there. She wasn't sure why she wasn't falling apart. Maybe it had all been too much, this gradual stripping-away of what she believed true about her life and herself. Her brain must be protecting itself, not allowing too much to register.

Because oddly, at this potentially most devastating of her losses, under the pain she felt almost relieved. Like this had to be bottom, right?

Downstairs she heard Duncan saying goodnight, the front door closing.

She rose and bent close to the screen, waiting for him to appear below, in the yard. The moon hadn't yet risen; the air was soft with moisture. Rain was scheduled for the next day. She'd have to find indoor things to do in the morning with little Jake.

Duncan appeared, walking confidently.

'Hey there.'

He turned, taking a moment to find her, then waved. 'Hey.'

'Going home?' She felt stupid. 'Obviously.'

He put his hands on his hips, a gray masculine shape down on the grass, dim light catching him from the living room windows below her bedroom. She hoped neither of the Pattersons could see him.

'Yeah, gotta get up early.'

'Can . . .' She closed her eyes, hating how pathetic she sounded. 'Can I come by?'

His hesitation made her cringe. She opened her mouth to avoid rejection by telling him to forget it.

'Okay.'

Pleasure swept through her. 'You're sure?'

'Yeah.' He slapped at what must be a mosquito on his arm. 'But come soon.'

'I will.'

He turned and walked away, Olivia following his progress until he faded into the darkness. Outside her door, she heard the Pattersons' footsteps on the stairs, their murmured conversation, a laugh from Georgia, then their bedroom door closing. They belonged to each other. Sex for them was a way to connect, to renew, to cement their commitment and their love.

Olivia might not have that for a while. But she did have Duncan. The enormity of what she was facing after watching herself puke all over the screen would inevitably take hold, but tonight, at least for an hour or two, she'd again be able to lose herself in the joy of shutting out everything about her life but her physical self. Second best, but she was immensely grateful for it.

She waited ten more minutes in case Georgia or Stuart re-emerged to do something forgotten, then tiptoed into the hall, down the stairs and outside.

Crap. No flashlight. Olivia wasn't going to risk going back inside. She'd have to feel her way.

A few stumbles, but easier going than she expected. Her eyes gradually adjusted to make use of the faint glow in the misty sky and the lights of Belfast across the channel. She breathed in the humid air, the scents she loved, luxuriating in the peace.

Maybe this week she could explore the idea of buying a summer house. A second home, a place to escape to, the way Mom had escaped LA, leaving Jillian Croft behind, reverting to Sylvia Moore. Up in Stirling, the Braddocks got to play at being an average family, cocooned and protected. No Dad traveling to lecture around the world. No Mom leaving home to be on set. No 'friends' hanging around for glimpses of famous parents. No whispering that the girls didn't deserve whatever they'd gotten because of who they were. Olivia might start looking around, maybe farther south near Portland.

Her brief burst of excitement faded. She needed to be thinking about where she'd move to next, what her life would entail.

Ugh. She was tired. She wanted Duncan.

He was waiting for her, not in the altogether as she'd hoped, but standing in the doorway looking slightly apprehensive. 'C'mon in.'

Olivia stepped into his cabin, becoming wary herself. Had she done something wrong? Had he lost respect for her because she didn't die well covered in fake blood?

She wanted to roll her eyes. Immediately she'd assumed that whatever was bugging him was about her.

'You okay?' she asked.

'Fine. You?'

She gave him a cheery smile. 'Better now.'

He nodded gravely, hands shoved in his back pockets. 'You seemed down tonight.'

'Kind of. Got anything to drink?' She asked without thinking. Did she even want a drink?

'Sure.' He headed for the kitchen area, got a couple of beers, popped the top off hers and handed it over.

Olivia lifted the beer to her mouth, the first sip giving her an answer: no. 'I was bad. In the movie.'

Duncan shrugged. 'Not so bad. You were young. Come sit.'

'Young is no excuse.' She sat on one end of the couch, stung when he took the chair instead of settling next to her. 'I'd done the work. I knew the role. I just couldn't handle it.'

'Okay.'

She lifted an eyebrow. 'Okay?'

'What was I supposed to say?'

'Nothing. Nothing. I'm sorry. It was just sort of . . . the

death of a dream.' The second the words were out, she wanted them back. What was she doing inflicting this on him? Olivia shouldn't have come. She didn't know this guy. He couldn't fix her life. More to the point, he was under no obligation to try.

'That sucks.' Duncan spoke sincerely, but she couldn't let go of the feeling he wanted her out of there as soon as possible.

'Am I using up too much of your oxygen?'

He exhaled. 'Look. I don't know what's going on here. The sex is . . . fantastic. But I can't . . . I can't be your support. I can't . . .'

She felt the slow crawl of panic and the rise of temper that protected her from it. 'Who's asking you to?'

'You came tonight because you were upset.'

'And? Don't you think it would be nice if you had a giant orgasm waiting when you were upset? I thought that's what this was about.'

'It is. It is. I'm just not . . .'

She waited. 'Not what?'

'Not sure what's happening.'

'From what I can tell, I'm sitting here holding a beer, you're sitting there doing the same, and we are not quite communicating. Additionally, we are not having sex.'

Duncan nodded slowly. 'That about describes it.'

'My sister would say the universe provided us for each other at a time we needed it to.'

'Yeah? What would you say?'

'I dunno . . . Don't look a gift universe in the black hole?'

He didn't seem to find that funny. Olivia thought it was pretty good. 'Maybe that's what I'm doing. I just can't seem to manage this right now. Manage you . . . us, and what we . . .' He let his head drop. 'God, I suck at this.'

'No, you don't.' Olivia kept her voice gentle, wanting to

howl like a werewolf. 'You're just trying to find a sweet way to say get lost.'

'It's not quite like that.'

'Do you want me to leave?' She got to her feet, steeling herself for his answer. 'It's totally fine if you do. I invited myself over.'

Duncan stayed with his head down for another few seconds, then lifted it. 'No. But I'm not sure I can . . . Maybe just talking tonight.'

'Sure.' The opposite of what Olivia had come here for. But if that was what he needed from her, she'd do it. Anything was better than lying in her lilac-strewn bed, thinking.

She moved over to the double doors facing the ocean, open to the breeze and the view of twinkling lights across the harbor. Homes in which families were tucking kids into bed, watching TV, fighting, fucking. Some with simple, satisfying lives, others with complicated messes. All of them at home.

'I don't have a place to live anymore.' She spoke the thought aloud, soundtrack to her musing.

'Why not?'

'I gave my house to my ex.'

'Olivia.'

She turned back to him, struck by the tenderness mixed in with his exasperation. 'Why am I telling you this? You just said I was asking too much emotionally, and the first thing I do is ask more from you emotionally. I am sorry, Duncan. I have no filters. None. What's in my brain shoots straight out of my mouth.'

'It's okay.'

'It isn't.' Olivia sighed, wondering when her mind would finally snap. 'My life is completely insane, and I think I'm getting there myself. I can't make sense of anything anymore.'

'I know what you mean.' Duncan brought his beer toward his mouth, then took it down without drinking.

'You're right. You do. I do not have a lockup on pain and weirdness here.' Olivia longed to sit next to him, take him in her arms, offer comfort he didn't want. 'In one of our last discussions, among other charming compliments, my husband accused me of being self-centered.'

'Sounds like a really great guy.'

She stared at the plank floor, feeling as if even moving her mouth would be an effort. 'I think he was right.'

'We're all works in progress.' Duncan shrugged, but his eyes were kind. 'Better to find out late than never.'

'True.' Yes, she had hoped he'd say her husband was a fool, that she was every shade of generosity and light. And yet, as always, she found herself grateful for his honesty. This man was not Derek. He had no reason to lie or pander to her. If she hung around people like him long enough, she could end up a better person. For the past several years, she'd felt herself steadily becoming a worse one.

'Why did you give your house to such an asshole?'

'He was blackmailing me over a family secret.'

Duncan's eyes shot wide. 'Are you making this shit up?'

'No, I'm not making this shit up. I would love to be making this shit up.'

'You married a skank.'

'You married a man.' Olivia bit her lip as he rolled his eyes. Well done, girlfriend. 'Sorry, Duncan. I did marry a skank. You're right.'

'Have you called the police? Last time I checked, blackmail was illegal.'

'I can't prove it. With all this other stuff still raging around the Internet, if I accuse him, things will get even uglier. Better to give him what he wants and hope he goes away.'

'He won't go away.'

'Then I'll have to shoot him.'

Duncan recoiled. 'Uhhhh.'

'What?' Olivia blinked sweetly. 'Do I make you nervous?'

That got her one small smile. 'There are many things you make me, but not afraid for my life.'

'Your sanity?'

He pretended to think that over. 'Possibly.'

She walked over and perched on the edge of the sofa. 'Do you think you'll marry again?'

'Jesus, Olivia, my divorce hasn't even come through yet.'

'You must have thought about how you'd rebuild your life eventually.'

'Yes. I have.' He stood and ambled over to the open doors, to the spot where she'd just been standing. 'I love this town. I love my job. But I can't help looking at this time as a chance to throw everything out and start over. Sometimes I wonder if by staying here I'm just doing the easy thing. At the same time, my child's mother is here, and Jake needs him.'

Olivia couldn't help a snort. 'That is confusing.'

'You're telling me.' He stretched both arms out wide. 'I'm feeling a little . . . trapped.'

'You want to get on your boat and go.'

He turned swiftly, as if she'd said she had the Ark of the Covenant in her suitcase. 'That's exactly what I want to do.'

'I want to leave this planet and start my own.' Olivia got up to stand next to him. If he moved back to the window, she'd get that he needed space and stay away. But she wanted to try one more time . . . one more time just to be close to him. 'Have you ever lived alone?'

'Until I got married, yes. I lived here in the boathouse my senior year of high school. I lived on my boat through my years of college.'

'You lived on your boat?' She loved the idea. 'That is so cool.'

Duncan looked sheepish, as if he was embarrassed to have done something she admired so much. 'Cheaper than a dorm. I biked to my classes.'

'Women must have fallen all over you.'

He shrugged. 'I had some fun. Why, have you ever lived alone?'

'Nope. I never have. I had roommates in college, roommates after college.' She put her beer down. 'I could afford my own place, but I've always needed people around me.'

'You're an extrovert.'

'That's a nicer way to put it than high-maintenance.' She pointed across the channel at the lights of town. 'I was thinking about all those nice houses, wishing I was at home in one right now. Safe and settled.'

Duncan stood looking with her. 'It's pretty common to feel as if everyone else is safe and settled when you're not.'

'Nope. They all are. I'm sure of it.' She swept her hand contemptuously across the view. 'Disgustingly okay. Ecstatic, actually.'

'Little bastards.'

'Happy, fulfilling lives, every single one of them.'

'*Lucky* little bastards.'

'All their wives are staying female.'

'All their husbands still have sperm.'

'It's enough to make you sick.'

Duncan put his arm around her shoulders. She moved closer and rested her head against him. Maybe this was all she wanted, too.

'What are you going to do tomorrow, Olivia?'

She smiled. That was the kind of question she needed as much as sex. Maybe more. The relationship questions, the stupid ones no one else asked because no one else cared. What are you going to do tomorrow? Good morning, how did you sleep? What did you have for lunch? Is your constipation better?

'In the morning, I'm hanging out with the world's cutest boy. In the afternoon, I'm going to visit my dad in Blue Hill. What about you?'

'Working.'

'On?'

'We're refurbishing an old Herreshoff sailboat, a beauty from the early 1900s. Has some wood damage, and some of the brass needs replacing. She'll be fantastic when we're done.'

'Can I come see it – her?' Olivia lifted her head. Duncan's arm fell away. 'I could bring Jake. You could show us around, then we could all have lunch.'

'Uh . . .'

'Oops.' She held up a hand to stop him having to explain. 'Too girlfriendy, sorry. I was just interested.'

'It might be weird.'

'I know.' She stepped away from him, feeling overly hurt, even though his rejection made perfect sense. 'I should go.'

She waited a beat, hoping he'd tell her to stay, even though she knew from the dullness of his eyes that it wasn't going to happen.

'It's probably a good idea. I'm sorry.'

'You have nothing to be sorry about.' Olivia put out her hand and held the backs of her fingers against his sternum, meeting his eyes and feeling a surge of longing. She was being cut loose. She would need to start handling her life's crises on her own. Duncan had been a godsend, but Olivia couldn't keep depending on him for the work she needed to do herself. She retrieved her beer and handed it to him. 'Thanks for the drink.'

'You had about as much as I did.' He followed her over to

the door, taking a moment to set the bottles down by the sink.

'Yeah, weird night.' She turned, hating herself for showing even more weakness. 'Just so I'm clear, we're platonic going forward?'

'Ah, Olivia.' Duncan sighed, put a hand up on the jamb over her head. 'I don't know.'

'Do you honestly not know?' She watched him, trying not to look anxious. 'Or are you too nice or too chicken to give me the kiss-off?'

His grin sparked their chemistry – that part was so, so good. 'I'm neither nice nor chicken.'

'Okay then. Goodnight.' She took hold of his shirt and moved quickly, finding his sexy mouth impossible to resist, though she made sure the kiss was sweet and light. 'You know where to find me if you change your mind.'

With that truly fabulous exit line, delivered about a thousand percent better than anything she'd said in *Friendship Never Dies*, Olivia turned and walked a few steps toward the Pattersons', peeking back to see the light through Duncan's door narrow then go dark.

She was absolutely not going to cry.

Fumbling her way, she continued a few yards farther down the path, then reared back with a gasp. In front of her was the enormous shadow of the person she least wanted to see right then. A man who apparently didn't use a flashlight either. A man who was standing with his hands on his hips, watching her approach.

She did not like the feel of this. 'Hi, Stu—'

'What are you doing here?'

Nor did she like his tone. 'Visiting Duncan.'

'Leave him alone.'

'*Excuse me?*' All the control and maturity she'd managed to summon with Duncan fled, and she was once again a royally pissed-off, barely stable diva. The return of that power made her feel strong. Also sick to her stomach.

'I said leave him alone. He's going through a lot right now. He doesn't need you messing with his head.'

'Why would you immediately assume that's what I was doing?'

'Because that's what women like you do.'

'Oh, that's just brilliant, Stuart. Really. Women like me. Because you know me so *well* by now, having spent about two hours in my company.'

'I know enough. Duncan needs someone right now who can *give*, not take. Who can support him when—'

'You don't know shit about me.' Her voice rose to a hoarse shout. 'Nor do you have any right to tell me what I can and can't do.'

'You're in my house. I make the rules.'

'What *exactly* is your problem with me, Stuart?'

He laughed, an ugly, cartoonish sound. 'Why don't you talk to my sister?'

Olivia's jaw dropped. She'd suspected Lauren might have been Stuart's poisoner where she was concerned, but it hurt a surprising amount to hear it. 'Why, what does she say about me?'

'Plenty.'

'Let me guess. I'm spoiled, I'm selfish, I'm self-centered?'

'Keep going, you're doing fine.'

Tears sprang into Olivia's eyes. Her power receded, leaving sickness in her gut. She couldn't even come up with a retort.

In the silence, she heard footsteps behind her.

'What's going on? Olivia? Stuart?'

Olivia closed her eyes. Great. Fabulous. On the very night when he'd gently and kindly been trying to extricate himself from her drama, she was dragging Duncan back in by his ankles. 'Just another psychotic episode in the life of Olivia Croft.'

'Braddock,' Stuart barked. 'Your name is Olivia Braddock.'

'I fucking changed it. It's *Croft*.'

'You just want your mother's—'

'Stuart.' Duncan's voice was low but icy. 'Lay off.'

'He's trying to protect you—' Olivia bit off the words 'from a bitch like me'. Duncan would figure it out.

'Thanks, don't need it.' He moved up close, his chest making contact with Olivia's shoulder. The warmth and shelter of his body were so comforting, she nearly bawled. 'Stuart, were you coming over to talk to me?'

'I was coming after *her*.' He pointed, as if he could possibly have meant anyone else. 'She wasn't in bed.'

'You checked to see if I was in *bed*?' Olivia blurted out, not at all helpfully. 'That is just massively creepy.'

Stuart spluttered, nearly covering Duncan's snort.

'I invited Olivia over, Stuart.'

'You don't need to be messing around with that.'

'*That*? Did you just call me—'

Duncan touched her waist. 'I appreciate you looking out for me. Olivia and I are both in tough spots. It helps to talk it out.'

'I saw more than talking.' Some of the vicious certainty had drained from Stuart's voice. 'She kissed you.'

'We're grownups.' Duncan's deep voice and quiet strength were working to defuse Olivia's rage, slowing her heartbeat, calming her stomach.

'I want you to be careful, Duncan.'

'Stuart.' Remarkably, Olivia was able to leave the she-devil shrieks behind. 'I am not out to hurt Duncan. As he said, it's comforting to hang out with someone else who is half out of his mind.'

'Hey.' Duncan gave her a teasing nudge.

Stuart took up his baseball cap and scratched his head. 'Well.'

'Well,' Olivia said.

'Well.' Duncan moved back a step. 'I think it's everybody's bedtime.'

'I agree. Goodnight. Thanks for talking to me tonight, Duncan.' Olivia moved swiftly past Stuart, unwilling to walk back to the house with him. Maybe she'd spend tomorrow night at Dad's, give Stuart some extra space, before her Croft temper made him any worse of an enemy.

On the threshold of her room, a memory popped up. Olivia, angry at how Mom and Dad's latest fight had scared her sisters, marching into Mom's pink, ruffly, over-the-top bedroom and demanding an explanation for her parents' inability to have a civil discussion. She must have been what, eleven? Twelve? Thirteen? Before she knew about Dad's affair. Old enough to think she had the world figured out. Young enough to have no idea she never would.

Mom had sat her down, drawing Olivia's stiff, angry body close. Jillian had smelled so beautiful, like the rarest perfume in the world. Later Olivia recognized Chanel No. 5, sold everywhere, but to her, Mom had smelled rare and special. 'You have a temper too, Olivia. My temper. You inherited that along with my talent. We can help each other. Okay?'

Olivia had been thrilled. Not only was she like her famous mother in yet another way, singled out for this honor over either of her sisters, but also they were going to team up! Make a secret pact to help each other!

It had not worked that way. Next time Mom yelled, Olivia had run into the kitchen, earnest in her effort to help, and was told to get the hell out of the room and mind her own damn business.

Olivia's temper wasn't from Mom. Nor was her acting. Nor her figure. Or her hair. All the parts of herself she was so sure had initially belonged to her fabulous, famous mother.

For the first time, Olivia let the big question appear front and center.

Where had she come from?

She got ready for bed, started to turn out the light, then stopped and reached for the second of Mom's diaries, the one Eve had sent. She started turning pages restlessly, skimming here and there, not ready to dive in, but wanting to know something about her mother's plan to fool the public into thinking she'd borne Daniel's daughters, hoping for some clue about the stranger who was her biological mother. She read bits – of Jillian's excitement and her father's reluctance to go along with the plot; of Mom's pain when she sent her husband out to impregnate the three women carefully chosen to bring her the babies she wanted.

Then she came to the entry dated October 5, 1989, and read the whole thing. Twice.

I think Daniel is having an affair. I don't know if it's with Mother #3 or someone else. Part of me doesn't blame him. My body isn't what men want. I try to understand that he needs to be with a whole woman. It's how God meant the world to be. I helped create his hunger by asking him to have these children for us. How could he help but want more? But it hurts, hurts, hurts, sometimes unbearably. I have started drinking too much. I was wrong that I could handle it. And I can't stop taking my lovely pills. I'm afraid I will have to get help again. People will know again. People will talk again. I'm about to turn forty. The work is not going to be around much longer. I can't let addiction be a bigger legacy than my art.

The only thing I hate more than having to drink is having to stop.

May God help me and everyone I love.

A brief, disbelieving pause. Then the temper Olivia had not inherited from Jillian Croft roared back to life.

Her mother had known about the affair.

Her mother had known.

Worse, that knowing had pushed Mom back into drinking, back into the self-destruction that had eventually led to her death, robbing her three daughters of the mother they loved.

She closed the diary, let it drop to the floor beside her bed, not bothering to turn off the light, knowing she wouldn't sleep.

Talk to my sister, Stuart had said.

Olivia would be happy to. She'd be going up to Blue Hill the very next day. She was finally going to stop pretending to tolerate her stepmother and let Lauren know the devastating extent of the damage and pain she had caused Olivia's whole family.

It was going to be ugly.

Olivia couldn't wait.

Chapter 15

October 16, 2000 (Monday)

I'm turning fifty tomorrow. I'm so afraid. My forties were difficult, so turbulent, so complicated. But now my fear is not about becoming old, but becoming useless. Hollywood does not celebrate older women. The parts are there, but few, small and simple at a time in my career when I'm ready for many, big and complicated. Men get to make this transition to meatier roles as they age. But women are rewarded first for youth and beauty, second for talent.

I wanted to change that. But even I, with all my star power, all my financial power, could not. I suppose I was naïve to think I could.

What does the rest of my life look like now? Who am I without the big screen? Who is there to care? I will become invisible except in the past. I want to exist in the present. And I want to have a future.

Jillian

Olivia lay on the floor in the Pattersons' sunny den, surrounded by paper and crayons, rain pattering on the roof. Opposite her, his face a cherubic frown of concentration, breath noisy from the summer cold he'd come down with over the weekend, lay

Jake. Each of them was hard at work on a masterpiece.

Georgia had taken one look at Olivia's face when she came downstairs and offered to switch shifts so Olivia could go back to bed. Olivia had accepted, and texted her father and Lauren to let them know she'd be coming for dinner that evening instead of at noon.

After a nap, which brought her sleep total for the night to four hours, she took a run through the miserable fog and drizzle, and ate breakfast that, given the hour, was more like lunch. She had little appetite, but forced down a piece of toast and a couple of eggs for protein. In spite of its late start, the day would be long, or would feel that way anyway. As soon as Sam picked up Jake after work, Olivia would drive over to Blue Hill to see her dad and finally confront Lauren.

Remarkably, maybe because the emotion center in her brain had finally short-circuited, she was calm.

Calm-ish.

Nervous rather than raging, sad rather than bitter. The planned vengeance wouldn't bring her mother back, nor would it erase the pain Mom had suffered because of her adored husband's infidelity.

But in case Lauren thought she'd gotten away with the affair, she needed to find out that her choices had turned into serious consequences for a whole lot of good people. Yes, Dad had been part of the problem, but he certainly hadn't forced Lauren into an affair. She'd been free to find her own damn husband and build her own damn life, which she bloody well should have.

'What are you drawing, Livia?'

'This is the view outside my family's house in Maine.' Olivia turned the paper around so Jake could see better, loving it when he dropped the O from her name. It reminded her of the song Mom used to sing when Olivia was little, one of the three she and Dad had made up for their baby daughters. 'It's farther up the coast from here, past Bar Harbor, even past Milbridge, if you know where that is.'

'I heard of it.' He glanced at the paper. 'You see islands? We have islands around here, too.'

'This is what it looks like in the sunshine. And this . . .' she selected a gray crayon and scribbled all over the page, 'is what it looks like today!'

Jake dropped his head. His contagious giggle turned into a cough she hoped wasn't. 'That's funny.'

'What are *you* drawing?'

'Mom and Dad at the beach. In my swimming pool. The one that got wrecked.'

'Hey, that's great.' Two stick figures in red and blue pants, arms growing straight out of their heads, with twiggy fingers and vertical hair. The pool was a blue circle, swirling around the right-angles of their legs and feet. 'They look like they're having a good time.'

'They are.'

The morning's reported disaster from Jake had been the discovery that his rock swimming pool had been rudely torn apart by the tide. His mournful description had been adorable, his vow to rebuild admirable. Georgia had apparently told him that the sea nearly always got its way, and Jake had decided the sea was a spoiled brat like his friend Peggy.

'Is my mom coming soon?'

Olivia pushed herself to her knees. 'Soon. Five minutes.'

'Good.'

'Yeah? I'm boring you?'

His grin was immediate. 'Noooo! Mom and I are going to Owdonna Wimsy to buy a present for John. His birthday party is soon.'

'Owdonna Wimsy?' She couldn't make head or tail of what he was saying. 'What's that?'

'A *toy* store,' said like Olivia should have figured that out and what was she, stupid?

Her phone confirmed that he was right. Out On A Whimsey was on Main Street in Belfast. 'That sounds like a fun place.'

'Yeah. Sometimes I get something too, but usually not.' He finished coloring a green cap on his mother's head. 'What are you doing?'

Olivia sighed. 'I'm going to see my dad and my stepmom.'

He looked up. 'How come you don't look happy?'

'I have to have a difficult conversation with my stepmother.'

'Why?'

She thought carefully how to answer. 'Because she did something that was kind of cheating. And I want to tell her that's not okay, which is hard.'

'Why?'

'Hmm.' Olivia started gathering up crayons that had rolled out of the way and putting them back into the familiar orange and green box. She loved their smell, loved the waxy way they put color on paper. Eve had been a big fan of colored pencils, but they'd been too fussy, too narrow for the way Olivia liked to draw. Rosalind loved markers, into bold colors from the earliest, same with her paintings now and the wacky clothes she designed. Three such different women. 'Have you ever thought something your mom or dad did was wrong?'

'Yup.'

'It was hard to tell them that, right?'

Jake looked surprised, then went back to coloring a pink hat on his father's head. 'Nope.'

'How about if a friend of yours did something wrong?'

'I'd yell at them. Or tell the teacher.'

'I guess I'm just a weenie, then.'

He finished Duncan's hat and dropped the crayon. 'Maybe my mom could go with you if you're scared.'

'Thanks.' She offered him the box and pointed to the pink, which he picked up and put back. 'I need to do this by myself, though. Maybe I should just put worms in her coffee. That would help her understand how I feel, right?'

His face split in delight. 'Nooooo!'

'No?' Olivia gave him a look of confusion. 'What if I told her she smelled stinky, so I could hurt her feelings. That would be good, right?'

'Nooooo!'

'Hmm, I don't know *what* to do, then.' She heard the door open downstairs. 'Sounds like your mom is here.'

'Okay.' Jake hesitated, laughter clearly at the ready. 'What else would you do?'

'Let's see . . . I need a grown-up and healthy way to handle this.' She tapped her chin, frowning. 'Wait, I know! Dead rat in her bed. Good, huh?'

'Noooooo!'

'Hey, what's going on, buddy?' Sam walked into the room, wearing shorts over hairy legs with too-slender calves. He bent down to hoist his son into his tattooed arms.

'Olivia doesn't know how to be a grownup.'

'No?' He looked at her curiously from long-lashed eyes. 'Why is that?'

'I told Jake that the mature way to handle a problem you're having with someone is to put a rat in her bed.'

'Ah.' Sam's grin lit the room. 'What do you think of that, Jake?'

Jake was shaking his head so hard, Sam had to tighten his grip. 'No. You have to be honest, but always kind.'

'That's right,' his mother said. 'That's what we do at our house.'

'You're *sure* it's better than spitting in her soup?'

Jake dissolved into giggles. 'Yes!'

'All right.' Olivia shrugged exaggeratedly. 'If you say so.'

'Hey, Jakey, I think Georgia has a snack for you in the kitchen before we go.' Sam put the little boy down and he galloped toward the front of the house, flapping his arms. His mother called after him, 'Wash your hands first, though, okay?'

His 'Okaaay!' floated back.

Olivia started to follow, then saw Sam looking at her the way people looked when they had something to say.

'Thanks for spending time with Jake. He's really taken to you. He talked about you all weekend.'

'He's a great kid.'

Sam nodded, rubbed his patchily stubbled chin. 'So, uh . . . I wanted to ask you something.'

Olivia went on red alert. Whatever he wanted to ask was making him nervous.

'It's not really any of my business, but . . . is something going on between you and Duncan?'

Olivia took a step back, color flooding her face. Good God.

'It's okay.' He held up a hand. 'It's fine. I just . . . wondered.'

'Why? How? I mean, wait.' She put a hand to her hot temple, pushing back her immature impulse to deny the whole thing. Rude and insulting, especially since Sam must know. 'We are both in a bad place. There's nothing really—'

'No, no, you don't need to explain.' He took a deep breath. 'It's weird, I admit. It hurts. But this whole situation is weird. I mean, look at me. Duncan did not sign on for this. I get that. And he's a man. And you are . . . amazingly beautiful.'

This was not the difficult conversation Olivia was supposed

to be having today. 'It's over, though. I mean, it wasn't really anything, but Duncan stopped . . . whatever it was last night.'

She thought.

'He did?' Sam did not react the way Olivia expected him to. Not pleased or relieved, but surprised.

'He said it was too much.' She was annoyed to hear her voice thickening. 'But how did you know? Or suspect?'

Sam stooped to pick up Jake's drawing, then the box of crayons. 'It was his face when I started talking about you.'

'He probably felt guilty.'

'Maybe. I've known Duncan my whole life. We married because it seemed like the right thing to do, but we are still, and I suspect always will be, very close friends. That means he can't put one over on me. I could tell he had some . . . feelings for you.'

'No, no, no.' Olivia was practically laughing. 'It was not like that. Believe me. No feelings. Just fun.'

'Yeah?' He studied her carefully, and she felt again that disturbing flash of attraction. 'Maybe I misread.'

'Definitely. I mean, there's no way. We barely . . .' Olivia shook her head, blushing again in front of Sam's handsome and utterly serious stare. 'That's not possible. It was pure rebound fun. For both of us. And a place to bitch about how hard divorce is.'

Please God, get me out of this conversation as soon as possible.

'Okay.' Sam put the crayons on a shelf, kept the drawing. 'As long as you're sure.'

'Yes, I'm sure.' As long as? Would Sam be more or less upset if Olivia wasn't sure? Something strange here. 'I'm also curious why you'd ask me about all this instead of Duncan.'

Sam looked up slowly from Jake's picture. 'Because I want you to be careful.'

243

'We—' Olivia had been about to tell him that yes, they'd used condoms, when thank God it occurred to her that he might mean something completely different. 'Careful how?'

'You're a wealthy, sophisticated Hollywood celebrity and Duncan is a boatbuilder from small-town Maine.'

'Oh, okay. Because being rich and sophisticated and from Hollywood means I'm not honest or caring? Whereas honesty and caring are second nature to everyone from a small town?'

'You know what I mean.'

'No, I really don't.' She couldn't stand reverse snobbery, any more than other kinds of prejudice or stereotyping. 'What makes you think I would hurt Duncan?'

'You publicly cut the balls off your ex.'

'I did. Yes. I did. Just for fun, because that's an inherent part of being from Hollywood.' Olivia threw up her hands, let them slap down against her thighs. 'In fact, if you would like to buy some balls, I have an immense collection.'

She froze. *Oh shit*. Given Sam's situation, she should *not* have said that.

To her immense relief, he laughed. 'Point taken.'

'Seriously, Sam. I hate to say it, since calling Derek out felt really good at the time, but I do regret it. I have a terrible temper, I was in a terrible state, I opened my cakehole and out it came. Derek was a scumbucket who deserved at least some of it. I will never know Duncan one millionth as well as you do, but even I can tell he's not the type to provoke anyone to that degree. *Even* a raging selfish Beverly Hills bitch like me.'

'You're right.' Sam stared down at his child's drawing. 'I'm being overprotective of him. Maybe a little . . . jealous, too. Sorry.'

Olivia released her hunched shoulders. Honest and always kind. This was the type of conversation she had with Duncan, and would have liked to be able to have with Derek. Also with Lauren later tonight. If she could keep her raging selfish Beverly Hills bitch temper under control. 'You're absolutely entitled to be both. You're his wi— spouse, and were for a long time.'

'True.'

'Hey, Mom.' Jake bounced into the room. 'I ate my snack. I'm ready!'

'Okay.' Sam curved his still-delicate hand around his son's head, letting it rest under his chin, holding the little body lightly against his side. 'Say thanks to Olivia for playing with you.'

'Thanks, Livia.'

'You're welcome. I'll see you again tomorrow, okay?'

He nodded, tugging on his mother's hand. 'C'mon, Mom.'

'Thanks for talking this out with me.' Sam smiled his female smile. 'I feel better now.'

'Mo-om!' Jake made the word into two impatient syllables.

'Okay, we're off. See you tomorrow.' He let his son pull him out of the room.

Olivia waited a few beats, not sure she'd handled that as well as Sam seemed to think she had, then followed them into the hall and climbed the stairs to her room for her keys, purse and a change of clothes.

Honest and always kind.

She'd try to be that way with Lauren. But Olivia had been there for Mom's last dinner, New Year's Eve 2001, when Jillian had fallen apart so completely over steak Diane, sobbing with her head on the table, the first time Olivia had ever seen Dad not rush to comfort her. Olivia and her sisters had been stunned and shaken – to the point where she had hesitated about going out to party that night. Dad had been insistent. Her mother was okay. Olivia should go enjoy herself.

She had gone, to her now endless regret. If she'd stayed and taken care of her mother, dried her tears, found one of the many things the two of them loved to do together, maybe Mom wouldn't have been so upset and misjudged how many pills she needed.

But no, while her mother had been wrestling with despair alone in her bedroom, Olivia had been getting surreptitiously smashed with friends at the celebration centered around Hollywood and Vine, dancing like a fiend, squealing with excitement. While Rosalind had been dialing 911, Olivia had been counting down to midnight with Carmen Electra, then hugging and kissing strangers, throwing confetti to U2's 'Where the Streets Have No Name'. Then she'd called her family to share the joy and been summoned to Cedars-Sinai.

Olivia would never know for sure what had made Mom sink so low that night, but she could guess it was one of two things. Either her career. Or Lauren.

She forced herself to twist away from the grief grinding at her insides, change out of her kid-proof clothes and into a yellow sundress with matching sandals, then she ran downstairs to the kitchen, where Georgia was cleaning up jelly smears from Jake's snack.

'You off?' She tossed a crust into the sink and put Jake's plastic Batman plate into the dishwasher.

'Yes.' Olivia wanted to add, 'Pray for me,' but since Georgia was Lauren's sister-in-law, it was probably not a good idea to hint that she was going into battle. 'I won't be late.'

'Drive safely. Say hi to Lauren and your dad for Stuart and me.'

'I will.' She gave Georgia an affectionate smile and let herself out of the house.

The drive to and through the adorable town of Blue Hill was easy, under an hour, the usual summer traffic on Route 1, though nothing like the crush farther south in the state, where tourists flocking from all over slowed traffic to an exasperating crawl.

A few miles later, Olivia turned into the Pine Ridge retirement community grounds and made her way through the small maze of streets along which the independent-living cottages were built. She parked outside the unit that belonged to Dad and Lauren – at least until they died and the next couple moved in. The same with any house, Olivia supposed, but more immediately inevitable in a place like this.

For a full minute, she sat in the car, reminding herself to stay calm, breathe, and not to throw actual punches.

The front door opened. Olivia sighed, picked up the mixed bouquet she'd bought along the way and stepped out of the car. Just as well Lauren had come out. Olivia probably never would have decided she was ready. They'd find her years from now, skeleton in a car, dry bones still holding the steering wheel.

Lauren gave a small wave, then stood clutching both her elbows. She was wearing a badly fitting blue-and-green-striped dress and a funny crooked smile – as if half her mouth wasn't sure about joining in. Her salt-and-pepper hair was in a new, unflattering style, either a short cut that had grown out or a longer one badly trimmed.

How could Dad have followed a woman like Jillian Croft with *that*?

'Hello, Lauren.' Olivia held out the flowers, an impulse buy she now regretted. *Here are some flowers; I attack at sunset.* 'How are you?'

'Oh, how pretty.' Lauren accepted the arrangement, looking to either side of her stepdaughter. 'Your dad's inside.'

'Thanks.' Olivia passed her and stepped into the little house, which smelled like roasting ham. Her father stood leaning on a cane, smiling at her, bringing on a rush of overwhelming love for him, probably the only thing she and Lauren had in common. 'Wow, look at you, Dad. You got to graduate from the walker. Congratulations.'

'Come.' Her father held out an arm, then grabbed her for a hug – she had to bend down farther now, to his reduced height. But he held her for a long time in the strong embrace that had comforted her all her life.

'Dad, you're making me cry.'

'You're so brave,' he whispered. 'I could kill that bastard.'

'I'd be delighted if you did.'

'Look what Olivia brought us, Daniel.'

'Pretty. Very pretty.' He released Olivia from the hug, but kept hold of her shoulder, gazing at her with his still-sharp dark eyes. 'How are you holding up?'

'Pretty well. Stuart and Georgia are taking good care of me.' She managed to look over at Lauren. 'Thanks for arranging the getaway. It's so nice to be back in Maine. I always feel closer to Mom here.'

'Yes. Well. Lauren, find a vase for the flowers. We'll have a drink before dinner.' Dad walked stiffly toward the sofa in the living room, an open area that included the kitchen at the front of the house and a breakfast nook at the back, which looked out on a lovely view of the wooded hillside, with Mount Cadillac misted over in the gray distance.

'What would you like, Olivia?' Lauren was in the kitchen, reaching for a vase from one of the cabinets. 'We have wine, beer—'

'No, no, bring out the Scotch.'

'Daniel, you shouldn't have—'

'I don't care what I shouldn't have. One night won't kill me. My daughter's here, we're going to celebrate. I have to take much too good care of myself in this place. Takes all the fun out of life.' He bent forward carefully, then let himself drop butt-first on to the blue sofa cushion. 'Lauren insisted on cooking for you. That means we can eat at a decent hour, thank God. The dining hall serves at five thirty, finished by seven. It's bloody uncivilized.'

'We've gotten used to it, though, haven't we?' Lauren calmly filled the vase with water.

Olivia was grinning. She hadn't heard one of her father's tirades in way too long. He was definitely improving. 'Can I help, Lauren?'

'No, no. You sit with your father. I've got everything almost ready.'

'You're too thin.' Dad scowled at Olivia from under bushy eyebrows. 'You need to eat more. Protein. Fat. You look starved.'

'Life has been complicated, Dad. Half the world hating me doesn't do much for my appetite. Neither does facing a divorce.'

'Sooner the better. That asshole never did deserve you. You have a good lawyer? I can call Alan Houser. Best in the business.'

'Alan passed on, dear.' Lauren brought over a tray on which sat two glasses containing meager servings of Scotch over ice, a bowl of peanuts, and a square block of white cheese accompanied by wheat crackers.

'*What?* When?'

'Five years ago. We went to the service. You must have forgotten.'

'Oh. Yes.' Her father's take-charge bluster evaporated. He passed a hand over his forehead. 'Damn brain doesn't work like it used to.'

'We won't worry about that now.' Lauren handed Olivia

and her father their drinks. 'Welcome, Olivia. I'm sorry you're on our side of the country in such bad circum—'

'What is this?' Dad held up his glass. 'A quarter-drink? Am I a child?'

'It's an ounce and a half, which is plenty. There's wine with dinner.' Lauren raised her glass of ice water toward Olivia. 'Here's to you getting past all this and on to a new life soon.'

'Hear, hear.' Her father drained half his Scotch.

'Thank you.' Olivia sipped more cautiously. 'How's life been around here? Dad, you seem a lot better. What have you been up to?'

'Lauren keeps us hopping. Lectures, painting classes, recitals, outings with other geezers. If you have to be in a place like this, it's a nice one. I'll say that.' He finished his drink and held the glass up. 'A little more. I promise I won't die on you tonight. A gentleman never kicks the bucket at a fine dinner party. Certainly not when his beautiful daughter is with him.'

'All right.' Lauren pushed herself up, broadcasting disapproval from every pore, and went into the kitchen for the bottle.

Daniel winked at Olivia, who took another sip and toasted him, grinning. 'Did you have to get the pacemaker?'

'No!' He practically shouted his triumph. 'My ticker has been ticking just fine. I told them where they could put the damn thing, and it wasn't into my chest.'

Olivia cracked up. 'Bet they loved that.'

'Of course they did.' He gave her knee a fond pat. 'Tell me about this family of boatbuilders you're staying with, princess.'

'My brother Stuart and his wife Georgia, in Belfast.' Lauren poured them each a mere touch more, then screwed the cap on firmly and took the bottle back into the kitchen.

'I *know* who they are.' Daniel looked deeply insulted. 'They were at our wedding.'

Olivia wasn't so sure he had remembered. 'They're sweet. Georgia especially.'

'What do you do all day? I'd go nuts living in someone else's house. I don't even feel at home here.' He glared at Lauren as if it was her fault he'd had a stroke.

'Belfast is beautiful. The Pattersons' property is across from the harbor, right on the water. I can kayak or go hiking.' Neither of which she'd done, but it sounded good. 'Plus I'm helping watch their son's best friend's kid. Jake is four, and the sweetest little boy around.'

Her face must have shown pain, because Dad reached his big hand to the back of her neck, the way he'd done when she was little, holding on, maybe a gentle squeeze to let her know he was there. 'You deserve your own little one. When I think what that man stole from you . . .'

'I know, Dad.'

'Your mother. Oh my God, how she wanted you and your sisters. Both of us did.' He waved his glass a bit unsteadily. 'She went through hell on earth to have you. It wasn't much easier on me. There were times when I—'

'Supper's ready, Daniel.' Lauren made a beeline for her husband, clearly afraid of what he might say next. 'Let's get Olivia something to eat.'

'Yes. Of course. She's too thin. Did I mention that you're too thin?'

'You did, Dad.' Olivia stood on the other side of her father from Lauren and took his arm, worried that he hadn't recovered quite as much as she'd first thought. 'Would you like to escort us to dinner?'

'I'd be honored. Two such beautiful women.'

They installed him at the table, on which sat a platter of ham slices, buttered noodles and a bowl of steamed broccoli and pearl onions. Lauren wasn't an inventive or adventurous cook, but she knew her way around a kitchen.

'This looks delicious, Lauren, thank you.' Olivia unfurled her napkin. Dad was already reaching for the wine, a French Viognier.

Once everyone was served, and glasses filled – Olivia's full, Dad's only half, in spite of his glare – they began eating. Conversation started out strong, Dad reminiscing about their lives and his career, repeating himself now and then but not seeming as bad as Olivia had feared after his first slip-ups. She had no doubt that he'd continue to recover to his full strength.

However, by the time Lauren put down bowls of sliced strawberries and whipped cream, he was clearly fading. As much as Olivia hated seeing him with such reduced stamina, if he went to bed, it meant she and Lauren would have time to talk.

She wasn't looking forward to it.

Her father's head started to droop. Lauren and Olivia's eyes met. Olivia nodded.

'Daniel, sweetheart.'

He jerked upright. 'Sylvia?'

Olivia gasped.

Lauren shook her head and mouthed, *It's okay.*

Olivia wanted to roll her eyes. She wasn't worried about Lauren's feelings. It was the shock of hearing her mother's real name from Dad's mouth, the way he'd always spoken it, with so much care and tenderness.

'How about a nap, dear?'

'No, I don't need a nap.' But he let Lauren help him up, not glancing once at Olivia. Had he forgotten she was there?

She started to get up to take his other arm, but Lauren gave a quick shake of her head.

Olivia waited until they'd disappeared into their bedroom, then moved quickly to clear the table. By the time Lauren came back in, Olivia had put the food away in the nearly empty refrigerator – she was always searching for room in hers – and had loaded the dishwasher with everything but two wine glasses, which she'd refilled.

'My goodness, you work fast. You didn't have to do all that.'

'No problem.'

Lauren checked her watch. 'You'll be wanting to drive back before dark.'

'No, actually.' She gestured to the glasses. 'I thought maybe we could sit and chat for a bit.'

Her stepmother's eyes widened, and she gave a smile that faded almost immediately. A blush crept up her face. 'I would like that very much.'

Her bewildered pleasure was startling. All these years Olivia had assumed their dislike had been mutual. Certainly Stuart's attitude could not have been spawned by affectionate reports from his sister.

Maybe age had softened them both.

They sat in the breakfast nook and even went so far as to clink glasses before taking awkward sips of wine.

Honest and always kind.

Olivia swallowed and tried to smile brightly, nerves making that nearly impossible. She wished she'd suggested they sit somewhere side by side, so they wouldn't have to look at each other like this. 'Being at Stuart's house has made me realize . . . I really know nothing about your childhood in Maine. Machias, right?'

Lauren's pink face grew pinker. She pushed her glasses up

her nose and blinked a few times. 'That's right. My father worked at Machias Savings Bank. My mother was a homemaker, but she also did sewing, repairs and tailoring. They were Baptists, good people, very strict. There were three of us, me, Stuart, and our younger brother Ben. We weren't rich, but we did fine.'

Her mouth snapped shut as if she'd run out of power. During her speech, she'd glanced at Olivia a couple of times, but most of the monologue had been delivered out the window or into the living room.

'What kind of kid were you?'

'Oh, very ordinary. A little mischievous.' She twitched guiltily, as if she'd said more than she was supposed to. 'I got some trouble going now and then.'

'Like what? What happened to you?'

'Oh, not *me*.' She shook her head, smiling now. 'I caused the trouble. I was never caught. I was much too careful.'

'I can't imagine that.' Gee, what a shock to discover Lauren had plenty of practice sneaking around. 'Tell me.'

'Well, let's see. There was a boy my age, a neighbor of ours. Jim, I think his name was. He was giving this girl Patty a hard time. Patty was not very attractive – big teeth and bad skin, one of her legs shorter than the other. Jim kept pestering her. I thought that wasn't right.' Lauren paused for a sip of wine. 'Isn't this delicious? Your father knows wine. I started out so naïve, but I have developed a taste for it.'

'It is good.' Olivia waited for her to continue the story. And waited. 'What did you do to Jim?'

'Well.' Lauren put her wine down on the coffee table. 'I tricked one of his younger siblings into telling me which window was his. There was a big oak right outside. One night I climbed up so I could see into his room. Hit the jackpot.'

'What do you mean?'

She chuckled. 'Next time he tried to pester Patty, I told him that if he ever bothered her again, the whole school would know he slept with a pink stuffed bunny. I told him I'd taken a picture, which was a lie, but he bought it. That was that. Very satisfying.'

'Did you ever find out what happened to Patty? Is she CEO of some company now?' That was how Olivia would write the ending.

'Oh no. She died of a heroin overdose. But maybe I made her high school years more peaceful anyway.'

'That's awful.'

'It certainly is.'

'Did you . . . always intend to stay home after you married? I mean, not follow any career?' Olivia tried very hard to act nonchalant, like it was the most natural question in the world, though after their pleasant chat so far, she was feeling a little guilty for leading lamb-Lauren to slaughter.

Only a little.

'Oh no. I wanted to be an actress.'

Olivia didn't try to hide her surprise. She did, however, hide the jolt of anger and irrational outrage. An actress? Was that why she'd latched on to Dad? Did she think he could help?

'Stupid dream, but I wanted it terribly badly.'

'Is that why you married Dad?'

Her stepmother looked taken aback. 'Oh no. Those dreams were long gone by then. After high school, I got a job with the Machias Savings Bank in Stirling. I knew both your parents from that time. They had an account there.'

'So I gathered.'

Lauren picked up her wine and took an actual gulp, more

than Olivia had ever seen her drink at one time. 'Your mother was so lovely. And so talented.'

'Yes, she was.' Olivia wanted to tell her to shut up. What right did she have to compliment the woman she'd successfully tried to replace? Lauren wasn't fit to wash Mom's undies.

'She was a big reason my dreams had to go. I knew I could never hope to be that good.'

'No. You couldn't. No one could.' All Olivia's sympathy had fled. What about Jillian's dreams, the many years of life she was cheated out of? Olivia put down her glass. 'So. When did you and Dad start having an affair?'

Lauren grew very still. Outside, there were friendly greetings as neighbor passed neighbor. *Hello there. Lovely night. See you tomorrow.*

'How did you know?' Her expression stayed neutral, but her voice barely sounded.

Olivia had expected anything but this calm and immediate admission of guilt. 'I heard you on the phone with him once.'

'When?'

'Does it matter?'

'Yes, it does.'

'I don't remember. I was a teenager.'

Lauren seemed the slightest bit pleased. 'I see.'

'So? Anything you want to tell me about that? Because I have things to say.'

'Oh, Olivia.' She sounded as if she was offering comfort, knuckles white on the stem of her glass. 'I'm sure you do.'

'Mom knew Dad was seeing someone. Did she know it was you?'

'No.'

'You hurt her horribly. Did you ever think about that?'

'All the time.' Lauren was terribly, freakily, grimly calm.

'That's why your father and I were nothing more than friends until a year after she died. Out of respect for her, and for you three girls.'

'Oh, come on.' That was just insulting. 'I'm not a child, Lauren, I know how affairs work.'

Lauren blinked, her calm seeming even more impossible the more upset Olivia became. 'But it's true. We talked on the phone once in a while. We had lunch a few times when he traveled close enough to see me. We were friends.'

'You don't need to hide a friendship.'

'From Jillian Croft you do.' She put her wine down with the first sign of emotion, making the liquid slosh back and forth. 'She was insanely jealous of every woman he talked to. If she'd known about our friendship, known how he depended on me to cope with the hell she made his life, you would—'

'Stop it. That's my *mother* you're lying about.'

'No, I won't stop.' Still freaky calm, but with steel in her voice. 'I know how you worship her, but you need to hear the truth, Olivia. To know what she was really like. When she found out your father had a platonic friend, she went off the rails. She threatened to go public, smear his name all over the press, make a major scandal and arrange to cut him off from the three of you. If she didn't get her way, she became hysterical, cruel and—'

'Stop trying to justify your behavior.' Olivia was nearly shouting. If Lauren wasn't bothering with honesty, Olivia wasn't bothering with kindness. 'You broke up my family. You all but fed Mom those pills that killed her.'

'I broke up nothing!' Lauren got to her feet, strength pouring off her, anger and power that Olivia had never thought she possessed. 'Your father stayed. All I did was give him the only happiness he had in those years. Hadn't he sacrificed enough to her ego? Didn't he deserve something better than the nothing she gave him?'

Olivia stood too, shaking with fury. 'I'm not going to stand here and listen to this bullshit. Until you apologize to me and to my mother's memory, our relationship is officially over.'

Lauren flinched. 'I don't expect you to believe me. But if you want to hear the same truth from a source you will believe, go see your Grandma Betty. She has something for you.'

Olivia stalked across the room, grabbing her purse. 'Say goodbye to Dad.'

'You'll want to see this.'

'I guarantee I will not.'

'Olivia.'

Something in her stepmother's voice made Olivia turn at the door. '*What?*'

Lauren took three steps toward her and stopped. 'It's something for you. From Jillian.'

Chapter 16

January 5, 2001 (Friday)

Daniel and I had Silas Angel over for dinner tonight. He is such a sweet man! So attentive to our daughters. Most of my friends show up at our house, compliment the girls on their beauty, maybe ask a question or two about school, then they just want their cocktails. First time Silas came over, he sat down with Olivia on his knee and read her a story – it was so adorable. This time he brought her a gift, a little antique doll that she adored. Rosalind wanted to show him a tumbling routine, and he went outside with her to see it as if he really wanted to! Only Eve can't be charmed. She scowls. But then she's quite the serious little thing. I'm sure she'll grow out of it.

Over dinner Silas brought up a movie he wants to make, about a middle-aged woman who becomes chronically ill and has to fight the system to make sure her disabled daughter will be taken care of. There's a romance with a doctor and a fabulous surprise ending. He all but told me the part is mine.

I can't even begin to describe how I feel. As if my life were no longer careening toward disaster, but starting over. I am reborn! This is my part! This is my reason for being.

This will be The One.

Ecstatically yours,

Jillian

*

Georgia was waiting for Olivia when she let herself into the house after the drive back from Blue Hill.

'Hey, Olivia.' She looked tired. Or worried. Something was off. 'How was your visit?'

Hellish. 'Lovely. Dad seems much stronger. He and Lauren send their best.'

'That's nice.' She stood with her hands at waist level, lacing and unlacing her fingers. 'I'm glad you had a good time.'

'Is something wrong?'

'No, well . . .' Lace, unlace. 'I wonder if I could ask you a favor?'

'Of course. Anything.' By now Olivia was alarmed. Was Stuart ill? Even she wouldn't wish that on him.

'I took a loaf of banana bread down to Duncan earlier. He didn't seem . . . himself.'

Olivia became even more alarmed. 'How so?'

'Just . . . down.' Georgia took a hasty step forward. 'I know this is none of my business, but Stuart said you and Duncan had gotten . . .'

'To be friends?'

'Yes.' She rushed on in relief. 'And I thought maybe you wouldn't mind giving him a call or going down to see how he's doing.'

'Of course.' Olivia would be delighted. She'd been planning to give Duncan the space he'd asked for, though after the way he'd rushed to her defense last night when Stuart attacked, she didn't think he meant to cut her off entirely. But if he needed help, she could try to cheer him up, and benefit selfishly as well, because hanging out with him was her favorite part of Belfast. 'I'll go right down.'

'Oh, but you just got back.' Georgia was obviously protesting for the sake of politeness. 'You must be exhausted after driving all that way.'

'No, I'm fine.' Olivia wouldn't mention that an hour in the car in LA would be a super-speedy daily commute. 'Happy to do it.'

'Thank you so much.'

Still clutching her purse, Olivia pivoted and walked back through the door, down the hill and on to the shore path through the woods, more comfortable with the darkness than she'd been the previous night, to the point where she didn't even bother turning on her phone flashlight.

On the drive from Blue Hill, she'd had to talk herself down from the fury, then try to make sense of what Lauren had told her. By the time she made it back to Belfast, she'd found her answers. Lauren was bitter. She didn't measure up to the woman she'd somehow managed to replace, and never would. Add in guilt over the affair and it only made sense that she'd villainize her rival, try to make Olivia think less of her mother – the only weapon she had. The idea that Jillian could be that vindictive toward the man she loved so deeply was ridiculous. Using her daughters as bargaining chips? Absurd. Mom had her flaws, but cruelty wasn't one of them. Threatening to cut Daniel off from Olivia and her sisters would be impossibly cruel.

She knocked on the boathouse door.

No answer.

'Hey, Duncan. It's Olivia. You got a hot date in there?'

A faint 'Nah.'

Footsteps. The door opened. Duncan's hair looked as if he'd been rubbing a towel over it for maximum disarray. A smudge of dirt crossed one cheek. He wore a T-shirt with a hole in the shoulder and shorts with fraying legs.

'Ooh, off to the prince's ball?'

He rolled his eyes.

Maybe not the time for humor. 'Come out with me tonight?'

'Uh . . .' He gripped the back of his neck, tipped his head to stretch what must be tired muscles. 'No, thanks.'

'How come? What are you doing?' She put her hands on her hips. 'You're brooding, aren't you? Come on. We could both use a drink and friendly company.'

'I'm not really in the—'

'A couple of beers downtown. It'll do us good. I had a really crappy evening. Looks like you did too.'

'Yep.'

'I'm sorry.' The words were heartfelt, whereas when Derek put on his miserable act, Olivia just got impatient. 'I confronted my stepmother about the affair she had with my dad while he and Mom were married. What did you do?'

He raised his eyebrows. 'Always the drama.'

'I'm talking one beer.' Olivia held up a finger, refusing to be baited. She'd heroically shaken off the ghastly battle with Lauren; the rest of her evening was going to be pure pleasure. 'If I can't make you laugh, I'll even pay.'

'For a *whole* beer?'

'The *entire* thing.' She nodded slowly, eyes wide for emphasis. 'And I'm warning you that if you say no one more time, I will stop bugging you, so think carefully.'

Duncan groaned, tipping his head back to consult the ceiling. She waited, fingers figuratively crossed. Sitting around feeling like death wasn't going to do him any good. Even with Georgia's banana bread. They needed each other tonight.

'Okay, I'll go.'

'Great.' She made sure she didn't look triumphant; in fact canceled plans for a victory dance. 'You won't regret it.'

'We'll see.' He stepped back, gesturing her in. 'Let me get ready.'

'Wait, why?' Olivia blinked in fake surprise. 'You look great as you are.'

He gave her the look she deserved. She couldn't stop grinning, watching him climb the stepladder to his loft room. This was a brilliant idea. One of the few she'd had lately. A quick beer, get Duncan talking, see if listening would help or if she needed to take more drastic action. Like buying him a second beer.

In a very short time, Duncan was climbing down the ladder dressed in black jeans and a black tee under an open gray shirt. Olivia forced down the longing to rip it all off him and roll around for the rest of the evening. Friendly company. So be it.

'Let me wash up.' He crossed to the sink, scrubbed his face, then wet a comb and got his hair to behave. 'Okay. I'm ready.'

Olivia shook her head at his grim demeanor. 'We're not going to the gallows.'

Duncan walked past her. 'Knowing you, someone will choke to death at the next table, or the bar will be held up by aliens.'

'Knowing me, we'll dance naked on the wharf and have the time of our lives.' She waited while he closed the door, then headed with him back toward the Pattersons', determined that he'd be feeling better by the time they said goodnight. 'Where would you like to go?'

'Rollie's. Good beer. Been around forever.'

'Sounds perfect.'

It *was* perfect. He drove them over the Passagassawakeag bridge – Olivia still couldn't look at the sign without laughing – and down Belfast's steeply sloping Main Street to a building near the wharf. They were even able to snag just-vacated seats at the bar, where they ordered a couple of draft pints.

'Cheers.' Olivia drank deeply. 'Oh, that's good.'

'So?' Duncan set his glass down, still looking lifeless. 'What made you decide to confront your stepmother today? Not enough chaos in your life?'

Olivia held up a finger. 'Tonight we are talking about fun topics.'

'Isn't this what you needed me for?'

'No, Duncan.' She could cheerfully smack him. '*You* are the needy one tonight. This is your chance to shine.'

'I didn't mean it that way, sorry.' He covered her hand briefly with his. 'I need this too or I wouldn't be here. Tell me about your day.'

'Only if you promise to spill after I do.'

He groaned, rubbing his eyes. 'Okay, I will spill after you do. Now tell me what made you go on this idiotic quest.'

'All righty.' She beamed at him. 'Last night I read an entry in one of my mom's diaries. I didn't know she'd suspected my dad of having an affair. Her pain was terrible. I thought I should . . .' She tried to think of some way to frame her motivation that didn't sound like *pummel my stepmother into a pulp*.

'You thought you should stir up more shit.'

'No.' Olivia concentrated, trying to keep her thoughts clear. She'd done the right thing confronting Lauren with the consequences of her selfishness. 'I wanted her to know that my mother knew.'

'So you could hurt her.'

'She hurt our whole family.'

'And that became your battle because . . . ?'

He was making her cheer-up mission difficult. 'I'm the only one brave enough to fight it.'

'Or crazy enough.'

She huffed, annoyed at his logic and the challenge that would force her to rethink her behavior yet again. 'You've got it bad today.'

'Yeah.' He gripped his glass with both hands. 'I guess I do.'

'Okay then, your turn. How come?'

'Olivia . . .' He hunched his shoulders. 'I really don't want to talk about it.'

'I gathered. But saying the words out loud, hearing yourself talking, getting a reaction . . .' She poked his arm. 'Not that I did a single thing I'm not one hundred percent proud of, you understand.'

'Of course.'

'But you did make me think.' She wished he'd look at her, hoping he could hear the sincerity underneath her I'm-so-perky tone. 'Talking to me is cheaper than therapy. I care, and it's safe, because who am I going to tell?'

Duncan kept his head down. Why was it harder for men to talk about emotions than women? Was that socialized behavior or wired? Mom had been the epitome of overshare. Olivia tended to be the same way. Was Sam able to talk easily about private things? Would he become impaired in that ability after his transition to maleness was complete?

'I guess you're right.'

Olivia nudged him affectionately. 'Well, duh.'

'So . . .' He circled his head, trying to loosen tension. 'Being on this end of a gender transition is nothing compared to what Sam is going through, but there's a lot. Grief over the loss of the woman I knew, and of our life together. Fear for what kind of life Sam has ahead as a transgender man. Fear for Jake. Sam is a strong person, but he's anxious over his change, and Jake feels that. He's clingier, worried more often. That could get worse when he starts going to school in the fall and sees how people react to his mother.'

'I'm sure there will be a lot of support too. Society has come a long way.' Olivia searched for more words of comfort. 'Having a trans mom is becoming Jake's normal. You can teach him to feel sorry for people who don't understand.'

'That would be nice.'

She bunched her mouth, wanting to offer more, thinking about the conversation with Lauren, the curveballs Duncan had thrown that had struck her outrage into uncertainty. 'Grief makes it so hard to figure stuff out. It's like having a pink vase that's suddenly gray, then suddenly blue. You get confused over what the real color is. And divorce is all about grief. Mine is complicated by hatred and blackmail, and yours is complicated by a gender switcheroo, so it will take time. But then we're done, on the other side. And we'll still have a lot of life left.'

He nodded, rubbing his chin. 'Olivia . . .'

'Yes, Duncan?' She hoped that had helped. She thought it was a pretty good speech.

'Did you really just say gender switcheroo?'

Olivia snorted. Served her right for expecting kudos. She liked the way Duncan punctured her ego. Gracefully, without malice or spite. 'I'm afraid I did.'

'Thanks for the pep talk, and for dragging me out tonight.' He was still hunched over his beer, but the creases in his forehead had relaxed. 'It always seems easier to shove the bad stuff away, but it hits back at you one way or the other.'

'Ah, you've described my entire life.' She lifted her glass. 'Here's to denial, my best friend for many years, always ready to lend a helping hand.'

'Yuh.' He signaled the bartender for another beer; Olivia put her hand over hers to show she was fine. 'You know, Georgia worked with pregnant teens for a while. Some of them had to be handed the babies that had just come out of their bodies before they admitted to themselves that they were pregnant. It's a pretty powerful force.'

'Unfortunately, what I've been discovering lately is that the longer the denial goes on, the more it hurts when it stops working.'

'Yeah.' Duncan finished the last of his first beer and sat staring at the bottles behind the bar while Olivia let him work out whatever it was, tapping her foot to the beat of a song she'd never heard before while waiting for him to come around. Fun bar. Seemed to be a nice mix of locals and summer types, not that she could reliably tell the difference.

'How did your stepmother react today?' Duncan straightened with a jerk, as if flinging off devils perched on his shoulders.

'Oh, she was *thrilled*.' Olivia cackled evilly. 'She invited me over tomorrow to do it all again.'

'I bet.' He reached to touch her back. 'Sorry.'

'That's what I get for shit-stirring, right?' She shoved her hands between her knees. 'It was difficult. She tried to turn it around so that *she* was innocent, and it was all my mother's fault.'

'That's pretty cold.'

'Isn't it?' Olivia leaned out of the way of a patron reaching for his drinks. 'I don't know what I expected. I supposed I wanted her to crumple and beg for forgiveness. People need to grow up and admit their mistakes. I, myself, have a million of 'em.'

'No way.'

She pulled up her hands to count. 'Mistake to get engaged so quickly. Mistake to stay married after the infatuation wore off. Mistake to tell the world Derek's little secret. I'm also starting to think that . . . it was a mistake to pursue acting for so long.'

Duncan finally turned and really looked at her. 'Why is that?'

'Mom used to tell me all the time, "Keep giving them you until you is what they need. Every opportunity brings you one opportunity closer to getting what you want." But lately I've been going through the motions.' She grimaced, finding it harder to stay cheery and flip. 'Probably have been for a long time. I don't seem to have the hunger in me anymore.'

'Then quit.'

'How do I know I'm not just tired from all the recent shit?' She paused while the bartender set a fresh beer in front of Duncan. 'How do I know the role of a lifetime isn't right around the corner, with a director who can inspire me to do it really well?'

'You don't. If you decide to give it up, you have to make peace with that.' He picked up the new glass. 'What would happen if you quit? Your biggest fear?'

'Oh, that's easy. My biggest fear is finding out I'm no good at anything.' Olivia's voice cracked. 'That I'm nothing special.'

She laughed nervously, waiting for Duncan to make fun of her, or worse, to jump in with easy reassurances. He took a slow sip of his beer and put it down deliberately; she was getting to understand that this was his way of delaying an answer until he could think it over.

'A lot of people are afraid of that.'

'But not a lot of people are told over the course of their childhoods that they are special, that they're going to go on to become even more special, the exact nature of that specialness described over and over until they internalize their future specialness as fact.' She was shocked to hear bitterness threading her voice, and tried out a careless laugh that fell utterly flat. 'What happens when they grow up and start to suspect they're not special enough to fulfill their own super-special destinies?'

'That's a horrible thing to do to a kid.' Duncan sounded furious.

'What do you mean?' Olivia gaped at him. 'Acting is what *I* wanted. *I'm* the one who couldn't handle it.'

'How do you know it's what you wanted?' He waited, brows raised, eyes flashing. She had no idea how to respond. 'How do you know what you would have wanted if she hadn't gotten her hooks into you?'

'No, Mom wasn't like that. She didn't push me. She encouraged me. In fact, she was only a stage mother once, when I was overlooked for a lead. She thought it was a political decision.'

'Sounds pushy to me.'

'One time! And she was right.'

He shrugged. 'Okay, okay, she was a goddess. A goddess who tried to make your life all about her.'

Olivia was so appalled she could barely speak. 'No.'

'You think I tell Jake every day that he's going to spend his life building boats, that he's going to be the world's best boatbuilder, and that he should never, ever give up until he *is* the best? Before he's even old enough to understand what that means? Who does that?'

Olivia hunched her shoulders, feeling ill. 'It wasn't like that.'

'Okay. I'm sorry.' Duncan turned back to his beer. 'It sounded that way to me.'

It did. But Olivia did not want to deal with any more vitriol against her mother today. She'd file his comments away, take them out to look at later, when she was braver. Stronger. Not tonight.

'So. I've laid myself bare.' She flipped her hair back over her shoulders, trying not to show how badly he'd shaken her. 'Now you have to tell me your worst fear.'

'Oh no. I only signed up for the why-was-your-day-crappy? package.'

269

'C'mon, Duncan. Play with me.'

He rubbed the bridge of his nose, looking adorable again now that his features were no longer made of stone. 'I guess my biggest fear . . . is screwing up my kid.'

'That's every parent's biggest fear. Doesn't count.'

He glared at her for a few exasperated beats. 'Okay. Then . . . I would say my biggest fear is being alone.'

'Alone like alone in a room? Or alone like without friends? Or alone like without a woman? Because if it's the last one, there is no way women anywhere will leave you alone. You are hot enough to start forest fires.'

He started blushing. 'I wasn't fishing.'

'I don't care. You're kind, you're sexy and you're employed. Bingo. In fact, Duncan . . .' she put a hand on his arm and fluttered her eyelashes, 'you are *special*.'

He stared up at the ceiling, laughing. Briefly, unwillingly, but he did laugh. 'That's *your* fear.'

'No, no, it's the same one. Think about it. A good partner, a really good one, makes you feel fabulous every day – sexy, smart, good-looking, worth every ounce of oxygen you use up, right? Which is pretty much another way of saying special.' She tapped the bar smartly: signed, sealed, delivered. 'Our fears are the same.'

'Okay, but since you're not a superstar, and I'm on the way to being single, we both need to find a way to feel good by ourselves.'

'God, no. That's much too much work. Hire someone.'

He laughed again, then turned to face her, a warmth in his eyes that made her sit up and pay attention, heart thumping, breath going shallow.

'You, Olivia, are *truly* unique.' His voice turned husky. His brown eyes were totally, intensely sincere. 'I have never encountered anyone like you before.'

Olivia's laughter faded. She'd assumed he was teasing her, but then the words had come out so gravely. Even Duncan looked startled.

She jumped on a way to give them both an out. 'You, on the other hand, would make a great actor. That was almost convincing.'

'Hmm.' He ducked his head. Drank some beer. Shifted on his seat. Drank some more beer. Olivia was unsure where to go next or what was happening in his head, so she waited, tapping her foot again. Perusing the customers. Checking out the beer taps. 'If you aren't going to keep acting, what are you going to do when you leave here?'

'Ah. I'm happy to say that I have *no* idea. Very proud.' Olivia raised her glass in a victory toast. 'When are you going to stop living in a boathouse?'

'Soon as I get my head out of my ass.'

She clapped a hand over her mouth to keep from spewing beer. 'Do not do that to me again.'

'Sorry.' He wasn't. He was grinning like he'd won a prize.

'I don't want to live in LA anymore.' There. Olivia had said it out loud, a little scary, but she wasn't panicking. In fact, the idea of starting over seemed more exciting tonight than it ever had. Maybe it was the beer. Maybe it was Duncan.

'Where would you like to live?'

'I don't know. The world is my oyster, right? Paris, London, Greek isles, East Podunk, Nowhere. Why, where would you live if you could live anywhere? On a boat?'

'Here.'

'Here over *anywhere* else? I love Maine, but I think I'd lose it sometime in early January.'

'You *and* Georgia. I'd love to do more sailing. Long trips up and down the East Coast, or down to South America or the

271

Caribbean. But after a few months, I'd want to come back here. This place is inside me.' He thumped his chest. 'I'm a Mainiac.'

'D'oh! I get it.' Olivia loved the idea – home when it was beautiful, travel and adventure when her California blood couldn't take the long, cold winter. 'That could work. Spring, summer and fall here, then winter sailing somewhere warm.'

He turned deliberately, eyes finding hers in a way that made her insides go shivery. 'Could work for which of us?'

She felt a blush rising, feeling off-center, mortified to have been picturing them sailing off into the sunset together. 'You. Of course. Your dream. What did you think I meant?'

He sat watching her through narrowed eyes while Olivia fidgeted, dropped her gaze, then met his again until she couldn't stand it anymore. '*What?*'

'Would you like to come home with me?'

Olivia caught her breath. *God, yes.* 'I thought we weren't doing that anymore.'

'Something changed.'

'What changed?'

'I'll tell you later.' He was already on his feet, throwing money on the counter.

'No, no.' Olivia reached for her purse. 'My treat.'

'You made me laugh. That was the deal.' He grabbed her hand and pulled her out into the parking lot while she giggled like a smitten dork.

Hadn't she said this evening would be all about fun?

Duncan probably broke a few speed limits driving the Jetta back, and they didn't make it up the ladder to his bed before they were at each other, undressing in a frenzy on the futon, their frantic movements becoming calmer as they made love, luxuriating in the sensations before passion carried them to a

272

climax. Afterward they took their time returning blissfully to themselves and to the warm room around them.

'Round one complete.'

'Mmm.' Olivia smiled, a sated, purr-like-a-cat smile. 'I like the way you think.'

'Yeah?' Duncan stretched and pulled her closer. 'I like the way you fu—'

'Hey, watch that.' She twisted to a more comfortable position, savoring the warmth of his chest against hers, the way their legs meshed perfectly. 'Now. Tell me what changed your mind about the nookie.'

'Well . . . it *could* be the guy thing. Me. Hot girl. Chance to get some.' He touched her cheek, expression turning serious. 'Or maybe it was the look of longing on your face when I talked about our sailing life together.'

'No!' She struggled to sit up, gave in when he was too heavy to budge, but kept her hand firmly pushing at his chest. 'That is not what I thought you were talking about.'

He was acting smug as hell. 'What did you think I was talking about?'

'You sailing by yourself.'

'Oh, right, you looked totally starry-eyed at the thought of the guy who doesn't want to be alone being alone.'

'*Starry-eyed?* You are reading way too much into—'

'Why do you think I asked you to come back here?'

'Same reason I came back here. We like each other and we're horny.'

'I can prove you wrong.' He grinned as if he knew something she didn't, then kissed her like he meant it. Again and again, light, sweet kisses, sometimes full on the mouth, sometimes each corner, upper lip, lower, perfect kisses that stole her breath, made her heart pound, her chest ache with longing.

For what? She wasn't in any shape to decide. Her vase was every color of the rainbow.

Then he did something much worse. He lifted his head, opened his beautiful brown eyes and stared into hers, connecting the two of them absolutely.

Olivia looked away, back, away again. 'Stop that.'

'Why?'

It was on the tip of her tongue to make something up, protect herself, deny what she was really feeling.

Fuckarini. She couldn't. This was Duncan.

'Because . . .' Deep breath, summoning courage, much more than what she'd needed to confront her stepmother, more than to lay the trap for Derek, or to come to this town and live among strangers. 'I don't want to be this vulnerable. Not to anyone. Not to you. I can't. This wasn't the plan.'

'Shh. Okay.' He sat up, helped her to sitting, watching her with concern . . . and a touch of triumph. 'You want to leave?'

'I should.'

'Should, but do you want to?'

'That's not fair.'

He chuckled with infuriating satisfaction. 'You're as gone as I am, aren't you?'

'No, I'm . . . No.' Her denial didn't even come close to convincing.

He was laughing at her, and she really wanted to punch him. The urge got stronger when he started to sing, tuneless but utterly charming, in a deep, resonant voice. 'My name is Ol-i-via, I live in De-nial. Give me a wor-ry to cir-cu-lar file.'

'Goddammit, Duncan.' Olivia let herself fall back, giggling, then covered her eyes with the back of her hand. 'I can't bear any more pain . . .'

'I'm not out to hurt you.' He settled next to her, laying a

possessive hand on her stomach. 'But I'm tired of analyzing, tired of trying to follow the shifting path of supposed-to rather than what my instinct tells me is right. I want you and me for as long as we can have it.'

Tears thickened Olivia's throat. Not putting a stop to this now could be a huge mistake, one that would add serious damage to what they were already suffering. Damage that would turn their upside-down lives inside out.

Duncan kissed her again, the bastard, totally sure of himself and his power. She'd given away too much, too soon.

Except the way he was kissing her didn't feel like victory or conquest; it felt like giving, sharing, and the look in his eyes as he pulled back to gaze at her contained a touch of awe.

Olivia sighed and pulled him down again. Rosalind had been right. She'd been reckless and stupid and self-destructive her entire life.

But maybe this time she'd finally get it right.

Chapter 17

April 4, 2001 (Wednesday)

Daniel and I are fighting all the time now. I finally confronted him about the affair. I was hysterical. He swore he's not having one. I would love to believe him. But it's not true. I know it's not. If only I was born a real woman. If only I was born with enough to satisfy him.

If only I could go out and cheat on him in return, so the lying bastard could feel what this hell is like! I told him that if he ever left me, he would never see his daughters again. Never. I have never seen him look scared like that. It made me feel deeply triumphant and powerful. Sometimes I don't even recognize myself anymore. I need Silas's part. I need to work. Without it, I am terrified I'll go crazy. I have no idea when he'll be ready to start or to cast the rest of the film or anything.

I despise having my fate in someone else's hands.

Olivia took one last look at her face in the mirror. No one she saw today, including Grandma Betty, would give a rat's ass what she looked like, but old habits died hard. She'd had a relatively calm week after the blissful night spent in Duncan's arms, and the not-blissful glare from Stuart when at the crack of dawn Tuesday morning she'd stumbled groggily up to the house to go straight back to bed. A calm week compared to those that preceded it, not compared to any normal person's life.

She'd found a yoga studio in town and a massage therapist, and had continued working out and babysitting the adorable Jake. She and Duncan had gone on a sunset kayak trip, and she'd taken a solo hike on a portion of the Hills to Sea Trail. Stuart had been gradually thawing, and Georgia continued to be a fun companion and source of unflaggingly cheerful support and great food, though Olivia had successfully argued her way into preparing several more meals.

Also this week, the Internet had moved on to hate other people, making Olivia feel she was running out of excuses to stay in Belfast. She tried to spend more time in the boathouse to keep Georgia and Stuart from feeling invaded, but still felt uneasy. Finally she'd made a comment about overstaying her welcome to Georgia, who had scoffed so convincingly that Olivia had even less impetus to wake herself from this very pleasant hibernation.

The only grim moment had come a couple of days earlier, when, after talking with her lawyer, she had called Derek to suggest they attempt a collaborative divorce. The idea had been inspired by Duncan and Sam, who'd cut both cost and conflict that way. The concept went counter to Olivia's fight-or-fight-harder method of handling disputes, but she'd jumped on it. Maybe she was evolving. Maybe she was just tired.

Unfortunately, Derek was not in the mood to be collaborative. But at least he didn't resort to blackmail again, raising Olivia's hopes that he really would be satisfied with what she'd already given him, and that his threats would go away somewhere warm and lovely and stay there.

Today, with Jake staying at his dad's, she'd decided not to

put off the visit to her grandmother any longer, curious if Lauren had been telling the truth about Grandma having something for her from Jillian. Betty had readily agreed to her visit, sounding the same as ever, which meant cranky and self-centered.

Downstairs, Olivia poked her head into the den, where Georgia was spending her Saturday morning relaxing with a magazine, feet up, windows open to let in the humid breeze from the bay.

'I'll be back by late afternoon probably. Can I bring something for dinner?'

'Stuart and I are eating with friends tonight, so get whatever you want for yourself. Did you need to take anything for the trip?' Georgia lowered the magazine and leaned forward, preparing to get up.

'Do not move.' Olivia pointed emphatically at Georgia's chair. 'I have everything I need. What's more, I can get out of the house and into the car all by myself.'

'No, you can't. No one can get anything done around here without me.' Georgia waved Olivia cheerfully away and turned back to her reading. 'Drive safely. See you tonight.'

'Thanks.' Olivia stepped into the kitchen to retrieve the lunch she'd made to take with her – subject to Grandma's pre-approval, of course. Olivia would rather starve than show up at mealtime and eat anything Betty had prepared. The woman could ruin even the simplest recipes. A true talent. Dad had nearly had a fit the first couple of times he'd had to force down her cooking. After that, he and Mom always arrived loaded with food.

She pushed through the front door out into the oppressive heat, tossed lunch into the passenger seat of her car, buckled herself in and put on her oversized sunglasses.

Let's do this thing.

The drive northwest to Jackman was fairly easy, about two and a half hours on small highways, so not much tourist traffic. The largest town Olivia passed through was Skowhegan on the Kennebec River, home to the annual Maine State Fair. Beautiful country. Not many people knew much about Maine beyond Acadia National Park and the most famous cities – Bar Harbor and Portland. Bangor if you were a Stephen King fan. Freeport if you loved L. L. Bean.

She drove with the windows down, letting the wind mess up her hair, blaring favorites from her teenage years: Sheryl Crow and Tori Amos, Red Hot Chili Peppers and Green Day. *It's the nineties, baby.* She was still in grade school, Mom was alive and sober, she and Dad were happy. Pudding-faced Lauren hadn't shown up yet. Olivia was going to be a movie star.

Life was good.

With one stop for a potty break, she reached the outskirts of the little town just after eleven thirty. Grandma Betty ate her meals on an exact schedule every day: breakfast at 7 a.m., lunch at 11.30 and dinner at 5 p.m. When her daughters had activities after school, or her husband worked late, they'd had to fend for themselves. Grandma wasn't going to have her household routine disrupted by anyone. Tornado carrying off the house? Didn't matter, she'd be sitting at the table, napkin in her lap, chewing whatever tasteless, overcooked masterpiece she'd produced.

Crazy lady. Rigid as a femur.

And yet she doted on Olivia, not that anything Grandma Betty ever did could be interpreted as doting by an outsider. According to Mom, baby Olivia had been instrumental in ending the estrangement between parents and daughter that started when Sylvia Moore ran away from home at age seventeen, set herself up in a ladies' residence in Manhattan and began her acting career at the Stella Adler Studio. Young Sylvia had assuaged her guilt by writing letters to her family every week. Only her sister Christina ever responded. Apparently Betty had forbidden Sylvia's name to be spoken in the house — she was dead to them.

For all her young-girl eagerness to escape from home, Mom had never quite been able to eject Jackman and Maine, nor Arnold and Betty, from her soul. Thirteen years later, some months after Olivia was born, Jillian had declared enough was enough. She and Daniel had flown to Bangor, rented a car and shown up on Grandma Betty's doorstep unannounced.

The reconciliation had been rocky, but not the disaster Jillian had feared. As Mom told the story, as soon as Betty realized who was standing at her door, she'd made a move to close it in their faces. Just in time, Olivia had let out 'the cutest coo ever in baby history, as if God made you do it'. Betty had been unable to resist her first grandchild, and though she never forgave her daughter for running away, an uneasy truce had been established. Poor Dad, born to a wealthy, sophisticated New York family, had weathered the awkward visits with his country-folk in-laws, whether in Jackman or at the Braddocks' house in Stirling, with tightly clenched teeth.

Radio turned down to spare residents her taste in music, Olivia drove through the little town, population somewhere around seven hundred. Not much had changed since she'd last visited, what, five years ago? Somewhat dutiful visits, since hanging around Betty was at best amusingly exasperating. In fact, given that Olivia would be arriving at the house at 11.38, Grandma would be greeting her already annoyed.

She turned on to Bartley Street and pulled up beside the little white house with green trim, also looking just as she remembered it, though maybe a little more in need of painting. While she was gathering up her purse and lunch from the seat next to her, she heard the door open. Grandma Betty emerged from the house at the same time Olivia climbed out of the car into the slightly cooler air.

'Hi, Grandma!'

'You're late.'

'I know, sorry.' She marched up the steps and hugged her bird-boned grandmother, inhaling her familiar scent, somewhat mustier than it used to be. 'You look great. Not a day over ninety.'

'I'm plenty of days older than ninety, thank you.' But Betty was smiling, her wrinkled cheeks turned pink, gazing up and down at Olivia. 'Royal blue is your color. Though you are still too beautiful for your own good.'

'Thank you.' Olivia held up the bag containing egg salad sandwiches on bread she'd baked the day before, carrot sticks, peaches and chocolate chip cookies. No point trying out anything fancier on Grandma. She wouldn't touch it. 'Here's lunch. Sorry to be late.'

'I'm all right. Come in.'

'You first.' Olivia held the door open, not surprised when Betty glared at her.

'My house. You first.'

She knew better than to argue. 'Okay then.'

The house was stuffy and in appalling shape, rug dirty, same crappy furniture covered with the same ratty quilts and blankets gone even rattier. A layer of dust on everything. Had Betty stopped taking care of it or could she simply not see the dirt?

'Grandma, you seriously need a cleaning lady in here.'

'What?' Immediate outrage, which happened so often the

281

family labeled it business-as-usual and moved on. 'What do you mean? It's fine.'

'It's really not. I can help you some this afternoon.'

'My house. My rules. It's clean.' Betty stomped toward the kitchen. 'C'mon, dish up this lunch of yours. I'm famished.'

'Okay . . .' Olivia followed her into the kitchen, remembering how often she'd stood there dying to reorganize and to whip up something that actually tasted good. That room showed its age too, the beige linoleum cracked and mottled by an assortment of dirt splotches. 'Your floor could use a scrubbing.'

'I did it last week.'

'Or replacing.' She put the bag on the table, already set for two.

'I'm not spending money on that.'

'You should have plenty from what Mom kept depositing for you. What did you do with all that?'

'Saving it.'

'For what?'

'Someone who isn't you. Now sit.'

Exasperating woman.

'I don't need the money, Grandma.' Olivia sat on one of the chairs, which let out a rude sound as the vinyl seat poofed out air. She reached into the bag. 'The house could really do with a top-to-bottom. Why don't you hire—'

'Egg salad!' Betty nodded firmly. 'I do like egg salad. Thank you.'

'You're welcome.' Olivia put the container of carrot sticks on the table and a small bag of potato chips. 'Mom wanted you to use the money to make yourself more comfortable here, to travel, to have nice things.'

'I don't need her money. I'm saving it for my other daughter.'

Betty bit into her sandwich. 'Mmm. You do make a good egg salad.'

'Your other daughter . . . Christina?' For one awful moment Olivia feared her grandmother had forgotten that Jillian's sister had died nearly ten years earlier.

'Of course not. What would *she* do with it?'

Olivia rolled her eyes. 'Nice, Grandma.'

'Facts are facts, and dead is dead.' She took another large bite. 'I'm talking about Christina's friend Phoebe Jansen. *She* stayed in Jackman when both of my daughters refused to. *She* took care of me. *She* visited. *She* cared. When she moved to marry some guy she met on the computer, I was happy for her. Phoebe deserved a good man, and she deserves all my money when I kick the bucket. Your mother didn't think this house was good enough to stay in. I'm not using her blackmail money to make it anything other than what it always was, and should be. *My home.*'

Olivia started on her own egg sandwich, wishing she'd used more seasoning – mustard or thyme. 'Mom was trying to help you, Grandma. Not blackmail you. She wanted—'

'Putting on airs, acting like she was better than us, assuming we needed her money. That dad of yours was worse. He did it to her, that's what I think. Your grandfather . . .' She crossed herself. 'Your grandfather and I were not rich, but we weren't poor either, and we didn't need any of her condescension.'

'She loved you.' For some reason.

'Funny way of showing love, to leave home without saying a word, and us with no idea what had happened to her.'

Olivia gave her sandwich her undivided attention. Eve had visited Grandma a few months earlier and reported that Betty had been hung up on the 'ungrateful daughter' rant then, too. Olivia should have known better than to try and argue, especially on a topic concerning Mom. 'Where did Phoebe move to?'

'She fell in love with a horse guy in New York. The racing town, what is it?'

'Belmont? Aqueduct?'

'No, no, starts with an S.'

Olivia put down her sandwich. 'Not Saratoga Springs?'

'Yes, Saratoga Springs.' Betty crunched on a chip. 'Why *not* Saratoga Springs?'

'But that means . . .' She stared aghast at her grandmother. Her sisters had mostly honored Olivia's ban on the subject of Jillian's infertility, but she knew Mom's diaries had been sent anonymously to Rosalind and Eve in packages postmarked Saratoga Springs. 'So Phoebe had Mom's diaries?'

'What? No.' Betty spoke impatiently, as if Olivia were dense. '*I* did. Your mother sent them to me.'

'When? Why?'

'Right before she killed herself.'

Olivia gasped at her grandmother's cruelty. 'Grandma! Mom didn't kill herself. She overdosed.'

'She overdosed to kill herself.'

'*Accidentally*.'

'No.' Grandma Betty shook her head and reached for another chip. 'She told me she'd given up on life and it was over. Fine thing to tell your own mother. Where are you going?'

Olivia found herself on her feet and sank slowly back down, sick and dizzy with horror. 'She told you that she was going to kill herself?'

'She sent me the diaries because she didn't want anyone finding them after she died.'

'How do you *know* that?' Olivia was sounding hysterical. She wanted to scream at her grandmother to stop making up these hideous lies.

'How do you think?' Grandma Betty glared at her in exasperation. 'She wrote me a letter. I still have it somewhere, along with your diary.'

Olivia pushed her plate away, afraid she was going to throw up. '*My* diary?'

'The one Lauren wants you to have.'

'Lauren?'

'Why are you repeating everything I say?' Betty peered across the table. Her jaw dropped. 'Oh my. You better lie down. Go to the sofa in the living room.'

'No.' Olivia tried to keep her breathing low and regular so she'd stay conscious. Her grandmother was unhinged. Mom would never, ever give up like that. Nor would she abandon Olivia. Or Eve, or Rosalind, or Daniel, or her public. Dad had probably sent Grandma Betty the diaries so she'd realize how badly she'd misjudged her daughter. 'I'm okay. It was just . . . a shock.'

A shock hearing Betty spout such vindictive bullshit.

'Then you can imagine how I felt when I got the letter. *Dear Mom, I'm going to kill myself tomorrow, can you please keep my diaries?* My God, it was cruel.' She gave a nasty laugh. 'I shouldn't have been surprised. Always thinking of herself.'

'Mom was *not* a cruel person.' Olivia stared at her grandmother, wondering if they'd entered some alternate universe where it was always 'opposite day', one of Jake's favorite games.

Some of what she was thinking must have shown, because Betty's thin gray eyebrows shot up. 'What would you call it then, if not cruelty?'

'Protecting her family.'

'She wasn't protecting *me*! Sending me those books all about herself and her every thought as if she were the center of the universe.'

'You didn't protect her either.'

'From what? Being a movie star married to a rich man, living in a castle making a billion dollars by making faces at a camera and reciting words she didn't have to write? What was there to protect her from?'

Olivia took a deep breath to control her temper. Betty was old, stubborn and probably narcissistic, possibly losing it. Clearly it was, and likely always had been, impossible for her to understand anything but her own point of view. There was no point arguing sense. And if Olivia made her angry, she might not give up the diary.

'That must have been hard on you.'

Immediately her grandmother's face softened. 'Oh, it was. I tell you, that girl was a trial.'

'She loved you, Grandma.'

'I did the best I could. She was beautiful. She was talented. She was also cursed.'

'Yes. You had it rough.'

'I did.' She was beaming now, making Olivia want to reach across the table and sock her in the solar plexus. 'But I raised her right, because that was my job. Mine and her father's.'

Olivia did her best to eat the rest of her sandwich, or at least enough to make it look as if she were eating, while her grandmother spewed more bile, about the idiots who'd torn down the town church and rebuilt it ugly, about the damn hippies who flocked to Jackman every summer to kayak the Moose River, about this friend who'd done her wrong, about that repairman who'd charged her too much.

Olivia made it through lunch – as much as she could stomach – then waited for her grandmother to take a breath. 'So . . . you have another diary here?'

'Just the last one left now.'

'Lauren said you had something for me. Something from Mom. Is that it?'

Grandma Betty lifted her chin, stretching the wattle-like folds of skin beneath it. 'Lauren said that?'

Olivia nodded, holding her breath.

'Well, she's the boss.' Betty snorted. 'She told me where and when and how to send each one, and I'd wrap it up, address it, and tell Phoebe to drop the box in the mail. The damn things never did me any good.'

'You didn't read them?' Olivia knew the answer even as she asked the question. Betty would never admit it, even to herself, but she was probably terrified of her daughter's true inner life, preferring to substitute the ugly one that suited her vision.

Betty scoffed. 'Why would I need to? She was my daughter. I already knew her.'

'Right.' Olivia got up and scraped her plate into the trash, which needed emptying, wondering if she could stand waiting until Betty finished her lunch to ask for the book. 'If you tell me where it is, I can go get it.'

'Awfully eager, aren't you?'

'She's my mother. She's been dead for nearly twenty years. Yes. I'm eager.'

'She had no problem ignoring *her* mother.'

Olivia bunched her mouth to keep her response from spilling out. Mom had written letters to Jackman every week for *thirteen years* with no response. Who was ignoring whom? 'Right.'

'It's upstairs in my closet. In a shoebox on the shelf, marked *Sylvia*.'

Olivia practically launched herself up the staircase, which badly needed resurfacing. Grandma Betty's room was at the end of the hallway, but Olivia lingered by the room her mother had grown up in, shared with Christina. The twin beds were still covered with pink spreads that made Olivia give in to the absurd impulse to see if she could capture any of her mother's scent still in them.

Not after this many years.

Disappointed, she made herself go on to Betty's room, which smelled as if the windows hadn't been opened in years. Rumpled clothes spilled out of the open dresser drawers, laundry made pyramids of chairs that must have belonged to Betty's own grandmother.

Getting old was a bitch.

Olivia stepped over a worn pair of slippers and peered into the open closet. Somewhat stunningly, it was perfectly organized, a throwback to neater days. Betty obviously didn't wear much of what was in it anymore.

On the shelf, as Grandma had said, a shoebox, *Sylvia* written neatly in black marker, next to another marked *Christina*. It did Olivia's heart good that the box wasn't buried away out of sight. Every time Betty looked into the closet, she'd see her daughters' names. Somewhere under the cranky wrinkles there had to be a real, feeling person.

Olivia pulled down Sylvia's box and lifted the lid, hoping for many treasures, finding only the one. Wrapped carefully in barely wrinkled tissue paper was the diary, soft green leather with her mother's stage name in gold. Olivia traced the letters, blinking away the blurring tears.

'Mom,' she whispered. She had jewelry from her mother, dresses, photos, a couple of hasty letters written during Olivia's first years in college, but these were Mom's uncensored words, her inner thoughts, unread by anyone else until now. It felt like a rare and miraculous chance to be alone with her mother again.

Hugging the small book to her chest, Olivia debated whether

to put the box back in place, and settled for folding the tissue paper inside, adding the lid and leaving it on Grandma's unmade bed, where she'd be forced to encounter it.

The box labeled *Christina* beckoned. The quiet, slightly strange woman had not been much of a presence in the girls' lives, either before or after Mom died. Olivia would take a quick look, then make sure she put everything back exactly as it was, since she hadn't asked Betty for permission.

Eagerly she pulled out the box, noticeably less dusty than Sylvia's. Inside were two bundles of rubber-banded letters, with another loose one on top; a clumsy bead necklace; a whelk shell and a heart-shaped key ring with one key. None of the items meant anything to Olivia. She glanced toward the hallway, as if Grandma might be flying up on her broomstick to spy, then opened the loose letter, written in her aunt's distinctive round handwriting. Dated April 12, no year. Was it written after the others or taken out of the stack by her grandmother recently and not filed back?

Dear Mom,

You made it clear what you thought of me last time we met. But I wanted you to have this picture, just so you could see her and not deny the truth, the way you did throughout my pregnancy. She's my child, your granddaughter. And even though I have to give her up, I want you to know how much I love her, how much I will always love her. I can't regret my choices. Sin can be more complicated than right or wrong, but I guess you have to be in it to see that. I know God will forgive me. I hope you will do the same.

Love,
Christina

Olivia gasped, put the letter down, picked it up and read it again. This was astounding news. Christina had lived a small, lonely life in a small house in a town even smaller than Jackman, far north in Maine – maybe as far away from Betty as she could get? She'd been a midwife, had assisted in the birth of all three of Jillian's daughters, then died in 2010 in her late fifties from the diabetes Mom said she'd never bothered to manage well.

Apparently sad, lonely Christina had had a good time with someone, at least for a while, though with anguished consequences. Having to give up a baby . . . Olivia couldn't imagine the pain. But it would certainly explain the pall of sadness that hung around Christina, making the contrast with her energetic, glamorous older sister all the more dramatic. Olivia, Eve and Rosalind had never particularly taken to their aunt, who spoke little and watched them with a hungry intensity.

Had Mom known? She'd never said a word about a baby.

Olivia read the letter a third time, as if the same words could give her additional information with another try. Who had the father been? How early in the process had he bailed? Poor Aunt Christina. Grandma Betty would not have tolerated 'fornication'. And knowing Betty, she'd be unlikely to answer any of Olivia's questions now.

After replacing the items carefully in the box, Olivia went back downstairs, wondering how early she could leave without being rude, then wondering why she even cared, given how rude her grandmother could be. She wanted to call her sisters, tell them what she'd learned about Christina, and about where the diaries had come from. They had an unexpected ally in Lauren. Despite her pledge to Dad never to reveal any details of Jillian's 'pregnancies', when the girls found out, Lauren must have felt it important that the three of them share at least this much of their mother. Olivia should probably feel grateful to her.

She'd read the diary first.

'There you are.' Grandma Betty had cleared the table and stacked their dishes in the sink. 'I want to show you family pictures I was organizing the other day. I want you girls to have nice memories when I die.'

Olivia was thrilled. The perfect opening to ask questions about Christina and her mother, unless images of Sylvia had been carefully razored out of the collection. Olivia wouldn't be entirely surprised. 'I'd love that.'

'I thought you might.' Betty stood and shuffled into the living room. Olivia squirted dish soap into the sink and washed up in a hurry. She'd just finished putting the last glass into the drying rack when Betty came back in, clutching a couple of photo albums.

'Oh, aren't you nice to do that. Thank you.' She pointed. 'There. Bring the chair around. We'll look together, here at the table.'

Whatever had turned her grandmother this sweet and generous, Olivia hoped she had a large supply and dipped into it often.

'This is what I've been doing. My God, it's an endless job. Too many photos. I might croak before I finish. Then you get the mess.'

'It's okay, Grandma. Thanks for working at it.'

As she turned pages, Olivia's desire to bolt lessened. There were pictures of Mom, pictures of Christina, the two of them with similar coloring, otherwise different like night and day. Christina plump, short, serious and plain, her older sister tall, willowy and joyous. Even at a very young age, it was clear that Sylvia's beauty would be extraordinary.

Pictures of Mom at Christmas, at Thanksgiving, in shows in high school – *Guys and Dolls*, *Harvey*, *South Pacific*. Olivia remembered her mother talking about her earliest performances, had read about them more recently in the diary. At least Betty had kept these photos. Even better, she seemed able to look at them without spitting poison.

'Would you like a cup of tea?'

'Sure, thanks.' Olivia stared at a picture of Grandpa Arnold, wearing his usual baseball cap, sitting on a rocker staring out into space. Nice man. Not the brightest bulb in the box, but kind and fair, at least to Olivia and her sisters. From what Mom had said, when she was growing up, her father was either out working at his carpenter/handyman job, or home smoking hand-rolled cigarettes that, no surprise, ended up killing him. His job was to bring home the paycheck, not drink too much of it, and take the belt to Sylvia and Christina when Betty decided they deserved it. Otherwise, unfortunately, he left their raising to his wife.

'Need any help, Grandma?'

'You think I don't know how to make tea?'

Olivia rolled her eyes and turned another page. A photo slid out and fell to the floor. She picked it up and peered curiously. Aunt Christina, exhausted Aunt Christina. In bed, holding an infant. A dark-haired newborn. The look on her face cut right to Olivia's heart. Love. Deep, hungry love – and anguish, just as deep. This could be the picture referred to in the letter upstairs. Betty must have taken it out of the box recently, which would explain why that letter was free of the bundle. Maybe Grandma had forgiven Christina eventually, Olivia hoped before her aunt had died.

The best part of finding the picture? Olivia could ask questions about the baby without admitting she'd been snooping.

'Christina had a child?'

'Christina?' Betty put the filled kettle on her tiny stove and turned it on. 'Of course not. She never married.'

Olivia rolled her eyes behind her grandmother's back. 'Weirdly enough, women's bodies don't know the difference. It's been known to happen.'

'Not in *this* family.' Betty came back to the table.

'Then what's this?' Olivia showed her the picture. 'Christina in bed holding a newborn. If it's not hers, whose is it?'

'Oh, that.' Betty scowled at the picture. 'I wondered where that went. I was going to put it somewhere else. I must have slipped it into this album by mistake.'

'If she didn't have a child, who is the baby?'

'The baby . . .' Betty took a deep breath, not meeting her eyes, 'is you.'

'*Me*.' Olivia's heart started pounding. Her face grew hot. Christina was her mother? 'But then . . .'

'She'd been up all night with your mother when you were born.' Betty reached to take the photo back. 'She was exhausted.'

Olivia's breath caught. She'd just been yanked in an entirely different direction. 'Up all night with my mother? Jillian?'

'Of course. What other mother do you have?'

For one crazy second, anything seemed possible, until reality crashed back in. 'My mother didn't give birth to me.'

Betty set her lips, then withdrew her hand when Olivia wouldn't surrender the picture. 'Your mother was there when you were born. Christina was up all night, and so was she.'

Olivia let her aching lungs empty, then filled them again. Of course not Jillian's child. But . . . Christina's? With Daniel Braddock? That would explain the absence of a man in her life.

She exhaled again as the whole scope of the truth hit. If Christina was her mother, then she and Jillian might not be mother and daughter, but they were the next best thing – aunt and niece. Real family. The only one of the sisters related by blood.

Tears rose that Olivia fought hard to keep back. This explained so much. Why Mom favored her. Why Olivia took after her most in face and figure. Why she had been groomed from birth to be the next Jillian Croft.

Joy bloomed in her, so deep she could scarcely contain it. All this time she'd pushed away the idea that her birth mother wasn't Jillian as something threatening and terrible. Now, though she still hadn't been given that prize, she'd won a very, very close second.

'Christina told me how she'd been midwife for Sylvia. How that night her blood sugar acted up because she'd neglected her health, hadn't eaten or slept in too long. So your father put her to bed, but he let her hold you. She was so happy to be able to help her sister. She was such a sweet girl. I still don't know why God didn't allow her to be happy in love. She wanted a husband and family so desperately.'

Aunt Christina had carried and given birth to Olivia, but had given her up . . . to her sister. There was the source of the equal parts of joy and anguish in her expression. The reason she always fixed her attention on her eldest niece as if Olivia belonged to her.

Olivia studied the picture longer, mind whirling.

Her birth mother. She hadn't wanted to know for so long, had been so terrified of finding out. Now that she knew the truth, she was ashamed of that fear and regretted her reluctance. She was Jillian's niece! That made her . . .

She caught herself, appalled. What did it make her? What exactly did it make her? *Special?*

She let the picture drop on to the album. What difference did it make whose kid she was? Olivia had grabbed at the idea that she might be a blood relation to Jillian Croft like a rope thrown down the well she was trapped in. Worse, she'd all but concluded that the relationship made her a more legitimate daughter than either of her sisters.

She was deeply ashamed.

If it was that important to be someone special, Olivia had to earn that honor herself, not by riding on the trains of her mother's designer gowns.

She let her head drop back, eyes closed, ignoring her grandmother's concern. Over the past few weeks, life had been building her a funhouse mirror set, in which her reflection had become both bloated and very, very small.

She was only just realizing what everyone else had probably figured out by the time they hit adolescence: that it was impossible to be anyone but yourself.

The next thought rose like an unpredicted tsunami. If Olivia stopped trying to be the woman her mother wanted her to be . . .

Who was she?

Chapter 18

December 14, 2001 (Friday)

I took the girls shopping today. Usually I just get Nancy to bring a selection of outfits to the house and the girls and I pick what we want. I can't always handle the circus. But today I wanted to go wild. It was time to buy their dresses for our annual holiday party. They were so excited! Olivia most of all, of course. She loves dressing up, like her mom. Rosalind, who spends her life in jeans, always wants the most colorful and loudest dress they have. Eve is my frustration. She is so conservative!

I don't want my girls ever to be ashamed of their bodies. They are all perfect, whole women, and they have nothing to hide.

Eve and I compromised eventually. I got her a beautiful blue strapless dress and a silk shawl she could wear if she wanted to. But no need. She has gorgeous bone structure and will grow up to be a stunning woman. Tall already, like her mom and older sister.

The party this year is scheduled for the 27th. Invitations have been sent to follow the hold-the-date cards we mailed out last month. Silas has already told me he's coming. I hope he'll have good news. I desperately need some.

Jillian

*

As soon as Olivia could politely – semi-politely – excuse herself from Grandma Betty's house, she drove north on Route 201 until she came to the familiar graveyard, where she pulled off the road, yanked the car into park, and half ran over to where her mother lay, her heart full, tears inevitable.

She knelt by the stone, put her cheek to its warmth, then touched the grass under which Jillian Croft still existed. 'I have your diary. Your last one. I want to read it while I'm with you.'

She sat on the coarse meadowy growth, heart thumping, opened the green cover and started to read.

An hour later, she trudged back to the car, crying again, but this time for a vastly different reason.

Lauren had been right about Mom.

Grandma Betty had been right about Mom.

Even Duncan had been right, and he'd never met her.

Jillian was exactly the needy, controlling, self-centered person they described. Where was the woman Olivia had idolized and imitated? Had she ever existed, or had Olivia always been blinded by her mother's aura, then and since? What happened to *Never let them see you ugly*? What happened to *Never surrender*?

Her mother had turned ugly, surrendered, thrown up her hands, refused to look ahead to that next audition, that next opportunity. She'd betrayed everything she'd lived by, every gospel she'd taught her daughter. Had those teachings been an illusion too? Part of Jillian's idealized version of what a star, a woman, should be?

Had she even known who or what she was, or had her own aura blinded her too?

Olivia got back into the Jetta and sat staring despondently through the bug-smeared windshield. The worst part was that she owed Lauren a humble, thorough and sincere apology. She might owe Grandma Betty an apology too, but Grandma Betty should have apologized for her own behavior so many times, Olivia would just deduct it from her account.

She had another good cry, then started the engine and set off back toward Belfast.

She arrived back two and a half hours later, barely aware she'd made the drive. Avoiding the Pattersons, she left the diary in the car to retrieve later, and headed down the yard in the now-stifling heat and humidity, past the gazebo and into the woods that embraced the boathouse. She needed Duncan.

Ten yards from his house, she stopped. All her life she'd gone running to a man when something went wrong. To Daddy when she was a girl. To boyfriends, then to Derek. Now Duncan.

Had she inherited that from her mother, too? Using men to attain goals or scratch itches? She believed Mom had truly loved Dad. But what if Dad had lost his job and his status? What about this past year after his stroke? Would the woman in the diaries have slogged through caretaking chores day after day with patience and good humor the way Lauren did?

There was no answer to that. But Olivia was not going to run to Duncan this time.

She walked back through the woods and was about to re-emerge into the clearing when she heard voices and saw Sam coming up the steps from the water, followed by Duncan.

Shit!

The last thing she wanted was to have Sam see her standing there, cheeks tear-stained, eyes swollen, hair a windblown fright, obviously having come boo-hooing to find her new lover, who was technically still Sam's husband.

Without thinking, she darted back on to the path, then leapt into the woods and crouched behind a fir, hoping Duncan and Sam would go up to the Pattersons' and give Olivia time to sneak around and pretend she'd just returned from her trip.

No such luck. From the crescendoing voices, she could tell they'd started down the path toward the boathouse.

Olivia crouched farther, sweat trickling between her breasts, wishing she'd worn a darker color. Preferably something green, with needles. If Sam and Duncan were absorbed in conversation and kept their eyes on the path or straight ahead, she might get away with this.

Please. She'd been through enough humiliation lately.

'Olivia?' Sam's voice, high with amusement. 'Are you sick, peeing or studying nature?'

Olivia blinked wearily. Fabulous. She stood up, fists clenched, and stepped over ferns and logs to get back on to the path, trying not to look as hot, sticky and mortified as she was. 'Yeah. I've been identifying some planty things.'

Sam's face sobered immediately. 'Olivia, what happened? Are you okay?'

'Fine.' She slapped at a mosquito. 'Why?'

'You don't look fine.' Duncan was holding a manila folder, expression split between concern and I-wish-I-was-anywhere-else. She didn't blame him.

'Just an allergic reaction to Saturday.'

Duncan turned to his ex. 'Sam . . .'

'Sure. I'll see you later.'

'No. Actually, no.' Olivia held up a hand to stop him. 'I was taking a walk, feeling sorry for myself, and when I saw you, I panicked. I thought we'd make a slightly awkward trio.'

'We slightly do.' Sam wrapped his arms around himself, the first time Olivia had caught him in a female pose. 'But whatever. Life is awkward sometimes.'

'Yes.' Olivia scratched at her upper arm, where one of the flying shitheads had left a mark, wishing she had half Sam's courage. Or Duncan's, for that matter. 'Anyway, keep talking. I'm headed back up. Just had a bad moment. Feeling much better now.'

'Olivia . . .' Duncan was clearly unconvinced.

'Really.' She communicated as much sincerity as she could.

'Tell you what,' Sam said. 'Duncan has business stuff to look over. He can do that without me. I'll come with you. I need to talk to Georgia about scheduling.'

'Sure. Okay.' Olivia gave Duncan a brief reassuring smile, then set off with Sam toward the house. 'Thank you for being so civilized about all this. I know it must be strange.'

He remained silent as they passed the big cedar and the steps down to the shore. 'Honestly, right now there is so much for me to navigate – getting divorced, changing gender, keeping my son sane – you're kind of a gnat among charging elephants.'

Olivia laughed loud and long, a welcome release. 'That is beautiful.'

They were approaching the gazebo when Olivia's exhausted brain functioned well enough to give her an idea.

'Are you busy right now? Would you mind if we talked for a while? I'd like to ask you some personal questions that are completely inappropriate coming from a virtual stranger.'

Sam snorted. 'Gee, I can't think of anything I'd rather do.'

'You don't have to, it's just . . . someone who was close to me had gender issues.' She found herself clutching his forearm and lightened her grip. 'I would have liked to understand her better.'

'Do I get to know who?'

'A college friend.' She hated lying, but she couldn't expose her mother's truth.

'How about in there?' Sam pointed at the gazebo. 'Bug-free and private.'

'Perfect.' They went inside and pulled two of the chairs arranged around a small table to face the blue-green sea and the green-carpeted hills, today smudged by a sheer white veil of humidity. It was cooler out of the direct sun, but the breeze was non-existent. A sailboat heading out of the harbor had to use motor power to move.

'Thank you for doing this.'

Sam nodded, scratching his chin, reminding her of the way Duncan did the same.

'So my friend . . .' The phrase sounded clichéd and ridiculous. Sam would probably think Olivia was talking about herself. 'She had complete androgen insensitivity. Have you heard of it?'

'Don't think so.'

'She looked like and identified as a woman, but . . .' Olivia swallowed, feeling as if she were stripping her mother naked in front of this man, 'she was born without female reproductive organs.'

'Oh, okay, yeah, I think I have heard of that.'

'What I'm asking is . . . I don't know what I'm asking. I guess it's possible that a condition like that could screw you up, huh?'

Sam laughed, but not like he found anything funny. 'It could. Or not. Depends on the person. But yeah, with any deviation there's going to be "I am who I am, but what I am isn't normal" or "isn't mainstream", which is a better term. That's hard, whether you're talking about gender confusion or being born with only one arm.'

'So how do you deal with . . . I mean, she was totally convincing as a woman, but—'

'Yeah, so was I.' Sam gave another mirthless laugh.

'But she wasn't happy.' Olivia's voice broke. 'She finally killed herself.'

'Ah.' His face took on a look of deep, weary pain. 'I'm sorry to hear that.'

'There were other factors, other things. But I wonder how much of who she was and wasn't . . .' Olivia gestured in frustration. 'It may have nothing or little in common with what you're going through, but I thought I'd give it a shot.'

'Sure. Suicide is tough to understand, because survival is such a strong instinct for most of us. I will tell you that for people whose internal and external genders don't match, the attempted suicide rate is about ten times that of the general population. Forty percent versus four.'

Olivia's stomach dropped. 'Forty percent.'

'Yeah, it's grim. I don't know what your friend did or didn't feel, but that's a pretty significant statistic.'

'No kidding.' Olivia frowned. There was something in all this, some coherent truth that would help her, but it floated around her brain in jagged puzzle pieces she couldn't quite join together.

'Here's a question that might help.' Sam watched the sailboat putt-putt toward open water, where its crew must be counting on more of a breeze. 'What do you think makes someone a woman?'

'Boobs,' Olivia announced cheerfully.

Sam raised his eyebrows. 'Boobs, okay. So if you have a double mastectomy, are you still a woman?'

'Right, of course.'

'What about a hysterectomy? What if you had to have some toxic treatment for a disease that made you grow a mustache and beard, are you still a woman?'

'Yes.'

'How do you know? If all external signs point otherwise?'

Olivia gave up on her puzzle pieces and tried to put Sam's together. 'I guess . . . I'd know in my head that I am.'

'Exactly.' Sam was grinning like Olivia had won a contest. 'The way I know in my head that I'm a man, even though my body didn't do me the favor of going along with the program.'

'So my friend . . .'

'Your friend lived as a woman and was comfortable being feminine?'

'Extremely.'

'Then she was a woman in her brain, where it counts. I was pretending to be one. I could do okay with it. I loved Duncan. Still do, actually.'

'He said the same.'

'Did he? That's sweet.' His face softened, becoming female again in that instant, making Olivia wonder if, as he continued to transition, those other-gender moments would fade further or disappear entirely. 'We were meant to be really good friends.'

'I'm sure you always will be.' Olivia pushed away jealousy, a normal human emotion in the circumstances, but she was newly sensitive to any of her thoughts evoking Greedy Princess.

'My therapist told me that if your basic needs go unmet, you can function for a while, but eventually your subconscious will start shouting louder and louder to get your attention. Which can mean you start acting out, with uncharacteristic or self-destructive behavior.'

'Like what?' Olivia shifted uncomfortably, thinking of her recent love affair with alcohol and in-your-face confrontations.

'Depression, self-harm, promiscuity or infidelity, drugs, alcohol, you name it. For me, it was depression and cutting. I was also angry, unreasonable, not nice enough to Duncan, not that nice to my family or to my son, who deserved it least of all. It really shook me. I thought I'd been wrong all my life in assuming I was a good person. Since I've started transitioning, those behaviors have disappeared.'

'Oh wow.' Olivia was saying the words half to Sam, half to the part of herself still working on her puzzle, but now with this new bounty of pieces.

Jillian's method of proving that she was female was to become the ultimate woman, not only to those around her, but up on screen in front of the entire world. Likewise, when she faked her pregnancies, she didn't just flaunt the costumes around town, she called *People* and became pregnant with extensive international distribution.

After the furor over her children died down, when her husband strayed emotionally, when movie offers dried up and talk show appearances and commercials fell off, her outlet for feeling publicly and fabulously female went with them – a need no longer being met. If Sam's therapist was right, that could have been enough for Mom to start spiraling.

'The bottom line is that I feel truly happy sometimes now. I have moments of optimism. This might sound trite, but for the first time I'm realizing that life might not suck.'

'That is anything but trite; it's a beautiful gift.' Olivia lifted her hair off the sweating back of her neck, moved by Sam's openness and honesty with someone he barely knew. 'You were brave enough to recognize what you needed and to do what it took to get that need met.'

'I don't feel brave. You want to experience terror, go out in public in the town you grew up in dressed as a guy, and watch how people react.'

Olivia shuddered and let her hair drop. 'I want to go back and apologize to every trans person I've gawked at.'

'We're all guilty of it. I do a double-take when I see a dwarf, no matter how much I don't want to. We're geared to pay attention to whatever doesn't fit our expectations.' He lifted his face to catch the hint of a breeze. 'Probably what kept us alive in jungles and caves.'

'You've given me much to think about, Obi-Wan.'

Sam turned, looking apologetic. 'I've been lecturing.'

'No, no, I wanted to hear this.' Olivia touched his tattooed arm. 'I meant that as a compliment. You've helped me work some things out.'

'Hey, ladies. I was—' Georgia reached for the gazebo door, then let go to smack her forehead. 'La-*dy* and *gentleman*. Sorry, Sam. I swear, I have the hardest time remembering.'

Sam waved away her embarrassment. 'Trust me, it's an adjustment for all of us. Come on in.'

'Thank you.' She stepped inside, hair pulled back in a ponytail that made her look about thirty. 'I haven't had a chance to ask lately, how are you doing? With the hormones and all?'

'Great. They're definitely working.' He smiled winningly. 'Every day I become more and more of an asshole.'

Olivia and Georgia shouted with laughter.

'Seriously, the changes are amazing. My skin is getting thicker. Muscles still growing.' He flexed an impressive bicep. 'Less ass, more belly, narrower range of moods.'

'Oh, now that last one, I believe. Emotionally, Stuart is five of the seven dwarves – Sleepy, Grumpy, Bashful, Happy and Dopey.' Georgia pulled up a chair next to Olivia, grinning while Sam and Olivia cracked up. She didn't appear to be sweating a drop.

'What else happens?' Olivia was fascinated. The only way she'd ever imagined her body changing was swelling up with a baby. 'Do your boobs go away?'

'Nope. I'll need surgery for that. Not quite ready.'

'Ouch.' Georgia and Olivia spoke at the same time, crossing their arms protectively.

'Olivia and I were talking about what makes someone a woman,' Sam said. 'What do you think, Georgia?'

'Oh, that's easy.' She put her feet up on the support railing inside the screen. 'The ability to do twice the work for half the pay without complaining, then go home and do *all* the work for *no* pay, *still* without complaining.'

Olivia hooted. 'You are hilarious.'

'Georgia May Patterson, I did not know you had it in you to be so cynical,' Sam said.

'Oh, I'm generally not. I'm content with my life.'

'What's your secret?' Olivia asked.

'Piece of cake – just don't expect much.' Georgia joined in the giggling. 'Half kidding. I'm a simple person. I love my husband, I love our life here until winter sets in, then I love going away. I love my boy, he's healthy and doing well. That's all I need.'

Olivia sighed. 'I admire you.'

'Oh no, don't you go admiring me. You're half my age and you already amount to a lot more than I do.'

'Two thirds your age, and look at all the people you make happy every day.' Olivia pointed up to the house. 'I make no one happy.'

'I think you make someone pretty happy.' Sam nodded toward where Duncan was coming out of the woods, wearing a backpack and clutching the file folder.

'What's he got there?' Georgia shaded her eyes against the afternoon sun.

'Divorce papers.'

'Oh God. I wish you two could have made a go of—' She

clapped her hand over her mouth. 'Y'all can take me out and shoot me now.'

'No offense taken,' Olivia said, taking offense.

'Hey, Duncan.' Sam got to his feet and headed out the gazebo door. 'How did everything look?'

'I made some notes, signed the rest.' He handed Sam the file. 'I'm going to take the little boat out. Who wants to come?'

'Me!' Olivia jumped to her feet.

Duncan nodded. 'That's one. Sam? Georgia?'

'I've got stuff to do.' Sam gave him a hug. 'Have fun.'

'I have to get dinner.' Georgia lifted her feet down. 'Do y'all want something to take with you on your trip?'

Duncan pointed to the bag over his shoulder. 'Got plenty of food here, thanks. Don't worry about feeding Olivia tonight.'

'All-righty. I'll get to it for the big man. Nice chatting with you ladies.' She growled in exasperation. 'Lord have mercy, I will *never* get it right. Sorry, Sam.'

'I'll help you practice.' He patted her shoulder and walked with her up the path.

Olivia stepped out of the gazebo and sauntered up to Duncan. He looked tired. Not totally stone-faced, but not great. 'You have the best ideas.'

'I agree. Ready to go?'

She hesitated. She should fix her cried-off makeup. 'I should get sunscreen.'

'Got some.'

'And a jacket.'

'Got that too.'

'Extra life vest?'

'Yup.'

Her excuses were evaporating. Did it really matter what she

looked like? Even Mom didn't wear much makeup when she was—

Olivia stopped herself. Enough comparing. Just *enough*.

'Then I'm ready.' She peered curiously toward the shore. 'Where's your boat moored?'

'Straight across.' He pointed to the opposite coast. 'I've got a tender down by the boathouse.'

'A who?'

'Small boat to take you to the big boat. Didn't you grow up on an ocean?'

'Yes, I grew up on an ocean, just not with tenders.'

'City girl.' He fell into step beside her. 'We'll find some breezes. Cool off a little.'

'Good.' She wiped sweat off her forehead. 'This humidity is dragging me down.'

'Didn't used to be this bad. Not this often, anyway.'

'Climate change, huh.'

'Looks that way.'

They walked a few more steps.

Olivia nudged him gently. 'Are we really talking about the weather?'

'Uh-huh.' He nudged her back. 'Sometimes it beats what's really bugging us.'

'What's really bugging you?'

'Nothing serious. Paperwork. Splitting policies, reassigning beneficiaries. It's all good.'

'But sad. And final.'

'Yeah, that.' He flashed her a smile. 'How was your trip today?'

'Shitty, and also not.' She didn't want to pile another planet on to his Atlas shoulders. 'My grandmother can be a horrible person.'

'Then why visit?'

'She had something I wanted. A diary of my mother's. Her last one before she died.' She tensed, hoping he didn't ask too many questions.

'That's pretty intense. Did Horrible Grandma let you have it?'

'She did.' They passed the boathouse and turned along its far side toward the water, where a black inflatable skiff waited. 'It was depressing reading. But I guess good to find out.'

'Truth hurts? I don't know how I feel about that.' He untied the tow rope from a tree branch. Olivia helped him carry the boat down to the water. 'Hop in. Keep your weight low, and stay in the cen—'

'I *know* boats. Just not tender ones.' She climbed aboard and sat. 'We're tough in LA.'

'If you say so.' Duncan pushed off with a boathook into deeper water, then started the outboard, sending them chugging across the narrow bay.

Olivia turned and inhaled deeply, relishing the breeze, trying to figure out which of the boats on the opposite side was his. She settled on a beautiful medium-sized cruiser, forty-plus feet, with a dark green hull and wooden deck, brass rails polished to perfection, and was delighted to find out she was right.

'She's beautiful.'

He grinned as if she'd told him his child would win the lottery. 'She is. But today we're taking the little guy.'

They pulled up alongside a motorboat about half the cruiser's size. Olivia again managed not to look like a dork climbing aboard, though it was comforting to know that if she pitched over, Duncan would just roll his eyes and go about getting her out of the drink. A good man. Unflappable. Ballast for her big moods and emotions.

'What can I do to help?' Olivia watched him move around, readying the vessel, totally in his element. She envied him this passion he'd been able to indulge throughout his life.

'You can get a couple of beers out of the backpack. Food too, if you want.'

'Beer's fine for now.' She took out two, twisted off the tops and handed him one. 'Okay if I go sit up front?'

'Bow.'

'D'oh! I knew that! Okay if I go sit up in the bow?'

'Absolutely.' He started the engine, put the boat in gear and started them buzzing toward open water.

Olivia climbed forward and settled herself, watching the green rise of land slide past, occasionally putting the bottle to her lips for a good pull. She let out a long sigh, interrupted by a rude belch.

'Oh, *nice*.'

She twisted around, incredulous. 'You heard that?'

'So did the dead.'

'Oops.'

'Breeze blowing this way. You still hot and sweaty?'

'Less so. Why?'

'Hang on.' He was grinning mischievously. She found out why when the boat accelerated to a breath-stealing speed.

'Woo-hoo!' She climbed up to kneeling, bracing herself against the railing, and spread her arms *Titanic*-style as the boat roared over calm water, heading for outta-here.

The day's troubles receded with the town. Olivia was flying, away from pain, away from misery and decisions, away from her troubled sad self. Going somewhere free.

'Yee-haw!' She chugged the rest of the beer, tossed the bottle gently behind her on to one of the cushioned seats and yanked her shirt up and over her head, exhilarating in the push of cool wind on her torso, the blur of rushing water, the salty splashes that trickled down her heated skin.

After this ride with Duncan, she was going to call her sisters, fill them in on what she'd learned from Mom's diary; about her disintegration, which they'd probably seen more of than Olivia had; the truth about Lauren and Dad; about Mr Angel and the role Jillian had refused; about Mom's suicide. She'd tell them her theories about what had driven Mom to her end. She'd wait to talk about being Christina's daughter until they were all together.

The three of them would help each other through this. Olivia would no longer be the sister on the outside.

In a fit of mischief, she unhooked her bra and swung it in a circle over her head, tipped her head back and roared out one of her mother's favorite songs from the good old days, which probably weren't any better or any worse than the days Olivia was in now.

We . . . are . . . fam-i-ly.

Chapter 19

December 28, 2001 (Friday)

I can barely write this. I can barely keep from sobbing in rage. Eve. My beautiful Eve. It's taking all my strength to keep writing. Silas needs to die a horrible death in hell over and over for what he did to her. It's all my fault. All of it. He wanted to go upstairs with her, she didn't want to. Smart girl, taking charge of herself. I'm her mother, it's my job to keep her safe, and I told her she was being silly, I told her how much Silas loves kids. How could I have been so blind? How could I have been so careless with my own child?

Worst of all, she will pay the price for my sin.

I tried to tell her to be strong. I tried to explain that she will always encounter men like this because of her beauty. That she is not a victim, she is a goddess. I don't think she understood. But if she doesn't rise up now and take charge of this nightmare, she will suffer all her life, and it will be my fault.

I am starting to think my girls would be better off without me. I'm starting to think everyone would be.

'Nice kick!' Olivia gently returned the soccer ball to Jake, who lunged, gave a tremendous swipe and sent it rolling diagonally toward the bushes. Olivia had probably burned a day's worth of calories going after his miskicks. But every time she suggested they do something else, he insisted on more, more, more. The kid was going to be a soccer star. She admired his persistence.

Of course if Olivia had someone to chase down all her mistakes and make none of them matter, she'd be happy to keep playing too.

'This time kick it like you're a monkey.'

'What?' He wrinkled his nose the way he always did when she was being goofy.

'Like this.' She did a really horrible monkey imitation, arms out like the plastic Barrel of Monkeys toys, scratching under her arms and hooting as she kicked the ball. Monkeys probably did none of those things, but it worked for her, and, more importantly, for Jake.

He burst into bubbling laughter. Olivia's heart nearly burst every time he did. Such a free and uplifting sound. This was one of the reasons people had kids, one of the reasons she so desperately wanted them herself. Kids reminded you of the fun to be had in life, that every day could bring joyful new things if you knew where to look or took the time to invent them.

Jake did his own monkey imitation, more like an ape, grunting and lumbering, lips thrust forward, brows in a scowl. This time his kick went right to her.

'Perfect! Look at that.' Olivia was grateful for the chasing respite. She and Duncan had stayed out late on the boat, then spent the night together. Not a whole lot of sleep had happened. 'You are an excellent monkey soccer player.'

He cracked up again, pealing the kid-bell of happiness. It meant so much to Olivia to be enjoying herself like this, troubles pushed away, focusing only on the simian now. Finding out about her mother's suicide had to be the end in this series of life upsets, the last in a linked line of handkerchiefs drawn from a magician's sleeve. Another and another and another, and just when you think they'll keep coming forever, poof, the last one flies out and it's over.

There were more tough times ahead, difficult decisions, more grief to process. But here on this bright, sunshiny morning with Jake, Olivia could kick like a monkey and laugh.

'Olivia.'

She turned, mid hooting romp, to see Stuart pulling his truck into the driveway, face stern.

Olivia sighed. What now? He didn't approve of her spending primate time with Jake?

Georgia came out of the house looking pale. 'Jake, honey, come inside now.'

'Why? I wanna say hi to Stuart.'

'Okay.' Georgia watched her husband climb out of the truck, biting her lower lip, then flicked an anxious glance at Olivia. 'Quick now.'

'Hi, Stuart.'

'Hey, buddy.' He bent down – way down – to kiss Jake's cheek.

'How come you're home now instead of later?'

'I have to talk to Olivia about something.' He lifted and replaced his grimy baseball cap. 'Why don't you go hang out with Georgia? I'll come inside in a little while.'

'Oh-kaaay.' After five angry stomps toward the house, Jake returned to monkey scampering. 'What animal am I, Gorgy?'

'I don't know, sweetie.' She beckoned urgently. 'C'mon, come inside.'

Olivia turned warily to Stuart. 'Am I in trouble again?'

'No. It's bad news, though, Olivia.'

Her heart stopped. She could barely manage a whisper. 'Duncan?'

For one bizarre second, Stuart looked astonished. 'No. Not Duncan. He's fine. Lauren called me. It's your dad.'

'Dad.' She waited, knowing already, but unable to stop hoping she was wrong.

'He had another stroke. A massive bleed in his brain. He's alive, but . . . there's no hope he'll recover. Or even wake up.'

'Oh no.' Her voice was high and breathy, not her voice at all. The bastard magician had saved one more handkerchief. 'No, no.'

'He was taken to St Joseph's in Bangor. He's on life support.' Stuart was breathing hard, as if he'd been running. 'Lauren is waiting for the three of you to arrive, then she'll have the breathing tube removed and let him go.'

Olivia squashed her possessive, knee-jerk reaction that it was not Lauren's decision to make. It was. Lauren was Dad's wife. More to the point, being allowed to die was exactly what Dad would want, and the same gift Olivia and her sisters would have given him. 'I'll go right away.'

'I'll drive you.'

'No.' An hour in the car with Mr Disapproval was the last thing she needed. 'I'll be fine. I'll go and get my—'

'Lauren will need me.' His features set. 'This is her loss too. He was her whole adult life. She needs family.'

'*We're* family,' she snapped without thinking, then wilted. 'No. Sorry. We're not. *I* haven't been. I've been unfair to Lauren. I was planning to tell her so next time I saw her.'

'You'll get the chance.'

Olivia opened her mouth to respond. Instead, her face twisted into ugly, tearless sobbing. Stuart stood immobile, except for the strange stuttering breathing, probably hoping an Olivia-sized sinkhole would open under her feet.

Then he shocked the hell out of her by pulling her into his

big arms, and she realized his funny breathing was a brave attempt to keep from crying.

Olivia returned the hug, wanting to give as well as receive comfort. His shirt smelled like sawdust and varnish, which made her wish Duncan was there, and then in the next second made her glad he wasn't.

This was her tragedy. She and her sisters would cope.

Her sobs quieted. She stepped back, holding herself tall. 'Thank you, Stuart. Is Lauren calling my sisters or would she like me to?'

Her offer clearly pleased the Great Unpleasable One. 'She's called them by now.'

'When did you want to leave?'

'I'll shower, pack a bag. Half an hour?'

'I'll be ready.'

'Okay.' He started to walk away, then turned back. 'I'm sorry about your dad.'

She managed a smile. 'Now you tell me.'

'I'm worried first about my sister.' His deep voice became raspy. 'Daniel was the love of her life. And he's been my brother for fifteen really good years.'

Olivia blinked. 'You and Georgia spent time with them?'

'They're an hour away, Olivia.' He turned away in disgust. 'They're family.'

Olivia folded her arms around her middle and followed him, chastened puppy, into the house. Jake ran to Stuart. Georgia gave Olivia a hug that smelled like chili powder and felt like true friendship.

'I'm so sorry,' Georgia whispered. 'Daniel is such a lovely man. Stuart and I had so many good times with him and Lauren. We'll miss him.'

'Me too.' Olivia pulled away before she could break down

again, ashamed that she'd never thought of Dad's other family, Lauren's family, and how much they must have meant to each other. 'I'm going to get ready.'

'Are you sad?' Jake was watching her from Stuart's arms.

'I am. My dad is dying.'

'Oh. My great-grandpa died.'

'You were sad too, I bet.'

'Not really.' He scrunched up his face. 'He didn't smile and he smelled funny.'

'Sam's grandfather had Parkinson's. I wish you'd known him before he got sick, Jake.' Georgia reached for the little boy. 'C'mon, baby. Let's let Stuart and Olivia get ready to go.'

'I'm not a baby.'

'Of course not. You two need anything for the drive?'

'No. Thanks.' Olivia headed upstairs, thinking that if she'd asked for baked Alaska, Georgia would probably have been able to whip one up by the time they left.

She'd set one foot into her room when the phone rang. Rosalind. Olivia's breath caught. This would be so hard.

'Hi, Rosalind. Lauren called you?'

'Yes. I'm on my way to LaGuardia. Are they . . . are they sure he won't recover? He came back so far from the last one. He was in a coma for a week before he woke up. Who's to say he can't do that again?'

'Rosalind, sweetie, his brain was destroyed this time.'

'I know, but . . .' Gentle sobs came over the line, then Rosalind exhaled forcefully. 'Sorry. I'm in denial, I guess.'

'It's hard to take in.'

'Yes.' She took a shaky breath. 'My flight arrives in Bangor around four. When will you get there?'

'In about an hour and a half. You need picking up from the airport?'

'No, Eve is driving up. She'll get me.'

'Okay.' Olivia had to work hard to keep the tears back. 'See you late afternoon, then. I love you.'

'Love you too.'

Olivia ended the call, thought of calling Eve, but decided to get ready first, to make sure Stuart didn't have to wait for her.

Eve called when she was half undressed. Olivia pounced on the phone. 'Eve.'

'Hi, Olivia. How are you doing?'

'Still in shock. I'm sure you are too.' Her voice broke. 'I just saw Dad last week. He was so much like his old self. We had a drink together, he teased me . . .'

'I know. It's brutal. How are you holding up? It's bad for me, but life has been using you for target practice lately. And you're all alone there.'

'I'm okay.' Not alone; among family and friends. 'I can't wait to see you and Rosalind. I need sister time.'

She closed her eyes, thinking of all the complicated and emotional things she'd planned to tell them. Those might have to wait.

'I'll see you tonight, sweetie. Rosalind and I should be there in time for dinner.'

'Can't wait. Love you.'

'Same here.'

Olivia managed a smile. Rosalind could say *I love you* to her mail carrier. The words were harder for Eve.

She showered quickly and changed into white capris with a teal top. A cheerful outfit to combat gloomy reality.

No time for elaborate makeup. She'd only cry it off anyway.

'Olivia?' Georgia was calling up the stairs.

Was Olivia late already? Was Stuart impatient?

'*Coming.*' She grabbed up a few pairs of panties, a couple of shirts and a pair of shorts to bring with her. No telling how long she'd be gone.

A knock came on the door.

Olivia rolled her eyes. 'I'm *coming.*'

'It's me.' Duncan stepped into the room. 'I couldn't get away sooner, I'm sorry. I was with a client.'

She stopped where she was, holding her deodorant and cosmetic bag, drinking in the tall, solid, brown-eyed sight of him like he was a cold beer in a hot baseball park. 'I didn't expect you.'

'Why not?'

'Because . . .' She was at a loss to explain. 'You don't owe me . . . I mean . . .'

He grinned. 'Because me showing up to support you through a terrible time smacks of serious commitment?'

'No.' Olivia's chin started to wobble. She'd always gone running to men for support. She'd never had one come running to provide it. 'It's just really sweet of you.'

He walked over to her. 'I'm so sorry about your dad, Olivia. I know how much you love him.'

Her chin wobbled harder. 'Stop being nice to me.'

'Okay.' He touched her cheek. 'You look so beautiful without expensive shit on your face.'

Olivia loved him . . . like Rosalind loved her mail carrier. For rescuing her from a precarious state by being a jerk at the perfect time. She tossed the deodorant and cosmetic case on to the bed. 'Thank you, I think.'

'You'll be okay? I can take the afternoon off if you need me.'

She loved him more. Maybe less like the mail carrier. 'I'll be fine. My sisters will meet me there.'

He watched her, measuring.

'Truly, Duncan. I can do this.'

'If you're sure.' He kissed her so sweetly, it took all her strength not to have a snot-filled meltdown in his arms. 'You have my number if you need me.'

'Yes.'

He held her for a long time, cheek pressed against hers. Tears began spilling, peaceful, calm tears. There would be harder ones later.

'Take care of yourself.' He drew back. 'Don't forget to eat.'

Olivia nodded, emotion that had nothing to do with grief swelling in her chest until she could barely breathe. It was as if she'd finally pecked through a cynical shell and emerged, wobbly and vulnerable, into a new world of feeling, terrifying in its intensity.

She wanted to push him away, run from the room and back into safety.

'Let me know when you get there.' Duncan walked to the door, paused for a simple lift of his hand. 'Have a safe trip.'

'Thanks.' Olivia watched him leave and allowed herself to savor him, the emotion, the transformation she'd felt in his arms. She was halfway to falling in love. In time, either the rest of that love would come, or the first half would evaporate. Time meant staying in Belfast, finding her immediate future – maybe the rest of her life – here.

A door opening in the hallway forced her to shrug off her Duncan hypnosis and rush to retrieve her overnight bag.

Pack. She needed to pack. She would much rather stand around mooning, but she had to drive for an hour in a car with a guy who hated her in order to sit in a hospital waiting for her father to die.

Deep breath. She was strong. She was invincible. She was going to be late if she didn't get moving.

Five minutes later, she'd stuffed her bag with whatever felt necessary – there were stores in Bangor – and ran downstairs to find Stuart waiting, looking unlike his usual self in neat khakis and a button-down shirt, even a clean cap.

'Sorry it took me so long. My sisters called and then—'

'Don't worry.' His voice and face were kind. 'Georgia, we're off.'

Georgia emerged from the kitchen with a bulging plastic grocery bag. 'I packed you some—'

'Georgie, it's an *hour* drive.'

'I know, love, but hospital food is awful, and I need to feed people.' She thrust the bag at him. 'Mom was the same. Soon as someone took sick or a family member died – ours or any family – she'd run to the kitchen. Y'all are lucky I didn't try to fit a whole ham in there.'

Olivia totally understood, because she felt the same way. How many plates of cookies and brownies, pots of chamomile tea and artfully arranged fruit platters had she brought to her mother during her dark times? A frightened kid trying to cure mental illness with sweets.

With a jolt, the obvious became so ridiculously obvious that even she, Queen of Denial, couldn't miss it. She hadn't always been an actress. She'd always been a cook. Whatever she found to do from here would involve her lifelong passion, a passion she'd never taken seriously, simply because her mother hadn't.

'Thank you, Georgia.' Olivia hugged her new friend affectionately. 'I'm not sure how long I'll stay in Bangor. Sorry to back out on any time with Jake.'

'Don't you give that a thought. Not for a minute.' Georgia turned to Stuart. 'Give Lauren my love. And Daniel. Talk to him, both of you. I read that hearing is the last thing to go. He might be able to understand.'

'Sure.' Stuart pushed open the door and stepped outside.

Olivia followed him, a little shaky, not quite ready for what was about to happen, either to her father or to her in the car with Stuart.

They loaded their bags and got into his slightly battered pickup in silence. He pulled away with one last wave to his wife, who stood in the doorway absorbing tears with the corner of her apron.

'This won't be easy.' He glanced at Olivia. 'Letting your dad go.'

'No.' Olivia desperately wanted to stick buds in her ears and shut out whatever else he was going to say during the trip.

'You're close to him, I take it.'

'Yes. Lauren told you that?'

'She did.'

Olivia leaned her head against the window, feeling as if she had washed clean the distorting lens through which she'd always viewed her childhood. 'Dad did the bulk of raising me. I idolized my mom, but our time together was . . . more about her.'

'You helped raise your sisters?'

'No, no, of course not. I was busy working on my primadonna lifestyle.'

Stuart snorted, put on his blinker and passed a slow-going sedan. 'I want to apologize for being angry about you and Duncan.'

Olivia peeked over at him, but he looked as sincere as he sounded. 'What changed your mind?'

'Your face when I said I had bad news.' He gave a quick shake of his head. 'Duncan was the first person you thought of.'

Olivia shrugged. 'Yeah, well.'

'Yeah well.' He chuckled, clearly having seen through her

attempt at nonchalance. 'And then *his* face when he walked into the house and demanded to know where you were. Never seen him move as fast as he did up those stairs.'

'He's a good person.'

'He is.'

'I care about him a lot.'

'I'm glad.'

They drove for some time in a silence that wasn't as painfully awkward as Olivia would have thought. She didn't even take her earbuds out of her purse. In fact, she actually broke the silence herself. On purpose.

'Tell me what you know about my dad.'

'Good guy.' Stuart checked his rear-view mirror and made an unflattering remark about tailgaters. 'Best thing about him is how happy he makes my sister.'

'You and she are close.'

'Yep. Our younger brother, Ben, had some problems. Mom and Dad weren't around much. They had to work. She protected me from him, from a lot of things.'

'Was he – Ben – mentally ill?'

'Maybe. Back then we called him a mean drunk.'

Labels changed, too bad the behavior didn't. 'So Lauren helped raise you?'

'I guess she did.' He threw Olivia a wry half-smile. 'No chance to become a prima donna around her, though. She was a drill sergeant.'

'That's what my sisters said. I was pretty much out of the house by the time she and Dad married. I do know she cured Eve of her goth period pretty quickly.'

'Sounds like her.' He muttered again as a sports car roared by them.

'When did you meet my dad?' She was shamelessly prying,

curious how much Stuart knew about Dad and Lauren's affair. About Jillian's condition.

'When they started dating.' He cleared his throat. 'After your mother died.'

After your mother died. He was careful to point that out. And quite the dramatic throat-clearing, too. 'You knew they were having an affair.'

Long silence. 'Yes.'

'I knew also. Stumbled over it. Did Lauren tell you?'

'Nope. I read a letter he sent her. Given who he was, I never dreamed it was personal. I read one of his books when I was a kid.'

'You wanted to be an actor?'

He laughed as if she'd asked if he wanted to shove a spike through his head. 'Not me. Lauren did, though. She had the book around. I was angry with her at first. I thought he was messing with her, that she was naïve.'

Olivia rolled her eyes. 'You really respect and trust us celebrities, don't you.'

'Not much.' He glanced at her; she made sure he could enjoy her scowl. 'I thought Lauren was being a fool, wasting her life on someone she couldn't have.'

'What did she think?'

Stuart shrugged. 'She thought it was love. The real deal. Turns out she was right.'

Olivia relaxed back into her seat. She still turned queasy at the thought of her father and Lauren's affair being about true love. But Mom's third diary made it easier to stomach, as did having heard the story from Lauren's point of view.

A little easier. It would still take time to internalize so much new information.

'All I had to do was see Daniel with her and I knew she was

safe. Around this great man, this hugely successful person, she was still totally herself. He adored exactly who she was. That meant a lot to me.'

Safe. Totally herself. The words lingered in Olivia's mind. She hadn't really felt safe with Mom, whose moods swung radically with her illness and level of sobriety. She'd felt safe with Dad, but given his gruff, judgmental nature, she had undoubtedly altered her behavior to please him. With Derek, she'd felt loved, she'd felt committed, she'd felt passion and the thrill of effortless comradeship. But not safe. The danger had been exciting. She'd told herself she'd be bored with a different kind of man, but she'd never stopped to wonder why she'd instantly agreed to Dad's demand for a prenup, why she still kept her accounts separate, why she'd occasionally sneak peeks at Derek's phone, something she told herself over and over not to do, but seemed compelled to. With him, Olivia had felt like a needy, neurotic control freak.

The discussion with Sam came back to her, like a cheesy movie flashback. When your basic needs weren't being met, your subconscious started shouting to get your attention, forcing you into uncharacteristic behavior.

Olivia felt safe with Duncan. She felt totally herself.

She moved so suddenly her elbow banged the door of the truck and scored a funny-bone bullseye, sending pain and tingles through her forearm.

Rub it. Her mother's recipe for curing anything from cold to itch to pain.

'Dad is a total control freak. Everything in the house had to be up to his standards, including the people in it.'

'The way I figure it, Lauren needs someone to take care of, and your dad needs someone to take care of him.' Stuart lifted his hands briefly from the wheel. '*Voilà*.'

Voilà. Basic needs met. It sounded so simple. Olivia would have liked it to be that simple for her too. She'd have liked to meet the right guy after college, get married and have a boatload of kids exactly as smart and cute as Jake.

Olivia didn't choose simple. She'd chosen Derek.

The rest of the trip passed without much traffic or talking. The closer they got to Blue Hill, the more reality intruded on this hour of suspended action, and the more anxious Olivia became. By the time they pulled into the main parking lot at St Joseph's, she was shaky again, afraid she'd faint or cause a scene, remembering her out-of-control grief after learning Mom was dead.

But she was twenty years older now, and better prepared for what would happen, what had to happen. Now that they'd arrived, she was also unexpectedly grateful for Stuart's gigantic, calm presence. He'd be the buffer she needed between her and Lauren until she could get herself stable enough to say what needed to be said.

Eating humble pie had never been Olivia's forte. She had more experience throwing it.

She and Stuart found their way to the ICU and spoke to a blond nurse, who led them into a small private room where Daniel Braddock, teacher of generations of actors, inspiration to thousands more, lecturer, writer of books, husband to one of the world's greatest stars, father of three adoring daughters, lay terrifyingly still, a horrible tube extending from his throat. There was no sound in the room but the creepy inhale-exhale of the respirator breathing for him, and the beeps of a huge computer lit with red graphs, dials, and numbers.

Beep. Beep. Beep.

Lauren sat with her back to them, leaning across the bed, holding her husband's hand, gazing into his face.

'Lauren?' Stuart spoke hesitantly from behind Olivia in the doorway.

Lauren jumped and turned, face lighting at the sight of her brother.

'Hi, Lauren.' Olivia stepped reluctantly into the room.

'Stuart.' Lauren got up from the chair and made a beeline for her brother. He enveloped her small, plump form in his big arms, eyes squeezing shut, forehead creased in sympathy and pain.

Olivia turned away, feeling like an intruder. She approached her father, hating all the needles, tubes and machines, and laid her hand on his warm arm, thinking of the cold that was to come. 'Hi, Daddy. It's Olivia. I'm sorry you're . . . not doing so well. Rosalind and Eve will be here in—'

Her father moved his head. Olivia gasped. 'He moved. Dad moved. He heard me.'

'The nurse says that's involuntary. Like a newborn.' Lauren sat again and pulled her chair closer to the bed, sniffing, wiping her eyes. Stuart positioned himself sentinel-like beside her.

Again Olivia felt like the intruder in a situation she belonged to, a special role she'd earned all on her own, through years of fighting this woman's legitimate role in her life.

'There's not enough of his brain left undamaged for him to be able to respond consciously. He might hear us, though. There's no reason not to hope.'

Beep. Beep. Beep.

'Olivia's here, Daniel.'

Olivia kept herself from pointing out that she'd just *told* him that. She'd promised to do better.

'Stuart's here too.'

'Hi, Daniel.' Stuart had taken off his cap and held it at chest level, squashing and unsquashing it. 'It's good to see you. Georgia sends love.'

He glanced nervously at Olivia, clearly out of topics to discuss with a brain-dead brother-in-law.

Beep. Beep. Beep.

Olivia took a deep breath. She hadn't prepared for this either. 'Dad. I'm still staying with the Pattersons. It's been really nice, and so nice of them to have me. I'll be moving on soon. I don't know if I'll go back to LA. I'm divorcing Derek . . . uh, you know that.'

She turned helplessly to Stuart and Lauren, who stared helplessly back.

Beep. Beep. Beep.

What could she possibly say to him that would matter now?

'Tell him things you remember about him as a father,' Lauren suggested.

Olivia was embarrassed for, what, the four millionth time? All she'd talked about was herself.

'Dad . . .' *Beep. Beep. Beep.* 'Can we stop those fucking machines?'

'Olivia.' Lauren looked stunned. 'They're keeping your father alive until your sisters get here.'

'No, God, no.' Olivia put her hands to her head. 'I'm sorry. I meant the beeping. Can we stop that?'

'Oh.' Lauren started to get up.

'I'll ask.' Stuart put his cap back on and left the room.

Beep. Beep. Beep.

Alone with Lauren. It was time.

Olivia got up and hurried after Stuart, touched his sleeve. 'Can I . . . have some time with your sister? There are things I need to say. Good things.'

He nodded, looking pleased. 'I'll get us something to drink. Text me when you want me to come back.'

'I don't have your—'

'Lauren gave me yours when you first showed up. I'll text first. Just respond when you're ready.'

'Thank you.' She put as much sincerity and depth into the words as she could, reaching to touch his sleeve again. 'For a lot of things, Stuart.'

He nodded, embarrassed now, gave her the nicest smile he'd ever summoned for her, and lumbered toward the exit.

Back in the room, Olivia found Lauren with her forehead resting on the mattress next to the lump under the blankets that used to be her husband.

'Lauren.'

She sat up, wiping her reddened eyes, fumbled for her glasses and put them back on. 'Yes.'

Olivia's heart contracted in sympathy. She sat back on her side of the bed. 'I wanted to apologize to you for the way I acted last time, for the things I said.'

Lauren turned sharply toward the door of the room, as if she expected someone to appear at any moment. Olivia knew her well enough not to follow her gaze. Long habit born out of her shyness.

'I went to see Grandma Betty. She gave me the diary Mom wrote toward the end of her life. I've read it.'

Beep. Beep. Beep.

Lauren gave a brief nod, flush visible in the V of her floral print shirt.

'I have a better understanding now of who she was and why she made the choices she did. But I also have a better understanding of your relationship with Dad. I am . . .' The next words were still hard to say. 'Sorry that I judged you so harshly.'

Lauren looked over at the machine showing her husband's vitals. 'I took your mother's place. It was natural that the three

329

of you would resent me for that. Especially given who your mother was . . . and who I am.'

'I was by far the worst. I'm sorry for how I've treated you.'

The flush was well up Lauren's neck. 'Thank you, Olivia. I accept your apology.'

'I do have some questions.'

'Yes.' She folded her hands in her lap. 'I expect you do.'

Beep. Beep. Beep.

'Hi there.' A fresh-faced brunette nurse entered the room. 'I'm Heidi. You must be one of Mr Braddock's daughters?'

'Olivia.'

'Olivia, hi. I'll turn off the noise, okay? As long as someone is in here with him. Your sisters are coming soon?'

'In a few hours.'

'We'll be taking out the breathing tube then.' She fiddled with the machine, and mercifully the electronic symphony cut out, though its loss made Dad's artificial inhale-exhale that much louder, a dubious improvement. 'I'm right outside. Call if you need anything, okay?'

'Thank you.' Olivia waited to turn back to Lauren until Heidi was gone. 'How did you know Grandma had the diaries?'

'She told your father. He said to burn them. I contacted her and told her not to.'

'Really?' Olivia was stunned. Behind Dad's back? She wouldn't have thought Lauren capable. Obviously she hadn't known her stepmother well at all.

Lauren stood abruptly, fiddling with her wedding and engagement rings. 'You should know that I did not approve, never approved of the way your mother and father chose to keep the circumstances of your births from you and your sisters. But it was not my decision. I honored my promise to Daniel to stay silent until Rosalind told me last summer that you'd found

330

out about your mother's infertility. At that time your father was just recovering from his stroke, in no shape to deal with any of it. I . . . had to make decisions on my own.'

Olivia nodded. Lauren had made the right ones. She'd acted with more honest integrity than either Daniel or Jillian. 'You told Grandma to send the diaries to us?'

'I thought it might be easier if you got them anonymously.' She sat back down, looking uncertain. 'Needless drama maybe, but if you knew I'd sent them, I was afraid you'd come here looking for answers and upset your father. If you'd known your grandmother had them . . . well, who knows what Betty would have said about your mother. I thought Jillian should be able to speak for herself. I don't know, maybe that was a mistake.'

'I have no idea. But thank you.' Olivia watched her dad make another random head movement, thinking how much easier it was to talk to Lauren while they could both concentrate on a man they loved. Or on what was left of him. 'It's so strange to see Dad lying there but know in some sense that he's gone.'

'Yes.'

'Do you think he's in pain?'

'They said not.'

They sat in silence, listening, watching the machine count out the rest of Daniel Braddock's life. Pulse rate. Oxygen rate. Heart rate. Respiration rate. Morphine level.

'Lauren.' Olivia cleared her throat. 'When I was with Betty, I found out that Christina was my birth mother.'

Lauren turned to stare. 'Christina?'

Olivia was taken aback. Lauren had known who Rosalind and Eve's birth mothers were. Why wouldn't she know about Christina? Had Dad never told her?

'Grandma Betty showed me the picture of her holding me as a newborn.'

Lauren continued to stare, her face hot pink, fingers twisting her rings. Olivia stared back.

'Betty must have been confused. Christina gave up her baby girl for adoption. We don't know where she is.'

Olivia went back to watching the living corpse that was her father, disappointment cutting. Another tie to Jillian severed. 'Do you know who my birth mother is?'

Lauren's breath went in sharply. 'Yes.'

Olivia turned to her. Lauren was no longer looking at Olivia or her husband, but down at her fidgeting hands.

'Who?' Olivia could barely get a whisper out. 'Who is my mother?'

Lauren swallowed convulsively.

'I am.'

Chapter 20

December 30, 2001 (Sunday)

Silas Angel offered me the part. The part of a lifetime that I know will finally get me that Oscar I deserve, that will get my beautiful career back on track.

That will literally save my life.

I told him to shove the part up his ass, and that if he ever came near one of my girls again, I would shoot him myself. He said I'd never work in Hollywood again. I told him that line had been used so many times it was beyond pathetic, and so was he.

He was also right. I will never work in Hollywood again.

I am finished.

'You.' Olivia stared at her stepmother's – no, good God, her *mother's* – profile. '*You.*'

'Yes.'

She made an incoherent sound and jumped to her feet, fists clenched. This woman. *This* woman was her mother! This little . . . overweight, bland, pink—

Listen to yourself, Olivia.

Thank God she at least had enough decency to be ashamed. In the next second, she was furious. 'You lied to me. You

333

said you and Dad never . . . did that while my mother was alive! You said you waited until after she—'

'No. I did not lie.' Lauren stood, composed now, though her face still glowed with color. 'I was the first woman Daniel and Jillian picked for their secret baby scheme. They held open auditions in Maine for a movie part. I didn't get the part, but Daniel chose me out of the group. It was a business deal. Jillian knew every time we were together.

'After you were conceived, it was over between Daniel and me physically, until a year after Jillian died. I never said anything to contradict that. It's the truth.'

Olivia's brain tried desperately to find something, anything to latch on to, to keep her from spinning further into this bewildering void. 'But you stayed in touch with him.'

'Yes, we stayed in touch.'

'How? Why?'

'I suppose this will seem impossible to you.' Lauren's tone turned bitter. 'But over all the months it took to conceive you, your father and I fell in love.'

'Dad loved my mother.' Olivia hurled the words at her.

Lauren didn't flinch. 'Yes, he did. But she drained him. She took everything he had and gave him nothing back. For years and years and years.'

He felt safe with Lauren. Olivia understood it as clearly as if Lauren had explained using those exact words.

'But I still—' Olivia turned toward her father's passive body in horror. 'Can he hear us?'

'I think it's fine if he does.' Lauren put her hands on her hips. 'This conversation should have happened when each of you was old enough to understand. Barring that, it should have happened immediately after Jillian died. It's the only thing I asked Daniel for that he refused me. He believed he was honoring your mother's wishes and her memory. He believed absolutely that the three of you would never find out.'

Olivia sank back into her chair. She had no idea how to deal with this. Arguments she knew how to do. Hissy fits? She was a pro. But how to nurture outrage when everything Lauren said rang true? When Olivia had read her mother's diaries and gotten a glimpse of the woman Lauren described? When every bit of this absurd situation had been created and maintained by Jillian Croft with little thought as to what would happen to her daughters if the secret ever came out?

Obviously, like her partner in the scheme, dying slowly on the bed next to them, she never thought it would. The perfect crime.

Tears came. Slowly, but without stopping. Finally Olivia ceded control, put her hands to her face and bent double, body heaving with sobs until she could regain her calm. At some point during her spell, Lauren crossed the room and put a hand on her shoulder.

'I'm sorry. I know this isn't the story you wanted for your life. Not one anyone would want. I'm well aware that you and I . . .' She squeezed. She had strong fingers for a small woman. 'I'm sure I'm not your first choice for a birth mother.'

Olivia sat up and wiped her eyes, knowing Lauren better than to try to lie. 'Maybe not. But it's hard to see Jillian Croft as much of a first choice either anymore. I feel as if I didn't know her at all.'

'Of course you did. The parts you knew weren't fake. They're still there. And she loved you, Olivia, all of you, very much. Your dad said so over and over. He talked about her a lot, you know.'

'He did? To you?' Olivia forced herself to leave her lavish self-pity party. 'You didn't mind?'

'It was hard. But I understood.'

She understood. Olivia tried to imagine herself calm in *any* situation in which someone she adored went on and on about an ex. Hysteria would happen. 'Who knows besides you, me and Dad?'

'No one.'

'Grandma? Stuart?'

'The only other person who knew was the midwife to the three of you, Christina. Your father and mother did their job well.'

'God, this is so effed up.' Olivia swiped at her cheeks.

'I'll get you a tissue.' Lauren walked over to the box beside Daniel's bed, pulled out two and handed them over.

Olivia dried her eyes and blew her nose, breaths shuddering like a toddler's after a tantrum.

'I'm glad I skipped the mascara to—' She let out a huff of exasperation. 'Really? My dad is dying, my role-model mother turned out to be a horrible person, and I'm worried about how I *look*?'

'You were raised to care how you look. Your mother was obsessed. She had to be in her line of work. It makes perfect sense.' Lauren smiled down at her, then reached and pushed back a strand of hair that had gotten caught on Olivia's forehead.

A sweet mother-daughter moment.

Olivia was *not* ready for this.

'Well.' Lauren's beatific expression slumped.

Something in Olivia's face must have communicated her unease at the touch. For once, she felt guilty for the pain she'd caused this woman, whom she'd misjudged, misunderstood and underestimated for decades. 'What is it?'

'Nothing. I just . . . I've thought about this so many times – telling you the truth. Now it's here and I thought I'd . . .'

Lauren shrugged and looked away. 'Frankly, I'm finding it really uncomfortable.'

Olivia snorted. Lauren grinned, and they actually shared a giggle. A brief one, ending with them both awkwardly turning back to the faux-breathing ex-person on the hospital bed.

It was a start.

The rest of the afternoon ticked by dismally. Stuart was summoned back in. The trio watched and waited, attempted conversation, watched and waited some more. They took turns leaving to eat Georgia's loving gift of food, to get a drink or use the bathroom.

Finally, roughly two hundred years later, Rosalind texted that she'd landed. Then that she'd met up with Eve at the airport. Not long after, their footsteps and voices sounded in the hallway and their anxious, pale faces appeared at the door.

Olivia launched herself at them. More tears. Her sisters came into the room; each greeted Lauren and Stuart, then approached the bed. The mood returned to somber as they tried to comprehend the horror of what had happened.

More chairs were found; the mourners sat talking in low voices, to Daniel or to each other, until Nurse Heidi broke the tension by entering the room, then created more by the significance of her presence.

'Hi there. Everyone here? Are we ready?' She addressed Lauren respectfully, hitting the right tone, not too chipper, not too doleful.

Lauren nodded firmly. 'Yes.'

A dark burn of adrenaline traveled through Olivia's chest; she moved restlessly, noting Stuart, Eve and Rosalind doing the same. Lauren alone stayed calm and resolute, earning more of Olivia's respect. She wasn't sure she'd have half that strength in her place.

'I'm going to have you all leave for a moment, while I remove his breathing tube. It's probably not something you'll want to watch. Okay?'

Everyone was okay with that. In fact, after hearing a few of the sounds that traveled through the curtain, by unspoken agreement they all moved farther into the main ICU until Nurse Heidi came out for them.

Olivia followed her family back into the room, numb with dread. Dad still lay there, now minus the tube and mouthpiece and tape. It was good to see his face unencumbered, though his chapped mouth remained open and his breathing was straight out of a monster movie, rasping and uneven, requiring great heaves of his chest as his body struggled for life, even as it was leaving him.

Each family member took a turn, bending next to his ear, speaking words of love, forgiveness, humor – who knew what each person shared?

Then they sat, waiting expectantly, tear-filled eyes flicking to the machine, watching for the oxygen levels in his blood to fall below what could support his heart and brain. It was a serene, pure moment of sadness and of love.

Except half an hour later, they were still there and Daniel Braddock was still breathing.

And a half-hour after that.

By the next half-hour, they'd resumed talking to each other, shooting frequent nervous glances at the machine monitoring Daniel's vitals. Each time his oxygen levels dropped, conversation would falter. Each time, his heart rate would speed alarmingly, trying to make up for the loss. Through it all, the heavy, rasping breaths continued.

Olivia almost missed the beeping.

Nurse Heidi stole in every now and then to suction Daniel's

airways, moisten his lips. Once she dialed up the morphine level when she decided his breathing had become too labored.

On and on and on went Daniel Braddock's death, a bizarre suspension between living and not, until Olivia felt like urging him to let go, to leave them. There was no point prolonging this terrible limbo.

The next time Heidi came into the room, Olivia pounced. 'How long will this . . . take?'

'I'm afraid there's no telling.' She smiled patiently, in spite of the fact that desperate, grieving families had undoubtedly been asking the same how-does-death-work? questions as long as she'd been working there.

'Do we have time to go to dinner and come back?'

Heidi consulted Dad's machine. 'I would think absolutely. He's stable right now. I can let you know if anything changes.'

'I'm not leaving him.'

'Lauren.' Olivia faced her stepmother – her birth mother – and folded her arms.

Lauren folded hers back.

Neither of them needed to wonder where Olivia got her stubbornness.

'We can bring Lauren something.' Rosalind stood and stretched. 'I could use some food too. Eve? Stuart?'

'I'm in.' Eve got up and retrieved her purse.

'I'm staying with Lauren.'

'No, Stuart,' Lauren said. 'You don't have to. I'll be fine. You can bring something back for me.'

Stuart folded his arms.

'We'll bring back meals for two.' Olivia beckoned to her sisters.

They found a barbecue spot not far away and had a nervous, rushed meal. Olivia didn't even try to bring up all the things she had to tell them. There was too much. This day – and however much more time it took – belonged to Dad.

Before they drove back to the hospital, the sisters each made calls to the new men in their lives to update them on the day's agony. Duncan was sweet and concerned, urging Olivia to get enough rest, to make sure she didn't exhaust herself. From the more relaxed looks on her sisters' faces when they finished their calls, Olivia could safely assume all three of them had been at least somewhat emotionally fortified for the return to Dad's room.

They hurried back to St Joseph's and delivered the food to Lauren and Stuart, who ate it gratefully.

Then they settled back and waited.

And waited.

Raspy breath in. Raspy breath out. Oxygen levels up and down. Up and down.

They talked quietly, to Daniel, among themselves. Waiting.

Then Dad stopped breathing.

Lauren stood.

'Daniel,' she whispered tearfully.

He inhaled. Exhaled. Inhaled again. Involuntary sounds came from around the room, a mixture of relief and frustration.

Olivia saw no need for this misery to go on. The family had gathered, had their last moments with him, said what needed to be said, were resigned to saying goodbye, and now this ghastly uncertainty over when the certainty would happen.

'This is insane.' Lauren sank back into her seat, taking off her glasses, and pressed her fingers to her eyes. 'Dogs are allowed to die more humanely.'

'I agree.' Olivia massaged her temples. 'It's awful. Though I wouldn't want to be anywhere else right now.'

'No.' Lauren put her glasses back on and smiled at Olivia. Olivia smiled back. Warmly.

There was a first time for everything.

Another half-hour went by. Twice Daniel stopped breathing and the family rose as one, and twice, when the awful rattling sounds restarted, they subsided back into their chairs.

Then finally, finally the oxygen numbers plummeted and didn't rebound; Dad's breathing slowed impossibly, then stopped. They waited for him to start again, that boy who'd cried so many wolves, but this time . . . no.

It was so remarkable and so simple. Life was there, and then it wasn't.

Nurse Heidi came in. 'He's gone. I'm sorry.'

A communal inhale, exhale to release the miserable suspense, then tears and hugs all around. This moment Olivia had been on the cusp of praying for now seemed to have come impossibly too soon. Even having focused on nothing else for most of the day, she wasn't ready. How could she be? How could any of them be?

They waited for a doctor to pronounce Daniel dead, a quaint formality given the gazillion-dollar machine reliably indicating that every process in his body had stopped. But pronounce the doctor did, and then they were finished. They could walk right out and do whatever they wanted, leaving brother-in-law, husband, father Daniel Braddock lying alone on the white-sheeted hospital bed.

That was the worst to face. Damn near unbearable.

In silence, the Braddock-Patterson-Crofts walked out into the ICU and made their way outside, emerging into the soft night air.

Olivia took in a lungful with guilty relief, reminding herself that Dad wasn't really in the building anymore. He existed now only in the memories of those who loved him.

'There's a Marriott close by.' Stuart was consulting his

phone. 'Looks like there are rooms available with two queens. One for you girls, one for Lauren and me. That sound okay?'

'Yes. Thank you, Stuart.' Lauren sounded like she'd aged ten years. They all did.

'Let's head over.' He put his phone back in his pocket. 'I'll take Lauren. You three can follow me.'

He walked his sister over to his truck, his big arm supporting her. Olivia looked after them for a long beat, moved by Stuart's tenderness, then joined her own siblings at Eve's Mercedes.

'I'm so glad you both came.' Olivia waited by the rear door for Eve to unlock. 'I needed you.'

'I'm so glad we did too,' Rosalind said. 'We all needed to be together.'

Olivia collapsed into the back seat while Rosalind tucked herself into the passenger side, turning back with a half-smile. 'Since when do you leave shotgun for your little sister?'

Olivia blinked sweetly. 'I'm working on becoming a nicer person.'

'Whoa, that's weird.' Rosalind reached back and squeezed Olivia's calf affectionately.

'That was really hard up there, but really important too. And kind of amazing.' Eve buckled up and started the car, then pulled out of the parking place and up behind Stuart's truck. 'Now I want to sleep for about a million years.'

Rosalind touched Eve's shoulder, yawning. 'I think we all could use a million or two.'

On the short drive to the Marriott, Olivia texted Duncan that her father was gone, considered letting Derek know as well, and decided with her new generous and sweet heart that he could go screw himself.

At the hotel, Eve parked next to Stuart's truck and everyone headed into the lobby, carrying their bags. After check-in, they started tearful and emotional goodnights.

Olivia found herself hugging Lauren not only willingly but sincerely.

'You okay?' Lauren murmured.

'Somehow, yes. You?'

She nodded, a tiny smile trying to make it through her tears. 'I think that was the most pleasant conversation we've ever had.'

Olivia took a breath and set her shoulders. 'I . . . hope we can have more.'

The words freaked her out a little. So did realizing she meant them. Even a week ago, she would have thought it impossible she'd want to stay in touch with Lauren after her father's death.

Death! Her larger-than-life, sometimes insufferable but always remarkable father was dead. Even having seen it happen, she found it hard to comprehend.

A final wave, and the sisters parted company with Lauren and Stuart and found their way into the night's pleasant, spacious room.

As the door closed behind them, Olivia felt some of the day's weight lifting. 'When was the last time we had a sleepover?'

'God, I don't know. In Mom's room?' Rosalind pulled off her scarlet shoes and pushed them over by the wall. 'When we were kids.'

'I must have been practically a baby.' Eve frowned in concentration, unzipping her suitcase. 'Was there popcorn?'

'There was.' Olivia tossed her overnight bag on to one of the chairs. 'We'd watch movies, have ice cream. It was awesome. We did it a bunch of times.'

'I don't have popcorn or ice cream.' Eve held up a bottle of red wine. 'But I thought we might need a little help relaxing.'

'Uh-oh.' Rosalind feigned alarm. 'Drinking to relax is one of the signs of—'

'Intelligence.' Olivia strode over and grabbed the plastic cups by the refrigerator, bizarrely re-energized. 'Eve, you are a genius.'

'I guess I could use a little.' Rosalind accepted a cup from Olivia as Eve opened the wine. 'Pretty profound, this dying business.'

'Unbelievable.' Eve poured all around and raised her glass, choked up a little. 'Here's to Dad.'

'To Dad.' They each took a somber sip of the dark, rich Columbia Valley red.

'Yummy.' Rosalind managed a smile. 'Thanks, Eve.'

'Hits the spot, as Mom used to say.' Olivia kicked off her thongs, happy to keep her sisters' memories of Jillian intact tonight. She climbed up on one of the beds, not surprised, but not really hurt either, when her sisters chose to share the other one. 'God, what a day. This is exactly what I needed. My besties and a full glass of—'

Her phone rang.

'Oh for Pete's sake.' She peered at the display, hoping it was Duncan, then feeling unexpectedly liberated because seeing her ex's name on her phone hadn't brought on anything but severe disappointment. 'Oh *crap*. It's Derek.'

'What does *he* want?'

'Probably to make the day worse.' She made a face, glad she hadn't answered, wondering if the news of Daniel Braddock's death could possibly have leaked out this quickly. 'He's left a message.'

'Let's hear it on speaker,' Rosalind said. 'I could use a laugh.'

'I'm not sure it will be that funny.' Olivia hit play, hoping she wasn't making a mistake, but deciding that in the unlikely worst-case event that Derek was asking for more money, she'd have to tell her sisters what she was already planning to tell them.

At least she hoped that was the worst case.

'Yeah, so, um, hi, baby, hope you're doing all right.'

All three women blew long, heartfelt raspberries, then burst into giggles, shushing each other so they could hear the rest of his message.

'I've got something to ask you. I'm in a kinda rough spot right now, and uh . . . I could use some . . . help. Well, anyway, call me.'

Olivia's heart sank. Yes, it had been a mistake to play his message out loud. *The little bastard.* She hadn't expected it, not this soon anyway. Another of her trips to Planet Denial, a forlorn last-ditch hope that yes, okay, her husband had turned out to be a blackmailer, but gee, maybe he was only a *one-time* blackmailer, because that wouldn't be *as* bad, right?

Pathetic.

'Whah?' Rosalind looked outraged. 'What kind of rough spot?'

'Who cares?' Eve snorted. 'You owe the little prick nothing.'

Olivia took a deep breath, hating to inflict more misery on her sisters. 'He wants money. He's blackmailing me.'

'What are you talking about?' Eve looked dumbfounded.

'Somehow he found out about Mom's . . . physical issues.'

Rosalind gasped. 'That little shit. You haven't given him anything, have you?'

'Oh, not much.' Olivia gave a sick laugh. 'Just the house.'

'Olivia!' Eve's face was a study in sisterly horror. 'The house! You love that house!'

'Not so much anymore. It's full of too-expensive furniture and shitty memories.'

'No.' Eve came out of her shock to display uncharacteristic temper. 'You do not reward the little asshole.'

'I had no choice, Eve. He was going to broadcast it worldwide.'

'At least tell me this was just a verbal transaction. You can get out of that easily.'

'So far, yes.'

'But how did he find out?' Rosalind was predictably stricken. 'About Mom?'

'*I* sure didn't tell him.' Olivia tossed her phone on to the bed. 'I wouldn't even admit it to myself. He said some woman called him. Who knows if she's even the original source.'

'Shelly would never tell anyone.' Eve was shaking her head. 'Nor would Clayton. Even my scumbag ex Mike has more integrity than that.'

'Bryn wouldn't either.' Rosalind frowned, thinking. 'Nor Grandma Betty. Who else knows besides Lauren?'

Silence.

'What about the person sending the diaries from Saratoga Springs?' Eve asked.

'Nope.' Olivia resettled her pillows. 'That was Phoebe, the woman Grandma Betty all but adopted. Grandma had the diaries. Whenever Lauren told her to send one, Betty sent it to Phoebe, already wrapped and addressed, and Phoebe dropped the box in the mail. She had no idea what was in it.'

'So *that's* how it worked.' Eve rolled her eyes. 'Crazy.'

'There's another diary. A third one. The last one.' Olivia spoke flatly, anticipating her sisters' pain after reading Mom's last words. 'I'll send you each a copy when all this is—'

'Oh *no*.' Rosalind clapped both hands to her head. 'Oh *crap*. I just thought of someone who might know, someone we have no reason to trust. I bet it's my fault.'

'Who?' Olivia asked.

'Last summer, right after we found Mom's diagnosis, I called the doctor's office where she was seen after she and Dad got engaged. I wanted to know if they could prove or disprove that Mom had the disorder. I gave them her maiden name and the diagnosis. If the woman I was talking to knew that Sylvia Moore was Mom's real name, she could have figured it out. I bet it's her.'

They all thought that through.

'Why wait until now, though?' Olivia said. 'And why give the information to Derek and not just blackmail one of us directly?'

'She probably knew we'd simply deny it.' Rosalind looked miserable. 'But when your and Derek's infertility poop hit the fan, she must have figured she'd have a willing buyer for the information. Then she could drop out and let him do whatever he wanted with it.'

The sisters sat in dismay. That made sense. They hated it.

Olivia put her wine on the table next to the bed. 'If that's true, she deserves a slow roasting in hell.'

'We can't prove it's her, short of asking Derek.' Eve sighed. 'He certainly wouldn't tell us.'

'Well, you can't let him get away with it,' Rosalind said fiercely. 'Call him and tell him to stick his demands up his ego.'

Olivia shook her head. 'He'll go public.'

'Who'll believe him?'

'A lot of people.' She picked up her glass again. 'There will be digging. A big mess. This family doesn't need that right now.'

They settled glumly back to thinking.

'Call him.' Rosalind pointed to Olivia's phone. 'We can record him blackmailing you and send it to the police.'

'That won't work.' Olivia grimaced. 'He'd still tell everyone about Mom.'

'From jail,' Rosalind said.

'Maybe that wouldn't be so bad.' Eve spoke slowly.

'Derek in jail? It would be fabulous. But not at that price.'

'No, not Derek in jail.' Eve got up on to her knees, her cried-out eyes oddly lit. 'Everyone finding out about Mom.'

'Absolutely not.' Olivia reacted so strongly she nearly spilled her wine. 'Mom would— No. We can't do that. Derek would make it public in the worst possible way. I can totally picture the headlines. "The shocking truth of Jillian Croft's barren womb, and the women who—"'

'Not have *him* tell everyone.' Eve was looking directly at Olivia, clearly willing her to be convinced. '*We* would tell everyone.'

Olivia's stomach burned. 'Eve . . .'

'So the world hears the truth about Jillian Croft.'

'My God, Eve. Yes.' Rosalind turned to Olivia, who was now outnumbered, two sisters to one. 'The truth. Coming from the people who loved her best.'

Chapter 21

December 31, 2001 (Monday)

Dear Mom,

I'm writing to you tonight, New Year's Eve, the last night of my life. In a short time it will be midnight, the end of the old, the beginning of the new. I'm the old; it is time for me to end and make room for the new.

I am sending you my diaries. I want you to know who I am. Who I was. I want you to understand something, anything about me that might change how you think of me in the future. I want you to miss me. I want you to think of me lovingly, as a mother should, as I will think of my girls from heaven, or hell, wherever I end up. Please keep these safe. What's left of me on screen is beautiful, but it isn't real. These diaries are not always beautiful. But they are real.

Know that I die in peace and with no regrets except any pain I cause my daughters. I know in my heart they will recover, and that they are better off without me. My husband is now free to marry this woman he loves, one who will doubtless set a better example for their womanhood than an aging, drunken has-been with a broken body and a shattered spirit.

I love you,
Sylvia

*

Olivia held binoculars up to her eyes. She was standing in front of the wall of windows in her new house's three-season room, shamelessly spying on Rosalind and Bryn, who were out for a life-changing walk on the rambling property Olivia had bought on the opposite shore of Belfast Bay from Stuart and Georgia.

'See anything good?' Duncan slid his arms around her. She nestled back against him, enjoying his solid strength. He'd been her rock over the past few tumultuous months since Dad had died, and she was falling more deeply in love with him every day. Around him she'd become a better person. Calmer. Less neurotic and less defensive. More tolerant. He seemed to be similarly crazy about her, which still hadn't stopped being amazing. She had to be the luckiest girl on the planet.

Though doubtless Rosalind was about to feel she'd earned that title.

'They've stopped.' She gripped the binoculars, so excited she was having trouble holding them steady. 'They're talking.'

'Maybe give them some privacy?'

'Privacy? Are you kidding me?' Olivia stopped spying long enough to throw a scowl over her shoulder. 'You think I'd miss my sister getting proposed to?'

In late August, Bryn had called her. Rosalind had been dying to see Olivia's new home, and he had decided a mid-September trip to Maine would be the perfect time and place to propose marriage to his sweetheart.

Olivia had jumped at the chance to be in on the surprise, and had added her own contribution, which was currently waiting nearby. Over the past month she and Duncan, with help from Georgia, and even Stuart on occasion, had just about lost their minds getting the house ready for the celebration. It was worth every gallon of paint and hurried purchase, every panicked, exhausting moment. The house – still not quite finished – looked fabulous. That morning, Olivia had filled the place with flowers and welcomed the caterer, whose staff were hiding in the kitchen. Somehow Bryn, as curly-haired, adorable and hilarious as ever, had managed to use his considerable charm to convince Rosalind they needed to walk the grounds that afternoon before coming inside.

'What's happening?' Jake, looking ridiculously cute in his first jacket and tie, ran up next to her and peered through the French doors. He'd started pre-school and was loving it. Olivia and Duncan had been careful to keep their relationship platonic around him – Duncan was still living in the boathouse the weeks he had his son – to give Jake more time to adjust to his parents' divorce and his mother's transformation, but he and Olivia were continuing to bond. 'Is there a boat sinking?'

'Bryn is going to ask Rosalind to marry him.' She hadn't told him earlier. Four year olds and important secrets were not meant to stay together.

'Are they getting married now?'

'No, just promising that they will sometime soon.'

'Will they have kids?'

'Probably.' Her own desperate need to have a child had subsided over the past months as her happiness and fulfillment grew, though she and Duncan hadn't ruled out the possibility.

'When will Rosalind turn into a man?'

Olivia nearly choked trying not to laugh.

'Rosalind will stay a woman.' Duncan ruffled his son's hair. 'Your mom is special.'

'Are you and Olivia getting married too?'

Duncan suddenly had a lot of throat-clearing to do, which earned him a gentle elbow to the ribs. 'We might. You have to be sure you fit together before you decide that, which can take time.'

Olivia brought down the binoculars. 'You think you'd mind if I became your stepmother?'

'Nah, that'd be okay. You make good cake.'

'I'm glad you think so.' Movement outside made Olivia cut short her stepmotherly smile and jam the binoculars back on to her face. 'Bryn's kneeling! Oh my sweet little sister. This is so amazing. Look at her face!'

'Let me see! Let me see!' Jake tugged at her skirt. 'What happened to her face?'

'She's happy.' Olivia knelt next to him. He might as well watch. With her eyes swimming with tears, she no longer could.

Jake looked at her somberly. 'Why aren't you happy?'

'These are happy tears.'

'Happy *tears*? That's silly.'

'It is, you're right.' She held the binoculars up to his perfect little face. 'Can you see? What are they doing?'

It took a while for him to focus. 'Yech! Kissing!'

Olivia grinned up at Duncan. 'Yech indeed.'

'It's time to tell all the people to come into the house,' Duncan told Jake. 'You ready to do that for us?'

'Yeah!'

'Great.' Olivia wiped her eyes with a tissue she was smart enough to have tucked into her skirt waistband, and hauled out her phone, where a pre-typed message to Georgia waited. 'Just touch that little arrow there.'

Jake touched it and the one word text sent.

Now.

'Lots of smiling.' Duncan had the binoculars now. 'No moves to come back to the house yet. I think we've timed this perfectly.'

'I'll go watch for the troops.' Olivia hurried to the marble foyer of the nineteenth-century ship captain's house she'd fallen in love with at first sight, which had miraculously stayed on the market the entire time she was waffling over whether to leave Belfast.

Falling the rest of the way in love with Duncan had clinched her decision. Both of them were still going through divorce fallout, but by now Olivia had enough faith in the two of them and enough love for this part of the country to take the risk. So far she'd felt nothing but joy and anticipation over her decision to stay.

She planned to open the house as a B&B, from which Duncan would take guests out on his boat for weekend excursions ranging from sightseeing and whale-watching to fishing and overnight trips up to Nova Scotia, possibly longer winter trips as well. Details involving Duncan's possible absence still had to be worked out with Stuart. Cooking for people, hosting people, star of her own little kingdom – the new career would suit both Olivia's strengths and her neuroses. Maybe someday she and Duncan would decide Belfast no longer fit, but for now it looked perfect on both of them.

'Are you watching for real ones?'

She started, not having noticed Jake following her. 'Real what?'

'You said troops were coming. Will they have guns?'

'No, no, it's an expression. I meant our party guests.' She opened the front door and pointed eagerly. 'See? Here they come.'

'Oh.' He made his adorable disappointed face. 'Just regular grownups.'

'You can go get the roses now. You remember where they are? And what I told you to—'

'*Yes*. You told me about a *million* times.'

Had she mentioned that her need for children had subsided?

Grinning at her joke, and from the joy of what was about to be, Olivia stood waiting to welcome her family, some members of which she had yet to meet.

First up the front walk were Georgia and Stuart. Georgia looked beautiful in a pale yellow dress, and Stuart quite dashing in a coat and tie. Olivia's heart warmed to see them so elegantly turned out. They had done so much for her and for Duncan. Such lovely, generous people, though Stuart still worked hard to hide his warmer side. He and Olivia were getting to a better place, however, and starting to trust each other.

Behind them, new-to-Olivia family members – Rosalind's auburn-haired birth mother Leila Allerton, dazzling in a purple jumpsuit with a black embroidered jacket, and her Reese Witherspoon lookalike daughter Caitlin, all in white. Rosalind had told her that Caitlin had started business school at Boston University this past fall and was loving it, and that Leila had one more role to sing this fall, but had otherwise given up traveling and performance and settled into a job as a music teacher at Princeton High School. From the rest of her sister's chatter over the past year, she felt she already knew both women.

After the Allertons, Eve, rocking a floral sundress, her boyfriend Clayton, tall, dark and elegant in summer beige, and his daughter Abigail, wearing a white tuxedo with a black blouse. Olivia couldn't wait to get to know the two of them, though the way Eve talked about Clayton, she would bet there was plenty of time. Like until death did them part.

Next, linked arm in arm, childhood best friends: Eve's Aunt Shelley, looking slightly uncomfortable in a glossy grey pantsuit, and Lauren, actually chic in a boxy coral suit Olivia had never seen before. Maybe without Daniel Braddock dictating every facet of her life, as he'd so loved doing, someday Lauren would be free to blossom herself. At sixty, she was still young enough to try again.

Olivia welcomed the crowd into the house, greeted each person with a hug, whether they'd met before or not, then directed him or her toward Jake, who somberly handed out red roses, reveling in his importance.

'The happy couple's coming back,' Duncan called out.

'Excellent.' Olivia put her arm around Eve and beamed up at Clayton. She liked the way his face lit when he looked at her sister. 'Everyone please line up here in the foyer, ready to go across the hall. Duncan will direct you after that. When it's your turn to greet Bryn and Rosalind, please hand the bride-to-be your rose.'

The next half-hour was an orgy of delirious reunions, happy gasps – and squeals from Rosalind – from the stunned couple as they greeted the unexpected newcomers, loud congratulations and best wishes winding around and through the euphoric bursts of chatter.

After the last rose was added to the bouquet in Rosalind's arms, Olivia signaled the caterer. Champagne was next, because . . . well, duh.

The party lasted all afternoon. By six, only the three sisters remained at the house. The rest of the guests had set off on a tour of Belfast and the boatyard under Stuart's lead. In an hour or so they'd be coming back for takeout pizza, but Olivia had conspired with Duncan to get this precious time alone with Eve and Rosalind.

'God, Olivia, this has been the best afternoon of my life.' Rosalind had never been more beautiful. Her cheeks were pink, eyes shining with happiness. 'I can't thank you enough.'

'You're welcome, sweetie.' Olivia gave her a hug. 'Wait here. I have another surprise.'

She went into the kitchen, where the caterers were busy cleaning up, and pulled out champagne from the refrigerator. Veuve Clicquot La Grande Dame had been their mother and father's favorite special-occasion drink. Olivia had bought the 2008 vintage so the three of them could share it.

She put the bottle in a bucket filled with fresh ice, and brought it out with three plastic tumblers, not remotely worthy of what they'd be serving, but unbreakable on rock.

'I saved this for us. A Grande Dame. Who wants to go down to the water and drink it?'

'Oh, Olivia.' Rosalind clasped her hands over her heart. 'What a gorgeous idea.'

'Mom and Dad's favorite.' Eve's eyes filled. 'Olivia, you are amazing.'

'I know I am! It's incredible.'

Her sisters rolled their eyes. As they should.

Laughing, Olivia led the way down the path recently rescued from the wilderness with a combination of crushed stone and mussel shells. The previous owners of the house had all but clear-cut the front yard. She and Duncan were encouraging selected newly sprouting birches and firs to grow to maturity, in order to create a sense of privacy and landscaping without boxing in the house or eliminating the ocean view. Given that the building stood on a small rise, they had years before they had to worry about not being able to see the bay.

As they neared the water, Olivia pointed out where they planned to build a larger version of Stuart and Georgia's gazebo to accommodate bug-free outdoor parties. Also in the plans, a dock from which Duncan could pick up and unload passengers. She let Eve know she hoped for her expert help with some of the designing, and told Rosalind she'd love to hang some of her paintings in the house, and place a few of Bryn's landscape sculptures in the grounds.

Her sisters were enthusiastic on all counts.

They climbed down to the rock-strewn shore on steps made of carefully placed stones – for their guests' use, Olivia and Duncan would have to build proper steps with solid railings. The light was slowly pulling back from the intensity of the day into a glow painting the water, shore and tree trunks a light coral that reminded Olivia of Lauren's suit.

Olivia in the middle, the sisters settled on an obligingly flat ledge, letting their bare legs dangle. Olivia carefully opened the champagne so the pressure released with a soft *thunk*. Rosalind and Eve applauded her skill.

She poured for all of them and lifted her cup. 'Let's drink first to how our family has grown, to all the new people we had no idea were part of it. So far, we even like all of them.'

'Imagine that.' Eve hoisted her champagne. 'Here's to newly discovered family.'

'Hear, hear.' Rosalind joined them in the first sip.

Oohs and *aahs* and *omigods* followed as the remarkably complex flavors crossed their palates.

'Mom and Dad weren't stupid.' Olivia took another sip, very pleased that she'd been so busy chatting all afternoon, she hadn't downed more than half a glass. This stuff was worth waiting for. 'I can't believe it's been over a year since we found out about Mom's diagnosis.'

'No kidding.' Eve found a safe niche for her cup and stretched her arms high. 'Not much has gone on since then, huh.'

Rosalind faked a yawn. 'I know *I've* been bored.'

'If only something would *happen*,' Olivia said.

'Where do you think we'd be if we hadn't stumbled over that paper?' Rosalind sipped her champagne and rolled her eyes blissfully. 'My *God*, that's good.'

'You know, that was the last sheet in the last file in that end-less box.' Eve brought her arms down. 'I was so tired at that point I almost threw it away. We were all sick to death of the job by then.'

'And of each other,' Olivia added sweetly.

'That too.' Eve retrieved her cup and took a contemplative sip. 'It's a good question, though, Rosalind. For me . . . if we hadn't found out, Lauren wouldn't have sent me to Washington Island to stumble over Shelley. Lauren really put my new life in motion. I wouldn't have found Clayton. I might still be living with Mike, designing bathrooms. I owe her a lot.'

'We all do.' Olivia and Lauren had done a lot of talking while they'd been planning Dad's memorial. They were inching toward a better relationship, neither putting pressure on the other to make one happen. Whatever would be would be. 'I wouldn't have said this two months ago, when I was still so firmly in denial, but I'm truly grateful she decided we should know the truth.'

'Same here. She told me where to find Leila. Without that, I wouldn't have found Bryn. I wouldn't have gotten the con-fidence to show my paintings. I'd still be working a million different jobs and avoiding life.' Rosalind lifted a lock of her natural-brown bob. 'With purple hair.'

Olivia watched a boat making its way into the harbor for the night. 'I know where I'd be.'

The girls waited.

'Ye-es?' Eve prompted.

'On Maui with a surf bum?' Rosalind suggested.

'In Paris with an *artiste*?'

'Confined to an institution,' Olivia said.

'That was my next guess.' Rosalind winked at her.

'Well, I'm glad you're here.' Eve slung an arm around Olivia's shoulders.

Olivia took a moment to enjoy how much she loved her sisters, and to think about how ironic it was that discovering they were only half related had ended up bringing them closer. 'It's funny. I miss Mom differently now.'

'How do you mean?' Rosalind asked. 'Though I think I know.'

'I miss her more distantly.' Olivia chose her words carefully, not having admitted the feelings out loud before now. 'I no longer wish so much that she were still alive and around every day to talk to. Is that awful?'

'If it is, I'm awful too,' Eve said. 'We lost her nearly twenty years ago, but in some ways we lost her even more after that third diary. Though for me there was also the comfort of finding out she'd turned down the big role that sex-offender jerk offered her.'

Olivia let out a growl. 'I'd still like to dig up that guy, bring him back to life, and then kill him.'

Eve snorted. 'I'll bring the shovel.'

They sipped their champagne, watching the waves rush the shore then gurgle sheepishly back.

'I was rereading our *People* story last week.' Rosalind put down her tumbler and leaned back on her hands. 'Even without Derek forcing the issue, I'm so glad we did it, and that Mom's story came out the way we'd hoped.'

'Agreed.' Eve ran her fingers through her hair, a luminous pink-blond reflecting the sunset. 'There was no reason to keep it secret anymore. I hope our efforts inspired other women not to feel shame.'

'The reaction to the article wasn't awful either. I was worried,' Olivia said. 'We were *all* worried. Though I did get called a few new names. Nice to see people can still hate so creatively.'

'I was thinking of one passage in particular,' Rosalind said. 'It was when the interviewer asked why we'd chosen this moment to come forward with the story. We all looked right at you, Olivia. I was so proud of your answer, how you decided not to mention Derek.'

Olivia squeezed Rosalind's arm. She was not going to forget that moment soon. The question had been anticipated. In discussions prior to the interview, Eve and Rosalind had deferred to Olivia on whether she'd answer truthfully or not. She'd gone in still angry, still unsure what to do. But when the question had come her way, she'd realized there was no decision to be made. Her answer had been three words: it was time.

She no longer needed to dive down to Derek's level, had no more need for him to suffer as she had. Though she wasn't above being glad about the call she asked her lawyer to make after the magazine article came out. Derek would now be free to make his own way in the world, financially speaking. Olivia wasn't giving him a penny more than she had to. She'd rescinded her gift of the Brentwood house, and was considering renting it out to starlet wannabes for next to nothing, a riff on the ladies' residence where her mother had lived in those early days in New York. A tribute, in fact, to what Mom had accomplished.

'Duncan has been good for you. And from what I heard from Georgia, you've been good for him too.' Rosalind exchanged glances with Eve. 'I'm thinking we'll be having one of these parties for you two soon.'

'Not that soon. We don't want to move too fast for Jake's sake.' Olivia nudged Eve. 'You'll be next.'

Eve blushed prettily. 'I do have some news.'

'No way!' Rosalind sat bolt upright, eyes lit with pleasure. 'Olivia, get the bottle. I need a refill.'

'No, no.' Eve started laughing helplessly. 'Not *that*.'

'Doesn't matter.' Olivia poured them each another glass. 'We all need a refill.'

'Clayton is moving to Massachusetts after the new year.'

'Eve! That is fabulous,' Rosalind said.

'Moving in with you?' Olivia asked.

'Yes.' Eve blushed even harder and held up crossed fingers as her sisters cheered their approval. 'It seems so soon. I hope it's not a mistake.'

'It's not a mistake. I've never been more sure of anything.' Rosalind leaned across Olivia and wrapped her arms around as much of Eve as she could reach. 'You two are meant to be together.'

'Agreed.' Olivia hugged Eve when Rosalind finally let go, feeling a deep swell of love for the sister she'd been least close to. They seemed to have evolved toward each other. Another blessing.

She sipped more of the superb bubbly; then she was ready to tell them her news. 'After the *People* article, I got a call from my agent.'

'I thought you didn't work with an agent anymore,' Eve said.

'I don't, but she thought I'd want to hear this. Sandra Bullock wants to produce a movie about Mom's life.' Rosalind's eyes widened. Eve's narrowed. 'They offered me the leading role. The chance to play Mom. Major motion picture.'

Both of her sisters gasped.

'Oh my God, Olivia!' Color flooded Rosalind's face. 'This is amazing! Your dream come true! I can't believe it. After all you went through!'

Eve tilted her head, watching Olivia. Her mouth curved in a slow smile. 'You turned it down, didn't you?'

'What? Of course she—' Rosalind broke off, staring at Olivia. 'Oh my God. You did.'

Olivia nodded.

'Of course you did.' Rosalind's face cleared. 'I was thinking of old Olivia.'

'Hey.' Olivia bristled. 'Who you calling old?'

'You're practically *forty*! What else would you call it?' Eve nudged her affectionately. 'You did the right thing. Your life here will be ten times better than anything they could offer.'

'Yes.' Olivia shook back her hair, grinning blissfully, still with zero regrets at turning down stardom. Practically zero. C'mon, she was human. 'I agree.'

The sun dipped lower behind the hills, the coral glow faded toward gray. Olivia smiled with a sudden thought. She started humming.

'What is that?' Rosalind turned to her. 'Do I know it?'

'It's one of the songs Mom used to sing to us.' She hummed another few bars. 'Our baby songs.'

'Huh?' Eve looked confused.

Olivia pretended horror. 'You don't remember?'

'Uh . . .' Rosalind scrunched up her face, thinking. 'It's sort of familiar.'

'I'm so glad I thought of them.' She beamed, delighted she could share such a good memory. 'Mine was hilarious, sung to the tune of "Lydia the Tattooed Lady". Rosalind, yours was to "Everything's Coming Up Roses". Eve's was to "Amazing Grace", for her middle name.'

'Sing.' Rosalind leaned back, ready to listen.

Olivia cleared her throat, patted her chest. 'I hope I can remember them all. Here's mine:

> *Livia, Livia*
> *Have you met Livia*
> *Livia the faboo baby . . .*

> *She has a face we adore so*
> *And a torso even more so*
> *Livia, the queen of them all!*

She finished with a flourish. Her sisters applauded madly.

'Hilarious.' Eve was still giggling. 'Did Mom write it?'

'She told me she and Dad collaborated. I remember her saying they had a great time cracking each other up suggesting lyrics. I bet some of them were unprintable.'

'Wouldn't surprise me.' Rosalind's face had softened. 'They did have fun together.'

'They had a *lot* of fun together,' Olivia said. 'We can't forget that.'

'Sing Rosalind's now,' Eve demanded.

'Okay.' Olivia fortified herself with another sip of champagne, thinking through the lyrics. Then she started in with her best belting Ethel Merman imitation:

> *You are swell, you are neat*
> *You have all of the world at your feet*
> *Startin' here, startin' now*
> *Honey everything's coming up Rosalind!*

More applause. Rosalind hooted. 'I *love* it. I'm going to make up songs for my kids too.'

'Don't name your son Chuck.' Eve shook her head sadly. 'Very bad rhymes.'

'Sing Eve's now.' Rosalind was already giggling.

Olivia's laughter faded. 'This one's different.'

She sat straight and lifted her chest, wanting to do the song justice, to sing it as simply as she knew how.

When she started, her voice found its natural place, emerging with clarity and resonant power. She sang slowly, with all her heart, as the last rays of the sun disappeared, picturing Jillian Croft's pure happiness cradling baby Eve in her arms.

Amazing Eve Grace, how sweet the child
Such perfect hands and feet
How precious this new gift of love
She makes our world complete.

When she finished, tears were rolling down Rosalind's face. 'Oh, Olivia.'

'I'm so glad you didn't forget those songs,' Eve whispered. 'We need to write them down.'

'Yes.' Olivia thrust her glass up toward the darkening sky. She had to clear her throat twice before she could speak. 'Here's to Daniel Braddock, brilliant teacher and scholar, for the legacy he left American theater and academia. And here's to Daniel Braddock, devoted husband, who loved two such remarkable women.

'Here's to Jillian Croft, actress par excellence, for all the talent and joy she brought to the screen and to the world. And here's to Sylvia Moore, to the woman she was and all that she went through. Long may they both be honored and remembered.'

Her sister's glasses joined hers, streams of golden bubbles coursing up toward heaven.

Olivia smiled through her tears. 'And finally, from the hearts of their three loving daughters, here's to Mom and Dad.'

Want more of the intriguing family secrets
and compelling romantic entanglements of the
Braddock family?

Look for Rosalind's story in *Private Lies* and Eve's story
in *Hidden Truths* – the other enthralling titles in the
Fortune's Daughters trilogy.

Honest Secrets

Bonus Material

Discovering Maine

As you can probably tell, I have a special place in my heart for the state of Maine. In the early 1950s, my grandfather, a professor of music at Hamilton College in Clinton, New York, was invited to visit a fellow professor at his summer house on the coast of Maine. My grandparents fell in love with the area at first sight. When a house and twenty acres came up for sale next door to his friend, my grandfather snapped it up. Back then, $1,000 was a lot of money, but it seemed worth it.

Are you kidding me? $1,000? It *was* worth it. Because although my grandparents and their children – my mother and aunt – are no longer alive, all of them adored the place and went every summer until their last. Thanks to them, my brothers and I started our annual pilgrimages to the coast before our first birthdays. We adore the place, as do our spouses and kids. Three generations later, we are still close to that same 'next-door' family (their house is actually some distance through the forest) who invited my grandfather nearly seventy years ago.

Our little corner is not heaven for everyone. There's no insulation, and no electricity. That means no dishwasher, no computers or Wi-Fi or TV. When I was growing up, it also meant no phones. The plumbing is temperamental, and creatures periodically believe the house belongs to them.

But no electricity also means we talk to each other, we read books, we do jigsaw puzzles and play games. During the day, we spend a lot of time outside, kayaking, hiking, exploring other gorgeous areas of the coast, near and far.

Or we sit at the edge of the sea, performing a kind of unconscious meditation, smelling the gorgeous air I describe in all three Fortune's Daughters books, listening to waves, lobster fishermen and gulls. We watch clouds passing, tides rising or falling. We spot eagles, seals, heron and loons. We toss our city hurry, focus on experiencing rather than accomplishing, accept the natural rhythms of nature. We settle under its spell.

When I was a girl, I was certain that if everyone had a bit of nature to retreat to like ours, the world would be a much more peaceful and happy place. I wouldn't be surprised if there was a bit of truth buried in there somewhere. In any case, I find as the years pass that I take the place less and less for granted, and am more and more grateful that my grandparents left us such a beautiful and precious gift. I hope they know how much we love it.

Chicken with Bacon and Leeks

This recipe is adapted from one of Julia Child's episodes of *The French Chef*. It's delicious the first day, even better the second, therefore a perfect do-ahead meal. Julia served it with parsley chive biscuits – you can find her recipe online or make your own. Leftover chicken can be boned, shredded, stirred back into the sauce and ladled over pasta or rice.

Ingredients
4 rashers smoked streaky bacon (that's regular bacon in the US)
2 medium onions
4 cloves garlic
2 leeks, cleaned
¼ cup flour
½ tsp each salt and pepper
1 chicken, 1⅓–1¾ kilos (3–4 lb), cut into serving pieces
1 tsp dried rosemary
1 tsp fennel seeds
350 ml (1½ cups) dry white wine
350 ml (1½ cups) chicken stock
2 tbsp chopped parsley
½ tsp grated lemon zest

Method
Brown bacon in a Dutch oven, drain on paper towels and crumble.

While bacon cooks, chop onions and garlic and thinly slice leeks.

In bacon fat in the same pot, sauté onions over medium heat until softened and lightly browned.

While onions cook, place flour, salt and pepper in a small paper or plastic bag. Shake to blend. Add chicken pieces in two batches and shake until coated.

When onions are cooked, remove from pot. Add more fat if necessary and sauté chicken in two batches until browned on both sides. (If the bits at the bottom of the pan start looking too brown, you might want to haul out another skillet for the second batch to avoid a burned taste.)

Leave last batch of browned chicken in the Dutch oven and remove from heat.

Sprinkle half of each of the following over the chicken in the pot: bacon, onion, rosemary, fennel, garlic, leeks. Season with salt and pepper. Add the rest of the chicken and the remainder of those same ingredients.

Pour over enough wine and stock to nearly cover chicken (I used 1½ cups of each, but it depends on your pot).

Cover pot, bring to boil over high heat, then lower temperature to a simmer and cook, covered, for approximately 45 minutes. Be sure to check periodically, since the temperature can climb. If serving the next day, cool for an hour with lid off, then refrigerate. Reheat gently.

Just before serving, sprinkle finished dish or individual plates with the parsley and lemon zest mixed together.

The Fortune's Daughters Trilogy

A compelling and enthralling series of family secrets, romance and self discovery . . .

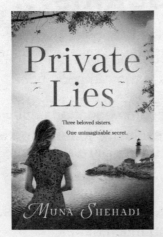

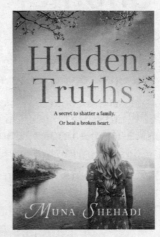

Available from

REVIEW

When one book ends, another begins...

Bookends is a vibrant new reading community to help you ensure you're never without a good book.

You'll find monthly reading recommendations, previews of brilliant new books, and exclusive features on and from your favourite authors. We'll also introduce you to exciting debuts and remind you of past classics.

There'll be a regular blog, reading group guides, competitions and much more!

Visit our website to see which great books we're recommending this month.

welcometobookends.co.uk

f /welcometobookends

🐦 @teambookends